Living Legend
Bo Diddley

Cover Photograph: Pictorial Press Ltd.

Printed by: Staples of Rochester, Kent.

Published by Castle Communications plc, A29 Barwell Business Park,
Leatherhead Road, Chessington, Surrey KT9 2NY.

ISBN: 1 86074 130 4

Living Legend
Bo Diddley

by

George R. White

Foreword
by Don Everly

After hearing Bo Diddley for the first time in 1955 my idea of music was forever changed. He opened the door to rhythms and music that reached to the very soul of me. His original sound is evident in all forms of music, rock and roll, rhythm and blues and country.

I think his influence is very evident on my intro to *Bye Bye Love* which was my attempt to connect to that same rhythm he alone originated.

Bo Diddley is truly a rock and roll hero of the first magnitude and I'm honoured to be able to call him my friend.

Don Everly
September 1995

Acknowledgements

This book is a labour of love, born out of a lifelong fascination with Bo Diddley and his music. The product of over twelve years' painstaking research, it is an attempt not only to chronicle the life and career of one of this century's most innovative and influential black performers, but also to look inside the man and understand how his personality and cultural heredity express themselves through his work.

The prospect of accurately charting Bo Diddley's eventful career through forty equally eventful years of popular music was indeed a daunting one and, had it not been for the initial encouragement of my good friend Charles 'Dr Rock' White, I doubt I would ever have had the courage to embark upon such an ambitious venture.

I am eternally grateful to all those friends, fans, researchers and collectors who came forward to help, especially Paul Alford, Jim Bardsley, Mark Bennett, Bob Brunning, Tony Burke, Steve Cairns, Trevor Cajiao, Wallace Chadwick, Chris Clark, John Collis, Barry Cornell, Norman Darwen, Martin Davis, Steve Davis, John Dunn, Svein Eide, Ron Ellis, Les Fancourt, Trev Faull, Paul Fenn, Neil Foster, Byron Foulger, Julian Gilchrist, Derek Glenister, John Goldman, Peter Goldsmith, Ferdie Gonzalez, Fred Goulding, Bill Gray, Phil Groia, Peter Guralnick, Steve Hall, Mark Harris, Graham Harrison, Martin Hawkins, Dick Heckstall-Smith, John Ingman, Wild Willie Jeffrey, Leroy Jenkins, Willa Jenkins, Paul Kattelman, Klaus Kilian, Bob Koester, John Koenig, Spencer Leigh, Bill Lewis, Dave Luxton, Mike Lydon, Xavier Maire, John Marriott, Hugh McCallum, Craig Moerer, Jim Newcombe, Mick Nightingale, Stewart Parker, Dave Peabody, Davy Peckett, Steve Potts, John Reeves, Paul Roberton, Dave Robinson, Fred Rothwell, Wayne Russell, Dave Sax, the late Screamin' Brian Simmons,

Peter Shertser, Dick Shurman, Ken Smith, Gary Sneyd, Neil Spencer, Andrew Steel, Tom Sturt, Graham Spittles, Brian Taylor, Don Toews, Paul 'Sailor' Vernon, Steve Wallace, Ian Wallis, Peter Ward, Dr Edward Wawrzynczak, Jim Wilson, Gerry Woodage and Mike Wylde.

   In particular, I would like to thank Bopping Brian Rushgrove for the mountain of press cuttings he donated; Dave 'Daddy Cool' Booth, Bill Millar and Cliff White for allowing me access to their extensive files; Christoph Ebner, Robert Pruter, Ray Topping and Chas White for additional interview material; Steve Armitage, Graham Barker, Ron Courtney, Daddy Cool (Showtime Archives Inc), Lorenzo Ferguson, Paul Harris, Norbert Hess, Cilla Huggins and Bez Turner (*Juke Blues*), Ellen Mandel, Bill Millar, Michael Ochs, Jim O'Neal (*Living Blues*), Robert Pruter, Lady Bo, Steve Richards, Mike Rowe (*Blues Unlimited*), Brian Smith, Mike Vernon, Cliff White and Val Wilmer for their help with my photo wants; Paul Harris and Ridings Reprographics Ltd, Leeds for their help with preparation of the artwork; Liam Keenan, John Poole, Morten Reff, John Skea and Tony Wilkinson for their unremitting efforts in tracking down dozens of Bo Diddley-influenced recordings and cover versions; Leon Campadelli (Phonogram Ltd), Janine Cooper (*Guitar Player*), David Dalton (*Music Week*), Joan Deary and Marge Meoli (RCA Records), Andy McKaie (MCA Records), Patti Jannetta, and the staff of the Birmingham News Co, Bradford and Leeds Central Libraries, the British Film Institute, the British Library Newspaper Library, the Fresno County Library, the International Communication Agency, the National Film and Sound Archives for their assistance in locating other obscure but vital information; Alan Balfour, Barry Hampshire, Colin Miles, Roger Osborne, Tony Watson and Chas White for their invaluable advice on a variety of technical matters; Steve Sher for keeping me up to date with latest developments Stateside and conducting urgent last-minute research; and, last but not least my wife, Verena, for the many hours she spent helping me to prepare and check the final manuscript, and for her steadfast support and encouragement at times when my own confidence and enthusiasm wavered.

   I am also deeply indebted to Peter Jacobs and Johnny Toogood (Stallion Artists) and Bo's manager, the late Marty Otelsberg, for making possible my many meetings with Bo Diddley; to Chris Barber, Ethel Christopher (Bo's mother), the Rev Kenneth Haynes, Paul Johnson (Guitar Red), Gloria Jolivet, Peggy Malone (Lady Bo), Kay McDaniel and Marty Otelsberg for granting me interviews and being so generous with their time and recollections; to all the copyright-holders who permitted use of their material in this book; and to my editor, Penny Braybrooke, whose talents and hard work helped bring this project to fruition.

Finally, very special thanks are due to Bo himself, who endured many hours of close questioning about a variety of personal as well as professional matters with a friendliness, dignity and patience that turned a potential chore into a very real pleasure.

George R. White

For Mum

Contents

Introduction

'An' now I must tell you somethin' that I'm pretty sure you wasn't aware of...'

The man on stage blinks through his thick, bottle-bottom glasses and grins.

'You are in my classroom now. *I* am the professor in here, an' you will do as I say.'

People start to giggle.

'You *will* have a good time! You will jump up an' down an' act like a *maniac*! You will go completely *out of your skulls*! That means young *an'* old! Dig it? Tonight, you will do somethin' that you didn't think you knew how to do...'

Wolf whistles. Cheers. Laughter.

'In other words, when I've finished with you in the next few minutes, you ain't gonna know where you've *been*! Dig it? This is *rock 'n' roll*!'

The crowd responds with an almighty roar of approval.

'You all ready?' he enquires.

'Yeah!'

'I said: are you *ready*?'

'YEAH!!!'

'Well, you better hang on, 'cause I'm goin' *crazy* – an' you're comin' with me,' he warns, launching into a powerful kickass boogie that has everyone on their feet within seconds – chanting, stamping, clapping.

No matter how often you see him, a Bo Diddley show is always a special, almost magical experience. An electrifying performer with an awesome stage presence and more than a modicum of showmanship, he's been in the limelight now for forty sweat-filled years, thrilling audiences all over the world with his unique brand of musical entertainment. Widely acclaimed for his talents as a composer, arranger, guitarist, singer, humorist and raconteur, he has pointed the way for successive generations of rockers, and the epithets bestowed upon him over the years speak for themselves: Genius... Master... Hero... Legend... the Originator... the King... the Most. Barely five foot seven in his stockinged feet, Bo Diddley is a musical giant.

How he came to rise to such prominence from the very humblest of beginnings is an enthralling and, at times, heart-rending tale of a poor black boy's struggles to free himself from the shackles of the ghetto and make it to the top. Illuminated by Bo's animated and often candid accounts of his experiences along the way, it offers a fascinating insight not only into the life and times of one of rock's first superstars, but also into the soulless and frequently brutal machinations of the popular music industry. This, then, is the story of Bo Diddley – the man with the most famous beat in the world!

Chapter 1

My Story

I was born one night about twelve o'clock,
I came in this world playin' a gold guitar,
My papa walkin' 'round, stickin' out his chest,
Holler: 'Mama, this boy, he gonna be a mess!'

People came from miles around,
Just to hear my little guitar sound.
Now some of 'em said I got what it takes,
If I keep on practisin', I'll be famous one day!

Early in the middle of the night,
A car drove up with four headlights,
A man stepped out with a lo-o-o-ng cigar,
Said: 'Sign this line an' I'll make you a star!'

I said: 'What's in it, man, what's in it for me?'
He said: 'Play your guitar, son, an' wait 'n' see!'
My first engagement was in Chicago.
I played for some people I ain't never seen befo'!

McComb, Mississippi

Down in the south-western tip of Mississippi known as Pike County, a dozen or so miles from the Louisiana border, lies the small, sleepy township of McComb. A cluster of clap-board houses and dusty roads bisected by the inevitable railroad track, it could be any one of a hundred similar settlements that pepper this vast expanse of woodlands, swamps and cotton fields. Nothing much ever happens here, although the town did achieve a short-lived notoriety in the closing months of 1977 after an aircraft carrying top Southern boogie outfit Lynyrd Skynyrd ploughed into the surrounding countryside killing four of its passengers.

Its real claim to fame, however, rests in another, less sensational event which occurred almost half a century earlier and passed by unreported and unnoticed by the world: on a small farm just outside town, a young black girl named Ethel Wilson gave birth to a baby boy: 'I was born December 30th, 1928, an' my real name is Ellas Bates. My father was Eugene Bates,[1] but I don't think he an' my mother were ever really together. I never cried over not seein' him or anythin' like that, but I do feel he could have been a man an' come by once to say "Hi", even if he didn't have nothin' to *give*. It would have been the greatest thing in the world![2]

'My mother had me when she was fifteen or sixteen years old – which, if it *did* happen at that age, I couldn't care less. I'm not gonna frown on her because she might have made a mistake of some sort. But, so far as I understand, she *didn't* make a mistake, 'cause I think I'm pretty well put-together. I'm healthy, you know, an' I hope to live a whole lotta more years.'[1]

'Bein' young, my mom wasn't financially set to raise me, so, when I got eight months old, she had to let me go. I was raised by her first cousin, which was Mrs Gussie McDaniel. This type of thing goes on a lot in black communities – in fact, Momma Gussie raised *my* momma.

'They never deprived me of knowin' who my mother was – an' I'm *glad*, because I think it's *disastrous* not to tell a child who his parents really are. That's not gonna make that child *dislike* you, but it *could* make him dislike you if he finds out one day that you *didn't* actually lay down an' birth him into the world!'[1]

'I *understand* my mother's position: she *had* to let me go with somebody else, 'cause she couldn't take care of me. She didn't – whatcha call it – throw me away, an' that's what I love her for: 'cause she's *momma*, you dig? I knew who she was when I was four or five years old, an', when

16

I got fifteen, I didn't lose faith in my mother.[3] Actually, it was *great*! I was a special kid. I had *two* mommas, y'understand: "big" momma an' "little" momma!' (Laughs.)

'I had three adopted sisters and brothers, which were my third cousins, I guess. My brother, Willis, just died recently. He was in the service during the Second World War an' came out with a nervous condition, man, that *freaked me out*! He never worked after that: there was just nothin' he could do, you know. He'd get up an' – I guess – walk around the block or somethin', go back in the house. Never worked since the War, just spent all those years sittin' around the house doin' nothin' – that's how bad off he was.

'It's a *shame* what happens to young cats that go in the service, you know, defend their country, an' then the government or your country look down their goddamn nose at you after you done got all fucked-up. They *forget* you, an' even the people you deal with on the streets every day look at you like you're some type of *moron* or somethin' – an' you're the sonofabitch that went out there an' stopped some dude takin' away the *freedom* they're enjoyin' every day!

'My sisters are both retired now. Lucille used to be a schoolteacher, an' then she worked at the post office long enough to retire from there. My other sister, Freddie, never worked. She was just a housewife all her life.

'I also have a real brother as well. His name is Kenneth Haynes, an' he's a minister in the Baptist Church. He was born a couple of years after me*, an' he was raised by my momma, but we all lived pretty close, so we used to play together an' all that kinda stuff.

'Kenneth is my only *brother*, but I also have two *half*-brothers. See, to me, havin' different fathers an' the same mother is *full* brothers; different mothers an' the same father is *half*-brothers – there's a difference there.

'One of 'em's name is Fred. I met him a couple of years back for the first time, an' he's got the same nose an' everythin', you know. I don't know what the other one's called. I'm supposed to have a half-sister too, but I've never seen 'em.[1]

'All my people – I think – descended from around Louisiana an' back down in the Delta country – the Cotton Belt – durin' slavery times.[4] My people never did think it was very important that they told me. It just happened to slip out one day.[3]

---

*11 October, 1930.

'I'm classed as a negro, but I'm not. I'm what you call a black Frenchman, a creole. Just like Fats Domino: French, African, indian, all mixed up.[2] My great-grandmother was actually supposed to have been a Blackfoot indian,[1] an' I got some people in my family that look like they're white!'[3]

Bo's memories of his childhood in Mississippi are hazy, although he does remember one incident particularly vividly... and not without good reason:

'One time I was followin' my sister, Lucille. We was goin' down to the creek to wash – we had a big ol' wash-pot right on the creek that we used to build a fire under, an' wash all the clothes, an' then take 'em back to the house an' hang 'em up – because it's a *drag* carryin' water! Nobody wanted to draw water out of a well. We didn't have one of those that you wind the bucket up on a thing; we had to pull it up on a piece of rope, an' nobody wanted to do this, so they decided we'd do all the washing down by the creek.

'I was about five or six years old – I can remember that far back – an' this is the only really freaky thing I can remember from back then: I almost picked a rattlesnake up!

'See, long time ago they used to make belts in a snake design – a lotta people used to wear that stuff. Lucille lost her belt out of the clothes bag, an' I went back to get it.

'I saw this thing layin' on the ground. I didn't see the head – it looked like a belt to me – an' I was reachin' down like this, you know, but I kept hearin' this "trrr, trrr". I didn't understand what was goin' on. Lucille came back to see what I was doin', an' she heard the noise an' told me not to move, an' the dude must've got back up in the bushes, you know.

'The reason why I didn't get bit is because – I think – animals have a thing of knowin' that I was a child: I'm not grown, I couldn't be a danger.

'The word "snake" is bad news. Everybody scares you by sayin': "Oh man, don't get bit by *this*!" an' you have no way of knowin' *what* your chances are if you *do* get bit. I don't know one snake from another, but I sharpen shovels man, like *razors*, so anythin' that run up on me in the woods is in *trouble* – long as the shovel stay on the end of that handle. Now, if it break off, I'm *leavin'*!'[1]

Sweet Home Chicago

Ellas did not remain in Mississippi for long. Life in the rural South of the thirties was hard and, as the Depression began to bite, thousands of poor blacks were forced to abandon the ailing cotton industry and head for large industrial cities like New York, Detroit and Chicago in search of a livelihood. When Gussie McDaniel's husband, Robert, died suddenly in 1934, she was left with no alternative but to uproot her family and join the stream of migrants heading North – taking little Ellas with her: 'We moved to Chicago 'round when I was six or seven years old, somewhere in that area – I really don't know to be exact. My Aunt Janie an' Uncle Herbert was there, an' we went to live with them: Herbert an' Janie Wilson, an' their three daughters – LaVern, Geneva an' Louise.

'My name was changed from Ellas Bates to Ellas B. McDaniel because they wouldn't accept me at school unless Gussie had legal rights for me to be in Chicago – I don't remember all the details. I just have that faint memory of goin' to court an' seein' a dude in a black robe sittin' up there, an' it had somethin' to do with my name. Later, when everybody started callin' me "Mac", it dawned on me what had happened.

'I was raised up at 4746 Langley Avenue, on the South Side*,[1] where you grow up an' take care of yourself, 'cause if *you* don't, somebody else *will!*[3] In Chicago, you *had* to learn how to take care of yourself, or the kids would beat your brains out! I don't know *why* they were like that, but that's the way it was.

'You *had* to fight! Everytime you stick your head out the door, there's a bunch of kids ready to beat the hell outa you. Maybe *you* didn't want it that way, but that's the way it was if you was gonna live 'round there, you know.

'I was the kind of little dude that hung by himself mostly. I had kids that I played with, you know, but I mostly ran by myself. I was a hefty kid, quite strong, an' I didn't monkey around. You didn't push me too far: see, my thing is that I will *not* be done a certain way. If you get me an' do somethin' to me, best thing for you to do is *keep* me: because, if you've misused me some kinda way – it might be ten years – if I live, I'm gonna pay you back.

'This is one of the things I learned comin' up in Chicago, when you had to fight ten or fifteen boys on the corner to try to get sixty feet down the street to your house. Fight a little bit, an' run a little bit. Like, you had to ring your bell, an' then somebody had to buzz the door so you could get in downstairs, you dig? If you didn't push it when it buzzed, you had to go back an' ring it again, an' you're fightin' in the hallway, tryin' to get to the damned door with fourteen or fifteen little dudes that's on your tail, y'understand me?

*Chicago's largest and least salubrious black ghetto.

'So, since I found out I couldn't whup 'em all at once, I'd catch 'em one at a time. Didn't make me no difference because I was a pretty strong dude, an' there wasn't too much they could do with me. I'd take one of 'em an' hold him, an' whup the other one with my right hand. But now I'm older, I wouldn't even *attempt* no crap like that. The easiest way now is to find myself a two-by-four!' (Laughs.)

'I'm sorry, but that's the crap I had to survive. I've had my money taken, man, I've been robbed. I've been hit upside the head with a *hatchet*! I've had two cats turn my eyes red: they tripped me, one of 'em sat on my legs, an' the other sat on my chest, kept me on the ground, an' just punched me in the eye. When he finished, my eyes looked like two *beets*!

'I remember one time this boy caught me in back of this place called South Center, which was a big department store. I was back there because there was a place called the Savoy Skating Rink – right next to the Tivoli Theater – an' I used to go back there an' dig in the sawdust every other day when the guy swept out the floor an' threw the sawdust out. I was fartin' around back there an' found fifty cents in the sawdust! Evidently nobody had ever did this, because it had been burned: the pile of stuff was a rubbish pile, an' every two or three days the guy would throw a match on it. When it all burned down, I'd go back there an' sift through, an' I'd find money, take it home an' shine it on my mother's rug, you know.

'Man, I was findin' *money* back there! Sometimes I'd have two or three dollars in dimes! Old burnt dimes, man, pennies, fifty cents. One day I found a silver dollar back there, an' that *really* started me to huntin', 'cause there *had* to be *some more* in there! I'd find cuff-links, buttons, ear-rings, all sorts of little things, you know, an' I'd take all of this stuff home, clean it up, an' hang it on a little chain on the wall in my room, or somethin' like this.

'So, one day I was back there, an' this dude evidently was peepin' 'round the corner an' saw me pick somethin' up, look at it, flip it up in the air an' put it in my pocket. I kept lookin', an' found a couple more quarters an' nickels an' dimes. Then I got up an' grabbed my wagon – 'cause I was supposed to have been fetchin' some wood for our stove... this is before oil heating came out in the States – an' this tall dude jumped out from behind the wall, say: "Gimme that money!"

'I say: "I ain't got no money", an' kept tryin' to walk away.

'He had an umbrella, an' he kept followin' me, says: "I'm gonna have to *whup your ass*!"

20

'This is a bigger kid than me – I was about fourteen or fifteen, an' he had to be about seventeen or eighteen, somewhere along there – an' I said to myself: "How am I goin' to get outa *this*?"

'Now, at that time, black kids used to speak "pig latin" to get over on the teacher at school: the teacher couldn't understand it. See, we couldn't write a note across the room in case she got it, 'cause then she'd know we was all goin' to a battle in the alley at three o'clock, or whatever we was talkin' 'bout doin'.' (Laughs.)

'So, the dude made the mistake of lettin' me get to where there was some long pieces of wood like old window-glass sides. He said to me: "Hey lil' ol' nigger, you gonna give me the money?"

'I turned round an' says: "I ain't givin' you *nothin*'!" an' went to walk off. The cat let me get far enough for him to reach out with his umbrella an' snatch me back, hurt my throat here, you know. I couldn't get out of it, because he had it hooked around my neck.

'I had another little kid back there with me, an' I told him, I says: "U gi-imi a bi-ig sti, imi a loni-on!" He understood me – I'd told him to "give me that big stick, that long one" – an' he picked it up.

'The cat says: "What you talkin' 'bout?"

'I says: "I'm not talkin' 'bout anythin'", an' the kid just stood there with the stick.

'Then I says: "Ow-ni!" – an' when I said "Now", the kid held the stick out, an' I took it an' hit the cat upside the head! The last I seen of him, he was holdin' onto his head, an' holdin' the wall like this, you know.

'I ran home an' sat on my porch like this, *scared to death*! Every police car I saw I thought knew about me hittin' him with that stick, y'understand? Cop car: "Oh my God here they come! They're gonna get me!" Just totally freaked me out.

'After I made my first record, I seen that dude: he moved next door to the house I was raised in! He spotted me, I guess, the same way I spotted him. I went next door an' asked the people that lived there where he was, 'cause I *wanted* him! They said: "He just moved." He'd been stayin' there for one or two weeks, an' when he saw me, he just upped, went an' got his stuff an' disappeared, an' I haven't seen him since.

'I don't like confrontations, an' if I can get away from a problem, I'll get away from it. That don't mean I'm chickenshit – 'cause I'm not chickenshit from a long way – it's just that I know trouble is so easy to get into, but it's a *motherfucker* to get out of, an' if I *do* get into a problem where I've gotta bash some dude, I'll drop a *MOUNTAIN* on him![1]

'I was raised with what we used to call the "iron hand", an' in a way I'm glad, because if I wasn't, I probably wouldn't be alive today from tryin' to be slick, you know. I'm *serious*. I'm not gettin' off on a kid trip, but discipline is very important, an' if I hadn't got the good ol' five-of-clubs, I'd be somethin' else.[5]

'My momma was *rough*, man. She didn't speak but once. Like she'd say: "Ellas, wash the dishes." She knew that my hearin' was superb. She didn't speak a second time.[4]

'She had a thing about whuppings that I said I didn't deserve. You know what her answer was to that? "That's for the shit I *didn't* catch you at!" An' she *would* be justified, because there'd always be *somethin'* I'd did that she didn't know about. I still didn't like it, because she didn't *catch* me at it, but that was their belief. Old folks back then, they did all the thinkin'. You just jumped when they said "Jump!" – an' if you *didn't* jump, you'd wish you *hada* jumped! That was a thing called "discipline".[1] I think maybe they overdid it, but at the same time I'm kinda glad, because the devilment I *do* think about, I would never do it: that trainin' keeps you from doin' it. I think if I hadn't had that, I'd be one of the worst hoodlums there was.[4]

'My mom an' Momma Gussie, I feel, is two of the greatest women that ever walked on the face of the Earth, 'cause they made a man outa me. I didn't like some of the things that I had to go through, but after I got grown I appreciated it. I could be a thug, a drug-user, all sortsa stuff. Or I could be dead. I have no desire for any of these things.'[1]

Church, Church, Church

An exacting parent, Gussie McDaniel was also a deeply religious woman who taught at Sunday School and participated in many other activities of one of the city's largest black churches – the Ebenezer Missionary Baptist on South Vincennes.

'My mother was strictly a Bible woman, strictly church. Nothin' else mattered in life but church. I went to church Sunday, Monday, Tuesday, Wednesday, Thursday, Friday, an' Saturday afternoon. When I got to be about fifteen, I got off a day: Friday afternoon, Friday evenin'.

'Every night after school, if I didn't have no homework, I'd be hangin' 'round that church somewhere with her. "C'mon boy, get ready. We gotta go to prayer meetin' tonight!"

'Lemme tell you somethin': I ain't knockin' it, because I'm thankful for what she put me through. I don't go anymore, but I didn't "stray away"; it's just that I don't think anybody actually hangs on to exactly what they were taught, because you have a brain of your own, man.'[1]

It was also at church that Ellas received a thorough musical education from the tender age of seven onwards. 'As far as singin' goes, I started in church. Most blacks do, you know. I never really bothered about it too much but, man, I could *holler*! They used to tell me to shut up because I was drownin' out the rest of the choir!' (Laughs.)

'One day, I saw a dude playin' a violin. I didn't even know what it was, you know, so I told my mother that I wanted one of them things that that man had a stick on it, you know. My mother couldn't afford to buy me a violin because my family was on relief at the time, so the church took up a collection an' bought me one. Then, I found I was havin' problems readin' the music, so she had to go get me some glasses as well!'[1]

'The Ebenezer Sunday School Baptist Band an' Orchestra were run by Professor O.W. Frederick an' his wife, an' both of 'em were damn good teachers.[4] Professor Frederick was a helluva good man!'[1] I mean he was good-*hearted*. Of course, he'd kick my ass every once in a while because he wanted me to *learn* somethin'. I used to get mad an' run out, but I understand now why he did it: 'cause if he hadn't've done it, I wouldn't have showed any interest.[3] An' so, I learnt. I won quite a few merit pins for performances.[4] He *made* me learn it, an' I'm glad he did, because if he hadn't've pounded it into me, I'd be a lost ball in high weeds today.[3]

'Everybody was playin' 'Drink To Me Only With Thine Eyes' an' concertos, but I wanted to play some jazz an' *get down*, you know*. I wanted to play, like, 'Honeydripper'**, an' stuff that was goin' durin' that time. I just wanted to see if some of this stuff could be played on a violin. I figured if all this other stuff could be played, you *gotta* be able to play some blues on it! I'd quit practisin' an' start playin' that stuff, an' the teacher would come back in the room an' I'd get beat up.[4] You know how kids do: teacher leave out the classroom, somebody's gonna goof off. Well, I was the goofer-off in the orchestra: everybody else was sittin' up in there tryin' to do all of this fast finger-work, an' I was sittin' there goin' "dum-dum-dum-dum".' (Laughs.) 'One day, he jumped on me, broke up a violin

---

*A fellow pupil, Leroy Jenkins, did actually go on to become a jazz violinist of world renown.
**Joe Liggins's 1945 hit [Exclusive 207].

23

bow on my back, because he wanted me *not* to play the blues on the violin, just *classics*. I love classical music, but I just wanted to try somethin' *different*.

'I had violin lessons until I was fifteen an' I broke my finger. After it healed, I could still play the violin – but it slowed my hand up, so I took up the trombone. I played in the Baptist Congress Band for a couple of years, but I didn't like it that much: I love string instruments,[1] but when it's somethin' you gotta blow, I don't want no part of it.[3]

'I took up playin' guitar because my sister Lucille gave me one for a Christmas present when I was twelve – an' here I am!' (Laughs.)

'I'm completely self-taught, an' I don't play like nobody else. I can explain to you where I got it from.[1] See, playin' the violin gave me an edge for bein' original because it made me play the guitar the same way, an' with the same licks – this is where the Bo Diddley sound came from.[6] I was runnin' up an' down the strings to see if I could play 'When The Saints Go Marching In', an' I learned that on one string, you know.

'Then, I figured out that there was more notes: one day I was foolin' around with the thing an' tuned it by accident. I wrote the notes down – played 'em on my violin an' wrote 'em down – an' the number of the strings. I name 'em by numbers: if I break one, I say: "Gimme a third", you know – an' I got 'em marked that way, not E, F, G, D or B, or whatever they are.

'If it hadn't been for the Ebenezer Baptist Church I don't think I'd be Bo Diddley today, because the violin was the railroad tracks, or lifeline, to me playin' a guitar. *I* know that, but don't too many people know it. I *know* where it came from:[1] I used the bow licks with the guitar pick, an' that's the reason for the weird sounds.[7] That was my way of imitatin' what I did with the bow on the violin strings, an' that was the closest I could get to it. My technique comes from bowin' the violin, that fast wrist action.[1]

'I do a lotta things, an' when I get to where I'm goin' on the neck, I know where I'm goin'. Cats that do a lot of fingerin' can't do that – so, there's a barrier. Somehow, my left hand knows where to get to when the right one says: "Be there when I get there!" When I'm doin' somethin' that's fast, I'm thinkin' *way* ahead – two or three seconds before I get to a certain point – what I'm gonna do when I get there.

'Some guys play with real mellow tones that I could never do. I'm not what you call a guitarist; I'm a *showman*, an' I'm not downin' myself when I say that. There *is* a difference: the cats that do all that pretty finger-work, now they are *guitarists*. I could never do that: my fingers are too slow... but my hands are fast, y'understand?⁵

'I could *not* play like everybody else. I *like* what everybody else do, but I can't do it, so I leave it alone. See, most guitar players – you'll notice – have got little bitty skinny fingers. Look at these *meathooks* I got! I wear a size 12 glove – that's *big*. So, I developed my own shit: I tune *in* a chord*, an' I learned how to play it *from* a chord – which makes it different. Instead of me playin' it the way that the average guitar player plays it, all I do is bar a note, bar a fret, an' I got the same key that he's got.

'That's the reason why I'm not even *worried* about nobody tryin' to copy a certain sound that I got, unless they learn to play like I'm playin'. My fingers are more educated now, but I didn't use to do no finger-work. I was *all* rhythm. I could drive you outa your tree with *chords*, you know, an' that fast wrist-work. This is the key to me, right here.'¹

'I wanted to do somethin' else'

'The schools I went to in Chicago was the Frances E. Willard Grammar School an' Foster Vocational. Foster Vocational was at 720 O'Brien Street – that's where I learned how to build instruments.¹ I made a violin an' a bass fiddle: cut an' warped the wood, molded it, an' you couldn't tell it from a store-bought instrument! I decided to make my own molds to make a hollow-body guitar. I got ambitious, my head got a little too fat, an' I quit school.

'I feel I made a *big* mistake by quittin', y'understand, I feel that in myself. But, would I be here talkin' to you now as Bo Diddley if I'da stayed in school? I think I made the right move at that particular time, but, if I pulled it today, I believe I'd be facin' starvation: it don't work that way no more.⁴ It's a lot harder today than it was when I was comin' up. I feel that, today, you *need* that education. You need *somethin'* to fall back on because, man, you can't even get a job *shinin' shoes* nowadays without a piece of paper in your pocket!

'I was really not interested in basic everyday school stuff; I was mostly interested in what I could build or invent, you know – because everybody can't learn readin', writin' an' 'rithmetic. I wanted to do somethin' else, an' I felt that I had the talent to do somethin' *other* than sit up an' learn.

'I was the dude that used to fix everythin' that break down in the neighborhood. If people's water-faucets would quit workin' an' stuff like

*Open E Major.

25

that, they'd say: "Go find Ellas!" You know. "Ellas, my mother says would you come over here an' fix a faucet for her?" An' I'd get my little pliers an' wrenches an' stuff, an' go fix it.

'That's the way I *survived*! I was the kid in the neighborhood that didn't sit around and twiddle my thumbs. When people found out I knew a little about everythin', I didn't have no problem in survivin', because I kept on gettin' work.

'I've *always* been a hustler: while everybody else was shootin' marbles an' playin' basketball, I was somewhere tryin' to make me a quarter or two. I did things like sellin' wood, or I'd hang around the grocery store an' carry people's groceries, an' stuff like this. I've *always* been that way, an' I'm that way today. My wife says I'm a workoholic, you know, but I saw that the only way you get anythin', man, is you gotta *work* for it!

'My mother wasn't able to buy me the things, or give me the things that a boy of my age would have liked to have, such as bicycles an' nice clothes, an' stuff like this. I used to see kids that were a little bit more fortunate than me an', quite naturally, I wanted these things, you know. It didn't look like I was learnin' anythin' at school, so I said the best thing for me to do was to get out an' start to buildin' my "survival kit" *now*. In other words, to secure myself for old age – because I didn't want to be in the predicament that my mom had fallen into: she didn't *have* nothin', an' it was too late to *get* anythin'.

'I didn't become a pocket-book snatcher like everybody predicted I was gonna be[1] an', if I'd gone on through school I *could* have been a doctor or somethin', but I don't really know if I'da been happy doin' that. See, people gotta realize one thing: you gotta be happy in what you're doin'. Your mind's gotta be at ease an' together.'[3]

Ellas was by this time already quite proficient on the guitar and, shortly before leaving school, formed a duo with his classmate, Roosevelt Jackson.

'Roosevelt, which is Nat Cole's third cousin, played washtub-bass. As far as I know, I was the first one that built one around Chicago, but they tell me that they'd been around for years. How did I come up with this crap, an' I ain't never been nowhere an' ain't seen nothin'?

'What happened was, I was standin' up beatin' on the washtub one day with my hands, an' I saw that it made a sound. So, I took a nail an' punched a hole in my mother's washtub, an' put this rope on it an' hit it, an' couldn't get a sound out. Then I figured out the same system as my violin was strung: that there had to be a *hard point* that the rope crossed over in

26

order to make it sound. Then I figured out that, if you pushed the stick over, the notes would get deeper, an' if you tightened it up, they got higher. Then I learned how to play it, an' I taught Roosevelt how to play it, an' that was the beginnin' of my whole thing – which really started after I'd left school.

'There was this dude called Sandman that used to carry a board, an' a bag of sand an' a swish-broom, you know, one of them "sweep-ups". He'd put the board down on the ground, an' dump this sand on it an' spread it around, an' then he would sing an' "sand" – it was kinda like a shuffle, but it was called "sandin'". It carried a rhythm with it, like a tap-dancer taps, an' not too many people around there could do it. When he finished his act, he'd sweep up the sand an' put it back in his little bag. His name was Samuel Daniel – the same name as mine – but everybody called him "Sandman".

'So, Sandman an' us, we kinda teamed up together, but he wasn't actually part of the group. Half the time, Sandman would go off an' work by himself: he'd go inside of a lil' ol' juke joint, put a dime in the juke-box an' imitate Billy Eckstine. I mean mark him *to a "T"*! Sometimes we would go with him, but they wouldn't let us no further up in there but right inside the front door because we were teenagers, an' after we'd played for about fifteen minutes, the bartender or the owner would say: "Okay, y'all go now!" We didn't think nothin' of it, because we knew that was all "gravy", bein' able to walk inside the door, y'understand?

'When we first started playin' together, Sandman was the boss. I didn't like that, so after a few weeks I told him, I says: "Now wait, this is *my* group!" So, we didn't see too much of each other after that. Last I heard of him, he was in the nuthouse: stood out in front of the Club DeLisa, took off all his clothes, an' said: "To *hell* with the world!" Just freaked out one night, an' they locked his ass up.'[1]

Ellas's group did not remain a duo for very long, however, for they were joined soon after by another aspiring guitarist from their neighbourhood, Joe Leon 'Jody' Williams.

'We called ourselves the "Hipsters" because everybody was runnin' around in the streets talkin' 'bout "hip cats", you know. Later on, I got tired of that, so we changed our name to the "Langley Avenue Jive Cats" – that's where I was brought up at, South Langley. "Jive" was the Big Word back then: there used to be a group, say: *"Hit that jive, Jack/Put it in your pocket till I get back/Goin' downtown to see my girl"*, dum-dum-dum,

27

da-da-da*. As soon as we could play half a tune, we went out on the corner to try an' earn ourselves a few nickels an' dimes.

'Earl Hooker was the one that got me interested in playin' on the street-corners with a band, because he had one an' I saw they were makin' all these nice coins, so I said: "Hey!"'

'Earl an' me, we was in the same classroom at school.[1] I used to hang around with Earl a lot. We ditched school together, we'd get caught by the truant officer, get suspended.[8] But Earl was not a responsible person. He'd say: "Ellas, come on down to so-an'-so-an'-so", an' I'd be lookin' for Earl, an' Earl'd be – uh – *forty miles* away! You could hardly ever catch up with him, but he was a great guy.[1]

'I saw him about a couple of months before he died, an' it was a shock to me to hear that he had passed.[8] Earl had always been very sickly, an' he hadn't been well for quite a while**. I guess it finally caught up with him.'[1]

Mama Don't Allow

Playing on the street-corners may have been a fun way for Ellas to earn himself a little extra pocket-money, but his mother and 'bunch of uncles who were preachers an' deacons'[9] strongly disapproved of him playing the Devil's music, and the lad's protestations that 'the Devil ain't never paid me'[9] fell upon deaf ears.

'They thought *everythin'* was bad! Baptist people think *breathin'* is bad, you dig?[1] I wasn't allowed to listen to blues music an' stuff like that. This is somethin' I kinda sneaked in there.[5]

'I wanted to do somethin' on my own. Not necessarily be a guitar player, but I wanted to be somethin' different than a violinist sittin' around church somewhere.[8] Playin' the guitar was my idea, an' my mother didn't dig it.[1] She hit the ceilin'! She didn't realize that this wasn't – uh – 1909, that this is a new day. She didn't realize that the day would come when Ellas would have to support himself, an' couldn't run to momma an' say: "Hey mom, throw me out a couple of quarters!"[8]

'I'll never forget the time my uncle walked up on me – my Uncle Al, which is a minister – an' me an' Joe an' Roosevelt, man, we was gettin' *down*! Dust was flyin', people were jumpin' an' clappin' their hands, an' we

---

*'Hit That Jive Jack' was originally recorded by the Nat 'King' Cole Trio in 1941 [Decca 8630].
**Hooker contracted tuberculosis in 1956 and eventually died from the disease on 21 April, 1970.

had the corner crowded. This was on the corner of 47th Street, not too far from my house. We was upside the wall: that's the Chicago scene.

'Somebody touched me on the shoulder. It was Uncle Al. He said: "I'll see you at the house!" Now, that dude was about thirty-five or forty then, an', do you know, he beat me home an' told my momma I was up there on the street-corner! I wasn't supposed to be on the street-corner: she didn't allow that.

'I had a big cake-bowl out there – I'd snuck out the back door with it, an' it was half-full of money from people – the "kitty" we called it. They didn't want me playin' the blues an' all this ol' kinda stuff, but I snuck around an' did it anyway because I was makin' *money*, you know: ten, twelve, fifteen bucks *a night*! Man, for a kid sixteen years old playin' on a street-corner – I didn't know but two or three numbers – that was a *lotta* money. Nickels an' dimes? Shoot, wasn't no way *nobody* was gonna stop me after I got a taste of that fifteen bucks!

'I was the richest thing around my neighborhood! If I'da stayed there long enough, I'm liable to have turned out a loan shark!' (Laughs.) 'Lend out a nickel, get seven cents back, you know.·

'Of course, all the other kids knew we was makin' money, an' they'd catch you an' jump on you, so you had to learn how to run fast, jump high an' disappear quick! We used to run in gangways an' stuff – you know the way buildings was later built, a piece of concrete down in there to make a foundation for the building? You'd run through the gangway an', if the catchers were far enough behind, you could jump behind this little piece of concrete in the dark, an' everybody would run past you.

'But the cats got slick: they'd leave a straggler behind, so if you doubled back an' went the other way, this other dude was there, an' he'd whistle an' holler: "Here he is!" – y'understand what I mean – just like chasin' a rabbit.

'So, I decided to carry me a blade, because I didn't want my eyes punched out, or my teeth knocked out. I had to protect *me*, an' I don't think there's nothin' wrong with protectin' me. I carry a gun *all* the time, because I'm afraid a lot of times now when I go to play. That's the reason I have club owners to pick me up from the hotel, an' drop me off at the hotel, an' all this ol' kinda stuff. It's *very* dangerous, an' I don't think that I should be the victim of some dude. If he figure that I got a heater in my pocket, then he's not gonna try an' mug me, or stab me or somethin'. I don't wanna *hurt* anybody, but I don't wanna be the sucker that's layin' on the ground, either. You know, lotta people standin' around sayin': "Ooh-wee, that looks like Bo Diddley."

"It *is*, girl!"

"Looks like they robbed him."

"Is he dead?"

'An' then, here come the cops: "Anybody see who did this?"

'I don't *want* that shit. I wanna be standin' up there sayin': "Yeah, there the sucker is. He attacked me, an' I shot him."

'I'd rather the police catch me *with* a gun or weapon, than for hoodlums to catch me *without* it. That sayin' comes from a time that I got picked up in Chicago because I had a knife: I was a teenager – about sixteen – an' the police took me down to the juvenile court. The judge said: "Don't you know it's against the law for you to have this?" I told the judge the same thing I just said, an' everybody in the courtroom bust out laughin'. He told me to get outa there an' go on home – because durin' that time kids was gettin' beat up an' killed an', like, I was a kid that ran by myself, man. I didn't have no backers to help me fight.'[1]

Like many other teenagers, Ellas was by now also beginning to find the atmosphere at home too oppressive to live with: 'You know how old folks are: they try to program you as a youngster the way that *they* want you to be, an' don't realize that one day they're gonna be gone an' that you are goin' to have to stand on your own two feet. So, you gotta start tryin' to make your own life at some point.

'I figured that I'd had enough church when I was a kid: if I didn't know God now, I never will know Him. So, I left home at sixteen: I moved next door!' (Laughs.) 'Didn't go too far, just next door.

'I thought that, by movin' out, I could get away from goin' to church every day – because I couldn't dig goin' through the rest of my life bein' a little church boy. Ain't nothin' *wrong* with church, understand me, but I just felt that I had been to church, church, church, church, church, until I was churched-out. It didn't work.' (Laughs.) 'She used to come an' get me out of bed, an' *drag* me to church! I said: "Wow, when do you grow *up*?" I prayed for the day that I could do what I wanted to do, an' it just seemed like it didn't get there fast enough.'[1]

'I was raisin' sand'

As they grew older and their repertoire increased, the Hipsters began travelling further afield to perform, often heading for the bustling open-air market on Maxwell Street – the heart of an old immigrant area known as 'Jew Town'.

'I think the reason they called it "Jew Town" is because most of the Jewish people brought all these little packs an' stuff, an' they'd set it all up in the street like a flea-market. After a while, a few blacks an' Anglos would be hangin' around down there, an' they had little stands too. So, every Saturday an' Sunday, they had a big day.

'You could buy *anythin'*. If it was made, you'd find it; it would be down there. Them sap-suckers would have – uh, uh – *dogshit* in a can!' (Laughter.) 'Be *anythin'*, somebody's be buyin' it! Cats come with a big ol' carrier, just old nuts an' bolts, an' stuff like that, anythin'. Probably had it for years, or either found it in somebody else's garbage can. What the heck, if he drove down there, an' you bought it, he just made two bucks!

'I admire Jewish people for that – because, to me, every nationality has a reason for bein' here, an' mostly all the Jewish people own everythin': they got all the money.' (Laughs.) 'Give him a thousand dollars, he'll turn it into *ten million*! How the heck they do it, I don't know.[10]

'When we went down there to play, we would put on ragged clothes, an' dirty old shoes with paint on 'em an' stuff, an' people thought we were real poor. We would go down an' walk through the streets, an' stop an' play, an' all the old dudes would run us away because we'd take all their customers. Them old blues dudes that's been down there for years couldn't stand the idea that we was comin' down there, see?

'We used to go down there, find us a vacant lot, an' draw all the people. We'd be there, "boom-boom-boom-boom", an' people would come up in there an' start throwin' money. Then, some old dude would come down there, or either he'd send a bunch of older boys down there to run us away. Bullies, you know. Sometimes the cat would have six or seven dudes around the corner, so we got us a car, so we could get away quick, 'cause that walkin' shit wasn't gettin' it![1] We saved a little money, an' we bought a 1937 Buick!

'We'd park it about a block away from the corner that we was gonna play on because we didn't want the people to know that we had a car. One day some wino followed us, an' when we got to the wheels, he says: "Ah-ha, y'all got some wheels." So, every time we played on the street-corner, he'd make a bee-line for us an' say: "Where's your wheels, man?"'[8] (Laughs.)

'We scraped up pop bottles an' stole milk bottles off people's back porches to buy gas.' (Laughs.) 'You know, get twenty-five cents, an' buy a gallon of gas. Man, we'd ride all day! That's the *truth*! We'd get a basket, sneak up on somebody's back porch an' get the milk bottles, put 'em in the basket, an' let 'em downstairs. You could get a penny apiece for 'em, but you had to make one shot: if the woman come out, drop the basket, an' *run like hell*!' (Bursts out laughing.)

'I got caught a coupla times. The woman says: "I *know* you, boy! I know where you live! I know your momma, an' I'm tellin' her!" Man, I didn't steal no more bottles for a *month*! My mother never said nothin', but I know if she *had* told my mother, I'da got *killed* for takin' that woman's bottles for that ol' piece of car we had.' (Laughs.)

'No driver's license, we'd drive it through the alleys 'cause we couldn't go out on the streets in it. We'd *push* it to the gas station, so if the cops seen us, they wouldn't say nothin'. We'd get the gas an' look down the street. "Ain't no police cars, man, get in!" *Zoom*!!! We'd ride up an' down through the alleys with it. I used to do some *strange* things when I was a kid, but nothin' to hurt people. I just didn't believe in that.[1]

'Music I liked at that time was Louis Jordan an' Nat 'King' Cole. John Lee Hooker too.[2] The first time I heard him, I said: "If *that* cat can play guitar, I know darn well *I* can." I remember that exactly.[1] So, I tried to catch his strange guitar sounds, but at first I couldn't understand him.[2] I didn't wanna *sound* like John Lee Hooker, but I knew I could make some noise an' make people listen to me.[11]

'By the time I was sixteen years old, I'd really started gettin' into somethin' that sounded like a tune goin'. I wrote my first song around that time, too: it's a blues tune called 'I Don't Want No Lyin' Woman'*, but I've never sang it. I've been savin' it, actually, till I get to be much older, if I'm still in the business. Really, it ain't heavy enough to be mixed in with all the heavies like Muddy Waters an' stuff like that, so I'll just save it.[1]

'Muddy has been some of my inspiration, 'cause I wanted to be so much like him, but I couldn't even *begin* to think about bein' the man he is in the blues bag. Muddy is the greatest!

'It's written in a book that I played guitar for Muddy Waters. Nobody ever asked *me* about that, an' it's a *lie*! I was not even up to his standard. Muddy was *way* advanced over me! There wouldn't've been *no way* I'da even been able to *audition* for Muddy, because I knew nothin' about nothin' at that time, an' Muddy was the Godfather of the Blues around Chicago. I didn't know but two songs![12]

---

*This is a different song from the one featured on the *London Bo Diddley Sessions* album.

'I used to go an' listen at Muddy Waters an' Little Walter play – this is before Little Walter put a record out, I think*. They used to play a club right across from the White Sox ballpark on 36th an' Wentworth called the DuDrop Lounge. It was a *helluva* place, an' that was the beginnin' of Muddy Waters' thing. When he was there, man, there was *lines*! His crowds was tremendous.

'I'd ride my bike all the way down there, you know, sneak in. I was a little bitty dude, short an' stocky.[1] Man, I got throwed outa there enough times 'cause I was under-age!

'They had a juke-box near the door. I'd get in the corner between the juke an' the cigarette machine, where I could split when I saw the man comin'.[2] I wasn't old enough to be in the joint, an' the bouncer would throw me straight out onto the streetcar tracks. The next couple of weeks, I'd figure the dude forgot me, y'understand? I'd paint me a mustache on, but the cat would catch me an' – out the door again!

'I said: "One day, I'm gonna play in that place." So, finally, when I got seventeen years old, I went in there one night an' took my guitar with me, an' they *didn't* throw me out. I got to the stage an' they asked me if I wanted to sit in, but when they found out I didn't have no Union card, they told me that they couldn't let me on stage.

'That's one of the things that the Law doesn't understand: I eat an' sleep like anybody else, like an adult. If I wanna work, then why not give me an *opportunity* to work? People say that kids that don't have nothin' to do will steal an' cause all kinda problems, but they fight the idea of kids havin' a job. They say you don't belong to the Union, or that you can't work in this club because there's liquor in there an' you're under-age. To me, that's deprivin' you of your rights to *live*. Everybody can't be doctors an' lawyers. So, I'm a musician, an' I can't work!

'I still ain't figured out whether not lettin' me play with Muddy Waters at that time was a thing against me because I was raisin' sand around Chicago on the street-corners an' in Jew Town. Man, I was *raisin' sand*! I won so many midnight amateur shows an' stuff that they quit lettin' me on! They told me: "Give somebody else a chance to win", or they'd say: "You can get on, but you can't be in on the prizes."

'We used to do a midnight show at the Indiana Theater. We'd go on, man, just take First Prize an' walk off with it! I think First Prize was fifteen

*1952.

33

bucks: we got five dollars apiece. Every Saturday night, we'd stand in the streets an' work on the corners, an' then, just about time for the show to open up, we'd haul ass to 39th an' Indiana to sign in for the amateur show. It got so that the man knew we was goin' to show up, y'understand, an' he'd put up there "The Hipsters". People would come in, man, an' we'd *destroy* the place! Me, Roosevelt an' Joe. We played all over Chicago. We was just a little group that people wanted to hear.

'I never did get to play with Muddy Waters because, by the time I'd got old enough to get in the damn place, the Urban Renewal came an' tore all that shit down.

'The first club I played was – I got a gig playin' one or two nights a week at a place called the 708 Club, on East 47th Street. To tell you the truth, I was actually nineteen, but I lied an' said I was twenty-one. I *had* to work, man, so I just point-blank lied – which hurt me very much because I'm *not* a liar – but I had to eat. I'm a *very* religious person, but I gotta *eat*. I preferred workin' rather than stealin', so I said I was twenty-one, went an' got me an affidavit an' got inside the club.

'The cops in my neighborhood knew I wasn't no damn twenty-one years old, so they used to come in an' look at me, say: "We ain't gonna bother you, but we don't wanna catch you drinkin' nothin'."' (Laughs.) 'They didn't know that I never drinked anyway. I was never a drinkin' man, but all these people that I used to hang with as a younger man, a lot of 'em drank. They couldn't function unless they had a beer in their hand. I could never understand that, an' I don't understand it to this day. When I go on stage every night – like I gotta go on stage here tonight – the only thing I have inside me is a pork chop!' (Laughs.)

'I drink a little bit now, but I drink so little, that I can almost say that I don't. I'll taste a little Grand Marnier or somethin' like that if my throat gets a little funny on stage, an' I've found that that helps me get through the show.

'See, I'm up there on stage, breathin' in a lot of different air, an' I'm pickin' up germs an' smoke an' everythin'. Your throat gets dry from standin' up there hollering – *plus* you got all those hot-ass lights onto you. It takes a helluva man to absorb all of that.

'Now, I understand a virus don't like alcohol so, if you can get it into your system, an' get it to where you can sweat, you *might* be able to turn it around. The way I look at it, the virus say: "Hey man, this cat's got some *heavy* stuff in his body! We'd better go back an' try some *weak* dude." So, they jump off you an' *run*, y'understand?'[1] (Laughs.)

Chapter 2

I'm A Man

'I've done somethin' of everythin''

Surprisingly, perhaps, music was not Ellas's main preoccupation during his teenage years: 'At that time, I was tryin' to figure out about growin' up an' moldin' myself to manhood an', since I knew I had to walk this dirt road alone, I might as well learn not to be scared. Boxing was it!²

'Eddie Nicholson's gym on 48th an' Michigan, that's where I used to hang at. We used to have boxing tournaments at places like Corpus Christi, which was a Catholic church. Roosevelt – the bass player from my group – was my sparring partner.¹

'It wasn't that I wanted to be tough, but I think that you should like somethin' *rough* to be a man. Man is supposed to be *built*. Look at the gladiators back in Roman days: these cats could walk up an' *deck* a horse by crackin' him on the jaw. Man is gettin' outa that: try it today, an' you break your hand. We are usin' the knowledge-box more, an' doin' less of a physical thing. We're gonna be all head an' no body after a while. I believe it should be more balanced than that.²

'An' so, I got to be a light-heavyweight – I was 167 pounds – but I quit fightin' completely not long after that.¹ I was gettin' ready to turn pro when

I got eighteen, but I was gettin' around an' married this chick, Louise, an' that blew that. I quit, got right out – an' I'm *glad* I quit, 'cause I could be half-crazy today.[3]

'It was *my* decision, but I did have problems outa Louise about me boxing, 'cause I don't guess it's very pleasant to come home with your lip all busted, an' all that kinda jazz. Dudes was gettin' bigger an' hittin' harder, an' if anybody ever said "The bigger they are, the harder they fall", that's a *lie*![1] They kept gettin' bigger an' meaner-lookin' every time I went out. They hit you too hard then: I'm strictly a "fun" guy.'[13]

Ellas's marriage to Louise Woolingham lasted less than a year: 'I married her when she was sixteen, I think, an' I was eighteen. We stayed together about six or eight months, somethin' like that, an' we just found out it was a mistake, so we got divorced. She was okay, you know, she just didn't wanna be married: she wanted to get away from home, an' that was it. Like most young people, you know. She never gave me any problems or anythin', an' I haven't seen or heard from her in all those years.

'My first job after leavin' school was at Ben Gay's grocery store on 47th Street, between Langley an' Evans. I just did whatever needed to be done, whether it was workin' behind the counter, puttin' out the vegetables, takin' the vegetables in, preparin' 'em for sale, cleanin' up – the whole bit. When I got old enough, I learned to drive the truck down there.

'After I got married, I had to put the grocery store down because there wasn't enough money involved there for me to support a wife, an' I started hustlin'. I worked at the Union Station for two or three months. I was a elevator operator at Superior Auto Fabric, which used to make car seat covers: I ran the elevator where they used to take in all the shipments. I worked in Wilson's packing house in Chicago, in the cooler. I had to go in there an' hang meat an' stuff, you know. In the wintertime, the temperature *outside* – snow on the ground – wasn't as cold as it was in the cooler! I started gettin' colds, an' I've never been able to shake 'em. I guess whatever fights for you in cold weather must have got confused an' stopped workin'.

'I don't talk about that job too much because it only lasted a couple of months.' (Laughs.) 'See, somebody told me that you'd get a job if you tell 'em that you from Mississippi, or Louisiana, or *anywhere* but Chicago: they wouldn't have anybody from Chicago because they'd all work a couple of weeks an' quit. So, I went out there an' told this lie, got the job just like the dude said. I got fired 'cause they found out I'd went to Willard grade school!' (Laughs.) 'Cat walked up to me, gave me two checks: I thought I'd got a *bonus*!

'I also worked at Gardner's, which used to be a punchboard factory – you used to punch little bitty things out of a board an' win stuff, you know. I used to make those things. Then I worked in the print shop screwin' big die-cut machines – those things with the big blade. I used to do all the kinda stuff that nowadays you need a *diploma* to run it. Same damn machines, but you gotta have a college education or a high school diploma to prove that you got sense enough to run it. Today, it look like you gotta damn near have a diploma to *wash dishes* – which is *ridiculous*!

'I've done somethin' of everythin'. I've even been a latrine cleaner, you know, I've done worked cleanin' bathrooms, an' all sortsa stuff. I don't frown on *any* kinda job: if you take the job, it's a *good* job. If you're gettin' *paid* for it, it's *not* a sucker's job. It's payin' your bills, you're eatin' – bottom line.

'I heard a little joke once: there's a dude standin' up on the 35th floor, in the window. Nineteen below zero outside, an' he's standin' up there in his shirt-sleeves. Cat open the window, stick his head out an' say: "Seventy-five degrees in here!" an' the guy downstairs workin' on construction in the streets holler back up: "$15.95 an hour".' (Laughs.) 'You got the idea? $15.95, an' he's probably gettin' $2.95 upstairs, but it's *warmer* up there, y'understand?

'Whatever job you get – I don't care if it's *sweepin' floors* – if you *take* it, an' they're *payin'* you for it, it's a *job*! To me, there's no such thing as a chickenshit job or a flunkey's job. The way I look at it is: if you don't like it, don't take it!'[1]

It wasn't until 1949 when he married his second wife, Ethel 'Tootsie' Smith, that Ellas finally succeeded in finding more remunerative work.

'I was workin' at a picture-frame factory curin' wood for frames, but after I got married I got a new job because Tootsie's father was workin' for A1 Blacktop, an' he found out I had a driver's license an' got me the job. I worked on construction for A1 Blacktop for a *long* time – I think about four or five years, six years, somethin' like that.

'I started as a spreader, used to spread all of the hot mix with the shovel, an' then they had two guys that didn't do anythin' but lute – that's to level it so that when the roller rolls it, it rolls almost level. I learned how to do that by watchin' the other guys, an' then I became a luter.

'I was the youngest thing that was there, doin' a gig that wasn't

37

supposed to be for guys my age: it took *years* to learn how to do this type of thing – because you didn't wanna see no ripples when the roller went over it.

'I had a system that I introduced – it just made sense to me – I carried me a little thing with a long stem that you put water in, for pourin' into flowers, an', after the roller had gone past, I'd pour water on it to see if it run off in the right direction.

'I became pretty good, an' became a little straw boss – which the old guys didn't like because they'd been there all this time, but nobody was interested in tryin' to become more than just a laborer. My ambition didn't stop right at the goddamn job. If it had, I'd still be there.

'I was always an energetic person: I don't like to sit around an' wait for somethin' to come to me. I've found out that it *don't* come to you; you gotta go *get* it, gotta *make* it happen! You can sit on your buns an', before you know anythin', you're forty – an' what have you done for yourself? Okay, why can't you take that Saturday an' Sunday every now an' then, or take off a day from that gig you're doin', an' look for somethin' that might *better* you? The dude that you're workin' for don't care *nothin'* about you: you are a *worker*, he's not *in love* with you. When he gets ready to shut the damn place up, it's shut, an' you don't even know what's happenin'!

'I found this out: I used to work overtime thinkin' that I was betterin' my conditions, that the boss of the place was gonna say: "McDaniel is a good worker. He works overtime and he stays here to clean up after time. He punches in early, he comes to do things around here. These are the kind of people we need!" I was the *first* sonofabitch that got laid off when lay-off time came!

'So, it don't mean a damn thing, an' I can understand why a lotta times people get real arrogant an' say: "Hey man, I'm not gonna do that! What am *I* gonna get out of it? Long as I give you eight hours a day, an' I'm *workin'* that eight hours, don't put no heavy shit on me – 'cause when you get ready to lay off people, I'll probably be leadin' the line!"'[1]

'It was noisy as hell, but it worked'

Struggling to exist on the pittance he earned as an unskilled black labourer, Ellas had little choice but to continue hustling for those all-important extra few bucks. Most weekends and evenings would find him on the city's sidewalks with his little group, playing on corners, in doorways and anywhere else people would let them.

Then, one day in 1950, a young harmonica player by the name of 'Billy Boy' Arnold saw the boys taking a break in a restaurant and struck up a conversation. 'I told them I played harmonica, so Bo said: "We're going up to the Midway Theater to do an amateur show. Come and go up there with us!" Midway was on 63rd and Cottage Grove. It was a regular movie theater, but every Tuesday or Wednesday they had an amateur show. I went up there with them, but I didn't play. I don't know if they won or not, because there were so many people in there and I was in the audience, you know.

'Bo gave me his address, said: "Hey, come down to my house on Saturday morning, and we'll play on the corner." I went down to his house. Man, I must have got there eight o'clock! I was sitting on his porch: he hadn't even got up.

'So then, here come little Jody – he was a little short guy and his guitar was bigger than he was – coming down the street. Jody rang the bell and we went on upstairs. Bo was up there asleep. We sat up there about an hour and Roosevelt came by with his tub. Bo got his guitar and we walked down the corner. We got there about eleven o'clock. It was summertime and the weather was warm.

'Bo knew how to deal with the crowds: he had experience, you know. He played that boogie, and he used to play 'Rollin' Stone'* in his own way, but it was real funky and the people liked it. I was singing a Sonny Boy Williamson song and people say: "Sonny Boy!" and they give us money in the hat.

'We got us a crowd and we stayed there for half an hour. Then we'd go on up around 43rd, or go over to the West Side on Kedzie. At that time, we go to the Indiana Theater, on 43rd between Indiana and Michigan. They had what they called a "Midnight Ramble": they'd show regular movies in them daytime, and at night – at twelve o'clock – you'd see the acts, the blues singers.

'Bo Diddley split the money fair: four ways. I think we'd have ten or twelve bucks apiece. The guy with the washtub didn't want me with 'em. He told Bo: "We don't need that lil' ol' boy playing harmonica!"

'Bo said: "No, he's alright, let him go".'

'Bo Diddley was a very nice person that way, you know. Very friendly,

---

*Muddy Waters's 1950 smash [Chess 1426].

warm-hearted guy. It could be nine below zero and, if your car was stopped and he'll be driving along, he would stop and say: "Hey man, what's wrong?" He'd get out the car, go up under the hood, and try to get you started. He was a good mechanic: he'd take a motor out of a car, and when he got through with it, each part of that motor would be no bigger than a cigarette! He could take a motor like that and put it back together. Very good like that.'[14]

Billy became a permanent member of Ellas's informal group and played the inhospitable South Side streets and rough drinking joints with them for the next couple of years.

'Man, we played some *smokey* holes,' recalls Bo, 'bars under the El* station, in store-front clubs, an' it was *hard* – so hard you was lookin' for the *worm* to pull the *robin* into the ground, you dig? You ask cats like Muddy an' Willie Dixon an' J.B. Lenoir, you ask 'em how hard it was to get five or six dollars together on a weekend![2] A lotta times we'd get five bucks split between four or five musicians.'[11] When you worked a club, you *worked* it! Sometimes I'd make less than I would on the street – because on the street they'd say: "How cute that boy is" an' put in fifty cents, but in a club you had to have it together or be *cut!*'[2]

Although he worked well with the group, Billy quickly became disillusioned when he realised that, unlike himself, Ellas had no aspirations of becoming a professional musician. Frustrated, he quit the band in 1952.

Ellas's creative mind was, however, far from stagnant, and the ensuing months witnessed some dramatic changes as he began turning his ideas for a new sound into reality. 'When I was still at school, I used to go in the back of my mother's big old radio when she wasn't around, an' I figured out that it had to be some way that the sound was comin' through that radio. There was one tube that was makin' blue lights in it every time that talkin' would come on, an' I'd sit back an' watch it. I got me two wires an' touched two of the pins, an' kept on till I found the two that the thing came through. That's how I electrified my guitar: I played it through the radio.'[1]

'The pick-up that I had was made out of an old Victrola record-player cartridge – you know them old Victrolas? I didn't *buy* me no electric guitar; shit, man, I had to figure out a way to *make* me one!'

'The first amp I ever bought was when I started workin' the 708 Club.

---

*Chicago's elevated urban railroad transit system.

I bought me a nice little Silvertone amplifier with one speaker sittin' in the middle, Sears & Roebuck. It looked like a big spaceman!' (Laughs.) 'That's the popular Silvertone deck, an' I'm *cool*, y'understand? Three tubes in it...' (Laughs.) 'One 6-L-6 an' two 12-AXL – an' I'm cool, man! I got about twenty-five watts goin', an' I'm the loudest thing in the neighborhood!'[10] The electronic things wasn't as good then, y'understand? Man, if you'd paid $69 for a amplifier, you had a *good* 'un!'[1]

'I never actually *built* an amplifier, but I would take the guts out an' put 'em in larger boxes, an' stuff like that. I also spent *years* tryin' to develop a clean speaker that I could use. What I did was, I'd take two Fender Bassmans – which has ten-inch speakers inside – I'd take 'em out an' build 'em into one big cabinet, because I needed eight or ten or twelve speakers to handle all that stuff I was puttin' through 'em. Ten-inch speakers are very clean an' clear. They take a *whuppin'*, you know.[1] This was before monitors, so I also put two speakers in the back of each cabinet, so the drummer could hear what was goin' on.[11] I spent *twelve years* tryin' to develop a good, clean sound because I *hate* distortion. You know what happened? Some guy built a *fuzz-pedal*!' (Laughs.) 'Busted my bubble! That was the beginnin' of a new sound.'[1]

'People thought I was some kinda electronics genius, but I wasn't. I could hook up my little things but, if I busted an amp, I either got it fixed or bought a new one.'[11]

Loud amplification was, of course, essential if Ellas was going to make himself heard in the noisy clubs and bars he played, but he used it in a way no one had ever done before, intensifying his fiery rhythm-lead guitar style with raw electric power to create a sound with an energy and intensity few could match.

'I was lookin' to get a bigger sound, an' I came up with that "freight train drive" – that's what I call it. There were three of us, an' I developed a style that would make us sound like six people at least. That's the monster *I* built!' (Laughs.) 'If you listen to the stuff I'm playin', you won't find any gaps in there: I play first an' second guitar at the same time, an' the minute I start playin', you *know* it! It's power-packed all the way. Pure energy.'[1]

'People were sayin': "Bo Diddley, you're too loud", but we only had fifty watts up there. Today, they're playin' with one hundred-forty watts *per channel*!'[11]

'Then, I came up with the idea of breakin' up the sound. I went an' got me a great big ol' wind-up clock that had a good, strong spring, an' I attached wires all to it, an' separators an' stuff. I got me some automobile parts, an' made it so that it would break *this* circuit an' connect *this* circuit, break *this* one, connect *this* one. Then, I wired it in-between my guitar an' amplifier, so that everythin' that came from the guitar had to go through this bullshit that I had hooked up on the floor. It was noisy as hell, but it *worked*!

'About six or eight months later, Diamature came out with a tremolo with some kinda crap in a lil' ol' bottle that shook around an' broke the circuit. This was exactly what I was lookin' for, so somebody else was on the same wavelength, but they *knew* what they were doin'. It was on the market, but I didn't have enough money to buy one, so I kept on usin' mine.

'Later on, Jody Williams bought one, but he didn't like it an' I bought his offa him. He couldn't use it, but it was just right for what I wanted. It was a *trip* tryin' to play with the sound disappearin' an' comin' back – you get all out of step – but I learned to play with it, an' when I learned that, that was the greatest thing in the world, an' I made that sucker work for what I needed it for.[1]

'I was the first to start usin' that in R&B, rock 'n' roll, whatever you wanna call it. Nobody else was doin' it. You might have heard a *few* dudes usin' it on slow numbers, because it had a tendency to make things feel like they were out of sync: the rhythm was off, you couldn't dance to it.'[5]

In a final flourish of inspiration, Ellas decided to add maracas to his group's instrumentation, embellishing his already distinctive sound with an irresistible shuffling rhythm that subsequently came to characterise much of his early work.

'I met Jerome Green after I met my second wife, because he was livin' downstairs. I was standin' on her back porch one evenin', an' saw this tuba comin' up the steps. I couldn't see nobody under it – you know what a tuba look like – an' Jerome was all wrapped up in it. He was a jazz fanatic: he was playin' a tuba in school, an' he'd brought it home for the weekend.

'I asked him, says: "Hey man, you wanna go on the corner with us? We need somebody to pass the hat." He looked at me like I was *crazy*, but I finally talked him into it after I'd seen him two or three times. He went out there, an' stood around an' seen what we was doin'. We let him keep the money. His pockets was *heavy*! He liked *that*, y'understand?' (Laughs.) 'He snatched the hat an' started goin' 'round gettin' quarters in it. See, at that age, five or six bucks in your pocket every night, that was a *whole lotta* money back then. Shoot, man, you were *rich*!

'Now, I needed more rhythm for what I was tryin' to do, but we couldn't carry a set of drums up an' down the street with us – there's too many of 'em – so I got me some maracas. I got this idea from listenin' at Sandman sandin' on a piece of board. I'd sit up in the house an' shake 'em, an' create rhythm patterns with 'em. I changed the whole thing that calypso dudes do, because that didn't fit in with what I was doin': I needed somethin' that sounded like a cat playin' with brushes, an' I finally struck upon that pattern.

'The first maracas I had, I took two of those copper weights off a bathroom – you know those pull-chains they used to have, with copper weights in there to let the water go down? I took one an' cut me a hole in it, right at the top, an' filled it up full of black-eyed peas. I had no money, man, to *buy* nothin', so I'd go round junkyards an' find old water tanks an' stuff, an' screw things out of 'em.

'After I'd figured out about as many rhythms as I could on 'em an' taught myself, I hit Jerome with it. I bought him a brand new bag of maracas an', surprisingly, I picked the right dude. That cat could shake the *hell* outa them things! He was better than "great"; Jerome was *fantastic*!'[1]

'I was starvin''

Jerome's shuffling maracas and Ellas's unusual throbbing guitar sound turned out to be real crowd-pullers. 'People were constantly askin' me what kinda music I was playin'. I told 'em: "I don't know, I just play it."[15] I sing a little blues an' dig it, but I like that uptempo stuff that makes people feel good. I like to play *happy* music.[3]

'Louis Jordan is one of the cats I tried almost to be like: I was doin' things like 'Caldonia', an' 'Hey Ba Ba Re-Bop', an' 'Honeydripper' – those things, you know, back in Joe Liggins's days. I was pickin' up so many things as a teenage kid – like kids today are pickin' up mine an' revivin' 'em, an' puttin' little kicks an' licks here, an' it sounds good. But Louis Jordan wasn't a blues artist. *I've* never been what you call a blues artist completely.[6]

'At first, when I started, I played what I heard everybody else play, but it didn't make sense for me to play what everybody else was doin', because they *already* had guys doin' that. Muddy Waters was Muddy Waters. John Lee Hooker was John Lee Hooker. Everybody had their own style. Elmore James had his. Jimmy Rogers had his. It was always blues, but you could always tell who was who.[16] I was tryin' to sing some of Muddy Waters an' all sortsa stuff, an' couldn't make it, man. I was starvin' to death, sure 'nough. Every time I went to get a gig, cats'd tell me, say: "You got somethin' *different*?" So, I'd start singin' Elmore James's 'Dust My Broom', an' cats'd say: "Wait a minute, we got Elmore here *next* week. We don't want *that*!"[10]

'I *didn't wanna* play like everybody else. I tried it because that was all I was around. If you couldn't play like Muddy Waters around Chicago at that time, or Little Walter, you might as well put your stuff up – because they had Chicago *sewed up*! I'm talkin' 'bout the real early fifties, like 1950. They were only playin' black places, but they were workin' each one of 'em every night, you know, different ones, sometimes doublin'. They were the hottest things goin'!

'In order to penetrate that chain, you had to come up with somethin' *different*. It took me quite a while to stumble upon somethin' an' create my own style.[1] My stuff is no copy: it's *original*, an' I'm the one that was the first one doin' it.[3] Today, you hear one band, an' it look like you done heard 'em all. The disco bands, all of 'em sound alike to me. That is *bad news*: somebody'll be goin' hungry pretty soon.'[16]

Bo still speaks of his entry into the world of professional entertainment with some disbelief: 'It's really *weird* to be playin' out there in the limelight, playin' for millions of people, an' they accept me for what I am. It really is a *gas*! I was just walkin' down the street a moment ago an' I seen some kid playin' on a banjo, an' it just looked like only a few years ago that *I* was on the street an' people used to throw money in my hat, an' now *I'm* doin' that. It just doesn't seem it's been that long.[3]

'It never dawned on me that people played for big money. The first contract I got, I sat up all night lookin' at it, because there wasn't *no way* you could tell me that somebody's gonna give me seven hundred bucks for *playin' a song*. Seven *hundred* dollars! I worked *all month* drivin' a truck – an' I mean *worked* – an' I didn't get no seven hundred dollars! It just didn't make sense. I sat up *all night* lookin' at that contract! I turned it upside-down, I turned it sideways. I knew there was a seven, but I thought it might've been a misprint.[4]

'When I started playin', I was never really serious.'[11] I never intended to be no guitar player out here in the public. This is all a accident because I got mad with my wife: that chick took my guitar an' smashed it. This is – I think – what made me get up an' do somethin'.

'I came in from work an' she was sittin' in the chair with her arms crossed, mad, no dinner on the table, no food cooked. She's mad enough to bite nails an' spit rust. I says to her: "Baby, what's the matter? It's Friday evenin', I gotta go play" – 'cause I'm playin' on a weekend at the 708 Club. She didn't want me to play, but she couldn't stop me, so she took a Pepsi-Cola bottle, jumped on my big blond eighty-dollar Harmony. She didn't hit it on the front, she hit it on the back, busted all the back in. Oh man, that just *tore me apart!* She was pregnant, an' she told me: "Now *hit* me! Just *hit* me!"

'I said: "No, I ain't gonna take a chance on hittin' you, but you did the right thing: you jumped on somethin' that couldn't hit back!"

'So now I says: "I'll get another guitar." I gets my amp out the closet, an' I takes the cover off of it an' looks in the back to see if my cord's in it. No tubes! She done teared *this* up also! She'd took the tubes out of it an' walked over to her momma's on the other side of town while I was at work, left 'em there.

'I say: "How we gonna pay the rent?" – 'cause I wasn't makin' enough on my day job to pay bills an' buy food, so I had this little gig on the weekend to try an' make ends meet.

'Then, I takes my gear outside, an' I'm sittin' out there on the sidewalk, tears runnin' down my face, all under my glasses an' everythin'. Everybody that passed by seed me there. I was so mad, that I just wanted to climb all over her – but she's pregnant, see? That threw up a break right there.

'My friend Roosevelt came over, say: "Oh-oh, you an' Tootsie have been into it again."

'I say: "No, we ain't been into it. Just look down there in the doorway at my guitar!"

'He stuck his head in the doorway an' looked, an' he told me: "Maybe you can borrow my friend's guitar. I'll go ask him."

'So, I ended up goin' to the club after all, made the gig: I played through another dude's amp what was there. I bought a guitar from a cat for fifty bucks, an' the other twenty-five went for Union taxes, so I worked three days for nothin'[10] – an' it probably only messed her out of a new dress, 'cause I went an' bought another guitar when she could've used that money to get some new clothes, or a new pair of shoes or somethin'.

'It was hard to get fifty dollars at that time. *Hard!* Man, I sold pop bottles an' played on the street-corners so I could pay for everythin'. I was payin' eighteen bucks a week for a room with a little hotplate stove in it, an' feedin' her an' one baby. You get the picture?'

'I remember I was on relief when Tanya was nine months old. I couldn't get a job noplace. I went to get some welfare, an' they told me I had to make one more trip down there before I could get any money. I told the people my kid was hungry an' sick *right now*. What was I supposed to do, turn off a valve to stop her from cryin' because she was hungry? The next step was to stick somebody up, an' I didn't wanna do that. When a cat that's dedicated to his family gets so his hind parts is draggin', an' he can't get work... I have been this way, I ain't just sittin' here talkin'.

'Every mornin', I'd get up an' walk from my home on 47th Street down to 125th Street, tryin' to find a job. Get on the streetcar till the conductor saw me, then jump off an' wait for the next one. I was lookin' for *anythin'*, plain labor, but you'd go into a place, an' they're talkin' 35–40¢ an hour. That's no money: that's about $29 *a week*! Are you ready for *that*? You wouldn't believe it existed in the fifties, but I worked on some of 'em. I unloaded boxcars, I drove dump-trucks.[2]

'See, black cats wasn't makin' what white dudes was makin' – an' *first* of all you had the wrong job anyway.[10] Everybody was told a black dude is *bad business*, a black dude ain't even supposed to *be* there. I just told people: "Hey, I'm a *man*. I don't give a damn what color I am. I didn't ask to come in this world no way."

'Truck-drivin' wasn't so bad, but there *was* discrimination against black drivers: I'd drive to the quarry, an' couldn't get no stone![2] It was just a whole fucked-up thing, man, that I did *not* understand: I figured a job was a job, you know, an' then I started findin' out that all of this "race" shit was goin' on in Chicago that I never knew about! My mother never talked about that shit, you dig? It was all under my nose, an' I never knew it, never heard it. When they said "segregation", that was a new word to me. I didn't know what the fuck it meant!

'An' so, my old lady really knew how to get to me, man. Everytime she got mad, she'd say: "You wait!" an' go right an' get my guitar, lay it on the floor an' jump on the neck, or some ol' shit like that, an' then jump up an' holler: "Now *hit* me!"

'I'd say: "No, I ain't gonna hit you", an' I'd walk off an' sit upside the wall. After I'd did that a couple of times, she quit doin' that, 'cause that didn't work no more.' (Laughs.)

'So then, she started callin' the police on me! Every time I look up, man, I was in jail! Every time I came home, the neighbors would all get on the front porch to see me get carried away, 'cause they'd know I was goin'.' (Laughs.) 'This became like a show in the neighborhood, y'understand what I mean? I'd come home, walk in the house, an' I'd notice people just keep sittin' on their porch. It wasn't *that* damn hot! Then the police show up, an' I says: "Well, y'all, I'm goin' again".'[10] (Laughs.)

Ellas was by now seriously considering leaving Tootsie, but was persuaded by his friends to persevere with the relationship for the sake of their two young children, Anthony and Tanya. An uneasy peace was eventually negotiated, this being conditional upon him being allowed to continue his music-making activities without any further hindrance. 'When it came to the guitar, I felt I was givin' up too much. I felt deprived of everythin' I wanted to do.'[1]

'Buttercup didn't last long'

Fired by Ellas's new-found determination, the Jive Cats now began to make rapid headway, building up a sizeable local following and frequently jamming with other young amateurs from the neighbourhood. In 1954, however, the group unexpectedly fragmented when Roosevelt was invited to join Uncle Sam's armed forces and Jody (who had by now become an extremely proficient guitarist) volunteered for almost equally hazardous duty in Howlin' Wolf's band. Undaunted, Ellas simply drafted in replacements from the growing circle of musicians around him and carried on.

A few weeks later, Billy Boy spotted the new-look outfit playing in a tavern and took the opportunity to rekindle their friendship.

'Bo had a guy named R.C. playing harp for him – he's a Black Muslim now – and he let me play a couple of numbers. He told me: "I'm fixing to get rid of R.C., so keep in touch with me." I gave him my address and everything. He came by my house in September and said: "Hey, I'm fixing to get a band together."

'So, fall of 1954, he had James Bradford on bass, with a boy named Buttercup playing second guitar – but he didn't last long with the band... I'll tell you why in a few minutes. We got a job at the Castle Rock, 50th and Princeton. A chick came in there, say: "Hey, my brother-in-law plays real good drums. Can he come down and play some?"

'Bo said: "Yeah, bring him down!"

'That was Clifton James: we didn't know him then. Clifton came down – his mother had bought him a new set of drums. He sat in and he worked real good with the group. He was a real good drummer.

'So, Buttercup's old lady would be down there. She was a heavy-set broad and one night she went berserk, wrecked the joint. I mean *totally destroyed* the joint!

'Some chick was talking to Buttercup – he had broke his ankle or something and he was in a cast – and Buttercup's old lady said: "I know you going with this broad" or something, and starts fighting with him.

'Then she took out after the broad: the broad had run out and we were standing there, trying to calm her down. And there was a lady there – had nothing to do with it – sitting at a table. Buttercup's old lady took a beer bottle and hit her, cut her face *wide open*! The lady had nothing to do with the incident!

'So then, when she'd did that, she started running down the bar – it was a long bar – throwing bottles and glasses, cutting and hitting people. She tore that place *up*, man! *Everybody* was up against the wall. She *wrecked* that place!

'The guy who owned the joint finally started shooting into the floor. He shot about four times into the floor to get her attention, 'cause she was just hitting people at random, just tearing the joint up. Then Bo ran up behind her – he was a *powerful* guy – put a Full Nelson on her, and took her out the door. So, that was the end of Buttercup's career: they couldn't use him no more.

'We were real successful there, but the place started going down because the guy that owned the club was fooling around with them chicks that was working for him and he wasn't handling things. He wind up owing us three weeks' back pay, so we left there and went to the Sawdust Trail, on 44th and Wentworth. Clifton lived on 44th and State, and we'd all go over there and drink after the club and everything. We had a big thing going, you know.

'We was real successful at the Sawdust Trail. We packed 'em in, the people our age. I was only eighteen or nineteen at the time, and all the young girls came in, you know – because Bo was young, Jerome was about my age, and Clifton was my age. We drawed the young people, an' so we were *very* successful.

'They used to have bands in there, but no band ever did like we did, 'cause Bo Diddley's style was very appealing to the young crowd: he would play a boogie woogie-type riff on the guitar and would dance with it, things like that.[14] He used to sing: *"Me an' my baby was playin' in the bushes/All of a sudden a mosquito bit her on the thigh/Went a little further an' sat on the grass/Mosquito bit her on her big fat... /Hey Noxema, hey*

Noxema/Hey Noxema, hey Noxema/Yes your baby know", da-da-da-da, do that boogie woogie thing, you know. He used all those 'Dirty Mother'-type of lyrics, and he used to crack the people up*.'[17]

Bo elucidates: 'I wrote that tune, but it was a copy in a sense, or a take-off, of Cab Calloway. See, they used to have these little machines that you put money in an' turn the handle, an' you'd see Cab Calloway on the screen dancin' an' singin', an' he'd holler: *"Hi-de-hi-de-hi-de-ho!"* – I think the song was 'Hey Ba Ba Re-Bop'. He'd sing stuff like: *"Old Matilda Brown told old King Tut/If you can't re-bop keep your big mouth shut/Hey ba ba re-bop!"* an' everybody'd: *"Hey ba ba re-bop!"*.' (Laughs.)

'But I decided I did not want to sing other people's songs, because there was *already* one of them, an' that was *enough* as far as I was concerned. He had his *own* style, let me create *mine*. So, what I did to keep from singin' that particular song was, I wrote 'Hey Noxema': *"I got a gal, lives on a hill/If she don't love me her sister will/Hey Noxema, hey Noxema/Yes your baby know"*.' (Laughs.) 'I changed the lyrics, but I found myself writin' in the same rhythmic pattern as 'Hey Ba Ba Re-Bop' – which was just as bad as singin' the song – so I decided to leave it alone.'[1]

Eventually, Billy persuaded Ellas to cut a demo record, which they could then hawk around the various record companies in the city and hopefully secure a contract. 'We made this record. See, Bo, he did construction when the weather was good, in the summer. In the wintertime you can't do construction in Chicago 'cause it's outside work, so Bo would get on relief, draw compensation because he had a wife and two kids. I'd already made one record – this Cool thing** – so I was always trying to make records all the time, you know. I said: "Hey man, let's make some records!"

'Bo had one of those little disk machines, and we cut 'I'm A Man' and 'Uncle John'. We took it to United Records and Leonard Allen told us: "Bring the band down and rehearse in Al Smith's basement about four or five days."

'So we rehearse and rehearse. Allen and Smitty come down and listen to it. Smitty say: "You really want a record?"

*Arnold later recorded his own variation on the theme, 'Dirty Mother Fucker', which appeared in 1979 on *Checkin' It Out* [Red Lightnin' RL-0024].
**'Ain't Got No Money' b/w 'Hello Stranger' [Cool 103], recorded in 1953.

'We say: "Yeah!"'

'He say: "Well, go up to Allen and say I want a record and I don't want no money".' (Laughs.)

'So then we went to Vee-Jay, and this broad – the secretary – was just going to lunch. She said: "What y'all want?"'

'We said: "We got a record here."'

'She said: "Let me hear it."'

'She put it on the turntable, played about a second of it, and said: "I don't like that."'

'So, we went across the street to Chess.'[14]

Chapter 3

Bo Diddley Is Loose

A Checkered Career

The Chess Record Corporation of 4750–2 South Cottage Grove Avenue was a small independent jointly run by two Jewish brothers, Leonard and Philip Chess. Sons of Polish immigrants, they had started out in business in the forties, running several clubs and bars on the South Side, branching out into the record business in 1947 after discovering that many of the popular black acts they engaged did not have recording contracts.

They called their company 'Aristocrat' and initially concentrated on jazz and jump blues, though the enormous popularity of the tough, country-styled blues recordings of Muddy Waters (one of their earliest signings – and a most fortunate one as it turned out) quickly prompted them to change direction. Within three years, they had already made enough to buy out their partners and move to better accommodation, changing the label's name to 'Chess' in the process. Much encouraged by this initial success, the brothers now began pushing to expand their business. Leonard in particular put in a great deal of effort, making innumerable trips down South and building up a vast network of contacts.

Probably the most significant coup of his career was the licensing deal he negotiated with Sam Phillips in Memphis: Phillips's recordings of Southern downhome music proved enormously popular with the thousands of expatriate blacks living in Chicago and other northern cities – so much so, in fact, that by 1952 they accounted for a good half of Chess's releases.

Given this impetus, the company began to blossom. A subsidiary label, Checker, was launched on 17 May, 1952 and a publishing arm, Arc Music Inc, on 1 August the following year.

Even at this early stage, the Chess brothers were already breaking new ground, taking a gamble with an unusual echo-laden harmonica instrumental called 'Juke' [Checker 758] and watching with glee as the record shot to the top of *Billboard*'s 'Rhythm & Blues' chart in the autumn of 1952. Leonard's son, Marshall – then just ten years old – remembers it well.

'Little Walter was Muddy Waters's harmonica player and had recorded 'Juke'. They were playing it, and there were some black women standing out of the rain under the canopy of the shop, and they were *dancing*! That's what forced us to put it out, 'cause we'd never put out an instrumental like that before and it was really the first kind of echo used on a harmonica. My father actually put it out because of the reaction he saw from these women. This was a very common thing. We put out a blues record on a Friday, and we'd make enough money to eat by Monday morning, you know.

'When there was a hit, the whole building rocked! The first studio we had, the control room was in the office, so you couldn't do work when we were recording*.[18] I don't believe to this day that we ever knew – maybe it was accidental that the records came out that way. All we knew is that, if it sounded good, it would usually sound good on the radio. It was just a "pure" thing, you know what I'm saying? Our office was in the middle of the ghettos, and my father and uncle had a very good pulse on what black people liked, so they'd experiment a lot with echoes and things like that. We *knew* what people liked.

'We had a guy in our shipping room – one of the heroes of Chess Records that I *never* hear written about – named 'Sonny' Woods: Eugene Woods, the oldest employee of Chess Records. My father hired him when he was fifteen or sixteen, and he was there till – you know – seventy.

'He used to drink so much gin that he couldn't see anything all day – he'd be high by four in the afternoon – but whenever we cut a record, he'd

*Because of the inconvenience of this arrangement, Bill Putnam's Universal Recording Studio at 111 East Ontario was often used instead.

be called in. He was the one, and if he started dancing when he heard it, you knew you had a good record. He was, like, the "groove-tester". He was the guy who went to get coffee, you know, load the trucks – but he had the *groove*. We had a couple of people like that, "testers".[19]

'Of course, we had certain little things: *backbeat*, we were *always* after that backbeat! Bass drum, bass drum! We felt that was a formula.[18] My father was *definitely* instrumental in putting the big backbeat on blues records. He played bass drum himself a lotta times when he couldn't get them to play it right,[19] and the echo sorta worked out till we had all kinds of unusual echoes:[18] we used a sewer-pipe with a speaker at one end and a mike at the other,[19] an echo-chamber in the basement where the rats would run through and make a noise on the record...

'We never called it "producing"; we called it "supervising". To make sure that you got three tunes in three hours, that was really the attitude. It was my uncle, my father and I – we would take turns even. It was just that someone had to be there, watching.[18] This was in the days before all this bullshit of record producers. It wasn't an ego situation; all the ego was, was to have a nice bank account.[19]

'It was a family kinda business. I started working there at thirteen years old, in the shipping room. My first job was stock boy: sweeping the floor, putting albums in sleeves.[18] I worked in the shipping room from thirteen to fifteen. Sixteen and seventeen, I worked a record press – actually pressed records! We always pressed our own as much as we could; if we had a bigger hit, we would job it out to other plants.

'We controlled everything, you know what I'm saying? We could cut a record on a Wednesday, and put it on the radio on Thursday. Sell it Thursday, next day. Overnight in the matrixing, you know, and then they pressed the next day. We had our own printing for labels even. We'd get backdrops printed, you know, but we could put the name on it ourselves.[19] We put the sleeves on the albums and put them into the cover. We did everything ourselves: a totally self-contained operation.'[18]

Perhaps the most significant difference between Chess and other record companies of the time was the way they treated their artists. Unlike many of their counterparts, Len and Phil took great pains to cultivate a benevolent, family type atmosphere in which all their employees felt comfortable and cared-for. As in most family businesses, everyone helped out when there was work to be done – whether it was playing back-up on other people's sessions or simply packing records into boxes – but nobody ever objected, for their future prosperity depended directly on that of the company.

The degree to which this approach was responsible for the many superlative performances laid down in the recording studio by Chess's artists must, of course, remain a matter for conjecture, though its commercial benefits were undeniable: by the mid-fifties the company was expanding apace, diversifying into pop, gospel, rockabilly and rhythm and blues – a new, catchy dance music which appealed not only to the young black audience, but was also beginning to attract many white teenagers as well.

This was a most exciting development, not least because records which 'crossed over' in this manner were guaranteed to sell many more copies – a prospect which inspired the Chesses to keep their eyes open for suitable talent.

Then, one day in February 1955, Ellas and Billy, demo in hand, knocked on their front door.

'We don't need nothin' right now'

'Little Walter was behind the counter, 'cause he was doing some mail order stamping for Leonard,' recalls Billy. 'He knew me because I'd been around where he played a couple of times, and he knew Bo too.

'Walter said: "We don't need nothin' right now. Y'all come back in a couple of weeks!"

'So, at that time, Phil walked out. I already knew Phil Chess because I'd auditioned there in '53. He said: "Hey, how you doin'? What you got?"

'I said: "We got a dub."

'So Phil put it on, 'I'm A Man', you know. Them lyrics was kinda catchy. There wasn't the 'Bo Diddley' thing, because there wasn't no Bo Diddley yet. Phil said: "Hey, well, can y'all come back? I want my brother Leonard to hear y'all. Can you come by tomorrow at two o'clock and bring your equipment?"

'We came back next day at two o'clock. He had a little studio in the back, so we hooked up our stuff and started playing. Leonard walked in, started listening to it. He asked Bo a few questions and said: "Can you come back tomorrow and rehearse again?"

'Rehearsed again. Muddy Waters came in and heard 'I'm A Man': "Man, I like that! I *like* that! I want that! Man, that's great!" Little Walter liked 'You Don't Love Me (You Don't Care)'.

'Muddy and Little Walter liked all these little beats that Bo had, and they thought Leonard was just gonna kick Bo out the door and take everything, you know, but Bo had a little something going and Leonard saw that. It was a different sound, you know. The gimmick was that he used a tremolo on his guitar – he got that organ-like effect – that's what Chess liked about him.

'They was going to call him Ellas McDaniel.[14] I remembered one time we was on the street and the bass player, Roosevelt, said: "Hey Ellas, there go Bo Diddley" – speaking of a comical-looking, bow-legged, little, short guy.[14A] To me, it was the *funniest* word I'd ever heard: I just cracked *up!* So, in the studio, I said: "Why don't you call him Bo Diddley?"

'Leonard Chess had never heard the word "Bo Diddley" and he said: "Well, I don't know. What does that mean? Is that some kinda discriminating word for black people? I won't put that on there, they wouldn't buy it."

'He said: "No, 'Bo Diddley' don't mean that. 'Bo Diddley' is just a comical word of a guy, maybe a bow-legged guy, a comical-looking guy, you know."

'He said: "We'll call you Bo Diddley" – and that's how he got the name.'[14]

If Leonard's astuteness in recognising the advantages of such a catchy stage name is to be admired, then Ellas's failure to do so – especially at a time when nicknames and pseudonyms were commonplace among black musicians – is downright baffling.

'I got it when I was a kid goin' to grammar school, an' I've been tryin' to find out ever since why the heck they called me that,' says Bo.[16] 'I can't tell you exactly what it means, but it kinda means "bad boy" – mischievous, you know. I used the name when I started to foolin' around in Eddie Nicholson's gym, but I only used it in the ring; all of my friends called me "Mac".[1]

'Now, my mother speaks of an old man, when she was a kid, that used to come around an' sing an' dance, an' played a harmonica. They called *him* Bo Diddley. This is in the days of when the slavery trip was fadin' out. This dude ran around an' made his livin' singin' an' dancin'. He used to come through the fields, an' stop by people's houses an' sing an' dance, an' people'd throw him nickels an' dimes, an' he'd go to the next farmhouse. All of a sudden, he disappeared.

'I've *always* had people old enough to be my *grandparents* or somethin' walk up to me an' say: "Where you been all these years? I knew yo' daddy, boy!"

'I look at 'em, I say: "Wha-? I think you got me tangled up with somebody else!" They say: "Is you the Bo Diddley we used to know from such-an'-such a place?"

'I say: "No ma'am, I ain't never been there." They say: "Ah, now you've got big time, you don't wanna know nobody."

'That's *strange*! I don't *think* I've been here before as Bo Diddley, an' died, an' came back again as the same dude.[16] But maybe it just so happened that the little spirit that brought me here, that's inside of my body, happened to come here in a black body, y'understand? *Same* little dude – like when I die an' leave here, I'm liable to go an' come back in a *indian*! An' this indian may turn out – twenty or thirty years after I'm dead an' gone, somebody liable to say: "You know how that cat act? He play guitar like an *old* dude, *long* time ago..."

'They say: "Who?" "Well, some old black dude that used to play *long* time ago named Bo... Bo... Bo Diddley – I've seen it in the history books, man. I've seen a couple of movies too – *old-time* movies, and that cat acts *just* like him!"'[1]

It seems there were several other Bo Diddleys too – even one in China, according to this reader's letter sent to a British magazine in 1963:

> *'In* TV Times *of July 27 I saw the name "Bo Diddley". Could this be the same Bo Diddley who used to sing at Del Monte's in Shanghai when I was a girl there in 1929? He used to sing 'Buddy Can You Spare A Dime', and the dollars used to ring out on the ballroom floor as everyone expressed their appreciation.'*[20]

Somewhat closer to home, the *Chicago Defender* of 20 July, 1935 contained an announcement that a certain 'Efus & Bo Diddley and band' would be appearing at the Midnight Club on Indiana Avenue. Unfortunately, nothing else is known about this act, although it is likely that they were a black dance and/or comedy duo.

Frustratingly, the origins of the name itself seem destined to remain obscure forever.

'I would *love* to know where that sucker came from!'[1] confesses Bo. 'The other day, I read that there was a instrument in the South, in the old days, called a "diddley bow": somethin' with one string on it, an' played with a bow*. I said: "Oh yeah? Uh-huh!",[16] but I don't guess I'll ever find out who invented it.'[1]

Shave And A Haircut

'When I first went to Chess, I was singin' a song that went: *"Uncle John got corn ain't never been shucked/Uncle John got daughters ain't never been... to school/The bow-legged rooster told the cock-legged duck/You ain't good lookin' but you sure can... crow".*' (Laughs.) 'An' Leonard couldn't record that.[1] He said: "The old folks ain't gonna dig it, and the dee-jays ain't gonna play it."[11] Durin' that time, you couldn't say *nothin'*, man!

'So, they told me to go home an' rewrite the lyrics. Somebody said: "Why don't you call it 'Bo Diddley'?"

'Man, it took me *all night* to figure out how to say: *"Bo-Didd'ley-bought-his-babe a-di'mond-ring"*, because that's where it got *tricky!* At first, I was sayin': *"Bo Diddley, he bought his baby..."*, you know, an' that just didn't fit. Took *all damn night* before I finally stumbled upon it.

'I went down to the Universal Recording Studio an' cut 'Bo Diddley', 'I'm A Man', 'Little Girl' an' 'The Surf-Soppers' Hop'.' (Laughs.) 'See, I'd thought of a comical name for my group: Filthy McNasty & The Surf-Soppers. That's where the "Surf-Soppers" came from. A "surf-sopper" is a dude which – when he's eatin' biscuits an' gravy – scoops it up like this, you dig, like he's usin' a *shovel!*' (Laughs.) 'Chess changed the title of it an' called it 'You Don't Love Me (You Don't Care)'.

'Billy had a tune called 'I'm Sweet On You Baby' that he wanted to do, so he sang on that, an' also on 'You Got To Love Me Baby' – which was my song – but Chess didn't do nothin' with 'em**. The cats that played with me on that session was Billy, Jerome, Clifton James an' James Bradford – which was all my band – an' Otis Spann, which was the piano player with

---

*According to Paul Oliver's note in *The New Grove Dictionary Of Musical Instruments*, the diddley bow is 'a single-string chordophone of the Southern USA' usually consisting of 'a length of wire whose ends are attached to a wall of a frame house, the house acting as a resonator. A cotton reel is frequently used as a bridge. A more portable version has the wire attached to a length of fence picket. The instrument is played with a glass bottleneck or nail.'[21] Many great blues slide guitarists including Elmore James, Big Joe Williams and Muddy Waters started out by playing the diddley bow as youngsters, while Mississippian Lonnie Pitchford (whose diddley-bow rendition of 'Johnny Stole An Apple' is one of the highspots of the film *Deep Blues*) now also uses an electrically amplified version. Although he always utilises 'open' tunings, Bo has never played slide himself – primarily because his fingers are too big to accommodate any form of bottleneck!

**Billy's cuts were eventually released in 1975 on *Blow The Back Off It* [Red Lightnin' RL-0012].

Muddy Waters at the time. We did a few takes of 'I'm A Man', an' then Leonard decided he didn't like the way Bradford was playin', so he got Willie Dixon to play bass on it instead.

'Then, they decided they wanted to change it around! They wanted me to spell "man", but they weren't explainin' it right.[1] They couldn't get me to spell "man"! I didn't understand what they were talkin' 'bout. They said: "Spell 'man'", an' I just kept sayin' "Man". They couldn't explain to me what the heck they were talkin' about. If Leonard Chess hada been a *singer*, they wouldn't have spent all that money tryin' to get me to do somethin' that was totally simple. They had an idea, an' they couldn't put it across to me. We spent eight hours in there, I believe, tryin' to get me to spell "man", you know,' (laughs) 'an' finally I said: "M-a-n, man", an' they said: "That's what we wanted all along!"

'I said: "Why didn't you say that?"[22]

'I don't know how many takes it was – looked to me like there was 350 of 'em[1] – but the recordin' studio, they didn't care: their little clock was still tickin'.'[22]

A tough, Muddy Waters-styled composition with bold lyrics about the singer's coming of age, 'I'm A Man' was the most accomplished of the three blues cut by Bo on 2 March, 1955 and a strong contender for the 'Rhythm & Blues' chart, while the catchy 'Bo Diddley' was the natural choice for the flip: an explosive combination of shouted vocals, reverberating guitar and thundering drums laced together with a thumping, hypnotic beat, it was louder, wilder and heavier than anything ever heard before – and totally devastating in its effect.

Although he was the first to commit this unique rhythm to wax, Diddley does not claim to have invented it, and indeed, what evidence there is suggests that its origins are in fact much older: veteran West Coast drummer Johnny Otis, for instance, remembers using what he terms the 'shave-and-a-haircut, two-bits' rhythm pattern in the late 1930s during his stint with Count Otis Matthews & His West Oakland House Rockers, while certain ethnomusicologists profess to have traced the 'rat-ta-ta-tat-tat, tat-tat' of the 'tradesman's knock' back to the Ishango and Ewe tribes of West-Central Africa.

While such statements can be accorded a reasonable degree of credence, it is hardly likely that Diddley learned it from either of these sources. The African connection is quickly discounted with a terse 'I ain't never been to Africa'[1], while a suggestion that he may perhaps have heard it played by one of the Deep South's fife-and-drum bands (a primitive but closely allied Black American tradition) leaves him genuinely mystified: 'Whatcha call 'em again? What are those? No, I can't say I've ever heard 'em.[1]

'Truthfully, I don't know *where* it came from exactly. I just started playin' it one day.[16] What I *will* say is, I think I probably picked some of it up from church.[1] See, we had sanctified churches – an' that's *art*! They did these sanctified numbers for fifteen, twenty minutes. Tambourine an' a old raggedy set of drums, an' you'd think Duke Ellington was in there playin'! They'd be gettin' it *together*![4]

'I used to stand on the sidewalk an' listen, or I'd climb on a milk-crate an' peep in at 'em.[2] The music they played an' sang hit a nerve, an' the people would be jumpin' all over the place.[11] I'd say: "One day, I'm gonna get me somethin' that sounds like that."[2] This is where I found out those drivin' rhythms was the thing: a rhythm that penetrates within the person.[4] I'm a rhythm *fanatic*: beats an' rhythm, man – this is my bag.[1]

'I figured there must be another way of playin', an' so I worked on this rhythm of mine. I'd say it was a "mixed-up" rhythm: blues, an' Latin-American, an' some hillbilly,[13] a little spiritual, a little African, an' a little West Indian calypso... an' if I wanna start yodelin' in the middle of it, I can do that too.[4] I like gumbo, you dig? Hot sauces too. That's where my music comes from: *all* the mixture.[2] I got those beats so jumbled up on 'Bo Diddley' that they couldn't sort 'em out![1]

'There's an old thing around called the "hambone" that they tried to relate it to. There *is* a similarity, but the hambone wasn't done with music.'[16]

The 'hambone' Diddley refers to is a technique of dancing and slapping various parts of the body to create a rhythm. A hangover from slavery times (when it was known as 'patting Juba'), this ancient folk art enjoyed an unexpected revival in Chicago during the early fifties, becoming so popular that bandleader Red Saunders even made a record called 'Hambone' [OKeh 4-6862] in 1952 to cash in on the fad.

Its real stars, however, were three hambone-crazy schoolkids: Delecta Clark (later singer Dee Clark), Ronny Strong and Sammy McGrier – who explains how the recording came about...

'When I was in Evanston*, a kid came up from Mississippi and he brought the hambone with him. It became a novelty around school: I'd say

---

*A suburb to the north of Chicago.

maybe ten percent of the kids picked it up. When my family relocated to Chicago, I attended Calhoun School, and I was the only kid there that knew how to do the routine. Then, a neighbor from across the street who worked for the *Morris B. Sachs Amateur Hour* television show submitted my name in audition. I appeared on the show and Red Saunders saw me, contacted my father, and wanted to know whether he would be interested in a novelty record.

'Red suggested we bring three other people besides myself down. We only knew of two other people that could do the hambone good enough: Delecta and my step-cousin, Ronny. Delecta had picked up the hambone quite readily, but he had one little ingredient that just made a world of difference: he patted the heel of his foot on the second and fourth beat, just to give it that extra little rhythm.'[23]

Sammy's father, Horace McGrier Sr, helped to rehearse the group and added two verses of his own to the traditional chanted accompaniment:

> *Hambone, hambone, have you heard,*
> *Pop's gonna buy me a mocking-bird.*
> *And if that mocking-bird don't sing,*
> *Pop's gonna buy me a diamond ring.*
> *And if that diamond ring don't shine,*
> *Pop's gonna take it to the five-and-dime.*

The record reportedly sold 50,000 copies within the first two weeks of its release, and ultimately more than 150,000, though it would doubtless have been even more successful had it not had to contend with cover versions by Phil Harris [RCA-Victor 47-4584], Tennessee Ernie Ford [Capitol 2017] and Jo Stafford & Frankie Laine [Columbia 39672].

Sadly, two follow-ups, 'Zeke'l, Zeke'l' [OKeh 4-6884] and 'Piece A Puddin'' [OKeh 4-6914] – the latter again covered by Phil Harris [RCA-Victor 47-4993] and Jo Stafford & Frankie Laine [Columbia 39867] – failed to connect, though 'Hambone' itself proved amazingly durable, being reissued in 1963 [OKeh 4-7166] to capitalise on its use as the theme for the New York children's TV show, *Sandy's Hour*, and for a third time in 1967 [OKeh 4-7282].

The 'Bo Diddley-is-Hambone' controversy proper started in the early sixties, fuelled largely by records like Carl Perkins's 'Hambone' [Columbia 42514], Paul Evans's 'Hambone Rock' [Guaranteed LP *Fabulous Teens*], Bill Haley's 'Pancho' [Orfeon LP *Whisky A Go Go*] and Dick Shawn's

'Hambone' [20th Century Fox 461], which combined the 'Hambone' lyrics with the 'Bo Diddley' beat.

'There *is* a similarity, but the idea of 'Bo Diddley' is not 'Hambone'. I would say it came from the same family – I'm not gonna deny *that* – but what is there out here that *don't* belong to the same family? You take Chuck Berry's 'Memphis': that's a stepped-up tempo of Jimmy Reed with syncopation in it. Mine is totally different. *Totally.* Melody, everythin', note-for-note. If you know *anythin'* about music or rhythmic patterns, then you *can't* be that stupid. When I sing: *"Bo Didd ⌢ ley bought his babe a di ⌢ mond ring"*, that's *not* like *"Ham-bone, ham-bone, have-you-heard"*. There's a *lotta* difference there.

'I guess I could have been influenced in some way, but I was playin' on the street-corners when 'Hambone' came out, an' I was *already* doin' this: I was playin' this 'Uncle John' beat around Chicago on the street-corners when Red Saunders made the record. If 'Bo Diddley' *was* the hambone beat, an' it *was* 'Hambone', why wasn't it copied many years before me? The reason is because mine is *different*, an' it's *not* 'Hambone'! It has a type of rhythmic pattern that you can do a lotta things to, but not necessarily the hambone itself.'[1]

The confusion is, however, further compounded by the fact that the two songs are lyrically also very similar, both containing substantial borrowings from an age-old lullaby of British origin which was (and still is) very popular throughout the South, 'Hush Little Baby':

Hush, little baby, don't say a word,
Mama's gonna buy you a mockin' bird.
If that mockin' bird don't sing,
Mama's gonna buy you a diamond ring.
If that diamond ring turns [to] brass,
Mama's gonna buy you a lookin' glass.
If that lookin' glass gets broke,

Mama's gonna buy you a billy-goat.
If that billy-goat won't pull,
Mama's gonna buy you a cart and bull.
If that cart and bull turn over,
Mama's gonna buy you a dog named Rover.
If that dog named Rover won't bark,
Mama's going to buy you a horse and cart.
If that horse and cart fall down
You'll be the sweetest little girl in town. *

This surprisingly popular ditty not only inspired several other Diddley compositions (notably 'Hush Your Mouth' and 'We're Gonna Get Married'), but also spawned a third variant, 'Mockingbird' – a massive hit in 1963 for Inez & Charlie Foxx [Symbol 919], and again for Aretha Franklin in 1967 [Columbia 44381], Carly Simon & James Taylor in 1974 [Elektra 45580] and the Belle Stars in 1982 [Stiff BUY-159]. What is more, its future survival seems assured, for, in an era hardly renowned for the preservation of folk traditions, the hambone itself continues to thrive to such an extent that regular competitions are still held in Chicago today.

Biggest Thing That Hit The Country

'The day I cut the record, I came home an' told my mother they stole my songs, that they tricked me.' (Laughs.) 'Boy, I was *mad* till I heard it on the air. I said: "They done ripped me off", an' my momma said: "No, no! Don't say that till you're sure." See, I was one of those dudes that don't trust nobody. I thought for sure they'd got me[3] – an' it was the biggest thing that hit the country!'[25]

Released in the last week of March 1955, Bo Diddley's first record, 'Bo Diddley' b/w 'I'm A Man' [Checker 814] became a double-sided smash, reaching No. 2 on *Billboard*'s 'Rhythm & Blues Best Sellers' chart and ranking eighth 'Most Played In Juke Boxes'. Had he not been black, it would probably also have figured prominently in the 'Top 100' pop chart, for initial sales of the record are estimated to have comfortably exceeded the one million mark.

Surprisingly, this overwhelming success in the secular music field did not precipitate the disapproval Ellas might have expected from certain

---

*This version collected by Alan Lomax in the 1940s from a black woman in Alabama.[24]

members of his family. His brother, the Rev Kenneth Haynes, explains: 'There was no resentment as far as the family was concerned, because we are very close, but we are not a demanding family. We let each choose their own direction in life, and we let him know that we were behind him one hundred percent.

'Now, the year that Bo made his hit was the same year I was converted and accepted Christ. Bo offered me a partnership with him. He said to me: "You won't have to work anymore. All you have to do is just follow me, and take care of my business for me."

'I *had* to turn him down! Naturally, that put our mother in the middle somewhere.' (Laughs.) 'So, she was standing there and Bo says: "Momma, did you hear what he said? He won't accept it!"

'Mother said: "Well, I had nothing to do with it".' (Laughs.) 'She said: "You made your choice, and he made his. I'll have to abide by both of 'em."

'My mother supports him without question, always has. As far as catching his gigs, I've never gone. Not that I *resent* it or anything like that but, actually, I've never been in the city where he was performing at the time. We were *all* behind him one hundred percent, always have been.'[26]

With a smash hit on his hands, Bo Diddley became very hot property indeed: 'My record broke, an' I was on my way. I quit my job, quit drivin'.[1] A few months before, my daughter had been sick, an' the boss told me that, if I took a day off to take her to the hospital, he'd make me take four days off without pay. So, I did what he would have done if it'd been his kid sick, I said: "Crazy! You get four days ready, 'cause I'm goin'!" "You need a rest," he said. Man, it was a *bad* scene for a black dude then!

'A while later I made the record. I walked up to him one day an' said: "Here's your keys, baby!"

'He looked at me an' said: "What's this?" "I ain't goin' this mornin'," I said.

'He said: "This record got anythin' to do with it?"

'I says: "Not really, but remember the day you threatened me a few months ago about how I needed a rest? Well, now I'm takin' a rest – a *long* rest, man!"[2]

'I didn't feel no different, just had a big record an' was *scared to death* that I had to go away from home on the road. I never thought I'd get out of Chicago, never thought I'd get as far as Gary – an' that can't be but thirty miles away!

'I went down to New Orleans for a week to do a show with Howlin' Wolf an' Smiley Lewis at a place called the Dew Drop Inn. We stayed at a very famous hotel down there called the Shalamar. At the time, I was drivin' a 1947 DeSoto – a six-cylinder flat-head DeSoto with a rack up on top of it like a stage-coach, an' we had everythin' tied up on top.' (Laughs.) 'It was *great*!

'We got lost goin' down there, because we didn't know how to read a map: we'd never been out of *Chicago*! I saw "New Orleans", or "Louisiana" or somethin', an' that's where I headed to – but it was New Orleans, *Ohio* or somethin'. Then a man showed us, he says: "Stay right on this road here where it says '51', an' don't get off of it. Keep right straight on down through Mississippi, right on into Louisiana." Ever since then, I've been readin' maps!

'I feel I should have been taught how to read a map when I was at school. *Never was* taught how to read the United States map! I was taught about Africa, or Germany, or England, an' all this kinda stuff. That don't make sense: you should be taught about your *own* homeland. Teach about the *meat* first, then give the gravy *later*. I gotta survive *here*!

'So, we worked down there in New Orleans for a week, an' came home. We made it back to Chicago with thirty-five cents. *Thirty-five cents*!

'After we got back, I got rid of the bass player, Bradford, an' there was just four of us: me, Jerome, Billy an' Clifton James. See, James Bradford – we called him "Cornbread" – he was a *very* nice guy, a friend of mine that lived on the same block my Aunt Alberta lived on in Chicago, but Bradford was kind-of a troublemaker. We got along fine, but he always thought that, if we was doin' somethin', an' he was involved in it, he was entitled to whatever anybody else was gettin', an' he'd just come in on the tail-end of it. Then, he would try to get a whole lot goin', try to get lawyers an' all this ol' kinda stuff. He was this type of person. Before you know anythin', he'd have you served with some paper or somethin'. He was just that way, but I loved him anyway.

'My career started right after that. At first, I was a little shook up because all these people was just sittin' there, lookin' at me, you know,' (laughs) 'but after the first couple of times I hit the stage, man, it was all go. I *destroyed* 'em!

'We went all over the place. We played all over the South, white on one side of the room an' black on the other side, or either black upstairs an' white downstairs, or vice versa. It was *crazy*! You know, you run over here an' play a little bit this way, then you run back over here an' play a little bit for this way, but you're playin' to a *blank wall*! Then you gotta run on *this*

64

side of the stage an' play over here to your right, then you run back over here an' play *this* way!' (Laughs.)

'That's how I decided to have a fifty-foot guitar cord – 'cause when you played down South, you didn't know *what* kinda hall you was gonna get. You set up towards the wall, then you'd go out an' sing this way, an' sing that way, then you'd run over here an' wiggle a little bit at them, then you'd run over here on *this* side an' wiggle a little bit over here.' (Laughs.) 'It was *crazy*!'[1]

'At that time, nobody knew what extension cords was. *Nobody* stood up back then* – even Muddy Waters would sit down. I developed my shit on the street-corners of Chicago: weren't no seats on the street-corner, you know, an' if you took one of your momma's chairs out the house, that was *killin'* time!'[10]

Further engagements followed, including a prestigious one-week booking on Tommy 'Dr Jive' Smalls's *Rhythm & Blues Revue* at the famous Apollo Theater in Harlem, where Bo broke the all-time attendance record previously held by Sammy Davis Jr: 'When I went to New York, man, I had lines from the front door all the way round the block: all the way up the street, round the corner, an' back round to the front door *this* side of the ticket box. I'm the *only* one that ever did that at the Apollo Theater, an' it's *never* spoke about!'[1]

Jungle Music

'When I first came out, the guitar players that were playin' in big bands was really on my case: we were all playin' by ear, so it was impossible to play it exactly the same way every time, 'cause you're not readin' notes. I couldn't read music for what I was doin' anyway, but I *scared* 'em. Then, guitars started sellin' like mad because kids wanted to play like Bo Diddley.

'Muddy Waters an' them already had the electric guitar thing goin' with rhythm an' blues, but I came in an' upset the whole applecart, because they'd never heard a guitar do what I had it doin'. And so, since they didn't understand what I was doin', they started callin' me a "rock 'n' roller".

'I remember I was one of the first cats on stage when the word came about sayin': "Here's a man with an original sound that's gonna *rock 'n' roll* you outa your seats!" an' then Chuck Berry came along right behind

---

*Apart from a couple of exceptions elsewhere in the country (notably Eddie 'Guitar Slim' Jones, T-Bone Walker and Johnny 'Guitar' Watson), Diddley is essentially correct.

me with 'Maybellene'*. Alan Freed came up with that word. Not Bill Haley, but the late, great Alan Freed.[1]

'But I'm *not* what you call a rock 'n' roller. I don't play Bill Haley stuff, or Joe Turner, or Fabian, or sing anythin' that sounds like 'em.[27] I've argued day an' night with somebody who said: "Man, you're rock 'n' roll." Man, I *play* the stuff, an' I don't know what it is! James Brown's rock 'n' roll. Chuck Berry's rock 'n' roll. There's just no comparison to us at all. I guess I can more identify with bein' rhythm an' blues than anythin' else: I'm right across the street from Muddy Waters – but I've got my *own* little bag.'[5]

A convenient if inaccurate label for a rag-bag of black and white musical styles, rock 'n' roll rapidly became a cause for concern for many parents.

Bill Haley was the first to furrow brows across the nation with his frisky 'Rock Around The Clock' [Decca 29124], though this was chiefly due to the song's association with juvenile delinquency in the 1955 movie, *The Blackboard Jungle*; Haley himself was certainly neither a teenager nor a delinquent, his record no more than a harmless and inoffensive novelty.

'Bo Diddley', however, was an entirely different proposition: one of the wildest sounds ever committed to wax, it startled and shocked a generation of adults conditioned to the sweet 'n' gentle outpourings of Tin Pan Alley, and the White Establishment were not slow to react: 'Man, they slammed the doors an' put up signs: "We don't *want* that mess", you know – because everybody was into Glenn Miller, Harry James, an' they couldn't turn it a-loose. New thing came.

'When I popped up, they said I was playin' "jungle music", talked about me like a *dog*![1] When the kids started jumpin' up an' clappin' their hands, their parents thought the Devil had got hold of 'em! Everybody was sayin' that rock 'n' roll is *wrong*. They thought I was the worst thing to ever happen in the United States. They thought I was dirty an' vulgar,[28] but I didn't do *nothin'* compared to what's goin' on now. I was a *angel*!' (Laughs.) 'All I did was wiggle my legs, y'understand? Just wiggled my legs, man, an' I got threatened with goin' to jail in Norfolk, Virginia.[1] I'd have notes sent to me backstage which said: "Don't wiggle on stage". Seems the little old ladies didn't approve. They said: "This town can't take no wigglin', Bo", but then I'd go to a juke joint just down the road, an' that smokey little place'd be boogiein' down!'[28]

---

*Chess 1604 (released May 1955).

'Then, they started askin' me a lotta questions 'bout 'I'm A Man', like what was I talkin' 'bout that I had in my pocket when I says: *"When I was a little boy/At the age of five/I had somethin' in my pocket/To keep a lotta folks alive"*. What the hell could I do at five years old? Just look at it! What do you do if you aren't devious-minded yourself? Why should your mind run into the gutter to try an' make *that* meanin' out of what I was sayin'? This is what all that mess was about then.

'Hank Ballard & The Midnighters had a similar kind of problem with 'Annie Had A Baby'*. Okay, so what's *wrong* with Annie havin' a baby? What's wrong with the idea of a *woman* havin' a *baby*? Is that some big secret? Kids aren't that stupid anymore. They know that they come from somewhere, an' they just found out that they *don't* be brought by no *stork*!' (Laughter.)

'You see, all these little bitty funny things that people frowned on, I don't understand. The Bible says it the way it is: *"Multiply and replenish the Earth"*. Now, them only way that I see that you're gonna do this *without* gettin' together, is this test-tube crap they've been doin'!' (Laughter.)

'All this crap came from our parents – way back – tellin' you it *didn't happen*: "Your little sister's comin' by a stork" – an' here's some stupid kid standin' on the roof, lookin' for him, an' he never gets there!' (Laughter.) 'Or a cabbage patch, or some ol' crap like this, you know. This is all *fantasy*. Kids ain't that dumb anymore.

'Entertainers today got it *easy*. They can do just about anythin' they want an' get away with it. I couldn't do that. Like, I had to put double seams in my pants to make sure that they didn't split. That is a *very* embarrassing place to be, on stage, with everybody lookin' up at you, an' your pants bust! *Plus* you didn't get a nice write-up if your pants bust on stage. You was written up as "nasty". They didn't take into consideration that I didn't *make* the pants, I just bought 'em an' put 'em on, an' they fell apart – just couldn't hold up under the pressure!' (Laughter.)

'I was quite a bit different from all of the other entertainers, an' I was told at one time that I wasn't "classy" enough. That's the crap I heard, but I've got over forty years under my belt now, so *somethin'* must have been goin' right.[1]

'Alan Freed was one of the few disk-jockeys I *liked*: I could go into his dressing room an' talk to him. I wasn't treated like a piece of shit. When I

---

*Federal 12195 (1954).

came out with 'Bo Diddley', man, he was the *only* one with enough nerve to play my record, an' he probably had bricks thrown at his house, you know, fires set in his yard, for playin' a black cat's record. This is the States, y'understand?[7]

'That era was somethin' else, because nobody knew what the hell was goin' on. The blacks couldn't figure out what the hell was happenin', an' I think a lot of sensible-minded whites couldn't figure out why there was all of this *dislike* goin' on, you know. It just didn't make sense. I didn't know about no color barriers. White, black or whatever, it didn't make no difference to me: if you liked my music, you liked it; if you *liked* me, you liked me.

'None of the dudes that was around Chess, around Chicago on *any* labels knew what R&B was, an' that's the truth! They didn't know why it was called "rhythm and blues", an' why a lotta radio stations wouldn't touch it. All I figured was that they didn't play that kinda music. Then it started leakin' out, little by little. They said: "Hey, we gotta try an' get your stuff played on the *black* stations."

'Later on, I found out that the same ol' crap was goin' down with the Musicians' Union: we found out that Local 208 was the local for all the *black* musicians. I didn't even know there was a Local 10! I didn't know that there was a white local an' a black local, an' that the scales were different: the black one was *lower*, an' *we* were makin' all the music! *Now* they merged, after the civil rights crap.

'When I did the Ed Sullivan show* – now, this is the clincher – I was the first black dude to be on the Ed Sullivan show, with the song 'Bo Diddley'.

'Tennessee Ernie Ford had 'Sixteen Tons' out at that time**, an' they heard me singin' it in the dressin' room, just messin' around, you know. I liked it because it was a folk-song. Bein' black, I related to that, y'understand? The old slave-songs, an' stuff like this, I never knew a lot of the lyrics. Here's one that I had the chance to hear all the lyrics an' understand 'em, an' I liked this. It was a *big* tune then.

---

*Diddley appeared on CBS-TV's *Toast Of The Town* with Jerome Green, Clifton James and newly recruited lead guitarist Bobby Parker as part of a special fifteen-minute *Rhythm & Blues Revue* segment screened on 20 November, 1955. Also on the show were LaVern Baker, the Five Keys and Willis 'Gator Tail' Jackson & His Orchestra. Film of Bo's performance has survived, and a one-minute clip found its way onto the 1985 RCA/Columbia video compilation, *Rock 'n' Roll – The Early Days*. His performance was released in its entirety in 1993 on the TVT CD *The Sullivan Years – Rhythm & Blues Revue*'.
**Capitol 3262 (1955).

'So, the guy came in, says: "Would you sing that on the show?" – 'cause he liked the way I was doin' it. I was on this show to do 'Bo Diddley', so now I think I'm supposed to do two songs, you dig? So, when the time come for me to go on stage, I went out there an' did 'Bo Diddley' first.

'*They* made the mistake, but *I* got cussed out for it: they said to me I was supposed to do only one number, 'Sixteen Tons'. But I was there to do 'Bo Diddley', an' Chess later told me that if I'da did 'Sixteen Tons' an' *not* 'Bo Diddley', that would have been the end of my career right there – which, they were *right*, 'cause they were pushin', tryin' to sell my record. So, Ed Sullivan says to me in plain words: "You're the first black boy" – quote – "that ever double-crossed me!" I was ready to *fight*, because I was a little young dude off the streets of Chicago, an' him callin' me "black" in them days was as bad as sayin' "nigger", y'understand?

'My manager, Phil Landwehr, an' all these other dudes there says to me: "That's *Mr* Sullivan!"

'I says: "I don't give a shit about *Mr* Sullivan! Who's *Mr* Sullivan? He don't talk to *me* like that! I didn't call *him* no names!"

'They pulled me away from him, 'cause I'd snatched my guitar off an' was ready to *fall* on the dude. I figured the cat was just doin' this because he was grown-up, an' I says: "No, you ain't gonna get away with this, buddy."

'An' so, he told me, he says: "I'll see that you'll never work no more in showbusiness. You'll never get another TV show *in your life!*" It scared the *hell* outa me! I could have been discouraged along the way an' quit. A few times they *almost* got me, because durin' that time of all the riots about the rock 'n' roll stuff is when they jumped me: they had kids runnin' round the doggone buildings in Alabama with signs sayin': "We don't want our kids to listen to jungle music."

'We went out the back door an' got a bunch of kids, gave 'em five bucks apiece – there was ten or fifteen of 'em – took down some posters, an' took a marking pencil... shoe polish it was, one of those little round things with a piece of cotton in it, an' we wrote signs sayin': "We *love* rock 'n' roll", an' the kids walked toward the people that was walkin' around the buildin'. This was the same place that Nat 'King' Cole had a problem, same buildin'*. We must have been there only a few weeks after that, because I remember the heat still hadn't died down.

---

*During his performance at the Birmingham Municipal Auditorium on 23 April, 1956 Cole was attacked by a group of white segregationalists and knocked unconscious.

'We thought all of that was *ridiculous*, but that came from race-hate way before I was even thought about. That was the roots of shit that was supposed to keep goin': keep tellin' your kids they're not supposed to associate together, an' all that kinda stuff.

'Music kinda brought a lot of people together, all different nationalities, an' white people began to find out that negro people weren't that bad, an' negro people began to find out that whites weren't that bad either, an' that all that ol' ancient crap that was told to 'em *sucked*!

'A lot of the things that the white man done in the United States toward other nationalities, I don't blame him – I really, truthfully don't blame him, because he didn't know no better: he was *taught* that. I blame his parents, an' then *their* parents for all that hatred that went on between nationalities – because, if you walk up to any dude on the street an' say: "Hey man, why is it you don't like me, an' you ain't never seen me before?", the only thing he can say is: "I just don't like you." To me, you must have a *reason* for your actions.

'I don't think for a minute that the white man in the South actually *hated* black people. It wasn't that *at all*. It was economical, or financial: there was a lot of inheritances bein' left, an' they figured if a white dude's kids got tangled up with someone that was of another nationality, then they would reap what their father had worked for, an' they didn't want that, see?

'White people *don't hate* blacks! I've *always* said this. That's a false wall that's put up to keep you outa their front yard, but in reality they *like* you, y'understand? Because, would you *eat* somethin' that I prepared for you if you *hate* me? If that *was* the case, the blacks could have poisoned the South! Do you understand what I'm sayin'? Black people could have poisoned every white person in the South in the United States Of America, because they cooked for all the whites. There was no hate there. I never went for that "hatred" thing. We all worship the same God, an', if the Bible's right, we're all sisters an' brothers. Now, check it out!'[1]

Chapter 4

Who Do You Love?

I Wish You Would

The runaway success of Bo Diddley's first record sent shock waves throughout the entire American music industry, and it did not take long for either artists or record company executives to realise that there was money to be made out of the new sound.

First aboard the bandwagon was Little Walter, who invited Bo into the studio on 28 April, 1955 to cut 'Roller Coaster' (an instrumental version of 'Little Gwynadere', a song the latter had written about a waitress at the Sawdust Trail), and a 'Bo Diddley'-influenced composition of his own called 'I Got To Go'. Dulled by alcohol, the harmonica ace's performances were, however, far below his best and the record [Checker 817] failed to chart.

A second shot – this time a rewrite of Bo's 'You Don't Love Me (You Don't Care)' called 'Hate To See You Go' [Checker 825] – lacked even the saving grace of Diddley's guitar and likewise fell by the wayside.

Muddy Waters, on the other hand, fared significantly better with his version of 'I'm A Man', despite an embarrassingly sugary backing chorus (reportedly overdubbed at Len Chess's insistence). Recorded on 24 May, 1955, 'Manish Boy' [Chess 1602] climbed steadily to No. 9 on the *Billboard* 'Rhythm & Blues' chart, sparking off yet another controversy.

'Everybody thought Muddy was copyin' me,' explains Bo, 'but my song was based on Muddy doin' 'She Moves Me''*.[29] Muddy's tune didn't *sound* like 'I'm A Man', it just makes you *think* of the same tune because of the word structure; the melodies are not the same.'[1]

Whatever the precise genealogy of the composition, both artists have come to be identified with it over the years, each recording it several times**. Long acclaimed as an R&B landmark, it has also been covered by Bacon Fat, the Band, the Baker Street Irregulars, the Barracudas, the Beavers, the Bintangs, the Chancellors, Bobby Comstock, the Creation, Dr Feelgood, the Flamin' Groovies, John Hammond, Jimi Hendrix [recording as Jimmy James & The Blue Flames], the High Numbers [from Chicago], Blind Joe Hill, Cub Koda, Lazy Lester, John Lennon, the Litter, Magic Slim, the Marquis, Our Generation, the Remains, the Rolling Stones, the Royal Guardsmen, Doug Sahm, the Serfs, the Sonics, the Starliners, Things To Come, the Who, the Yardbirds, the Yellow Payges and the Zakary Thaks, while others have picked up on its distinctive 'da-da, da-da' stop–start phrasing and added their own lyrics.

Etta James was the first with her 1956 'answer' record 'W-O-M-A-N' [Modern 972], and there have been many since – among them the Animals' 'I'm Mad Again' [Columbia EP *Animals No. 2*], Chuck Berry's 'No Money Down' [Chess 1615], Big Brother & The Holding Company's 'Women Is Losers' [Mainstream LP *Big Brother & The Holding Company*], David Bowie's 'The Jean Genie' [RCA-Victor RCA-2302], David Allan Coe's 'Death Row' [SSS International LP *Penitentiary Blues*], Johnny Copeland's 'Nobody But You' [Rounder LP *Boom Boom*], Driving Stupid's 'The Reality Of (Air) Fried Borsk' [ICR 0116], Little Sonny's 'They Want Money' [Enterprise 9021], the Moonlights' 'Love Me True' [Rarin' Various Artists LP *Doo-Woppin' The Blues*], Johnny Otis's 'It's Good To Be Free' [Epic LP *Cuttin' Up*], 'You Better Look Out' [Kent LP *Cold Shot*] and 'Bad Luck Shadow' [Blues Spectrum LP *Great R&B Oldies (Volume 3)*], the Pirates Of The Mississippi's 'Redneck Blues' [Capitol CD *Walk The Plank*], Marty Stuart's 'Me & Hank & Jumpin' Jack Flash' [MCA CD *This One's Gonna Hurt You*], Them's 'All For Myself' [Decca F-12094], TV Slim's 'I'm A Real Man' [Ideel 581], 'TV Man' [Excell 104] and 'Mean Man' [Speed 715],

---

*Chess 1409 (1952).
**Waters scored a repeat hit with the song in 1988, when his 1977 Blue Sky LP version was issued in the UK [as Epic MUD-1] after being featured in a Levi jeans TV commercial.

Johnny 'Guitar' Watson's 'Gangster Of Love' [King 5774] and 'Rat Now' [Goth 101], Hank Williams Jr's 'My Name Is Bocephus' [Warner Bros LP *Montana Cafe*], Mighty Joe Young's 'Big Talk' [Ovation LP *Chicken Heads*] and Jack Nitzsche's themes for the movie *Blue Collar*, 'Hard Workin' Man', 'Quittin' Time' and 'Blue Collar' [all on MCA LP *Blue Collar*].

The jaunty 'Bo Diddley', meanwhile, created an even bigger stir, with several companies rushing out cover versions in the hope of grabbing a piece of the action for themselves.

RCA fielded Joe Reisman's Orchestra & Chorus [RCA-Victor 47-6121], while Mercury made an equally desperate attempt with the Harmonicats [Mercury 70629], but Essex clearly tried hard with Jean Dinning [Essex 395] – to the extent of hiring Diddley's own group to back her, as Billy Boy recalls: 'They got Willie Dixon, Clifton James and me to play on this white lady's session. They wanted the Bo Diddley band, but Leonard was *smart*: he wasn't going to give 'em Bo Diddley playing that tremolo, 'cause that would have been the Bo Diddley sound. The record came out: we heard it when we went to New Orleans. Her record was blasting all down South.

'When we got back, I went by Chess to see if the money for this session we'd did for this white lady had come. Chess told Bo Diddley that I came in there with a pocketful of money, and was asking for money. Bo told me: "Leonard don't like you. If I were you, I wouldn't go back around there. I'll tell you what I'll do, I'll take you 'round to another record company to cut your stuff." So I said: "Okay, that's cool."

'We played on a show at the Trianon Ballroom and Leonard was there. I was singing and blowing harmonica, and Bo Diddley was playing.[14] We had a new number called 'Diddy Diddy Dum Dum' that I had wrote. It wasn't called 'Diddley Daddy' yet, it was 'Diddy Diddy Dum Dum'.[14A] Leonard liked the song and he told Bo Diddley: "That's your next record! I want that!"

'Now, Bo had told me that Leonard didn't like me and didn't want me, so I went to Vee-Jay with it. Calvin Carter said: "Why don't you change the lyrics around?" I went home and I got 'I Wish You Would' together in about an hour, the whole lyrics, everything. I was playing the same harmonica figure with Bo Diddley 'cause it was my song, but it was Bo Diddley's beat because I was a member of his band. I ain't saying *that*, you know, it's his style and everything.

'Carter say: "Well, look here, get you a band together", so I went and got Jody Williams and Earl Phillips – who was already recording for Vee-Jay

– and Henry Gray and Milton Rector. Jody had a song called 'I Was Fooled' – he wanted to record too. Al Smith told Jody: "Let Billy do the song 'cause, you know, some people's voices is more suited to that sort of thing." Jody didn't sing, you know. I was more downhome-ish, in a way, than he was. So, we cut two sides: 'I Wish You Would' and 'I Was Fooled'.

'The same day I was cutting for Vee-Jay, I was supposed to cut 'Diddley Daddy' with Bo. Bo had come by my house looking for me, and I was downtown at Universal Recording, so they held Bo Diddley's session up.

'So, next day, I went on down there, you know, and Bo started playing 'Diddley Daddy': ba-boom, boom-boom... Leonard told Bo: "Hold it! Hold it! Let Billy sing it."

'I *could* have did the song, because 'I Wish You Would' was totally different, but I said: "I can't do it."

'Leonard say: "What's the matter? You *chicken*, man?"

'I said: "I just recorded it for Vee-Jay", and showed him the contract.

'Little Walter was in the studio, and Muddy Waters, and the Moonglows, and several other people. Little Walter told Bo: "If it was me, I'd tell him to hit the road!" He was kinda jealous, didn't want a young punk coming up, might give him a little competition.' (Laughs.)

'Leonard say: "Goddamn, ain't this a *bitch*! We gotta get some words to it!" So, the Moonglows started writing it, and everybody wrote these lyrics getting ready for the session.

'I didn't play on it, 'cause I'd did 'I Wish You Would' and I didn't want to do the same thing, so Little Walter used my harmonica and my amplifier and played on the 'Diddley Daddy' side – that's him you hear. Anybody that's got any common sense can hear that *smooth* harmonica on there, know there ain't no amateurs around Chicago playing like *that*!'[14]

For the flip, Bo cut a short blues called 'She's Fine, She's Mine', although the strange chanted introduction and heavy percussion accompaniment made it sound more like some eerie African dirge. The disguise worked so well, in fact, that when Willie Cobbs remade it in 1961 as 'You Don't Love Me'* [Mojo 2168] using a more conventional arrangement, few people recognised the song. It was reworked in 1962 by Louisiana Red as 'I Am Louisiana Red' [Roulette LP *Low Down Back Porch Blues*]) and by the Megatons as 'Shimmy Shimmy Walk' [Dodge

*Not to be confused with Bo's 'You Don't Love Me (You Don't Care)', an entirely different song.

808/Checker 1005], and has since become something of a blues standard, being covered by artists like the Allman Brothers Band, the Blues Busters, Dr Feelgood, the Groundhogs, John Hammond, J.B. Hutto, Kaleidoscope, Al Kooper & Mike Bloomfield, Magic Sam, John Mayall, Billy Lee Riley, Savoy Brown, Sonny & Cher, Sooner Or Later, Booker T. & The MGs, Gary Walker (who scored a No. 28 UK hit in 1966 with his version), Junior Wells and Smokey Wilson – though to date, only the Pretty Things have attempted the original Diddley treatment. However, the most successful variation on the theme so far has been Dawn Penn's reggae blaster, 'You Don't Love Me (No No No)' [Big Beat/Atlantic A.8295], which deservedly made No. 3 in the UK charts in June 1994.

'She's Fine, She's Mine' was the last time Billy Boy recorded with Bo. With a Vee-Jay contract in his pocket, he was of little use to Chess and his disloyalty had soured relationships: 'I played about two or three shows with Bo, then we parted company. He brought my amplifier by my house and said he had another harp player*. I didn't care. I didn't have no intentions of making a career playing behind Bo Diddley or nobody else. I didn't start out trying to be no sideman, and I knew I didn't have no future with Bo.

'See, Bo had a little attitude: he didn't want nobody to take no show, so he didn't let anybody do much singing. I didn't know I *could* sing! To tell you the truth, I was trying to play harmonica. That was my intentions, you know, when I first got inspired by Sonny Boy Williamson to be a recording artist.'[14]

Nonetheless, Bo admits he regretted losing Billy's services: 'Billy Boy was a helluva harmonica player, an' I just wish we could have stayed together an' wrote songs together, rather than splittin' up like we did, but you can't think for other people.'[1]

Wigglin'

Shortly after Billy left Chess, his record, 'I Wish You Would' [Vee-Jay 146], began selling like hot cakes, reportedly shifting 14,000 copies in Detroit alone during the first week of its release. Indeed, the waxing had all the

---

*Arnold was temporarily replaced by Lester Davenport, who was in turn succeeded a few months later by Little Willie Smith. Smith's tenure was cut short at the start of 1956, when Diddley decided to drop the harmonica from his band's line-up altogether.

makings of a sizeable hit until Len Chess pulled strings and had it yanked off the air. The ploy worked, and 'Diddley Daddy' [Checker 819] went on to notch up massive sales that took it as high as No. 11 on the *Billboard* 'Rhythm & Blues' chart in the summer of 1955.

One of Bo Diddley's most memorable recordings, the song has since been covered by Dave Berry, the British Walkers, Bobby Crafford & The Pacers, Marshall Crenshaw, John Hammond, Ronnie Hawkins, Chris Isaac, the Jeckylls & Hydes, Delbert McClinton & The Ron-Dels, the Liverbirds and the Rolling Stones, and its distinctive 6-4-5-4, 6-4 ‿‿‿ 4-5-4 phrasing and emphatic 'bom-bom-bom' rhythm are easily identifiable on many other classic recordings of the period – among them Billy Boy's 'Rockinitis' [Vee-Jay 260], Bill Haley's 'Lean Jean' [Decca 30681], Elmore James's 'Stranger Blues' [Fire 1503], Lil' Millet's 'Rich Woman' [Specialty 565], Sandy Nelson's 'Drums Are My Beat' [Imperial 5809], Robert & Johnny's 'Broken Hearted Man' [Old Town 1043] and Ronnie Self's 'Rocky Road Blues' [Columbia 40989].

The success of Bo Diddley's second release was quickly consolidated by a nation-wide *Diddley Daddy* package tour promoted by Alan Freed and featuring a host of top-notch support acts including Nappy Brown, Al Hibbler, Buddy Johnson & His Orchestra, Ella Johnson, the Five Keys, Little Walter, the Moonglows, the Moonlighters, Dakota Staton and Dinah Washington.

Everywhere he played, Bo caused a sensation with his powerful sound and dynamic showmanship. Always the focus of attention, he drove audiences wild, strutting ostentatiously around the stage, striking dramatic poses with his axe, shaking his legs and wiggling his hips.

Enthused one contemporary reviewer...

'The crowd starts howling its delight when Bo lets go with the rock 'n' roll dance he does with his guitar. Smiling big, Bo never misses a beat as he hot-steps it around the stage to his cool music. When his left foot takes off, the fans know they're in for the sizzling rock 'n' roll step which is fast becoming a trademark. Bo usually starts stomping on one side of the stage and high-kicks, spins, dips, taps and waddles his way to the other. By the time he's across the stage, man, everybody's jumping! After he finishes his fancy footwork, the audience always begs for more – which proves you can't get enough of a great showman like Bo Diddley!'[30]

'Rock 'n' roll had a *meanin'* back then,'[28] Bo fondly recalls. 'I remember the time when teenagers would come into the theater with their lunch, an' the school would send the truant officer after 'em, an' *he* would have *his* lunch too![27]

'At one place we was supposed to be playin' at, the owner came up an' told us that he'd changed his mind, that he was givin' everybody their money back: he'd read somethin' in the paper about me where I had upset the whole stadium an' people was just goin' berserk, an' chicks was faintin', an' they didn't want that happenin' there. It was *crazy*, man!'[1]

Sadly, Bo's immense popularity proved to be short-lived: 'He caught one of the Dr Jive shows at the Apollo Theater[25] late in 1955, an' he came to see me afterwards. We had quite a talk, though I didn't know who he was.[31]

'He admired me enough to do what he saw me doin'. He snatched my little wigglin' idea, an' – it wasn't *his* fault – but when *he* did it, he clicked, an' I got shoved back in the corner.[29]

'I think when Elvis Presley came out, he had no intentions of copyin' a black dude called Bo Diddley, 'cause maybe I didn't even exist in his mind.[1] So, I'm not mad with Elvis: I got an attitude against the people that put him up to it.[7] I think the people that was havin' him knew about me, seen me, brought him to Harlem, stuck him in the corner of the Apollo Theater, an' had him watchin' me.

'See, durin' that time, I had lines all round the street, all the way round the block, an' they probably said: "If this *black* dude can do this, if *you* do the same thing, man, you can draw people – an' *more*!" An' they were *right*!

'See, in the fifties, if they found a white cat that was doin' what a black cat was doin', they'd shove the black dude back in the corner. That was all that "black" an' "white" bullshit that I didn't even know existed, you know.

'Elvis *had* to be brought there by somebody, because – I don't care *how much* nerve he had – he did *not* have enough nerve to come in Harlem, bein' white, an' go to an all-black theater. Things like that did *not* happen! No way!

'I was *black*, an' *I* was scared to be up there in Harlem – because you had a different type of people runnin' around up there: everybody was *mad* about somethin' – a militant attitude. People that live in Harlem feel that they have been totally misused by the white man. They don't see nothin' else but *hatred*!

'No *white* dude came into Harlem. From *Tennessee?* An' let it be *known* that he was from Tennessee? No way, uh-uh! Ain't *nobody* got *that* much nerve!

'I'm tellin' you what I *know*: if you value your ass, you don't go there. Even the dudes that live on Long Island don't hang around in Harlem after dark![1]

'I *am* somewhat bitter about people runnin' around sayin' Elvis Presley started rock 'n' roll. It's a *damn lie*! He didn't create *nothin'* of his own![25]

'At first, it was a rip-off to the public: he couldn't sing, he couldn't play, an' I couldn't see anythin' that merited the action that he got.[1] A *lotta* people were fooled, but I was the son-of-a-gun that would stand there, *right* there – *lookin'*. I'm livin' proof, y'understand? I *know* what was happenin': Elvis could not play no guitar. He could *not* play! I'm speakin' the truth![7] But, after he got out of the service, he really got his act together. I think Elvis was a *magnificent* entertainer – I want the records to be straight on *that*.[1]

'An', okay, he made it. That's great, you know. I'll swear on my mother I have no animosity toward the dude, even after he's dead an' gone, you know.[7] Man, I *hated* it when they talked about Elvis, the way they chewed him up, an' all their life they've been runnin' around... I wasn't *in love* with him, but he never did anythin' to me except rip me off my act, an' I wasn't mad with him as a *individual*.[1]

'He probably *did* copy quite a few things from me, but then, so did a whole lot more guys. I was at the head of the rock world, an' they were figurin' out how to get in, how to jump on the bandwagon. They came to me to get the message![31] I opened the door, an' everybody ran through it an' left me holdin' the handle!'[1]

Increasingly passed over by the media in favour of newer, younger and (generally) whiter artists than himself, Bo Diddley quickly slipped from his position at the top of the rock 'n' roll ladder. His popularity as a live attraction waned little, however, and he spent the remainder of the fifties touring incessantly, appearing on *The Biggest Rock 'n' Roll Show Of 1956* (which took him overseas for the first time – to Australia), Alan Freed's 1956 *Big Beat* and 1957 *Easter Jubilee* packages, Eli Weinberg's *Fantabulous Rock 'n' Roll Show Of 1957*, GAC's *Biggest Show Of Stars For '57, '58* and *'59*, and countless other spectaculars.

'I also made a radio commercial: Royal Crown Hairdressing asked me to make a commercial for 'em, so I just did a little comical thing*. Took two shots at it, an' that was that. They sent me a case of Royal Crown – which, at that time, most dudes was gettin' processes, you know, no more grease in their hair.' (Laughs.) 'Man, that stuff's like *axle-grease*!'[1]

'I'm a road runner, baby'

The life of an itinerant musician can be both demanding and eventful, and Bo recounts anecdotes about his many experiences on the road with an obvious relish...

'Lemme tell you about Ray Charles, man, lemme tell you what happened. We were in Chicago, an' I said: "Hey Ray, since you goin' to New York, can I go with you?"'

'He say: "Sure."'

'So, we get out on the turnpike an' Jeff, Ray's manager, is drivin'. I'm sittin' in the back talkin' to Jeff, an' Speedy – which also used to drive for Ray – is sittin' over on the other side, sleepin'. Ray's sittin' in the front next to Jeff.

'So, Ray gets this big idea, tells Jeff: "Jeff, pull this son-of-a-gun over!"'

"What's goin' on, you wanna go to the bathroom or somethin'?"'

'He say: "No. *Shit*, thirteen thousand miles in that damn car? I'm gonna *drive* it!"'

'Now, he is a man that can't see *at all*... an' I'm sittin' in the back listenin' at this shit!' (Laughter.) 'Can you *imagine* what I was thinkin', man? I'm on the New Jersey Turnpike about ninety miles from thataway, an' eighty miles thisaway. Ain't nothin' but a few little farmhouses here an' there.

'Jeff say: "Are you *serious*?"'

'He say: "Yeah! It's *my* damned car, man. Get over!"'

'So, he pulled over. Ray say: "Now, you get out an' come around, an' I'm gonna slide over. Now, you nudge me two times when I need to go to the right an' one time when I need to go to the left."'

'An' I'm sittin' in the back, man...' (Laughter.) 'I ain't diggin' this shit *at all*, but I can't say: "Let me out!" 'cause it's cold, kinda chilly, might start snowin' yet.' (Laughter.)

'So, I'm watchin' this shit, you know. Cat's goin' 'bout 35–40 miles an hour, an' the car's goin' like this an' – *boom*! – we're tryin' to climb the New Jersey Turnpike! Speedy wakes up: "Ho-lee shit!" an' tries to jump out!' (Laughter.) 'See, 'cause that was kinda scary, to look up an' see Ray

---

*This was probably around the same time Little Richard recorded his: October 1956.

sittin' up at the steerin' wheel with his head down like this, you know, an' the car wigglin' all over the road.'[10] (Laughs.) 'You wouldn't *believe* some of the crap that I've gotten involved in, man!

'I remember one time I got through eleven cars *in one month*! I was on tour, an' they kept on breakin' down. Now, I like to think I'm a pretty good mechanic, an' if I've got enough time I *will* fix it, but when you're tryin' to make a gig, you don't have time to take out the engine. So, only thing you can do is get you another, an' hope that *that* one gets you there, you know.

'An' so, I'd go on down the road to a used car lot, give 'em a coupla hundred bucks down, get my wheels an' make the gig. Next day, same thing would happen. I didn't have time to fix 'em, so I had to leave 'em standin' right there, on the roadside. When I got home, there was a pile of letters *this* high, you know, from the police!' (Laughs.)

'I *had* to make all the gigs, because if you don't get there on time, you don't get paid, you dig? Or either you got *sued*. *I'm* the one that got sued all the time. Not nobody in the group, but *me*. That's the reward you get for bein' the big-time leader. You know, the boss is always the Big Shit, an' everybody treats you just that way. You're the big-time leader, you know.

'My contracts always stipulated the number of people that was to be on stage with me: wasn't no good if one or two of 'em was missin'. So, I had two drummers – an' later on I also had two bass players – because everybody would get tired of bein' on the road all the time, an' then I'd call the other one out. My drummers, Clifton James an' Frank Kirkland, used to take turns on comin' out on the road with me. Frank would come an' work awhile, an' get homesick an' go home, then Clifton would come out, y'understand? They used to play these little games on me, you know.' (Laughs.) 'Or they'd get mad an' make a statement 'bout goin' home, an' the only thing was that I had somebody else left. Or either, *I'd* get mad an' *send* 'em home! But there was still a lotta times we didn't get paid.

'A dude once tried to put me out of a hotel – this was in New York – because he thought I was Little Richard's band. Now, I don't know how true this is, but he told me they ran outa there an' didn't pay their bill. I told the dude: "I don't even *know* Richard!"

'Cat say: "Yeah, I seen you before!" – this was durin' the time when all the whites thought all blacks looked alike.

'I says: "I ain't got that much hair on my head!"

'He says: "Yeah, you work with him. We don't want no rock 'n' roll in here", you know.

'But, see, a lotta times that entertainers did stuff of that sort is because the promoter would run off with the money. Now, what you gonna pay the hotel bill with? You done rented a hotel, got it all set up, got a six-piece band in there, six rooms, you know, an' cats done run up telephone calls, an' all this ol' kinda stuff. You're *lookin'* to get paid that night, an' the promoter run off. Now you're *scared*, an' the only thing for you to do is try to figure out how to get out of that hotel with all that equipment an' take a chance on payin' the dude later.

'I think I ran out on maybe two or three hotel bills in my life. One of 'em, when I had to leave, the desk wasn't open an' I had a plane to catch. Now, I'm not goin' to sit around an' wait until nine o'clock an' blow my flight just to give a dude $25, you know. An' the couple of letters I *did* get, I have paid.

'My wife could always find me when I was on the road, an' for a long time I couldn't figure out how she did it, you know. What she would do was, she'd find out where I was playin' that evenin' an', because there was only a few hotels durin' that time that catered for blacks, she'd know straightaway which hotel to call!

'When I was goin' through the South, I used to cook *all* the time. The reason for that was: here am I, gotta go in some white dude's *back door*, an' I've got ten – maybe fifteen thousand dollars in my pocket! I'm gonna get a 95¢ hamburger 'cause I can't go in the front door. So I said: "To hell with your *back* door! I'll go buy me some chicken an' put it in the trunk, get some utensils, put it all on the bus, an' I'll do my *own* cookin'! I *ain't* goin' to your daggone *back door*! You got a *black* cook sittin' up there cookin' up all this shit, an' gonna tell me I *can't come in* the front door? I gotta go round the *back* an' get a *hamburger* because of the color of my skin? *BULL-SHIT*!"

'So, people in the South lost a *lotta* money,' (laughs), 'because I had all them people. You know, places that we went to up an' down the road, an' spent maybe fifteen, twenty bucks a shot, two or three times, you know, buyin' hamburgers, pop, all sortsa stuff – we quit doin' it.

'We'd go in a grocery store, buy all our stuff an' stick it in our little cooler on the bus. When we got hungry, we'd just get up an' grab somethin'. Chuck Berry did the same – he always carried a little electric hotplate with him, you know.[1]

'One time, when we were ridin' through the South, everybody got hungry on the bus, an' Jerome had made a shopping bag full of sandwiches, an' had some beer an' everythin' sittin' in the back of the bus.

81

Cats got hungry, an' he knew they couldn't get nothin' to eat 'cause everythin' was closed, so he tells 'em: "Well, *my* store's *open!*" Man, he sold out in half a mile!' (Laughs.)

'Jerome was always a shrewd character. You could never tell what he was off into, y'understand what I mean? He never got into trouble, never got into anythin' *illegal*, but if there was some way to make money, he'd figure out how to do it!'[32] (Laughs.)

'Entertainin'' is a *weird* business. When you go on stage with big smiles, everyone thinks you're happy, but you've got more troubles waitin' back in your dressin' room than those people out there clappin'. You can get in trouble without knowin' how. Just bein' who you are gets you in trouble![27] 'Bein'' black an' travelin' all over the United States, I've been in a lot of funky situations.[1] I've had dudes come up to me, put a gun up to my head an' say: "Nigger, we're gonna blow the shit outa your brain", an' I'd always be *very* polite an' say: "Yessir, sho' you are", an' then *get the hell outa there*! I've been in the kinda trouble I don't even *care* to remember![33] When you look at the United States havin' all that ol' kinda crap in it, you think: "Wow! *America?*"'[1]

Make A Hit Record

Having established himself as one of the nation's top in-person entertainers, Bo Diddley was expected – not unnaturally perhaps – to match this reputation in the recording studio. Rising to the challenge, he wrote and recorded prolifically throughout the fifties, producing a succession of miniature masterpieces – each readily identifiable, easily distinguishable, instantly enjoyable.

Issued in November 1955, his third release [Checker 827] was typical, combining a bouncy African-style 'call-and-response' chant called 'Bring It To Jerome' on one side, with an endearingly naive love song featuring a stunning chopped guitar introduction on the other.

'Willie Dixon* wrote 'Pretty Thing',' recalls Bo. 'I remember Willie standin' over me, whisperin' the lyrics in my ear before I got to the next

---

*Often referred to as 'Leonard Chess's right hand', Dixon played a pivotal role at Chess Records from 1952 onwards, acting as talent scout, A&R man, composer, arranger, producer and session bassist for the label. He was responsible for literally dozens of hits during the fifties and sixties by artists like Chuck Berry, Buddy Guy, Howlin' Wolf, Little Walter, Muddy Waters and Sonny Boy Williamson, and has long since been acknowledged as one of the major figures of the post-War blues era.

line!' (Laughs.) 'He was nice enough to give me part of the tune. It should be on the credits: "McDaniel & Dixon".[32] Willie was a great influence on me, an' he helped me a lot in the studio an' stuff. He was *always* there. He was like a father, you know.'[1]

By late 1955, however, Bo was already beginning to strive for a heavier and more complex sound, and he asked a guitarist friend of his named Bobby Parker to join the group. Parker's presence was immediately noticeable on his first release of 1956 – the futuristic-sounding 'I'm Looking For A Woman' [Checker 832] – on which he wove a tough lead around Diddley's exquisitely shimmering rhythm-lead phrasings, and likewise on its Willie Dixon-inked flip, 'Diddy Wah Diddy'*, which he embellished with some exemplary bent-note playing. Here (as on other sessions during the mid-fifties) the basic Diddley outfit was augmented by Dixon on double bass and the Moonglows vocal group: Harvey Fuqua (lead), Bobby Lester (first tenor), Alexander 'Pete' Graves (second tenor) and Prentiss Barnes (bass) – the latter coincidentally another native of McComb, Mississippi.

Now rapidly maturing as a musician, Bo was also beginning to develop an idiosyncratic songwriting style, drawing together themes and ideas from a staggering diversity of sources and fashioning them into eccentric, wonderfully outlandish creations that were unequivocally and undeniably his own.

One of his finest concoctions ever was the spine-chilling 'Who Do You Love' [Checker 842], an epic performance in which he attempted to win the affections of a young lady named Arlene with a stunning display of voodooesque braggadocio. The story of how he came to write such a strikingly individual song provides a rare insight into the creative genius that lay behind many of Diddley's compositions: 'I'm tellin' this chick: "Who do you love, me or him?" – that's what I'm sayin', an' I'm tellin' her how *bad* I am, so she can go an' tell the cat that she's hangin' with: "This dude is *somethin' else!*" That's what it kinda meant: cat ridin' rattlesnakes, an' kissin' boa constrictors an' stuff.' (Laughs.)

'I was in Kansas City when I wrote that. There was a bunch of little kids signifyin'** with each other, chasin' each other, throwin' rocks at each

*This mythical utopia was also the subject of an earlier song, 'Diddie Wa Diddie' [Paramount 12888], recorded in 1929 by bluesman Blind Blake.
**Insulting.

other, talkin' 'bout each other's parents. Little bitty dudes! An' the *language* they were usin'![34] I leant out of the window an' told 'em they oughta be ashamed of what they were doin', an' they told me where to go!

'They had a rhyme that they were doin' with it, an' the melody they were singin' stayed with me. I liked it, an' I put it onto a dub. It was like an African chant, an' I wanted words that would suit it.[35] Muddy Waters was on this *"He's got a black cat bone"* thing* at the time, an' so I was tryin' to come up with somethin' – uh – *rougher*. You know, people tend to hang around whatever might be goin' on that seem to be the "click", an', if you don't know any better, you'll find yourself writin' stuff that's similar.[1]

'I had the line *"I walk forty-seven miles of barbed wire"*, but I couldn't get a rhyme for it. I thought of car tires, an' mule trains, an' couldn't get anythin' to fit. One day, I said: *"Use a cobra-snake"*, an' my drummer, Clifton James, added: *"for a necktie"*. We then did a verse a day, him an' me an' Jerome. They didn't want no part of the song, though: they said I could have it all. Of course, we didn't know it was goin' to be that big.'[35]

With its murky vocals, eerie – almost *surreal* lyrics, and the revolutionary guitar work of Jody Williams, (who had meanwhile replaced Bobby Parker), 'Who Do You Love' ranks as one of Bo Diddley's major achievements and has since been covered by Keith 'Guitar' Allison, the Band, the Blues Magoos, the Blues Project, Bobby Crafford & The Pacers, the Doors, Gina & The Strollers, the Great Impostors, John Hammond, Ronnie Hawkins, Roy Head, the Hoodoo Gurus, Jack Horner & The Plums, Ian Hunter, the Intruders, the Jesus & Mary Chain, Scotty McKay, Kingdom Come, the Milkshakes, the Steve Miller Band, the Misunderstood, the Mood, the Only Ones, the Pleasure Barons, the Preachers, Tom Rush, Carlos Santana, Bob Seger, George Thorogood, UFO, Townes Van Zandt and the Yardbirds, while versions by the Woolies, the Quicksilver Messenger Service and Juicy Lucy also made the charts in 1967, 1969 and 1970 respectively.

The ominous atmosphere of 'Who Do You Love' also pervaded the flip-side, an entertaining (if thinly-disguised) 'I'm A Man' rehash called 'I'm Bad', which saw Bo purposely debasing his menacing delivery with ridiculously inappropriate 'fun' lines like: *'You even asked me where the light went/When it went out'*.

---

*'I'm Your Hoochie Coochie Man' [Chess 1560], a 1954 R&B hit.

The follow-up, 'Down Home Special'* [Checker 850], was equally ambiguous, with an ostensibly happy theme (a migrant worker going home to see his girl) sharply contrasted by a haunting and strangely unsettling melody. The arrangement, too, was one of Diddley's most inspired ever: a masterful portrayal of a speeding express train, with stuttering guitars conjuring up images of lurching carriages, drums simulating the pitter-pat of the wheels, Jerome's maracas hissing like steam, and whistles blasting away all over the place.

'I just found one of the whistles – I don't know what happened to the big one. Somebody broke the end off it, but I think I can fix it. I found that whistle in New York on the Bowery, in a junk pile, you know.

'I'm the greatest junkman that ever lived: if I can get it home, I'll drag it home. Then, if one day I ain't got nothin' to do, I'll try an' figure out what makes it tick. I had trouble out of my momma about it, an' I got trouble out of my wife about it, you know, but I can't stop.

'Everybody's got their little thing that they like to do. I'm a normal person like anybody else. Is my likes an' wants supposed to *stop* because I'm Bo Diddley?'[1]

The flip of 'Down Home Special' was a departure of a different kind for Bo: a hilarious monologue about a guy in car who gives a lift to a stranger and is coerced into acting as getaway driver in a store robbery.

Originally recorded a few months earlier that year by its composer, Kent L. Harris (under the pseudonym 'Boogaloo & His Gallant Crew' [Crest 1030]), 'Cops & Robbers' proved to be a fine showcase for Diddley's raconteurial talents.

Bo hates it: 'That was one *weird* record! I didn't really wanna do it 'cause they had me talkin' like a cissy, an' I didn't want that portrait drawn of me, of that type of dude. I finally cut it, but I was mad when I did, an' I haven't performed it more than ten times since.'[36]

The year 1957 likewise turned out to be a fine year, with ideas continuing to flow thick and fast. For his seventh single, 'Hey Bo Diddley'** [Checker 860], Bo combined thundering drums with cannibalised 'Old Macdonald' nursery rhyme lyrics to conjure up images

---

*Later a UK hit for Gene Vincent under the title 'I'm Going Home' [Capitol CL-15215], as well as a party piece for blues–rock outfit Ten Years After [Cotillion Various Artists 3-LP *Woodstock*].

**On which the vocal backing was, for a change, provided by the Flamingos.

of a fabulous *'Bo Diddley's farm'* crawling with women: *'Women here, women there/Women, women, women everywhere'*. He contrasted this on the flip with an impassioned chant inspired by – and dedicated to – the unlikeliest of heroines.

'Mona was an exotic dancer that I had the pleasure of workin' with about 1956 or '57. I was in a place – the Flame Show Bar in Detroit, I think – an' I *admired* her performance.

'She told me she was forty-five years old, an' I looked at her, an' the dance that she did, an' said that I wish *I* was able to move around – when I got to be forty-five – the way this chick moved. You know, just be *in shape*. That was one of my things that I set out to aim to do. She *proved* that you don't have to come apart at thirty years old.'[37]

Another acknowledged Diddley classic (not least because it was the prototype for Buddy Holly's celebrated 'Not Fade Away'), 'Mona' (*aka* 'I Need You Baby') has since been covered by the likes of the Len Bright Combo, Mick Farren, the Haunted, Help Yourself, Buddy Holly, the Iguanas, Willy Jive, the Liverbirds, Mahogany Rush, the Milkshakes, the Nashville Teens, the Quicksilver Messenger Service, the Rolling Stones, Bruce Springsteen, T.C. Atlantic, the Teddy Boys, the Troggs and of course Craig McLachlan, whose version reached No. 2 in the UK charts in July 1990.

Bo's other release that year [Checker 878] – the first to be recorded in Chess's new studio at 2120 South Michigan Avenue – was surprisingly conventional by his standards: 'Before You Accuse Me' was essentially a straightforward blues shuffle interrupted only by two magnificently eccentric guitar breaks – each a chaotic jumble of missed notes, slurs and tempo changes, while 'Say Boss Man' saw him tackle another familiar theme in his own inimitable fashion, with lighthearted exaggerations of life's hardships (*'I got nineteen kids at home gotta eat/Eighteen of 'em need shoes on their feet'*) and a cheerful bar-room piano played by another Diddley session stalwart, Ellis 'Lafayette' Leake.

Bubbling Under

Astonishing as it may seem, not one of these remarkable records ever made it into the charts. Part of the reason for this apparently poor showing was that, for the first three years of Bo Diddley's career (when he was at the peak of his popularity), the *Billboard* 'Rhythm & Blues' chart only ran to fifteen positions – these being determined (like those of the 'Top 100' pop chart*) by a none-too-representative weekly survey of sales to distributors.

Since the majority of independents (including Chess) relied upon 'car-trunk' distribution methods, their record sales tended to reflect the progress of their pluggers around the country, 'breaking' in different areas at different times. This created a curious paradox whereby poorly distributed records were frequently kept out of the chart by better distributed, but less-popular titles.

This was certainly the case with Bo Diddley's mid-fifties releases, most of which were massive regional hits, though seldom concurrently.

'There was long periods in-between releases. It wasn't somethin' against me, it was the way that they did things: they weaned every dime they could get before they'd put out another one to kill *that* one – because, when you put out a new release, the old one dies immediately.

'This is the way I *learned*. They taught me 'bout how to get ahead: they worked for *nickels an' dimes*, when you an' I are tryin' to get *dollars*. That's the way Jewish people get ahead: all these cats are penny-pinchin', an' they own *everythin'* in this goddamn country!

'That's what Leonard Chess an' them was doin'. They penny-pinched every nickel they could get out of it before they killed it: "Hey, we ain't gonna release this until *next* week", or: "Let's see what this sucker's gonna do by next week".[1]

'At first, I had a lotta black fans, but they all disappeared. They held on for about three or four records – after that, I guess I got monotonous. I could tell that I was losin' the crowds when they started droppin' off to two or three hundred.[12] I was goin' to Skid Row when I was playin' for blacks,[38] so I said: "There's nothin' for me to do, but shoot for the other side of the fence.[12] So, I quit playin' what you call the "chitlin' circuit", you know, changed all over into the white vein, an' it's been *beautiful* ever since. I never played too many black places after I'd did that. I don't know why, but I never even get a solicitin' from black promoters. They don't know what to do with me, I guess.[1]

'As a rule, black people don't follow me. A few of 'em will come around, 'cause they're curious to see is he still doin' the same ol' chinketty-chink-chink. They can't understand why I'm still here.[12] Cats ask me: "Hey man, what are you *playin'*? I don't *understand* this stuff!"

---

*Renamed 'Hot 100' in August 1958.

'I'm kinda bitter about that, an' I'm not scared to say it.[1] It *hurts* me that I can't even draw my own folks, an' I'm playin' *our* music. I'm accepted as a brother, but they don't go out to see Bo Diddley.

'Blues, an' the stuff I was playin', was supposed to be puttin' our people back fifty years.[12] It was my folks said that.[38] Then, all of a sudden, everybody wanted to be *African*, you know: "I'm black an' I'm proud". Okay, that's great. I was playin' what I thought was our *heritage* music, but they *still* didn't like it.[1] I'm confused. *Totally* confused.'[12]

With the bulk of his records selling in white record stores from 1956 onwards, Bo's chances of getting a record into the 'Rhythm & Blues' chart diminished further, while the 'Top 100' proved an even tougher nut to crack – because of strong competition from the majors, as well as racial prejudice within the industry which denied him access to the same kind of exposure as his paler-skinned rivals.

Be that as it may, comparisons between Diddley and his close but infinitely more successful contemporary, Chuck Berry, are unavoidable. After all, both men cut their first sides only a matter of weeks apart, both recorded for the same company, and both were black – yet virtually every one of Berry's singles figured prominently not only in the 'Rhythm & Blues' chart, but also in the 'Top 100'. How is it that Berry did so much better?

For an explanation, one needs to appreciate the differences between the two men – musical and otherwise – and understand their corollary.

There can be little doubt that the chief reason for Berry's immense popularity was the topicality of his songs: his snappy lyrics about cars, girls and other teenage concerns immediately found immense popularity with large sections of both the black and the white audience ; Diddley's ghetto jive and off-beat black humour, on the other hand, were far less accessible (and frequently unintelligible) to the average white listener, no matter how sympathetic.

Secondly, Berry's records were always consistent in style and quality, and could be relied upon to sell. Quite naturally, this inspired confidence among dealers, who would happily place huge advance orders for his new releases. Not so Diddley's recordings, which – brilliant though they were – were generally regarded as unpredictable hit-or-miss novelties and accordingly drew a considerably more cautious response. Inevitably, the smaller order quantities for Diddley's records resulted in lower chart placings.

A third important factor in Berry's success was the high media profile he enjoyed: his clear, melodic singing and country-influenced 'chonka-chonka-chonka' guitar style made him eminently suitable for white radio airplay, and his immaculately groomed, clean-cut image ensured that he was also a safe bet for television and movie appearances.

Diddley, conversely, remained firmly rooted in the ghetto: both his music and his image were too loud, too raunchy, too *black* ever to 'cross over' in the same way Berry had. His records were frequently played on juke-boxes and at dances, but far less often on the radio. Television appearances were a rarity. There were no movie offers.

The Chess brothers probably understood these limitations better than anyone, and concentrated on promoting and developing Berry's career – to Diddley's detriment: 'America is gullible to the advertisement. I've never had the public relationship. No ads, no billboards.[39] You see records gettin' bullets, an' a star, an' all this kinda stuff – an' the record that's got the star you might not be able to get *arrested* with![1] A group can have no talent but, if the dee-jay plays their song, you'll find yourself hummin' it – an' if you *hum* it, you might *buy* it! I've never been treated that way.[39]

'When it came to makin' movies, I wasn't really bothered that they didn't want me. It *did* harm my career, though, because I was never given the opportunity to show people what Bo Diddley is all about. I *can't* put my performance on record – there are artists like that. People need to *see* me, an' they never got the chance.'[1]

When one such opportunity – perhaps *the* opportunity – to make it finally presented itself, Bo was cruelly deprived of it by an unscrupulous promoter.

'I was supposed to do Dick Clark's *American Bandstand* once, an' I never made it. You know *why* I didn't make it? Because the cats I was workin' for told me I'd better not leave the theater an' do *American Bandstand*, because there was people all around the block waitin' to get in to see me. I was supposed to miss one show to do *American Bandstand*, an' a limousine was gonna bring me back: it was right there in Philly, you know. They wanted this money, so they told me I'd better not go – I *couldn't* go – 'cause I'd never get through the crowds.

'They called up Dick Clark an' told him I wasn't comin'. Dick got mad with me, because here's a piece of the show he's gotta try an' figure out how to fill. An' he had a *right* to be mad, because he was *lied* to. It was made to look like I'd said: "Go fuck yourself, I ain't comin!"'

'I did not *never* say that! I *needed* that show! Chuck Berry, Chubby Checker, Frankie Avalon – everybody that's ever been there, Dick made 'em. Dick Clark *made* 'em! If it hadn't've been for *American Bandstand*, they coulda racked up their shit an' went back home. *American Bandstand* put 'em on the map!

'So, eight years ago, I just happened to come out an' tell Dick Clark's guy that takes care of all the business, an' the stage an' everythin' – Larry Klein – about that. Larry, by accident, had heard somethin' about the fifties an' me an' Dick Clark, an' he went an' got Dick, since when he's been tryin' to do everythin' in his power to fill that gap that was there.

'Everybody had been tryin' to poison me up, sayin' things like Dick Clark was a racist, an' all this ol' kinda stuff, an' I just didn't believe that shit, man. *American Bandstand* used to be kinda racist, you know, 'cause they didn't like blacks dancin' down there with the white kids – this was in Philadelphia, you dig – but it was the woman that *owned* it, not Dick himself. Dick had nothin' to do with that. He just had a gig, a job, you know. Dick Clark is a *beautiful* dude! He is a magnificent man, an' I don't have anythin' wrong to say about him. He's tops in my book, you know. I think he's done wonderful things for *all* of us.'[1]

Chapter 5

Say Man

Shuckin' & Jivin'

Although nobody would have predicted it at the time, 1959 and 1960 were to be Bo Diddley's golden years. Improved recording facilities at Chess and the expansion of *Billboard*'s 'Rhythm & Blues' chart (from fifteen positions to twenty on 25 January, 1958 – and then to thirty from 26 October) at last put the chance of a hit within his reach.

Indeed, his first release that year, another reworking of the 'Hush Little Baby' lullaby called 'Hush Your Mouth' [Checker 896], only just missed and, after an ill-advised (and unsuccessful) attempt to cash in on Sheb Wooley's chart-topping 'Purple People Eater' [M-G-M K.12651] with 'Bo Meets The Monster' [Checker 907], he indeed came up with a winner: a memorable doo wop-styled ballad called 'I'm Sorry'* [Checker 914], which entered the 'Rhythm & Blues' chart in March 1959 and climbed to the No. 17 slot.

---

*Unmistakably inspired by Don & Dewey's gentle 1957 offering, 'When The Sun Has Begun To Shine' [Specialty 617], Bo's composition was itself reworked in 1963 by the Ohio Untouchables as 'Forgive Me Darling' [LuPine 1010], tremolo guitar and all.

At least some of this success was attributable to the strong flip, 'Oh Yea', an entertaining drama in the 'Cops & Robbers' mould (this time written by Bo himself) in which he tried to stand up to his girlfriend's interfering parents, only to find himself unceremoniously escorted off the premises by the police.

'I *did* have some of those kinda problems durin' my life,' (laughs) '...but what really made me write that song was, Muddy Waters used to holler *"Oh yeah"*, an' I just took the word because it sounded good.

'When I was comin' along, I *had* to write stories! That's why you saw songs come out that went: *"Let me walk you home"*... now, what you gonna do after you walk her home? *"Can I get a kiss, goodnight?"*, you know. An' then you go on, an' if the girl wouldn't kiss you goodnight, you'd have to make sure that you put in there that you left, an' then you came back, or either you sat on her doorstep an' *cried*, you know, an' you went home an' you couldn't sleep, couldn't eat, you know, you go back an' say: *"Can I kiss you today?"*' (Laughter.)

'You *had* to make a story out of it some kinda way, but today all they do is holler *"Hey-hey-hey"* or *"Ring my be-e-ell, ring my bell"*. Right now, you can't understand what *nobody's* sayin'! Maybe *I* can't understand it: it's a different language.' (Laughs.)

'Okay, alright, but it's serious to me that I can't understand it, because I *would like* to know what's bein' said, so I can draw a better opinion, an' not get this "negative" thing about it.'[1]

Three months after the success of 'I'm Sorry', Bo bounced back with another strong ballad, 'Crackin' Up' [Checker 924], whose novel Caribbean flavour and catchy *'What's buggin' you?'* hook took it not only to No. 14 on the 'Rhythm & Blues' chart, but also No. 62 in the 'Hot 100' in the summer of 1959.

He excelled himself on the flip-side too, setting his ersatz folk-epic, 'The Great Grandfather', to a haunting melody reminiscent of Chuck Berry's 'Down Bound Train' [Chess 1615] and embellishing it with an imaginative free-form *staccato* guitar break.

Lyrically, the song resembles 'Old Dan Tucker', an old minstrel tune performed all over the South for many years by Polk Miller's quartet. Bo, however, disclaims any direct connection...

'I'm not familiar with that song at all. I guess I *could* have picked it up as a child, an' it's in the back of my mind somewhere, an' so I wrote those same lyrics an' *don't know* where it came from.

'But, a lotta song lyrics sound like you've heard 'em before. You know what does that? Your *key word*, the beginnin': see, you gotta go as close to the rhythm as possible, an' you are *led* directly to what's gonna sound like you got it from someplace else, y'understand what I'm sayin'?

'Take the song 'Rock Around The Clock': "clock" sounds like "rock". If I wanna find enough sentences to go with "rock", I'm gonna *have* to use those words to get to the point I'm tryin' to get to. There's nothin' else in the English language that you can put in it. You are *programed* to go directly to 'em, an' I just fell into these things automatically.

'I actually wrote 'The Great Grandfather' from a story I found in an old, old book that rats had ate. You couldn't even pick up the book hardly. It was thrown out in the garbage in the alley somewhere. I was a big name then, when I found that book. I was fumblin' around, lookin' for somethin' that I can come up with that's *different*. Somebody had throwed this old woven basket out of their cellar or somewhere, an' it had been for many years what you call a "mice hotel", you know.' (Laughs.) 'It *stunk* of mice, an' I found this old book in it.

'It looked like it was a hundred years old – do you remember when they used to print pages that were about *this* thick – an' it was *rotten*, so rotten that if you tried to turn 'em, it just crumbled. I picked up pieces of it that had nursery rhymes on 'em, an' kept 'em. I kept that book a *long* time, an' I wrote all these tunes from ideas of titles that I seen. I saw one title an' I came up with 'The Great Grandfather', then I seen another one an' I wrote 'Babes In The Woods'*. The word "lumberjack" was also in that book, I think.'[1]

Hot on the heels of 'Crackin' Up' came 'Say Man' [Checker 931], a novelty 'conversation' item on which Bo and Jerome traded good-natured insults over an infectious shuffle rhythm.

The origins of this unusual song, or *performance* rather, lie in the street-corner 'toast' tradition – a uniquely, exclusively male vulgar folk art descended from the much earlier 'shuckin' an' jivin'' insult games played by slaves.

'I did quite a lot of those 'Say Man'-type things: I'd say stuff like: *"Hey man, where you been?"*, *"Oh, I been in California"*.' (Laughs.) 'See, this is where the county jail is in Chicago, on 26th an' California.

---

*This song appeared in 1962 on the best-selling *Bo Diddley* album [Checker LP-2984].

'So, cat say: *"Yeah, I've been out in California".*' (Laughs.)

"'Say Man' was written down *long* before we went in the studio,[36] an' the recording of that is a funny story too:[1] me an' Jerome just happened to be actin' the fool, an' the cat turned on the tape[36] – a lot of the things I did in the Chess studios, we were just goofin' around. They'd put a new tape on, an' we were sittin' there waitin' – you know, after we'd had lunch – to finish the session. So, Phil Chess, or Leonard, one of 'em pushed the machine an' started it. They played it back, an' it *shocked* all of us! Of course, they cut out all the dirty parts.'[32]

For the flip, Bo came up with another novelty, 'The Clock Strikes Twelve', a slow, wailing 'after hours' blues instrumental. 'I caught myself bein' smart. That was a violin on it, an' nobody knew what it was*. For a *long* time they tried to figure out: "What *is* that?"

'I still pick up my fiddle every now an' then, you know, for maybe twenty minutes or somethin' like that, an' then I put it down: "Yeech!". It just don't fit in with what I'm doin'.'[32]

Released in August 1959, 'Say Man' shot to No. 3 on the *Billboard* 'Rhythm & Blues' chart and No. 20 in the 'Hot 100', presenting Bo with what was to be his biggest ever US chart hit.

Always ready to cash in, Chess issued a follow-up in similar style, 'Say Man, Back Again' [Checker 936], coupling it with a lively, gospel-flavoured chant called 'She's Alright'. Inevitably, the record failed to emulate the gigantic success of its predecessor, although it still sold well enough to make it to the No. 23 slot on the 'Rhythm & Blues' chart.

Now firmly re-established as a top recording artist, Bo found his services in greater demand than ever. 'I played behind the Kalin Twins on a session**. They had some songs, an' I just happened to be in the studio – that's how I got hooked up into playin' with 'em. I played on

---

*Interestingly enough, Chess's neighbours, Vee-Jay had tried a similar experiment a year earlier with Jimmy Reed's 'Odds & Ends' [Vee-Jay 298].

**The passage of time has fogged Bo's memory: Hal and Herbie Kalin were enjoying considerable success with Decca and therefore had no reason to moonlight. The duo in question were in fact two friends of theirs, Terry West and Stephen Foster of the Washington, DC outfit, Terry & The Pirates. The group's debut single, 'What Did He Say' b/w 'Talk About The Girl' (the latter actually written by the Kalins) had originally appeared in the spring of 1958 on Valli 100, a tiny label emanating from Silver Springs, Maryland, but was later distributed by Chess as Chess 1696. Len and Phil obviously thought the boys had potential and arranged the session Bo refers to here the following year. Sadly, none of the five cuts they laid down together was ever released.

a song that sounded like the Everly Brothers, almost like 'Wake Up Little Susie'. It was a quick thing an' *zoom*!!! – they were gone!' (Laughs.)

'Lemme tell you, Leonard an' them were *slick*! When the Everly Brothers did their thing an' started makin' it, Chess went out to try an' find two dudes that can sound like 'em. I think that's what happened with the Kalin Twins.

'Jo-Ann Campbell recorded one of my tunes: 'Mama (Can I Go Out Tonight)'*. She needed somethin' for a movie that she was doin' – the name of it was *Go Johnny Go* – an' I was runnin' around singin' this tune, so I gave it to her. I've never recorded it myself.'[1]

The new decade opened with yet more Diddley-style humour in the shape of 'Road Runner' [Checker 942], a wonderfully zany outing full of engine roars, zooms and beep-beeps, with Bo claiming to be *'the fastest in the land'*, giggling mischievously, and passing everything in sight.

'We have a bird called the "roadrunner" that is the national bird for the State of New Mexico**. That bird is *fast*, you dig, an' I was tryin' to say: "I move too fast for you girls, you can't keep up with me", you know.[1] I was bein' funny about it really, sayin' like I can climb straight up the side of a buildin', an' can't nobody else do it but me, you know, that type of thing. It's to keep people laughin', an' put a smile on their face, you know.'[32]

Issued at the height of the early sixties' hot-rod craze, Bo's platter undoubtedly captured the mood of the moment, earning itself a No. 20 'Rhythm & Blues' chart placing. One of his most memorable compositions, it has since been covered by the Accents, the Animals, Brownsville Station, the Count Victors, Wayne Fontana & The Mindbenders, the Gants, the Gibson Bros, Cub Koda, Les Miserables, the Liverbirds, the Master's Apprentices, the Phantoms, the Pretty Things, the Remo Four, the Roadrunners (naturally), the Rolling Stones, the Royal Guardsmen, the Shamrocks, Sooner Or Later, Stackwaddy, the Thin White Rope, Johnny Winter and the Zombies.

The flip-side, 'My Story', also had something of a contemporary feel to it, its lighthearted, pseudo-biographical narrative owing much to Bill

---

*Gone 5055 (1959).

**A large member of the cuckoo family, the *Geococcyx californianus* acquired its common name because of its strange habit of running down the road in front of travellers. This unusual creature has inspired at least three other 'Roadrunner' songs (by the [Seattle] Wailers, Junior Walker & The All-Stars and Jonathan Richman), as well as the plucky Warner Bros cartoon character.

Parsons's recent smash, 'The All-American Boy' [Fraternity 835], though the hilarious personalised lyrics and hypnotic, circling melody were undeniably Diddley's own.

On his next single, 'Walkin' & Talkin'' [Checker 951], Bo took a cue from the Coasters' 1959 hit, 'Along Came Jones' [Atco 6141] – a Wild West story seen through the eyes of a Channel 2 TV viewer. Obviously tickled by the unusual perspective of the Leiber–Stoller novelty, he employed the same drawled introduction to set the scene, but tuned to Channel 3 instead to watch a different drama unfold.

For the flip, he turned his attention to the well-known folk-song 'Crawdad Hole', transforming it almost beyond recognition into a thunderous barrage of trashcan drumming, wildly reverberating guitar and an echo-chamber working overtime.

Perhaps the subject matter was too familiar, or perhaps the songs were simply too off-beat, but the single flopped, ending Bo's unbroken chart run of over fourteen months.

Mighty Fine Wax Work
If Bo Diddley's flights of fancy were indeed too way-out for the mass singles market, then the increasing popularity of the extended- and long-playing microgroove album provided Len and Phil Chess with a timely solution as to what to do with his more esoteric offerings.

After testing the water in 1958 with an EP and LP of his old singles cuts (both simply labelled *Bo Diddley* and sporting identical covers), they became more adventurous, including on the albums that followed a wealth of imaginative and marvellously extravagant creations, many of which might otherwise never have seen the light of day.

Bo's second long-player, 1959's *Go Bo Diddley*, was a case in point – a veritable pot-pourri containing two bluesy leftovers from his first-ever session, 'Little Girl' and 'You Don't Love Me (You Don't Care)', a frantic gospel-inflected rocker called 'Don't Let It Go', a delightful instrumental medley appropriately dubbed 'Bo's Guitar', and eight hit single sides from 1958–59 including 'Say Man', 'I'm Sorry' and the Caribbean-flavoured 'Crackin' Up'.

His third, 1960's *Have Guitar – Will Travel*, continued the trend, showcasing four singles cuts including the seminal 'Mona' and an updated version of 'She's Alright' complete with vocal group overdubs in the style of the Isley Bros' recent success, 'Shout' [RCA-Victor 47-7588], the instrumentals 'Spanish Guitar' and 'Mumblin' Guitar' (the former, a sombre, drum-laden outing recalling that country's Moorish connections; the latter, a frenzied John Lee Hooker-influenced workout), and a whole bunch of truly outstanding vocal cuts like the bustling 'I Love You So' with its curious 'bleating sheep' hook, 'Run Diddley Daddy' (a 'jungle chase' song set to a fast calypso shuffle and packed with fanciful imagery from 'The Titanic' and several other toasts), the unashamedly poppy 'Come On', and 'Nursery Rhyme' [also known as 'Puttentang'], an easy going 'Bo Diddley'-beat item constructed around the schoolboy saying:

Q ' *What's your name?*'

A '*Puddin'-an'-Tame** – *ask me again, an' I'll tell you the same!*'

On his fourth LP, *In The Spotlight* (also released in 1960), Bo scaled new heights of excellence with three exuberant rockers ('Let Me In', 'Live My Life' and 'Deed & Deed I Do'), a couple of instrumentals ('Scuttle Bug' and 'Travelin' West'), another Caribbean experiment ('Limber'), yet more verbal sparring with Jerome Green ('Signifying Blues') and, just for a change, a ballad ('Love Me').

His strongest and most balanced album so far, *Spotlight* boasted a driving two-guitar lead, electric bass, and mixed vocal group backings that brought his sound closer than ever before to mainstream rock 'n' roll.

More than anything, the excellence of these LPs served to underline just how much Diddley had matured as a songwriter and musician: within the space of four years, he had progressed from being a straight-ahead, one-chord bluesman to a versatile artist able to work in a variety of musical styles with consummate ease.

The catalyst behind this remarkable transformation was the arrival in 1957 of Peggy Jones, a talented nineteen year old guitarist (and former dancer, model, actress, pianist and big band vocalist) who had first made Bo's acquaintance in New York the previous summer: 'One day, I was walking down 125th Street carrying my guitar, and this big guy comes up to me and asks if I can play it. I was just learning then, so I said: "Not yet."

'Then he says: "Well, let me know when you can. I'm Bo Diddley." "Yeah, *sure* you are," I said and walked on.[40] I went to the Apollo Theater that night and sneaked backstage to see what the real Bo Diddley looked

---

*Although the meaning (and even spelling) of this phrase is uncertain, it has also cropped up on other recordings such as the Alley Cats 'Puddin 'n' Tain' [Philles 108] and the Relations' 'Puddin-n-Tang (Is My Name)' [Lebby 7966].

like.[41] What a thrill! I can still feel it. That was *really* him in the street that afternoon! I couldn't believe it.'[40]

Once she had taught herself the rudiments, Peggy wasted no time in contacting Bo. 'She wanted to play like I play, so I let her hang around an' showed her this, that, an' the other. It wasn't like givin' her lessons, but she caught on real quick. She joined my group as a singer in 1957, an' after she'd learned to play a little better, I let her play guitar on stage with me.

'It just so happened that I was lookin' 'round for somethin' different to come out with. Joe [Williams] had just got drafted, so I came up with the idea of puttin' a girl guitar player in the group. That was somethin' *new*, you dig, 'cause there wasn't no chicks in groups playin' guitars at that time. The chick started playin', an' she was *dynamite!*'[1]

Peggy agrees the combination worked well. 'In addition to the "image" thing was the fact that I could always figure out what Bo was going to do. We really are on the same wavelength, and it's just fantastic how compatible we are.[42]

'I played on a lot of Bo Diddley's sessions.[41] We often just jammed on tape, and the music was later added to his LPs.[40] Bo's forte had always been a rockin' rhythm with no changes – and he would take it to the limit. His "open tuning" style was experimental for me at first, but I learned fast!

'I would play second guitar, doing all the lead fills, but I could also play 'double guitar' if required, using exactly the same tuning and finger patterns as Bo. Guitar parts were played simultaneously in unison at first, then cross-rhythms once the shock wore off.[41] A lot of the time, Bo didn't even play: I'd be using his equipment while he sang, and you couldn't tell us apart!'[40]

'Many songs were recorded without a bass player – the only unstable position in the band. Or, if we recorded with a bass player and Chess thought it wasn't right, they would get Willie Dixon to overdub it. At that stage, a decision would also be made to add extra vocals, harp or whatever, though the main tracks managed to stay untouched.

'I toured with Bo and the band part-time between 1957 and 1959, and full time from 1959 to 1961. In between, I sang in a duo called Greg & Peg with Gregory Carroll from the Orioles, played on sessions for other people and worked as a night-club singer. I played guitar in Bo's group until 1961, but by then I also had my own group – the Jewels – and I'd work with them when I wasn't working with Bo. As a matter of fact, my bass player, Bobby

Baskerville, played on *Bo Diddley In The Spotlight* with us. Then we put on the backing vocals – just Bo, Bob and myself. Clifton James was the drummer, and we had Otis Spann on piano.'[41]

Despite all this, Leonard and Phil Chess still felt Bo Diddley's material was too eccentric for mass consumption and vainly tried to channel his wayward talent in more commercial directions: 'The Chess brothers tried to go through some changes. They'd come up an' say: "Bo, you're in a rut", an' all that jazz, you know. So, I'd say: "Okay, I'll change, but I still want it to taste like Bo Diddley – an' the only person that can do that is *me*."'[3]

'I don't like humpin' into the studio, an' then comin' out an' expectin' somebody to taste it an' like it. If I'm ever goin' to record a number, I go play it two or three times in a little club or somethin' to see if I get hand-clappin', foot-stompin'. I try things out on stage first, to see if people are gonna react, an', if I'm not gettin' any reaction out of it, I leave it alone because it ain't ready yet.[5] You see, when you're original, it's hard to break you away from what's original, but when you're a copycat, you can go any kinda way. Can you dig what I'm gettin' at?

'So they said blah-blah-blah, an' this an' that, an' a whole lotta other crap, but it's *hard* for Bo Diddley to bring his style up to date, because there really is no date for my thing. I'm *already* up to date. I've already done been here, an' ten years ahead of it. The stuff that cats are doin' now, I already *forgot* about!'[3]

'So, I was programed an' told what to do, an' I had no say-so. Or, if I *did* say anythin', they'd listen to me till I left town on a gig, an' then they'd do what *they* wanted to do with it. I had no control over nothin' – an' that was *wrong*!

'That's why I wrote the song 'Live My Life': it was a message, in a way of speakin'. I was sayin' that, if I knew what I know now, I would do it a little bit different – meanin' Chess Records. That's what it was all about.'[1]

As if to emphasise Bo's point, Chess tampered with the cut, overdubbing his vocal with a piano solo, rechristening the result 'Scuttle Bug', and cheekily issuing both items back-to-back on the *Spotlight* album.

'There was a lotta names on records that shouldn't have been there. I named the songs somethin' else.'[1] There I am on stage, an' the kids start to yell to me to play 'Bo Diddley's Rumble' or somethin' – an' I have fans who know every note, every grunt, an' every breath on my records – an' I think: "I've never recorded a song called that." Then I learn I *have* recorded it, but Chess – for some unknown reason – have given it a title of their own.'[43]

'Like, I did 'Mule Train' – remember the song called 'Mule Train', by Frankie Laine*? I did that, an' I think I did a *helluva* job of it. An', you see somethin' called 'Travelin' West'? Leonard Chess an' them, after I'd left the goddamn studio, they took that sucker, an' when I said: *"Mule train"*, they sucked it off into a echo chamber. After that, when you listen to it, it go: *"WhooOOOooh"*. I said: "What the *hell* is this? How am I gonna do that on stage?"

'It was *supposed* to have been my version of 'Mule Train'. It didn't turn out that way. They *changed* it, an' made it into somethin' that I had no intention of doin'! They did it to *everybody*, man.'[1]

Love Is Strange

To his lasting credit, Bo Diddley withstood both his meteoric rise to stardom and punishing work schedule remarkably well, remaining essentially unchanged as an individual. Eschewing the destructive temptations of the rock 'n' roll lifestyle, he preferred to spend his time quietly: resting, working on ideas for new songs or helping younger musicians to develop their talent – pretty much as he had always done.

One budding artiste to benefit from his patronage was Larry 'Billy' Stewart, an eighteen year old singer/pianist with a striking *staccato* vocal style and an exuberant stage act developed during a lengthy apprenticeship with his family's group, the Stewart Gospel Singers.

'Billy Stewart was from Washington, DC. When we worked the Howard Theater all the time, I used to stay at the Dunbar Hotel. Billy worked a place near there called the Cellar Door – I think – an' I heard him playin'. It tickled me, the way he sang, you know, an' I said: "This cat's *different*!"'[1]

Bo promptly took Billy to Chicago, where they cut a single together in March 1956. The results, however, were rather disappointing: 'Billy's Blues (Part 1)', an instrumental, featured an attractive lead guitar part played by Jody Williams, but Stewart's piano accompaniment was markedly uninspired (and Diddley's rhythm guitar virtually inaudible) throughout; 'Part 2' (not a continuation, but actually a separate 'vocal' take beefed up by Willie Dixon on double bass) was marginally better, but was let down by the sheer amateurishness of its lyrics**.

---

*Mercury 5343 (1949).
**A third cut, 'Cryin'', remains unissued.

Released in March 1956 as Chess 1625 (and, for some reason, reissued seven months later as Argo 5256), 'Billy's Blues' saw some local chart action, but never amounted to much in terms of national sales, though it later achieved considerable notoriety as the subject of prolonged litigation by Chess against the RCA subsidiary, Groove.

Their complaint concerned a recording made by Mickey & Sylvia, a romantic singing partnership launched in 1955 by veteran New York session man, Mickey 'Guitar' Baker: 'What I had in mind with Mickey & Sylvia originally was something like Les Paul & Mary Ford. I saw 'em on stage and said: "Shit, I can do better than *that*!"

'At the time, I was a guitar teacher and Sylvia Vanderpool* was one of my pupils. I was working with Alan Freed, and Sylvia comes along begging me to get together again. So I said "Okay" – 'cause I'm thinking how Les Paul and Mary can't make it because they don't have a real "human" approach.'[44]

After four unsuccessful releases, the duo cut 'Love Is Strange' [Groove 0175] in October 1956. The catchy ballad shot to No. 2 on the *Billboard* 'Rhythm & Blues' chart and No. 13 in the 'Top 100' in early 1957, clocking up initial sales of 800,000 and aggregate sales well in excess of one million.

'We moved from a little, raggedy office to a big one when RCA sent me a check for $50,000 one day and $27,000 the next,' recalls Baker. 'They told me they had to stop pressing Elvis Presley records to keep up with the orders on mine. I've already lived *that* grand life!'[45]

Chess, too, had followed the record's meteoric rise with considerable interest and quickly filed suit against RCA, claiming the song to be derivative of 'Billy's Blues'.

'We had it with all labels,' explains Marshall Chess, 'but it was a good-natured thing, it wasn't really big trouble. Sure, they had fights *that week* or *that month* but, you know, it's only a record, only a piece of plastic. It wasn't worth fighting for life and death, you know, so all those kinda fights passed quickly: they only lasted until you had your next hit. We never thought "opponents". We knew all the people really well: it was like a big sort of fraternity, you know.'[19]

Be that as it may, the fight on this occasion lasted for four years, with RCA eventually emerging victorious on 27 November, 1961 when the US Circuit Court Of Appeals upheld the original January ruling that the songs

---

*Later Sylvia Robinson, president of Sugar Hill/All Platinum Records.

were *'not substantially or materially similar, and would not sound so to
the average listener'*, and that 'Love Is Strange' was not copied from 'Billy's
Blues' *'consciously or otherwise'*.

Notwithstanding this pronouncement, the two songs were in fact very
closely connected, as Bo explains.

'That keen guitar, that "dee-dee-dee-dee-dee" on 'Love Is Strange', that
was Joe Wiliams: he's the one that came up with that little guitar part. That
was a new guitar sound. I went to Chess an' wanted to record it – I
remember this distinctly – an' Phil Chess came up to me an' said: "Who the
hell do you think you are, Perry Como?" So that was the end of that.

'Anyway, how Mickey & Sylvia got hold of the song was: we were on a
show together, an' Joe was tryin' to make it with Sylvia. We knew she wasn't
Mickey's ol' lady, an' he thought she was just the prettiest thing he'd ever
seen, so he went in there an' started playin' it for her. He told her it was
my tune, but somehow or other all this shit got tangled up, an' it got said
that I ripped him off for his tune.

'I did *not* rip him off! I've never *in my life* took *anythin'* from any one
of my musicians that helped me to rise to the point that I have. *Never in
my life!* If I *owed* 'em money, I paid 'em. I even gave 'em money that I
never got back, you know. It hurt me deeply, when I'm the one that taught
Joe how to play, that he would think I would do somethin' like that to him,
but I've never run into him to straighten out my end of it.

'See, a whole bunch of funny crap went down. I told 'em: "Me an' Joe
put the tune together, so Joe's gotta get the music, an' I get the lyrics. He
is entitled to the music of the song."

'They told me: "We'll take care of Joe."

'So, I signed a contract for the lyrics, an' I don't know what happened
after that. I later sold my part of it to Sylvia, just before Betty Everett & Jerry
Butler recorded it*, an' somebody else recorded it, so they made quite a
few bucks off of it.'[1]

---

*Vee-Jay 633 (1964). One of Bo Diddley's most successful compositions, the song has also
been covered by the Everly Bros [Warner Bros 5649] and Peaches & Herb [Date 1574] – both
hits in their own right – as well as by Chubby Checker, reggae artist Jon Cundo, Dale & Grace,
Buddy Holly, the (post-Holly) Crickets, Johnny Hallyday, Luther & Little Eva, Rose Maddox,
the Millionaires, Sonny & Cher (as Caesar & Cleo), Johnny Thunders, Mike Wilhelm, Paul
McCartney's Wings, Liz Winters & The Bob Cort Skiffle Group, and more recently by K.T. Oslin
and Everything But The Girl. Baker even recorded a French-language version in the sixties by
Mickey & Monique.

Mickey & Sylvia followed up their smash with a double-sided hit, 'There Oughta Be A Law' b/w 'Dearest' [Vik 0267] – the latter another Diddley ballad which peaked at No. 85 in the 'Top 100' in July 1957.

'I was in that 'Love Is Strange' bag at the time. First of all, I had a tune named 'Paradise' – which was a instrumental – an' I wrote 'Love Is Strange' from that. Then, I came up with 'Dearest', an' a couple of other things. A girl named Pearl Polk helped me to write 'Dearest', an' she ain't never got a dime either. They ain't paid *nobody* for it!

'I wrote 'Love Is Strange' for my wife. If you look at the writer's credits, it should say "Ethel Smith": that's Tootsie. I was really havin' *bad* problems outa her durin' that time, so I decided to move away from Chicago to Washington, DC. I was tryin' to get Tootsie away from her parents so that we could do our own thing an' lead a sensible life – an' not, every time I turn around, her parents had her doin' this, tellin' her how she should do, you know, with me an' her. So I says: "I'm gonna buy me a house out of Chicago, get her away from her people, an' try to make our relationship better."

'It didn't work. She came over to my house in DC, broke into my safe, tore up all the contracts an' stuff I had from Chess, burned up a whole bunch of stuff. Then she went back to Chicago an' sued me for non-support. She didn't have no right to break into my personal things, but *I* ended up with the bad end of the stick, 'cause I didn't have any receipts to show the judge that I had paid her!

'I lived in DC for seven years an' got to know a *lotta* cats down there. Marvin Gaye used to hang out with me, he was a very good friend. Billy Stewart was around *all* the time. A whole lotta cats that came from DC used to hang down at my place: that's where they used to practice. My electric bill helped to teach 'em, an' I'm very happy I was able to do that.'[1]

One bunch of young hopefuls which Bo took under his wing were the Marquees – a vocal quartet comprising the teenage Gaye, James Nolan, Reese Palmer, Chester Simmons. Their collaboration is documented by two 1957 singles: Billy Stewart's second solo release, 'Billy's Heartache', b/w 'Baby, You're My Only Love' [OKeh 4-7095] (on which they sang back-up), and 'Wyatt Earp', b/w 'Hey Little School Girl' [OKeh 4-7096] – two magnificent slabs of Diddley-flavoured doo wop recorded in New York earlier that year with the cream of the city's sessionmen: drummer Panama Francis, saxophonist Sam 'The Man' Taylor and guitarist Mickey Baker.

"Billy's Heartache' an' the Marquees both came out on OKeh – which is Columbia Records – an' I didn't know nothin' about it! I was a *Chess* recording artist, an' didn't have no business cuttin' for nobody else. I was producer an' arranger on both of 'em, an' I also played guitar on Billy's record – but, if you look at the labels, you'll see other people's names on 'em. Who the hell is "Joe Sherman" on *my* record? I ain't even *heard* of Joe Sherman!

'The person that did this OKeh thing, I actually believe it was my manager, Phil Landwehr. We gave the tapes to Phil Landwehr, an' never heard no more about 'em. I can't *prove* it, but somewhere down the line I was ripped off.'[1]

Although neither disc hit the best-seller lists, Harvey Fuqua was sufficiently impressed by the Marquees to recruit them as replacements for his group when the original Moonglows disintegrated a few months later. Adding Chuck Barksdale from the Dells, the new line-up recorded for Chess until 1961 – when Fuqua left to form his own Harvey and Tri-Fi labels, taking Marvin Gaye with him to Detroit and stardom.

Billy Stewart, meanwhile, soldiered on until 1962, when 'Fat Boy' [Chess 1820] – a song he had co-written with Bo – launched him on a successful solo career that was to end tragically on 17 January, 1970, when his car plunged from a North Carolina bridge killing everyone on board.

'Billy was a *helluva* good performer,' recalls Bo, 'but he got very antisocial. His hat became too small for his head when he got famous – you know: "money make people funny" – but he's passed on now, so I don't want to say any more.

'We also had a girl named Maureen that used to sing like him – she was big, too – an' I cut her doin' a song called 'Show Me What I Said'. We didn't do anythin' with it, though, because she got a tumor an' passed away, died on the operating table – which was very, very sad. She left a little girl: she's still in Washington, DC. Maureen was a very beautiful person. I'm not speakin' nice of her because she's passed on, because I spoke nice of her when she was livin'. She *was* a beautiful person.'[1]

Bo Diddley's A Gunslinger

'Since I was already sorta livin' there anyway, I decided to make Washington my base. This was late '59, early 1960. I got Chess to send me $2,900 in advance, an' I bought me a Presto tape machine. A guy named Scott Hubbard hooked it all up in the basement of my house at 2614 Rhode

Island Avenue, an' we built a studio around this machine. That was about as good a studio a person like me could have back then, you know: everythin' was just two tracks.

'The Presto is daddy to the Scullys: the Prestos wasn't sellin', so they changed the looks of 'em an' called 'em "Scullys", an' they sold like a *son-of-a-gun*! Nobody liked the way the Prestos looked. I've still got mine, works great. A little *noisy* maybe, but it's fixin' to get cleaned up.'[1]

Not long afterwards, a young white girl from Albany, Georgia by the name of Kay Reynolds walked into Bo's life.

'The first time I saw him was in Birmingham, Alabama. I was about fifteen, and there was a concert, and he was coming in the back of my mind. I was a great fan, I had all of his records, knew every song backwards and forwards, knew which one came after what, you know, had the whole thing memorized.

'I was selling magazines – I'd gotten bored as a secretary and I'd gone on the road selling magazines door-to-door, just for something to do – and I met him in Washington, DC.

'I was taken backstage because a friend of mine had met an acquaintance who was on the show, and we went backstage. He sent this girl to me because he was rotten [looks at Bo, who bursts out laughing] and she gives it: "Bo Diddley wants to see you."

'I said: "If he wants to see me, he knows where I am."

'So, she went off, and then she came back with a new approach: "Aw, c'mon", you know, blah-blah-blah.

'I said: "Okay."

'So, I walked downstairs, and he's sitting there like King Tut, with his legs crossed. Took about *five minutes* for him to get to my face – started at the feet and worked his way up – and then he says: "I'm married and I've got two kids, a girlfriend here and one in New York. If you want to go out with me, you'll have to be here about ten o'clock: that's when I leave after the show."

'At the time, I'd never been out with anybody black – or anybody married – to the best of my knowledge, but he'd been separated for years and I figured, you know, he can't be too hung up in the marriage or he wouldn't be having all these girlfriends all over. All of the entertainers had warned me about how rotten he was, and that just made him *more* attractive. I thought about it a few minutes and said: "Okay."

'I spent the entire first night nailing acoustical tiles in his studio!' (Laughter.) 'And, it so happened that he was there for two weeks, and my magazine crew was there for two weeks, so I lived with him these two weeks. Then he went to Baltimore to play another two weeks, and we went to Baltimore, so I was with him a whole month. After that, I moved in his house.'[46]

From that time on, Kay became a major influence in Bo Diddley's life, not only providing him with the support and stability he needed, but also involving herself totally in his work, helping him to compose and record material, and acting as a sounding board for his ideas.

'What actually made me turn around an' look at Kay, is because she treated me like a *man* an' made me feel like *somebody*. I don't like to be cuddled an' all stuff like that – I'm a *very* stand-offish person – but it meant a lot to me that she was around. Didn't have to *do* nothin', just be around, you know. That's the type of dude I am, y'understand, an' she fitted that thing I was lookin' for.

'But, besides of that, what made me turn around an' look at her was that, in the South in the fifties an' sixties, a mixed marriage – or either runnin' around together – was a no-no. So, when she came down to see me, I said right then: "If she's got enough *nerve* to come down here to see me, knowin' what the problem may be, then, if anythin' comes of this, I'm gonna fight *to the death* about this woman!"

'See, that told me she was in my corner, that she *cared* about me – an' that was the highlight of my life. So, I asked her to marry me. They say that it don't work; it *do* work, you just have to *make* it work.[1] I was married two times before to black girls, an' we just couldn't make it, so I went across the fence.[47] We got two beautiful daughters, we got a nice house, you know, an' I'm doin' fine.'[1]

At the time, a purpose-built recording studio – even a home-made one – was something of a rarity in the capital and, before long, Bo and Kay found themselves running open house for a large number of local musicians – so many, in fact, that their constant comings and goings attracted the attention of the local police, who placed the property under surveillance, suspecting it to be a brothel!

'Because I was livin' in DC, I started usin' musicians from DC in my group: there wasn't too many of 'em in Chicago that would come out to DC. My bass players, Jesse James Johnson and Chester Lindsey, they was outa Washington, an' my guitarist, William Johnson*, an' my drummers

---

*William Johnson stood in briefly for Peggy Jones during 1961. He is not related to Jesse James Johnson, neither should he be confused with the Moonglows' guitarist, Billy Johnson.

also. One of 'em's name was Edell Robertson. We called him "Red". He was killed just recently. Some chick stabbed him, an' she's *walkin' the streets*! I don't understand it. If *he'da* killed *her*, he'd be in jail! My other drummer was "Dino" – Billy Downing – an' I understand that he's a preacher now. That's what I heard, but I'm not too sure about *that*! They played on a lot of my records an' on the road with me. They played a *long* time with me.

'Chester Lindsey, he was with me in-an'-out for thirteen, fourteen years or more.' (Bursts out laughing.) 'We called him "Dr Boo" because he was always goin' around sayin' he was a "ladies' specialist", but Dino an' Jesse were really the two fools that was in the group.

'They came back one day, police had 'em. They'd went to a store an' bought 'em some cowboy guns – these big pearl-handled .45s with holsters an' everythin'. Just cap pistols, but they looked so *real*.

'So, they're walkin' down the street with 'em on – an' they *loved* cowboy outfits, so both of 'em had on a great big hat apiece – an' the police grabbed 'em. They asked Jesse, say: "Come here, boy! What's your name?"

'Jesse say: "Jesse James" – an' that really *is* his name!

'So, cop got out of the car, an' walked up to Billy an' say: "Now, you tell me your name is Billy The Kid, an' I'm gonna beat the shit out of botha y'all!"' (Laughs.)

'An' he says: "But my name *is* Billy!"' (Laughs.)

'So, they came back to the house, an' Jesse say: "Man, I ain't *never* goin' out there with these no more!" An' so, they wore 'em one day, for about fifteen minutes.'[1] (Laughs.)

Not averse to the occasional Western himself, Bo took some time out to see *The Magnificent Seven* – a recent box-office smash – and was promptly bitten by the same bug. The macho image of the tough gunman dressed in black appealed to him, and he hit upon the idea of using it as a theme for his next album.

'The first tune I cut was 'Bo Diddley's A Gunslinger'. I had four or five hundred copies pressed up on my own label, BoKay, but ended up givin' 'em all away to people, you know, as a advertisement. I didn't know about gettin' a license an' all that kinda stuff back then, I just thought: "Get a name an' stick it on a label, an' it's yours!"

'After that, I did 'Sixteen Tons', 'Whoa, Mule', 'Cheyenne', an' five or six other things. Quite a few of my tunes around that time had a lot of what you might call a "country" feel, so the cowboy gimmick sorta fitted, you know.

'I sent the tapes to Chess Records, an' it wasn't a week before Leonard an' Phil showed up at my front door, really concerned, tryin' to figure out what the hell I was doin'. They got *scared*: "What'd you buy a machine for?"

'I *know* what they were thinkin'! They didn't come to *visit* me. They didn't care *that* much about me, that they would travel 714 miles, all the way from Chicago, just to see me.' (Laughs.) 'They came to the studio, tryin' to figure out what I had, came all that way just to check me out!

'I had that weird sound because I hadn't learned really how to run the machine to get the best quality out of it. But, I am the only one that knows how I did that, an' that remains a secret. I *will* tell you it wasn't done with overdubbing or anythin' like that, because the equipment wasn't advanced enough in those days for me to be able to do that: what I've always done with two-track machines, is "stack" music. You'd be *surprised* what you can do with a stereo machine

'Chess tried to duplicate my sound that I had at home, an' they *couldn't* do it. They even *bought* the machine from me, an' they *still* couldn't get that sound I had in my studio!'[1]

Notwithstanding the irritation Bo's bid for independence had caused them, Len and Phil liked the 'black cowboy' angle and decided to push 'Gunslinger' as a single [Checker 965], as well as making it the title track of his next long-player.

For reasons best known to themselves, however, they only released seven of the eleven cuts Bo had sent them, padding out the LP with 'Diddling' and 'Cadillac' (two blistering rockers from a recent experimental session with saxophonist Gene Barge) and an uncomfortably schmaltzy ballad called 'Somewhere'.

Aesthetic niceties apart, their decision was more than vindicated when the *Gunslinger* album finally went gold two years later. Bo Diddley's ambitious experiment with C&W had been a resounding success!

'I've always been a great lover of country music.[29] You know the radio station WLAC, in Nashville? That's where I got the idea to write 'Cadillac' from, because *"C-A-D-I-L-L-A-C"* sounded like *"W-L-A-C"*: the letter "C" is what keyed me off, an' made me somehow or other write 'Cadillac'. Like I said, I *love* country...' (Laughs.)

'Carl Perkins, Jerry Lee Lewis, Mickey Gilley – that's three people I *admire*!'[1] Johnny Cash... Ernest Tubb. Roy Clark – he's a *monster*, an outasite dude! I was also crazy about Amos Milburn's record, 'Let Me Go Home Whiskey'*, which had a lot of country feel. So, I started to teach myself to play a little of it.[29]

'I just played a nightclub in Texas a few weeks ago. I got out at the place, an' looked an' seed these cowboy boots up on the front, you know, an' I says: "Oh-oh, I'm in a trick bag!" Get inside, an' these cats is up there singin' Hank Williams, an' Johnny Cash an' everybody. I didn't have my own group with me. I says: "Where's the band that's gonna back me up?" Sure 'nough, it was the guys that was on stage. They backed me up, an' I went over *great* – an' it surprised *me*![32]

'In 1978, I produced a album for a young lady named Linda Ellas – who is a *country* singer.[1] Her real name is Linda Heron, an' she used to live right up the road from me when I moved to New Mexico**. She asked me would I help her, so I said "Okay", an' it's *unbelievable*! The songs I gave her, she did a *beautiful* job on 'em![32] As a matter of fact, I've been fixin' to put that stuff out for quite a while, but country music got really weird an' they told me it was "too country". They can't tell me that now!

'I *know* what the problem was: here is a *black* dude, with a *white* girl, an' I done produced a *country* album!' (Laughs.) 'This ain't supposed to happen, y'understand what I'm sayin'? I ain't supposed to be able to do that! These cats don't *know* that I know more about their goddam music than they do themselves, it's just that I don't choose to play it. I make it my *business* to know what the hell they're doin'.

'Listen, I'm a music *lover*! It might sound funny to you, but I like *Chinese* music. Just think, whoever was any closer to Chinese music than John Lee Hooker – but he's a *blues* artist! I like anythin' that sounds *funny*. Once I hear it enough, I try to pick out somethin' *new* to do with it – because it seems like they're in a rut, it all sounds alike. That may be the culture, I don't know, but there's *gotta* be another dimension of that culture that hasn't been explored yet, somethin' else other than just "ding-ding-ding-ding" you know. It's the same thing with reggae: what they're playin', they've been playin' for *centuries*! They don't change it.

'You know what I've been doin'? I've been tryin' to learn the reggae lick, but do it *my* way – which makes it *different*. It's still got that "thing", y'understand, but I'm not playin' it the way they're playin' it. I have always

---

*Aladdin 3164 (1953).
**1971–78.

109

loved Spanish music an' calypso music, too, but I never was around it enough to gather up any of the way that it was done, you dig, so I just *listened* an' proceeded to see if I could play any of it.

'I love *classical* music, but I can't get anybody to record me doin' a classical thing. *Me*, doin' a *classical* thing on a record? They'd laugh me out the fuckin' studio! But I think my fans would think it was a joke an' grab it, because they'd figure: "Bo Diddley doin' a *what*? I *gotta* hear *this*!"

'I get a lot of ideas from theater, from shows, music I've heard in movies that authentic African people are playin'. I don't pay too much attention unless it *is* authentic: like, some black dude with a bunch of feathers hangin' all off him an' beatin' on a drum, supposed to be African, an' he don't know the way outa his daggone *neighborhood* – that don't tell me *nothin'*! Lemme hear somethin' *authentic*, then I might say: "Hey! I like that beat." I don't want the *whole thing* – because it's already been done once – but it might give me a *key* to start it: I have enough goin' upstairs to change it to what *I* wanna do with it.'[1]

Bo's Guitars

The importance of Bo Diddley's contribution to the founding and subsequent evolution of rock 'n' roll cannot be overestimated. As one of the first on the scene, he played a leading role in redefining the boundaries of popular music by pioneering the concept of a purely *electric* guitar sound and making widespread use of electronic sound effects like tremolo, reverb and distortion, paving the way not only for ground-breaking novelties like Mac Rebennack's 'Storm Warning' [Rex 1008] and Link Wray's 'Rumble' [Cadence 1347], but also – more importantly – for later innovation by Duane Eddy, Dick Dale, Jimi Hendrix and others.

His powerful stage presence and dynamic act revolutionised musical entertainment in the USA, injecting a level of emotion and excitement hitherto unheard of (outside the still-unexplored confines of black music, at least) and casting him as a model for a legion of imitators from Elvis Presley through to the posturing heavy metal rockers of today.

Not surprisingly, over the years, rock's first guitar hero has also come to be renowned for his collection of unusual axes, all of which were either built or adapted to his own specifications. 'The first guitar I ever bought was a red Kay but,[1] man, I used to change guitars like I changed clothes!' (Laughs.) 'I've probably owned more than a hundred.'[11] After my Kay, I had an old Epiphone solid-body, then a Gretsch – I made my first recordings on a red Gretsch Firebird.[1] I had some Fenders – a Stratocaster an' a Telecaster – but I didn't like 'em. They're good guitars, but my hands are so big I have trouble with the necks: they feel like toothpicks to me!' (Laughs.)

'I had to get a guitar with a good-sized neck. I had a Gibson for a while, but I never liked the way they painted 'em[11] I also had six guitars that I designed myself, but four of 'em grew feet an' walked off, you dig?

'The first one I had was called the "Cadillac Tail" – 'cause I was into these Cadillac rocket-tails durin' that time, an' that was supposed to have been almost the 1959 Cadillac fins. I built that one myself – it had an old Supro neck on it – but I never got a chance to use it because it got stolen. I also built the very first square guitar – took the neck an' electrics off a Gretsch, an' put it all onto a square body – but that one got stolen too.[1]

'After that, I got Gretsch to make my guitars for me at their factory in Brooklyn*. They made 'em especially for me, an' they weren't allowed to sell 'em to anybody else.[11] The first one that they made for me was shaped like a arrow, but I had an accident on my motorcycle, an' that was the end of that. Then they made my square guitar – the "Big B" – in 1958, an' then a rocket-tail guitar a year or so after that. Later on**, they built a matching pair of rocket-tail guitars for me.[1]

'At one time, everybody thought that my guitars had that special sound because of their shape, but the shape had nothin' to do with it. It wasn't the guitar; it was the person playin' it:[1] it's the *touch*, an' rhythm patterns. It's the guitar only when it's electronics an' gimmicks – because man can only do so much[5] – but the average guitar player wouldn't have no need for it. I can get away with this because of the way I play, but he'd play one song an' it's all over.

'I use pedals in the studio, but all my stuff is built into my guitars: I don't like stompin' on stuff on stage. That's what amazes my audience: they hear somethin' come on, an' they don't know what did that, you know.[1]

'I'm always lookin' for a gimmick, an' my little gimmicks an' things proved out to be somethin' that everybody liked. I didn't *know* that they were gonna be liked, you know, they were just somethin' new to do.[32]

---

*Apart from specially modified DeArmond pick-ups, all of Bo's Gretsch custom solids were equipped with the company's standard hardware – only the body designs were different.
**1962.

'I started off with that "funny" sound – an' I thank God that I was the first to do that, because it created a unique style, a trademark that's *me*, you know.[5]

'I've *always* wanted to be a little different. Anythin' that I own, I gotta put my own little touch to it – because I got ideas of my *own*, so why should I accept everybody else's ideas all the time?

'That's the reason I decided to build me a square guitar: because, when I jump on stage, I would like the people to have somethin' to talk about: "Wow! That dude came out there with that *funny-lookin'* guitar! Never seen *that* before!" Somethin' to rap about, see, 'cause once your name leaves the lips of your public, you got a *problem*!

'I'd like to jump on the stage one time – just for the heck of it – in a polka-dot suit, just for somebody to say: "Man, that sure was the *ugliest* suit that dude had on!" – but you're gonna keep *somebody* sayin' *somethin'*.[3]

'I've got a *weird* mind, man, about things that are different in order for people to remember me, but I've had some of my ideas fall flat on their face too!' (Laughs.)

'I went out an' bought some expensive rabbit fur, an' I covered this Gibson guitar with it*. I only used it once or twice on the show, because every time I hit it, hair would fly all over the place!' (Laughs.) 'I didn't know the hair was gonna come out of it! I just wanted to do somethin' *different*, you know. It was a way of keepin' my name goin'.[37]

'I've also had round guitars, triangular guitars, an' spaceship guitars; guitars covered with carpet, an' guitars painted weird colors. Like I said, I've had a *lotta* guitars!'[11]

'It's a long time since I built any instruments: I've just got too many things I'm hooked up in now, an' I don't have time. I've been *plannin'* to for a while, an' two months ago I went out an' bought the wood, but I looked an' looked at it an' ended up makin' a bench of it.[5]

'When I was in Australia, I asked this cat, Chris Kinman – in Brisbane – to build me a new square guitar, an' he did a real good job on it. It's got echo chambers in it, an' a whole bunch of sound effects**. I call it my "Mean Machine". I had it built because the "Big B" was beginnin' to be almost obsolete. I had it rebuilt twice, had new stuff put in, but, even with

---

*A photograph of this guitar appeared on the cover of the 1961 *Bo Diddley Is A Lover* LP.
**The instrument's onboard schematics include a phaser and an analogue delay unit.

all of the electronics I had built into it, it's almost like the $29 guitar that my sister bought me back when I was twelve years old. My great-great-grandkids will try to figure out what the hell this is, y'understand?' (Laughs.) 'It's a *baby* compared to what you can put into a guitar today!

'I got the 'Mean Machine' in 1979, but right now, technology is movin'' so fast that I've already had to get me some new axes, just to keep up! I'm still findin' out what they can do.'[1]

'I opened the door'
Notwithstanding his prominence as a rock guitar pioneer, it is for his individualistic approach to rhythm that Bo Diddley is chiefly acclaimed – and rightly so, for the African, Caribbean and Latin-American influences he assimilated into his music not only inspired some of the greatest recordings of the rock 'n' roll era, but also set in motion a powerful undercurrent that is still very much in evidence today.

Most famous of all, of course, is the beat he premiered in 1955 on his first recording, 'Bo Diddley' – a classic composition since covered by the Animals, the Astronauts, the Barbarians, Bad Bascomb, the Beatles, the Bill Black Combo, Bonnemere, Les Carle, the Carroll Bros, the Cavemen, Creedence Clearwater Revival, Jean Dinning, Jimmy Elledge, Fleetwood Mac, the Fugitives, the Harmonicats, Ronnie Hawkins, Jimi Hendrix, Buddy Holly, Sonny James, the Juveniles, Buddy Knox, the MC5, the Meters, Mighty Manfred & The Underdogs, Stu Mitchell, the Moody Blues, Sandy Nelson, Art Neville, the New York City Band, Teddy Randazzo, the Rattles, Joe Reisman, Emil Richards & The Family, Billy Lee Riley, Jimmie Rodgers, the Royal Guardsmen, Bobby Saver (as 'Count Drac'), Bob Seger, the Shadows, the Starliners, the Three Reeds, Maureen Tucker, J.M. Van Eaton & The Untouchables, Bobby Vee & The Crickets, Link Wray, Warren Zevon and countless others. It was, however, only one of many Diddley innovations that made an impression on the sounds of the rock 'n' roll era.

Under the guidance of veteran guitarist Chet Atkins, the Everly Bros, for instance, incorporated many of his musical mannerisms into their melodic country songs – a reverberating opening chord on 'All I Have To Do Is Dream' [Cadence 1348]; chopped guitars and jerky rhythms on 'Bye Bye Love' [Cadence 1315], 'Wake Up Little Susie' [Cadence 1337] and '('Til) I Kissed You' [Cadence 1369]; chunky bass riffs and maracas on 'Muskrat' [Warner Bros 5501] – to create a distinctive (and highly successful) style of their own.

Buddy Holly's work, too, was peppered with Diddleyesque touches like the *'dum diddy dum-dum, oh boy'* chorus of 'Oh Boy' [Brunswick 55035], the strategically placed hand-clap on 'Love's Made A Fool Of You' [Coral LP *Showcase*], and the unusual, haunting melodies of 'Words Of Love' [Coral 61852] and 'Heartbeat' [Coral 62051] – clearly inspired by Mickey & Sylvia's 'Love Is Strange', a record he reportedly played *'over and over, all night long'*[48] in fascination. Indeed, after his death, home-made recordings of both 'Love Is Strange' and 'Dearest' were discovered and subsequently released by Coral on the LPs *Giant* and *Showcase*, respectively*.

Paradoxically, his most blatant Diddley borrowing, 'Not Fade Away' [Brunswick 55035], also proved to be his finest, and has since become a classic in its own right, being covered by artists like Michael Angelo, the Barracudas, the Beatles, Dave Berry, Black Oak Arkansas, Cochise, the Corporate Image, Cyril Davies & His Rhythm & Blues All-Stars, Dick & Dee Dee, Joe Ely, the End, the Everly Bros, the Flying Pickets, the Foul Dogs, Bobby Fuller, Fumble, the Grateful Dead, Group Axis, the Heartbeats, Steve Hillage, Eric Hine, the Jaybirds, John Lennon, Phil Ochs, Joe Pass, Raw, Tim Rice, Dick Rivers, the Rockers, the Rock 'n' Roll Empire, the Rubberband, Rush, the Scorpions, Bruce Springsteen, Streetboy, the Sutherland Bros & Quiver, Tanya Tucker, Frank White and, of course, the Rolling Stones, who turned it into an international best seller in 1964.

'At the time, I thought the Rolling Stones had ripped me off,' says Bo. 'I didn't find out until some time later that it was a Buddy Holly song, an' so *he* was the one responsible.'[35]

'I met Buddy just a coupla times – we were on shows together. He was the kinda fellow you didn't forget. Real nice guy, caught up all the time with his music. He heard me play 'Bo Diddley', said he liked it.'[31]

'An' so, he took my beat an' used it. That's great, you know, but if it *is* my beat he used, then why isn't there a credit on the label sayin' "Bo Diddley", tellin' people that this is a Bo Diddley lick? If it *was* my beat that he put in there, then I shoulda been *paid* for it. I never was paid.'[1]

'I was one of those artists, man, that *everybody* jumped on somethin' that I was doin'. They gave the people too much, too quick, so it hurt *me*, y'understand? It's like givin' too many shows in the same daggone town: after a while, somebody's gonna bring a show in an' *die*. People are that

---

*'Dearest' was retitled 'Umm, Oh Yeah' in the process.

way. You can give 'em too much. It got so bad, till it left no room for me to do my thing.'[22]

The popularity of Bo Diddley's unique rhythms was certainly undeniable, initially prompting a handful of imitations like Billy Bland's 'Chicken In The Basket' [Old Town 1016], 'Chicken Hop' [Old Town 1022] and 'Uncle Bud' [Old Town 1109], Cousin Leroy's 'Highway 41' [Ember 1016], the Crescendos' 'Let's Take A Walk' [Scarlet 4007], Marvin & Johnny's 'Ain't That Right' [Modern 974], Robert & Johnny's 'Broken Hearted Man' [Old Town 1043], and Sonny 'Hootin'' Terry's 'Uncle Bud' [Old Town 1023] in addition to the predictable flurry of cover versions.

By 1958, however, the trickle had become a torrent, and the ensuing years saw the market flooded with dozens of pastiches like the Abstracts' 'Bo Gumbo' [Vantage 704], Andy & The Live Wires' 'You've Done It Again' [Applause 1249], the Astronauts' 'Diddy Wah Diddy' [RCA-Victor LP *Orbit Kampus*], Chuck Berry's 'Jo Jo Gunne' [Chess 1709], 'Broken Arrow' [Chess 1737] and 'Brown Eyed Handsome Man' [Chess LP *On Stage*'], the Bill Black Combo's 'Hey Bo Diddley' [Hi LP *Movin*'], the Buddies' 'Beatle' [Swan 4170], Freddy Cannon's 'Buzz Buzz A-Diddle-It' [Swan 4071] and 'Abigail Beecher' [Warner Bros 5409], Eddie Cochran's 'Weekend' [Liberty 55389], B.B. Cunningham Jr's 'Tantrum' [Cover 5981], the Curios' 'Chicken Back' [Curio 102], Curley & The Jades' 'Boom Stix' [Music Makers 109], the Ecuadors' 'Say You'll Be Mine' [Argo 5353], Duane Eddy's 'Cannonball' [Jamie 1111], Tommy Facenda's 'High School USA (Virginia)' [Legrand 1001], the Gay Jays' 'Chicken Back' [Josie 893], Bobby Gregg's 'The Hulaballoo' [Veep 1207], Bill Haley's 'Skinny Minnie' [Decca 30592] and 'Lean Jean' [Decca 30681], Johnny & The Hurricanes' 'Beanbag' [Warwick LP *Stormsville*] and 'Old Smokie' [Big Top 3076], Myron Lee & The Caddies' 'School's Out' [Del-Fi 4180], the Monterays' 'Bo-Did-It' [T-Hee 701], Jay Nelson's 'Sleepy Time Rock' [Excello 2149], Rick Nelson's 'A Long Vacation' [Imperial 5958], Sandy Nelson's 'Jive Talk' [Imperial 5708], 'Drums Are My Beat' [Imperial 5809] and 'Diddley Walk' [Imperial LP *Beat That Drum*], the Night Riders' 'Pretty Plaid Skirt' [Sue 713], the Piltdown Men's 'Brontosaurus Stomp' [Capitol 4414], Pat Powdrill's 'Luckiest Girl In Town' [Reprise 0286], Elvis Presley's 'Never Say Yes' [RCA-Victor LP *Spinout*] and 'His Latest Flame'* [RCA-Victor 47-7908], Diane Renay's 'Watch Out Sally' [M-G-M K.13296], the Royal Playboys' 'Goodbye Bo'

---

*Itself later recycled by seventies group Smokie as 'Don't Play Your Rock 'n' Roll To Me' [RAK 217].

[Dode 101], Sam The Sham's 'Go-Go Girls' [M-G-M LP *Wooly Bully*] and 'Mystery Train' [M-G-M LP *On Tour*], the Carl Simmons Orchestra's 'Boodoo' [Dot 16076], the Sparkletones' 'Bayou Rock' [Paris 530], the Tokens' 'A-B-C, 1-2-3' [RCA-Victor 47-8210], Ritchie Valens's posthumously issued 'Instrumental' [Del-Fi LP *In Concert At Pacoima Junior High*] and Gene Vincent's 'In Love Again' [Capitol LP *Sounds Like*].

But, of all of Diddley's imitators, none was more prolific than Johnny Otis, who stormed into the charts in the summer of 1958 with his catchy 'Willie & The Hand Jive' [Capitol 3966] and never looked back, churning out 'Crazy Country Hop' [Capitol 4060], 'Castin' My Spell' [Capitol 4168], 'Mumblin' Mosie' [Capitol 4326], 'The New Bo Diddley' [Eldo 106] and 'Hand Jive One More Time' [King 5581] according to the same formula, albeit with ever-diminishing success.

After spending several years in semi-retirement, he resurfaced in 1971 with a remake of 'Willie & The Hand Jive' [Epic 8071], following on with 'Two Time Slim' (an unusually inspired toast-style adaptation of 'Who Do You Love') and 'Hey Shine' [both on Kent LP *Snatch & The Poontangs*], 'Drinkin' Wine Spo-Dee-O-Dee' [Alligator LP *The New Johnny Otis Show*] and 'Hand Jive '85' [Kent LP *Otisology*].

Not surprisingly, it was Otis's Capitol recordings which made the biggest impact – judging by the many cover versions they have inspired over the years: 'Willie & The Hand Jive' has been recorded by the Bunch, Sonny Burgess & The Kings IV, Jo-Ann Campbell, Kim Carnes, Johnny Carver, Eric Clapton, the Countdown 5, the [post-Holly] Crickets, Jerry Kennedy, the Keymen, the Moongooners, the New Riders Of The Purple Sage, Dan Penn, Johnny Preston, Cliff Richard & The Shadows, Johnny Rivers, the Sevilles, George Thorogood, the Tremeloes and Wynder K. Frog; 'Crazy Country Hop' by Bobby & Laurie, Eric Clapton, the Mark Four and the Skeletons; 'Castin' My Spell' by Joe Brown, the Measles, Stu Mitchell, the Pirates, Savoy Brown, Wilko Johnson, the Talismen and Geraint Watkins & The Dominators; and 'Mumblin' Mosie' by Cliff Richard & The Shadows.

If Bo Diddley's standing among the pop crowd was remarkable, then his influence outside it was even more so. Most black artists simply ignored him – Dee Clark's 'Hey Little Girl' [Abner 1029] and the Little Willie John Band's 'Bo-Da-Ley Didd-Ley' [King 5591] being notable exceptions – but not so an entire generation of young, white country rockers, whose vast legacy of 'Bo Diddley'-inspired recordings is a testament to the immense respect he commanded: Gar Bacon's 'Marshall, Marshall' [OKeh 4-7115], Leon Bass's 'Little Liegie' [Whirl-A-Way 1058], the Big Bopper's two versions of 'It's The Truth, Ruth' [Mercury 71451 and LP *Chantilly Lace*], Bill Carlisle's 'No Help Wanted' [Hickory 1383], the Collins Kids' 'Hoy Hoy' [Columbia 41087], Sonny Curtis's 'Bo Diddley Bach' [Liberty 55710], Chuck Darty's 'Lumberjack' [Chart 649], Lloyd George's 'Sing Real Loud' [Imperial 5837], Mickey Gilley's 'I Ain't Bo Diddley' [San 1513], Dale Hawkins's 'Liza Jane' [Checker 934], Ronnie Hawkins's 'Clara' [Roulette 4228], Kris Jensen's 'Lookin' For Love' [Hickory 1243], Al Jones's 'Loretta' [Imperial 5587], Jericho Jones's 'Black Magic' [Todd 1038], Sleepy LaBeef's 'Turn Me Loose' [Crescent 102] and two versions of 'Ride On Josephine' [Wayside 1651 and Picture 1937], Bob Luman's 'Svengali' [Capitol 4059], Joe Melson's 'What's The Use (I Still Love You)' [Hickory 1121], Arthur Osborne's 'Hey Ruby' [Brunswick 55068], the Pacers' 'Tennessee Stud' [Razorback LP *Presenting The Fabulous Pacers*], Jody Reynolds's 'Daisy Mae' [Demon 1507], Leon Smith's 'Little Forty Ford' [Williamette 101], Warren Smith's 'Uranium Rock' [Sun Various Artists LP *Put Your Cat Clothes On*] and Kip Tyler's 'Jungle Hop' [Challenge 59008].

The only rockabilly performer to show any lasting commitment to Bo Diddley's music, however, was Ronnie Hawkins, who launched his recording career in 1958 with 'Hey Bo Diddley' [Quality 8127] and subsequently laid down fine versions of 'Bo Diddley', 'Diddley Daddy', 'Say Boss Man' and 'Who Do You Love' for a variety of labels, earning himself a well-deserved reputation as one of the foremost interpreters of Diddley's material.

Mention his name and Bo's face lights up: 'That's my partner, one *great* dude! He's closer to me than anybody else, an' I know the cat better than I know most guys. We go right back to the fifties, right back to Arkansas when he was with Conway Twitty an' we played the same clubs. In fact, durin' the sixties, in Toronto, Ronnie worked the Hawk's Nest, an' he leased that upstairs dancehall from the guy I worked for downstairs. Ronnie's done a lot of my tunes real good an', although he'll mix up the lyrics, I like 'em a lot.[29]

'A lotta people have copied me in their own way, picked up on my rhythm patterns, you know.' I think a lot of 'em did *very good* jobs an' some of 'em were *butchered*! I don't really have any favorites. All I can say is, it was *their* approach to the Bo Diddley thing.[32]

'What I had *worked* – an' it's *still* workin'! The only thing that *hurts*, is that I don't get the credit.¹ I don't care nothin' about people *usin'* my stuff, but at least give me *credit* for it! But, you get *"Song arranged by so-an'-so"*, an' it sounds like somethin' *I* did years ago, so that's a crock of crap!⁴

'At one time, I was kinda hostile about it, because I thought people should go get their own stuff like I went an' got my own, you know, because I didn't know the value of bein' the originator, Number One.³²

'Do I resent it ? In a way, yes, in a way, no – because one can only go so far, an' maybe it *was* that I came up with the *idea*, but somebody else maybe put a little bit more to it: that's the way I look at it. It's a "professional" feelin', you know.'⁴⁹

Chapter 6

London Stomp

Twistin'

Bo Diddley may well have earned himself a place in music's history books, but in 1961 his future in the business seemed far from certain. Indeed, with Buddy Holly and Eddie Cochran both dead, and Chuck Berry, Little Richard and Jerry Lee Lewis out of circulation for other reasons, rock 'n' roll itself was well and truly in the doldrums by this time, left with just a handful of instrumental groups to battle against a rising tide of pretty-faced, white 'high school' balladeers championed by the majors.

Unable to compete either on physical or musical terms, Bo found his popularity beginning to wane. Ironically, he also recorded some of his most compelling rock 'n' roll material during this period, notably the superlative *Bo Diddley Is A Lover* album, which was shamefully ignored at the time of its release and to this day remains one of his least-known works.

If ever there was a record which truly did Diddley's immense talent justice, then *Lover*, with its dazzling guitar work and staggering variety of images and styles, was it. Here was Bo at his most inventive, encountering a girl who *'don't sound like where she's from'* in 'Hong Kong, Mississippi', chatting to acquaintances on 'Bo's Vacation' (a clever rap in the 'Say Man' mould with underlying inferences of marital infidelity), and experimenting with a Gilbert & Sullivan-style courtroom dialogue on 'Not Guilty'; here was Bo at his most seductive, boasting about his prowess as a lover on the title track, pleading with his girl to telephone him on 'Bo's Blues' [*aka* 'Call Me'], and trying a little tenderness with the ballad, 'Love Is A Secret'; here he was at his most intense, cranking out powerful instrumental versions of 'Road Runner' and 'Gunslinger' (retitled 'Congo' and 'Quick Draw', respectively) and supercharged rockers like 'Back Home', 'Bo Diddley Is Loose' and Milt Buckner's 'You're Looking Good'* in tandem with Peggy Jones, whose eloquent lead guitar accompaniments added an effervescent sparkle to the proceedings.

Sadly, both the *Lover* album and its spin-off single, 'Aztec'** b/w 'Not Guilty' [Checker 976], failed to connect, and the amusing 'Pills' [Checker 985] – written following a backstage mishap at the New York Paramount in 1959 (when Bo tripped over some untidy cables and was carted off to hospital with a broken ankle) – suffered a similarly ignominious fate.

Shortly afterwards, however, his flagging career received a much needed shot in the arm, as a new dance craze called the 'twist' swept across the nation.

A rock 'n' roll hybrid, twist music relied on a solid dance beat – something Diddley was well-equipped to supply – and the appearance of records like the Carroll Bros' 'Bo Diddley' [Cameo 213], the Dovells' 'Bristol Stomp' [Parkway 827] and Johnny Otis's 'The New Bo Diddley' [Eldo 106] and 'Queen Of The Twist' [King 5634] was all the confirmation Chess needed that the Bo Diddley sound was still 'in'.

Accordingly, the perennially popular 'Bo Diddley' was quickly reissued in November 1961 [as Checker 997], followed closely by the predictable cash-in album, *Bo Diddley's A Twister*. In actual fact, it was Chess who were the 'twisters' in this case, for half of the tracks on the new LP had already been out before – six of them twice!

Quite understandably, such repackaging displeased Bo immensely.

'Chess had a *bad* habit about takin' my old songs, an' a different picture, an' puttin' out another album. Then a kid go an' buy it, say: "Hey, I *already* got this tune on *another* album!" That was *bad* news, an' that

---

*Buckner's version appeared on his 1960 LP, *Please Mr Organ Player* [Argo LP-670].
**'Aztec' was actually a slow treatment of the 1947 Jan August hit 'Misirlou' [Mercury 5117] – a tune much favoured by the early sixties instrumental groups. Although credited to Bo, it was in fact arranged and performed entirely by Peggy Jones.

was one of the things that hurt me as an artist, because right away people got the idea that that's the end of Bo Diddley, that's all he can do, an' I didn't even *know* that they were doin' this durin' that time.'[1]

While Diddley's complaint is certainly legitimate, the Chess brothers perhaps deserve to be given the benefit of the doubt in this particular case. After all, they were attempting to revive his career by introducing him to a new audience... and what better way to woo them, than with a selection of some of his very best recordings?

The same could not, however, be argued for the new material they included – with the exception of the spirited 'My Babe'*, a largely forgettable collection of chants and half-finished instrumentals left over from Bo's final sessions with Peggy Jones in the spring of 1961.

'What happened was, this single I'd recorded with my group** – the Jewels – started hitting in New York and we had to go there to promote it. I never actually *left* Bo Diddley's group; I took "leave of absence", and he said I could come back whenever I wanted to. I was in and out for about another year, but then I got involved in a lot of other things and didn't see him again for ten years.'[41]

Following the local success of their single, the group commenced work on an album but internal strife caused it to disintegrate soon afterwards, with Peggy branching out on her own as Little Jewel to work the New York and Boston club circuits. In 1967, she married bass player Wally Malone and started the outfit she now fronts, Lady Bo & The Family Jewel***.

The June 1961 sessions also yielded two sides by a female quartet from Washington called the Impalas: 'For The Love Of Mike', a jerky, up-tempo outing graced by a short Diddley guitar solo reminiscent of 'Bo's Bounce' (cut at the same session) and 'It Won't Be Me', a ballad. The girls (Sandra Bears, Margie Clark, Carrie Mingo and Billy Stewart's cousin, Grace Ruffin) had started singing together while at school, and specialised in beautiful harmonies laced with sweet 'teen soprano' leads, usually sung by Clark or Mingo. 'I thought they had somethin', so I decided to help them,' says Bo matter-of-factly.

---

*A cover of Little Walter's 1955 No. 1 'R&B' hit [Checker 811], a Willie Dixon composition.
**'I'm Forever Blowing Bubbles' b/w 'We've Got Togetherness' [M-G-M K.13577].
***The 'Lady Bo' prefix was actually added later, following a surprise reunion with Bo at San Francisco's Fillmore West auditorium in July 1970. She has since recorded further material with Bo, and has frequently supported him on US and European concert dates.

LIVING LEGEND

The Chess brothers also thought the group had potential and put out
'For The Love Of Mike' as a single [Checker 999] in November 1961,
coupled with 'I Need You So Much' (another ballad, recorded at a later
date), but the record proved unsuccessful.

Rechristening themselves the Four Jewels, the girls cut half a dozen
more singles for Start, Checker and Tec over the next couple of years, again
without commercial success. In 1964, however, they signed with Carol
King's Dimension label and as The Jewels scored a year-end smash hit with
their first release, 'Opportunity' [Dimension 1034], which made No. 64 in
the *Billboard* 'Hot 100' and No. 18 on the *Cash Box* 'R&B' chart*.

Sadly, the follow-up, 'Smokey Joe' [Dimension 1048] did nothing, and,
despite a year-long stint with the James Brown revue, the group eventually
disintegrated due to family pressures. Carrie Mingo subsequently
resurfaced during the seventies singing lead with the Velons, and in 1985
briefly reunited with the other Jewels to recut some of their classics for
DJM [LP *Loaded With Goodies*]. More recently, the three other members
have reformed and are touring again on the oldies circuit.

Wake Up, America

For all its shortcomings, *Bo Diddley's A Twister* received a reassuringly
favourable reaction from record buyers – though the real breakthrough
was to come in the summer of 1962, when Bo's new single, 'You Can't
Judge A Book By The Cover' [Checker 1019], shot to No. 21 on the
Billboard 'Rhythm & Blues' chart and No. 48 in the 'Hot 100'.

A Willie Dixon-penned novelty warning people not to judge the singer
by his outward appearance, the song has since been acclaimed another Bo
Diddley classic, inspiring cover versions by John Anderson, Rey Anton &
The Peppermint Men, Long John Baldry, the Betterdays, the Bintangs, the
Blues Project, Roy Buchanan, Cactus, Wayne Cochran, Bobby Comstock,
Billy 'Crash' Craddock, Dion, John Hammond, the Jeckylls & Hydes,
Sleepy LaBeef, Patti Labelle, the Mark Leeman Five, the Liverbirds, Dell
Mack, the Merseybeats, the Mugwumps, Orion, Johnny Rebb, Billy Lee
Riley, the Rogue Show, the Rolling Stones, Tom Rush, Troy Seals, the
Shadows Of Knight, the Wild Oats, Hank Williams Jr, Stevie Wonder and
the Yardbirds.

Billboard did not publish an 'R&B' chart between 30 November, 1964 and 23 January,1965,
when the record was at its height, so the less-reliable *Cash Box* entry has been shown instead.

122

With its overly dramatic *'I know you don't love me no more'* storyline, the flip – 'I Can Tell' – also created something of a stir, although the song is not one of Bo's personal favourites. 'Some dude* ran into the studio with it, you know, an' I was readin' it off a piece of paper. I had to put some kinda music to it – uh – as quick as possible, but I didn't really wanna do it. See, if *I'd* have written that tune, it would have been very comical.'[32].

Both sides of the single were also included on Bo's next long-player, *Bo Diddley* (significantly, the first not to feature his likeness on the sleeve). This, too, sold surprisingly well, eventually peaking at No. 117 on *Billboard*'s 'Top LPs' chart in December 1962

While some concessions to the ongoing dance craze like 'Mama Don't Allow No Twistin'' (a witty update of Washboard Sam's 1935 singalong, 'Mama Don't Allow' [Vocalion 3275]), and the instrumental 'Bo's Twist' (with Billy Stewart guesting on organ) were perhaps inevitable, the album generally had much to commend it, including a tougher, sharper sound, trendy 'chugging' rhythms and some memorable compositions including 'Who May Your Lover Be', an angry, rockabilly flavoured reworking of the folk-song, 'Corrine, Corrina', the powerful 'Give Me A Break', whose thumping fuzztone riffs reappeared years later on Canned Heat's version of the Bob Landers one-chord stomper, 'Cherokee Dance' [United Artists LP *Historical Figures & Ancient Heads*], and the amazing 'Mr Khruschev', a patriotic rallying call to all Americans urging them to unite and defend their land against the growing Soviet threat... absurdly packaged in the familiar 'Hey Bo Diddley' call-and-response format with some appropriately bizarre vocal support by the Vibrations:

Bo:	*J.F.K. can't do it by his-self...*
Chorus:	*Hup, two, three-four!*
Bo:	*C'mon fellers, let's give him a little help!*
Chorus:	*Hup, two, three-four!*

© Arc Music Inc (BMI)

Released just weeks before the Cuban Missile Crisis erupted in October 1962, Diddley's prophetic political-message-as-popular-song was a phenomenon unheard of at the time, though it was of course quickly

---

*Composer Samuel Smith.

followed by a flood of pacifist 'protest' anthems from the politically conscious folk fraternity.

'I'm a firm believer that you have to *fight* to protect what you have. Shouldn't *have* to, but it look like that's the way the cookie crumble. I wanted to get in there an' defend my country, because I didn't feel like we should be dominated by other people.

'When the Second World War broke out, I was ready to go an' defend the freedom of this country – or any other country that was bein' threatened – but they told me I wasn't old enough an' sent my tail back home.

'Later on, when I was thirty-seven years old, I finally got a letter from the Selective Service. I went down there, filled out a few papers, an' went home. I was A1. A1 was eligible to go, but I never was called.

'If I *was* called then, or even today, I would *gladly* have went if I figured it was for a just cause – but there's no sense in us just tryin' to *destroy* each other. We're supposed to be the most intelligent thing that's walkin' the face of the Earth, but that is questionable. We haven't *changed*, we've just got *smarter*: we used to run through the woods, an' throw spears an' shoot arrows at one another; now, we push buttons on each other. *Same* bullshit! We're still fightin' about the same mess: territory or food.[1]

'Man has gotta get it *together* for himself! Do you know we are the only animal that kills for the hell of it? We preach love, an' practice hate; we preach peace, an' practice war. Harmony, man, people gettin' along with themselves an' each other, it would be *so* beautiful![2] We should be able to sit down an' *talk*. *Every* nation. An' the ones that *don't wanna* talk, *don't wanna* listen – then *suffer*!

'I don't understand the United States an' Russia screamin' an' hollerin' at one another like two mad, mischievous children, an' then *doin' business* with each other! If I don't like you, I don't think I'll do any business with you. Only thing I can say, is that we'd better get our acts together or there ain't gonna be no rock 'n' roll – ain't gonna be no *nothin'* – 'cause the world is gonna be screwed up by all these idiots with all these goddamn bombs![1]

'Really man, I'm surprised at people that are supposed to be more highly educated an' more understandin' than us "peasants", as they class us. They know what's *happenin'*, but they don't know the *possibilities* of what Mother Earth will react to. I don't know what this planet of ours is made of – I couldn't even begin to think – but I know one thing: we have *enough* problems with earthquakes an' tidal waves without man himself manufacturin' destructive weapons to cause some type of reaction that may not happen till maybe thirty days later, maybe six months, who knows?

'But why play with gasoline and a torch? Where human lives are at stake, I think they should think again an' say: "Hey man, you quit makin' those things, an' I'll quit too." An' if they *still* wanna fight, give 'em all baseball bats, let 'em go out in a big vacant lot an' *beat each other to death!* At least like that, the other cat's got a chance. With a bomb, there's *no* chance for a guy like me. What do I have to fight with? A-a damn house-brick? A Coca-Cola bottle that's been layin' in a alley? No good. These people are supposed to be *so* educated. Why is it that they can't be educated enough to understand what the hell people all over the world are talkin' about?

'There are scientists who make bombs to *kill* people with. I'll bet you there's not one of 'em that can make somethin' for some cat to *survive* an atomic blast – because they're too devoted to makin' somethin' *destructive*. They say it's for peace, but it's *not*! How can a *bomb* be for *peace?*[50] We shouldn't have *none* of this shit!

'Durin' the time I wrote 'Mr Khruschev', everybody in America was arguin' 'bout which schools black kids could go to, talkin' 'bout "black this" an' "black that" – but, when bullets an' bombs start fallin', they don't jump up an' say: "Oh, that's a *white* man, we ain't gonna blow 'him' up. We'll go an' get all the 'niggers'!" *Everybody's* ass go! That's why I wrote the line: *"We're fightin' over a six-wheel bus/That bald-head Khruschev's plottin' on us"*. I was tryin' – in so many words – to tell people that we'd better start lookin' after one another.

'I was *serious* when I wrote that sucker – serious as a heart attack – an' I'm *still* serious about it, but I wouldn't dare play that song now. It's a little – uh – political, an' I got *enough* problems!'[1]

Duchess & The Lumberjack

Peggy Jones's departure from the group presented Bo Diddley with a dilemma. Finding a suitable replacement had been relatively easy – guitarist William Johnson had already been standing in, on and off, for over a year, so he knew the routine – but wherever he played, Bo would hear discontented whispers in the audience: "Where's the girl? Where's the *girl?*"

'That's when I got Duchess. Her real name was Norma-Jean Wofford, an' she was from Pittsburgh, Pennsylvania. Her family was *very* nice to me, an' they were like a big family, you know. When I met 'em, they immediately accepted me as a *friend*, an' not just somebody that was famous. Her mother treated me as if I was one of hers. It was just like bein' home. It was really great: they were *beautiful* people.[1]

'In the days she was growin', I taught her how to play guitar, an' then I taught her how to play my thing, you know.[3] Then, after I hired her in the group, I named her "Duchess", an' I says: "I'm gonna tell everybody we're sister an' brother." You'd be surprised at how many people are here that's got these little bitty things goin' on that's good for showbusiness.[1] We kinda fitted the same family a *little* bit, you know, so we could get away with it, but in reality we are really no kin.[51]

'Part of the reason why I decided to go with that little lie was: it put me in a better position to *protect* her when we were on the road. See, a lotta times dudes get to hangin' 'round the chicks. Now, if I politely ask a cat to back off, an' he figures I'm her *brother*, he'll probably be cool about it but, if it look to him like she's my *ol' lady* or somethin', then that's a *whole different* buncha shit, you dig? He might turn *nasty*, y'understand? So, we went around tellin' everybody that we was brother an' sister, an' I think we avoided a whole lotta hassles.

'I think a lot of Norma-Jean. She was, like, a very honest person in the group. I mean *totally* honest, you know. She used to be my bank. I used to tell her to keep all my money, an' stuff like this, an' she would do this for me. I'm not sayin' the rest of 'em wasn't the same way, but they were *careless*, you know: like, the guys would get to carryin' on, an' somebody would rip 'em off.

'Duchess came from a very good family, an' I think I made a good choice because she *did* shine a light on the Bo Diddley aggregation. She stayed with me until 1966, but then she got married an' quit. She's out in Florida now – I'm not sure where[1] – but I expect she'll be back with me someday, because a *lotta* people are beginnin' to ask me where she's at, an' they wanna see her.'[3]

Bo's new partner was introduced to his fans via 1962's *Bo Diddley & Company*, a worthy if flawed successor to *Bo Diddley*: the Billy Davis–Brian Holland composition, '(Extra, Read All About) Ben', was a fine opener, with a crisp, punchy rhythm and amusing plot about a tough guy who survives all kinds of potentially fatal incidents only to die of a common cold, though the release of two other variations of the tune – 'Help Out' and 'Little Girl' – on the same album was ill-considered to say the least.

126

4746 South Langley (centre of picture) in 1987
Photo: Robert Pruter

Corner of 47th and Langley today
Photo: Robert Pruter

The Ebenezer Missionary Baptist Church, 4501 South Vincennes Avenue
Photo: Robert Pruter

Ellas, aged 12
Courtesy: George R. White

A rare sight: Bo Diddley playing violin
Photo: Lady Bo

Live entertainment on Maxwell Street
Photo: Cilla Huggins

The Hipsters (L to R): Roosevelt
Jackson, Ellas McDaniel and Jody
Williams
Courtesy: Jody Williams

Earl Zebedee Hooker
Courtesy: Blues Unlimited

Muddy Waters (seated) with pianist Otis Spann
Photo: Blues Unlimited

Little Walter
Photo: Brian Smith

Clifton James
Photo: Mike Rowe

Billy Boy Arnold
Courtesy: Blues Unlimited

First publicity photo
Courtesy: Bill Millar

Dynamic Duo: Bo Diddley and
Jerome Green
Courtesy: Bill Millar

The Hambone Kids with Red Saunders,1952 (L to R): Sammy McGrier, Dee
Clark and Ronny Strong
Courtesy: Robert Pruter

Touring days (L to R): Frank Kirkland, Alan
Freed, Bo and Jerome Green
Courtesy: Wayne Russell

Tommy 'Dr Jive' Smalls
Courtesy: Juke Blues

Bo's 'other drummer' Frank Kirkland
Courtesy: George R. White

The one that started it all: 'Bo
Diddley'
*Courtesy: Chess Records/Juke
Blues*

Bo rocks the Apollo, 1955. To his left is guitarist Bobby Parker
Courtesy: Showtime Archives

The Moonglows (L to R):
Harvey Fuqua, Bobby
Lester, Prentiss Barnes and
Alexander 'Pete' Graves
Courtesy: George R. White

Willie Dixon
*Photo: Jim Simpson/
Blues & Rhythm*

Jo-Ann Campbell
Courtesy: George R. White

Billy Stewart
Courtesy: Showtime Archives

Mickey & Sylvia
Courtesy: Robert Pruter

Harvey & The Moonglows, 1959 edition (L to R): Chester Simmons, Reese Palmer, James Nolan, Harvey Fuqua, Marvin Gaye, and Chuck Barksdale
Courtesy: Arthur Berlowitz

The 1959 Cadillac . . .
Photo: George R. White

. . . and the guitar it inspired
Courtesy: Chess Records

2614 Rhode Island Avenue, Washington DC
Photo: Lorenzo Ferguson

Bo and Kay in
London, 1982
Photo:
George R. White

Billy 'Dino' Downing
Photo: Ron Courtney

Jesse James Johnson
Courtesy: George R. White

The Jewels' first line up (L to R): drummer Brian Keenan (later with Manfred Mann and the Chambers Bros), Peggy Jones (guitar), and Bobby Baskerville (bass guitar)
Courtesy: Lady Bo

Richmond, Virginia, 1961: William Johnson (right) stands in for Peggy Jones.
Note also the customised speaker cabinets
Photo: Ron Courtney

The Impalas
(L to R): Sandra
Bears, Grace
Ruffin, Margie
Clark and Carrie
Mingo
*Courtesy:
Robert Pruter*

Bo , Duchess and
Jerome, 1962
Courtesy: Bill Millar

Billy Lee Riley
Photo: Graham Barker

Bo pictured with his
1962 best-seller
'Bo Diddley'
Courtesy:
George R. White

Dapper Bo arrives in England,
September 1963
Photo: Brian Smith

Bo appears on ABC-TV's **Thank Your
Lucky Stars**, 28 September, 1963
Photo: Brian Smith

The Flintstones
Courtesy: George R. White

The Big TNT Show, 1965 (L to R): Bo Diddley, Clifton James, Bo-ettes Gloria
Morgan and Lily 'Bee Bee' Jamieson, Duchess and Chester 'Dr Boo' Lindsey
Courtesy: Michael Ochs Archives

Bo puts in a typically energetic performance at the Flamingo Club, London
27 September 1965
Photos: Mike Vernon

Bo poses outside Le Coq D'or club, Toronto, 1966
Courtesy: Chess Records

The Black
Gladiator,
1970
*Courtesy:
Chess
Records*

Violinist,
Eddie
Drennon
*Courtesy:
George R.
White*

Accused: the Chess board (L to R): Leonard, Marshall and Phil
Courtesy: Chicago Tribune/Blues Unlimited

From Gunslinger to
Lawman in eleven years
Photo: Pennie Smith

Cookie Vee
Photo: Crunch McCrann

Toronto, 1969 (L to R): Bo, Clifton James, Cookie and Chester Lindsey
Courtesy: LFI

Bo and
Cookie play
Wembley
Stadium,
1972
*Courtesy:
LFI*

Bo in exuberant mood at the Lyceum, London, 11 March, 1979; (L to R):
George Thorogood, Bo, Joe Strummer of the Clash and Ray Campi
Photo: Val Wilmer

Offspring: Tammi Deanne McDaniel (left) and Terri Lynne McDaniel, 1982
Courtesy: George R. White

Bo with his friend and manager, Marty Otelsberg, in 1984
Photo: George R. White

Bo's pottery
Courtesy:
George R. White

Bo Cookin' – I
Photo: George R. White

Bo Cookin' – II
Photo: George R. White

Bo struts his stuff at the Brighton Dome, 15 November, 1985
Photo: Paul Harris

Photo: George R. White

Equally inexplicable was the inclusion of 'Put The Shoes On Willie', a dreadful hoedown treatment of an Earl Hooker song* that would ordinarily have been guaranteed a place in the garbage can.

Happily, such lapses of taste were more than compensated for by the brilliance of Diddley's own compositions: his uncharacteristically caustic observations of everyday life, 'Gimme Gimme', 'Lazy Woman' and 'Same Old Thing', the Italianate 'Mama Mia' (which anticipated the success of Elvis Presley's 'O Sole Mio' retread, 'It's Now Or Never' [RCA-Victor 47-7777], a few months later), and 'Bo's A Lumber Jack' (sic), an epic of similar proportion to Jimmy Dean's 1961 saga of 'Big Bad John' [Columbia 42175] which simply cried out for single release. As it was, the poorly selling *Bo Diddley & Company* yielded no seven-inchers at all, unjustly condemning this and several other outstanding cuts to an undeserved obscurity.

Dismayed and worried by the rapid decline in Bo Diddley's record sales, Chess opted for a different approach with his next album. Their solution was *Surfin' With Bo Diddley*, a collection consisting of one vocal cut ('Surfer's Love Call') and eleven instrumentals – most of which had been recorded fourteen months earlier... not by Bo, but by erstwhile Sun Records rocker, Billy Lee Riley.

'At the time, I was writing and producing and singing radio jingles at Pepper Sound Studios in Memphis, Tennessee. It was a jingle studio; it wasn't a studio that people were doing sessions in. But, working there, I did my sessions there – because studio time didn't cost me nothing, you know.

'I went and cut the album because I had a good record, 'Shimmy Shimmy Walk' by the Megatons**, which was my group. It was only a one-record deal, and I knew that LPs usually follow a good record, so I thought I'd go ahead and cut this, and take it to Phil Chess personally, fly to Chicago.

'I tried to make a deal with him, which is a *hard* man to make a deal with, you know: he wants it free, wants everything free. So, I made a deal with him for so much money on the front and so much percentage, and I

---

*Hooker's version appeared on Checker 1025 (1962).
**An instrumental version of Bo's 'She's Fine, She's Mine', the single was originally released on Dodge 808 out of Ferriday, Louisiana. When the small independent found itself unable to keep up with demand, national distribution was taken over by Chess. Renumbered Checker 1005, it reached No. 88 in the *Billboard* 'Hot 100' in February 1962.

got our money and everything and left, expecting the record to come out – and it didn't.'[52]

When Riley's recordings finally saw the light of day in May 1963, they were barely recognisable: 'They took the harmonica track off and put Diddley* on there. Everything else is us. All the tracks sound alike, so you can't say it isn't. They've only got me down for four songs, but that's not true: everything that was on that album – other than 'What'd I Say', 'White Silver Sands' and 'Hucklebuck' – was mine too. I wrote 'em, but Chess changed the titles.

'I was quite upset about it, but I didn't figure there was anything I could do. I *was* upset, but it didn't make me *all* that mad – I just didn't like the fact that it was *mine* with somebody else's name on it, that's the only thing. It didn't really *matter* because, by the time the record came out, music had changed, and we was into session work out in California. Apparently it didn't sell, and I *knew* I wasn't gonna make any money off of it anyway, so I didn't care, you know.'[53]

Understandably, Bo was himself far from delighted with the *Surfin'* album. 'That was one of the *worst* things I've done! Come to think of it, I was only on about three or four tracks anyway**. But it's not *me*, an' it hasn't done me any good at all.'[52]

Neither was he happy about being pressurised into recording Maurice McAllister's*** 'The Greatest Lover In The World' for his next single [Checker 1045]. 'This guy didn't write this for Bo Diddley. He happened to have it, an' he saw that I had an album out called *Bo Diddley Is A Lover*, so he caught me in the studio, ran in there with this little piece of paper, an' Phil or Leonard Chess – one of 'em – then says: "Hey man, this guy's got a song. He thinks you can do it!"

'An' I says: "Hey, I don't wanna be *bothered* with it!"

'They says: "What have you got against other people's songs?"

'I says: "I don't have nothin' *against* it, I just *don't wanna* do it, man. I have enough material of my *own*. I write my *own* stuff."[32] See, all of a sudden, I started gettin' all these geniuses rushin' into the studio at the last minute, sayin': "Hey man, I got a *hit* for you!"

'I'd say: "If it's a hit, why don't *you* cut it?"

---

*Actually Guitar Red (Paul Johnson); Bo failed to turn up for the session.
** 'Low Tide', 'Old Man River', 'Surf, Sink Or Swim' and 'Surfer's Love Call'.
***Of Maurice & Mac/Radiants fame.

'That's the way I felt.[36] I *don't wanna* be like nobody else. I *totally refuse* – an' this is my *right*! I'm very much against people poppin' up out of the woodwork, an' all of a sudden they know what's great for Bo Diddley. *Nobody* knows what's great for me, because if they *did*, they'd've found me before I found myself, y'understand?[1]

'It wasn't that I was prejudiced against other people's material, but I felt that they couldn't write for *me*, because I was a self-taught entertainer:[37] I could *not* put the *feelin'* into somebody else's shit.[1] This is what Bo Diddley was all about, as far as I'm concerned: I wrote all my own material, an' I didn't have to run around *scared to death* because nobody came up with a good song to keep me from fallin' on my face.[37]

'None of the stuff they ever wrote for me turned out to be *good* records. Some I *liked*, but they didn't click. The stuff I wrote myself was the stuff that made it. I *know*, because I'm the son-of-a-gun that was doin' it!'[36]

Bo Diddley's career had indeed reached something of a low ebb in the States by now, but four thousand miles away in Great Britain (where he was still virtually unknown), it was only just about to take off.

Yeah, Yeah, Yeah

The British music scene of 1963 bore little resemblance to its American counterpart. Rock 'n' roll had made its presence felt during the fifties, of course, but its impact had only been limited: racial segregation had never been an institution in the UK, so there was no alternative network of clubs, radio stations and record companies to promote the music, and no major social upheaval to give it notoriety. Instead, the industry remained firmly under the control of national dancehall chains, the ultra-conservative BBC radio monopoly and a handful of major record labels who had responded to the fad by grooming their younger signings into 'rock 'n' roll' combos (usually based on the Haley model) while simultaneously encouraging more wholesome alternatives like skiffle and, of course, ballads. Some of the music was good – most of it was awful – but either way, it was novel enough to keep the kids amused for a while.

By the time rock 'n' roll finally achieved mass acceptance in 1959 (thanks largely to Jack Good's influential television show *Oh Boy!*), the 'high school' ballad had already taken over as its foremost style – a development which falsely led many British record executives to surmise that the rock group phenomenon was dying out and that 'proper singers' were about to make a comeback.

What they failed to perceive from the seclusion of their London offices, however, was that the increasing blandness of the music they were purveying had sparked off a nation-wide reaction among teenagers, many of whom were now starting to turn to American rock 'n' roll in search of excitement. Liverpool in particular was a hotbed of activity, with a thriving, cosmopolitan club circuit worked by dozens of local groups, as well as its own distinctive sound, 'Mersey beat'.

Amazingly, this grass-roots backlash remained unrecognised and unnoticed by the record industry until the Beatles stormed into the charts in October 1962 with 'Love Me Do' [Parlophone R-4949], sending droves of talent scouts scurrying north to recruit similar-sounding talent.

As it turned out, most of their discoveries were ardent R&B fans, and their earliest recordings included many quaint, uniquely *English* interpretations of Stateside hits – among them covers of Diddley favourites like Dave Berry's 'Diddley Daddy' [Decca Various Artists LP *At The Cavern*], Wayne Fontana & The Mindbenders' 'Road Runner' [Fontana TF-404] and 'Cops & Robbers' [Fontana LP *Wayne Fontana & The Mindbenders*], the Merseybeats' 'You Can't Judge A Book By The Cover' [Fontana EP *On Stage*] and Rory Storm & The Hurricanes' 'I Can Tell' [Oriole CB-1858] (which was also covered by the Searchers [Star Club LP *At The Star Club*], the Shakers [Polydor NH-52-272] and Southern outfits Bern Elliott & The Fenmen [Decca EP *Play*], Johnny Kidd & The Pirates [HMV POP-1088] and the Zephyrs [Columbia DB-7199].

Very soon, however, the lure of the Top Twenty (accompanied by constant record company demands for greater commerciality) became too strong to resist, and the music rapidly degenerated into family audience pap.

The vacuum they left behind was quickly filled by a very different breed of group just beginning to emerge from London's underground jazz scene: unlike beat, which had never aspired to be anything other than working class entertainment pure and simple, jazz was 'serious' music associated with radical politics and a bohemian lifestyle, and tended therefore to attract predominantly middle-class intellectuals, many of whom took a keen, often studious interest in the idiom.

Although their first love had been traditional New Orleans jazz, their musical horizons broadened considerably during the latter half of the fifties, when bandleaders like Ken Colyer and Chris Barber began experimenting with other black music styles.

Trombonist Barber was also responsible for organising the first-ever UK appearances by influential blues performers like Champion Jack Dupree, Big Bill Broonzy, Sonny Terry & Brownie McGhee, and Muddy Waters – who stunned the *1958 Newport Jazz Festival* audience with his ferocious singing and stinging electric guitar playing, and inspired guitarist Alexis Korner and harmonica man Cyril Davies to amplify their own instruments.

After playing some experimental 'electric' sets with Barber's band, Korner and Davies formed their own group – Blues Incorporated – in 1961, only to find themselves banned from all the clubs belonging to the National Jazz Federation for contravening their 'acoustic only' rule.

Undaunted, they opened their own club in Ealing on 17 March, 1962 and received such overwhelming support that the NJF quickly relented, offering them a Thursday night residency at their Marquee Club on Oxford Street.

Although only 127 people turned up to their first gig, attendances grew so rapidly thereafter that a second night had to be added to ease the overcrowding.

Many of those who flocked to see Blues Incorporated were themselves musicians, and the exciting on-stage jams in which members of the audience would be invited to participate became a highlight of their performances. As the weeks went by, the group gained a number of semi-permanent 'satellite' members, who would appear with them on a rota basis, or stand in if one of the regular line-up couldn't make it.

It was this arrangement which led to a young Mick Jagger, Keith Richards, Brian Jones, Ian Stewart, Long John Baldry, Dick Taylor and Mick Avory deputising on the evening of 21 July, 1962 while the nucleus of the group guested on the BBC Light Programme's *Jazz Club*. The makeshift ensemble dubbed themselves 'the Rolling Stones' (after the Muddy Waters hit) and proved so popular that they were engaged as regular relief band on Blues Nights.

However, their habit of interspersing the hard, gutbucket blues of Muddy Waters, Willie Dixon, Jimmy Reed *et al* with rockers by Chuck Berry and Bo Diddley soon got them into trouble, their refusal to confine themselves to 'authentic' black music causing consternation among the club's doyens. After several personnel changes (through which they acquired the services of Bill Wyman and Charlie Watts), the Stones were eventually fired in February 1963, only to receive an immediate offer of a residency at Giorgio Gomelsky's Crawdaddy Club* in Richmond. Here, they met with even greater success, attracting so many youngsters that Gomelsky was quickly forced to look for larger premises.

Chuck Berry and Bo Diddley may not have been 'authentic' enough for the purists at the Marquee, but the kids down at the Crawdaddy had no such qualms: as long as the music was fresh, exciting and (preferably) danceable, it filled the bill perfectly. Indeed, along with the Chicago bluesmen, both rockers had by this time amassed huge cult followings, despite the fact that very few of their recordings had ever seen UK release.

In Diddley's case, these amounted to just one EP (*Rhythm & Blues With Bo Diddley*, released 1956), four singles ('Crackin' Up', 'Say Man', 'Say Man, Back Again' and 'Road Runner', released 1959–60) and one LP (*Go Bo Diddley*, released 1960) – all issued under licence through Decca's London American Recordings subsidiary.

Naturally, this scarcity created a substantial and rapidly growing demand for imports of their recordings – a trend that did not pass by unnoticed in Chicago. There was clearly a budding market in the British Isles for Chess product, and Leonard's son, Marshall, was duly despatched to London in May 1961 to negotiate a comprehensive licensing and distribution deal. Pye Records emerged the lucky appointees, and their Pye International subsidiary's 'R&B Series' rapidly went on to become the prime British outlet for black American music in the mid-sixties.

With ready access to a vast new audience now guaranteed, Bo Diddley – like many other Chess artists – was to benefit enormously from this deal. The *Gunslinger* album appeared in September 1961 (rather inappropriately, on the Pye Jazz label), while 1962 yielded a single, 'You Can't Judge A Book By The Cover' [Pye Int R&B 7N.25165]. The year 1963, however, witnessed the release of no fewer than five Bo Diddley singles, three EPs and three LPs, and his popularity soared as a result. A contributing factor to this sudden flurry of activity was Bo's scheduled appearance on a five-week Don Arden package tour in the autumn of 1963** – another unexpected but extremely welcome boost to his flagging career.

---

*Named after 'Doing The Craw-Daddy', one of the tracks on *Bo Diddley Is A Gunslinger*.
**Also on the bill were the Everly Bros, the Flintstones, Julie Grant, Mickie Most and the Rolling Stones, whose first single, 'Come On' [Decca F-11675] had just peaked at No. 21 in the UK charts.

A Slice Of Pye

Arriving on 22 September, a week before the start of the tour, Bo was immediately whisked off to Birmingham to film a spot for ABC-TV's *Thank Your Lucky Stars* (for broadcast on 28 September); on the 23rd, he recorded a session for the BBC Light Programme's popular radio show, *Saturday Club*; on the 24th, he journeyed to Manchester to appear on the Granada TV magazine programme, *Scene At 6.30*; the rest of the week he spent rehearsing and being interviewed by a succession of curious pressmen.

Despite the advance publicity, public reaction to the tour was initially disappointing. Fortunately, the surprise last-minute addition of Little Richard to the bill from 5 October sent ticket sales rocketing, and the show spent the remaining four weeks playing twice-nightly to packed houses throughout the provinces.

Although Bo had only been able to bring Duchess and Jerome with him (due to Musicians' Union restrictions), the trio worked well with their English bassist and drummer, and won many converts – including *NME*'s Chris Hutchins, who reported:

> *'The unusual style of Bo Diddley had Sunday's first house perplexed as the curtains opened... but the familiar strains of the song to which he gave his name earned Bo a warm reception that had turned to something approaching red heat before his startling, though comparatively brief set was completed.'*[54]

A great deal of interest was also expressed in Duchess's skin-tight gold lamé catsuit. Asked by one dauntless investigator how she managed to get into it, Norma-Jean responded by pulling out an oversized shoe-horn!

All in all, the tour was a happy affair and, as the weeks went by, friendships blossomed: 'The Flintstones were a group from London. I liked the way that the saxophone player was comin' across, but they didn't have no *direction*, so I gave 'em a tune of mine to do: I wrote 'Safari' strictly for them, just tryin' to help give 'em a identification – but I don't think it ever did anythin' because they split up or somethin' right after the record came out*.

---

*The instrumental appeared in 1964 [HMV POP-1266].

133

'The Rolling Stones were also on that tour. They welcomed me when I came to England,[1] an' I'll never forget that. They came to the Cumberland Hotel an' gave me a pair of gold cuff-links with my initials on 'em, an' that *said* somethin' to me.[4]

'The Stones are what you call my "jug buddies": we would share wine together, they would come an' watch all my shows, you know, we were real good friends. I even let 'em sleep in my hotel room – on the floor – when they didn't have any bread.[1]

'They were arguin' back then an' were about to break up, but I told 'em to sit down an' iron out their differences. I told 'em: "You're gonna outlast the Beatles because you play like *black* dudes.[28] If you don't be *bigger*, you gonna last *longer*."

'They said: "I don't know what you mean, man."

'I got Brian off to the side, an' I said: "Brian, you look like the one with the level head. Hold this group together, because you guys are goin' to be a *mother*! All you gotta do is stick together, get in a studio, an' put your heart an' soul into it, an' you've *gotta* make it – because what you are doin', the people wanna hear. That *'yeah, yeah, yeah'* jive the Beatles are doin' is gonna fall out *in a minute*!"[55]

'They took my advice – an' look where they are today:[28] the Rollin' Stones is one of the greatest rock 'n roll bands *ever*!'[1]

Pleasantly surprised to find himself once again beseiged by the media and mobbed by adoring fans, Bo took advantage of every opportunity that came his way to rebuild his career. By the time the tour was over, Diddleymania was upon the nation.

His latest UK single release, 'Pretty Thing' [Pye Int R&B 7N.25217], shot to No. 34 in the 'Top 50' – a remarkable achievement quickly overshadowed by even more remarkable album sales. Within the short space of five months, no fewer than four of his long-players made the top twenty: his recent US best-seller, *Bo Diddley*, the two year old *Bo Diddley Is A Gunslinger*, a retrospective compilation called *Bo Diddley Rides Again* and his latest Stateside release, *Bo Diddley's Beach Party*, a live album recorded in Myrtle Beach, South Carolina (epicentre of the 'shag' dance craze) on 5 and 6 July, 1963.

'There used to be a guy that hung around Chess that had a mobile unit – the only one that existed anywhere, I think. Had all his stuff built in a walk-in van. He could go anywhere an' record you. The whole thing ran offa airplane batteries: they are very quiet, you know.

'I happened to see it in Las Vegas – I think – an' I says: "Hey, why don't we do some live things?" The only thing I got 'em to do was *Beach Party*, an' that was one of the *biggest* albums I had!'[1]

Capturing Bo well and truly in his element, *Beach Party* turned out to be not only one of the best records of his career, but also one of the most exciting and atmospheric live albums ever recorded.

Side One explodes with a stirring instrumental rendition of Chuck Berry's 'Memphis', and the pace never slackens as Bo tears through old favourites like 'Gunslinger', 'Hey Bo Diddley' and 'Road Runner', and four new compositions: 'Bo's Waltz', an interesting adaptation of Wanda Jackson's 'I Wanna Waltz' [Capitol LP *Day Dreamin'*] with alternating passages of classical music and rock 'n' roll; the old campfire favourite, 'Old Smokey', attractively repackaged as a 'chugging' instrumental; 'Mr Custer', a comic number about a faint-hearted trooper at Little Big Horn (inspired, no doubt, by Larry Verne's recent hit of the same name [Era 3024]); and 'Bo Diddley's Dog', a frantic workout during which Bo whips the audience into a near-frenzy, barking, yelping and howling over some of the wildest drumming ever committed to vinyl.

Marshall Chess, too, has vivid recollections of these exciting performances – albeit for slightly different reasons: 'It was a remote recording, the first one I'd ever done. I had an engineer from Atlanta: a real thin, nervous guy – I don't know his name. They sent me down to do it, and I had it all miked up. It was, like, in some gymnasium or something, it wasn't really on the beach.

'Jerome got really drunk and high, you know, and jumped down with his maracas and started really sexually dancing with a white girl... and the next thing I knew, the police were there[19] – twenty policemen *with dogs* – threatening to take us all in jail, and I was *scared*:[18] I was the guy that was the *boss*. They threatened me with locking me up: "Take your people two weeks to find out where you were", "You could be beat up", you know, all *kinds* of shit!

'Bo Diddley wanted to *fight* 'em[19] – he had guns in paper bags behind the drums – but we ended up leaving peacefully.'[18]

Even though the technical quality of the *Beach Party* recordings left much to be desired, 'Memphis' was released as a plug single [Checker 1058] coupled with 'Monkey Diddle', a recent studio cut which Chess overdubbed with audience noise in a misguided attempt to make it sound as bad as the top deck. Released just two months after Lonnie Mack had graced the 'Hot 100's No. 5 slot with his inspired interpretation of the Berry classic [Fraternity 906], Bo's version never stood a chance.

His first release of 1964, 'Mama, Keep Your Big Mouth Shut' [Checker 1083], was much better, with a lumbering, hypnotic rhythm and multitracked vocals, and an eminently danceable flip ('Jo-Ann') besides, but its unwieldy title and offensive lyrics (written by Bo in the wake of a particularly annoying episode involving his mother-in-law) ensured that this disc, too, received only limited exposure.

Fortunately, he fared rather better album-wise, collecting a gold disc for sales of the peerless *Bo Diddley's 16 All-Time Greatest Hits* collection and receiving much praise for his outstanding guitar playing on 'Chuck's Beat' and 'Bo's Beat' – two lengthy workouts with his stablemate, Chuck Berry, which accounted for the bulk of the all-instrumental *Two Great Guitars*.

'All that happened was: Chuck came into the studio, an' I asked him how about me an' him doin' a tune together. So, we did somethin'. Then, he had to be down there the next day, so I came down, an' we did another tune.

'It's been said that I played with Chuck Berry on a lot of his recordings, but I never have. I would have *liked* to – because I think Chuck is a *superb* musician – but we only ever did this one thing, *Two Great Guitars*. That's the *only* time.'[1]

In Britain, these new releases were sandwiched between yet more compilations of back-catalogue material – in total three singles, four EPs and four LPs were issued during 1964 – but further UK chart success was to elude Bo until 1965 – strangely enough, as a result of his own popularity.

Long Hair & Maracas

Returning home in November 1963 after his triumphant first UK visit, Bo had left behind him not only a vast public clamouring to hear more of his exciting music, but also a group who could reproduce his sound so closely that they would soon depose him – the Rolling Stones.

Indeed, with a repertoire including 'Cops & Robbers', 'Crackin' Up', 'Diddley Daddy', 'Mona', 'Pretty Thing', 'Road Runner' and 'You Can't Judge A Book By The Cover', and an authentic-sounding R&B style closely modelled on that of their hero (even down to Mick Jagger's maracas), the Stones could hardly have failed to appeal to Bo Diddley's fans. In addition, however, they had two other advantages which enabled them to reach a much wider audience: they were young, English and white (which made them more readily acceptable to the indigenous teenage population), and they were permanently based in the UK (which meant they were always available for personal appearances).

Indeed, by 1964 it was already clear that they would soon become a major attraction in their own right: their second single, 'I Wanna Be Your Man' [Decca F-11764], got to No. 12 in January that year. Their third, 'Not Fade Away' [Decca F-11845], made No. 3 in March. The next five, 'It's All Over Now' [Decca F-11934], 'Little Red Rooster' [Decca F-12014], 'The Last Time' [Decca F-12104], 'Satisfaction' [Decca F-12220] and 'Get Off My Cloud' [Decca F-12263] were all Number Ones.

This phenomenal success was due at least in part to the Stones' defiant stance against authority and established modes of dress and behaviour – which not only garnered them all the publicity they could have wished for, but also the adulation of a generation of teenage rebels. It was this controversial image, underscored by the aggressiveness of their music, which helped to establish R&B as a mass culture in Great Britain, engendering an unprecedented proliferation of groups and clubs up and down the country. Writing in 1964, sociologist Peter Leslie analysed the effects of the R&B explosion:

'In the middle of 1963, six groups – all semi-professional – had a choice of two or three clubs in London at which their music could be presented once or twice a week. A year later, thirty professional and fifty semi-pro groups were continuously employed in the same area, with a further 120–130 maintaining steady club work in the provinces. In the same period, more than 280 traditional jazz clubs switched over wholly or partly to a rhythm and blues policy.'[56]

Although there were several different strains of British R&B, the dominant one during 1964 and the first half of 1965 was the 'long hair and maracas' style pioneered by the Rolling Stones.

Inevitably, a great many Bo Diddley-influence recordings appeared during the course of these two years – among them the Animals' 'I'm Mad Again' [Columbia EP *Animals No. 2*], 'Story Of Bo Diddley' [Columbia LP *The Animals*], 'Road Runner' [Columbia LP *Animal Tracks*] and 'Pretty Thing' [Decca EP *In The Beginning*], Rey Anton & The Peppermint Men's 'You Can't Judge A Book By The Cover' [Parlophone R-5132], the

Betterdays' 'Here 'Tis' [Polydor 56.024], the Birds' 'You Don't Love Me (You Don't Care)' [Decca F-12031], the Bo Street Runners' 'Bo Street Runner' [Decca F-11986], the Brand's 'Zulu Stomp' [Piccadilly 7N.35216], the Downliners Sect's 'Be A Sect Maniac' [Columbia DB-7300], 'Cops & Robbers' [Columbia LP *The Sect*], 'I'm Looking For A Woman' [Columbia LP *The Rock Sect's In*], 'Nursery Rhymes' [Contrast EP *Nite In Gt Newport Street*] and 'Sect Appeal' [Columbia DB-7347], Micky Finn & The Blue Men's 'Pills' [Oriole CB-1927], Alex Harvey's 'Bo Diddley Is A Gunslinger' [Polydor LP *Alex Harvey & His Soul Band*], David John & The Mood's 'Pretty Thing' [Vocalion V-9220] and 'Bring It To Jerome' [Parlophone R-5255], the Kinks' 'Cadillac' [Pye LP *The Kinks*], Manfred Mann's 'Bring It To Jerome' [HMV LP *Five Faces Of*], the Mark Four's 'I'm Leaving' [Decca F-12204] the Nashville Teens' 'I Need You Baby' [Decca EP *The Nashville Teens*], the Others' 'Oh Yeah' [Fontana TF-501], the Other Two's 'Grumbling Guitar' [Decca F-11911], Jimmy Powell & The Five Dimensions' 'I'm Looking For A Woman' [Pye 7N.15663], Shorty & Them's 'Pills' [Fontana TF-460], Them's 'All For Myself' [Decca F-12094], the Thyrds' 'Hide & Seek' [Decca F-12010], the Yardbirds' 'I'm A Man', 'Pretty Girl' and 'Here 'Tis' [all on Columbia LP *Five Live Yardbirds*], and the Zombies' 'Road Runner' [Decca LP *Begin Here*].

Hardcore Diddleyphiles even named themselves after their idol's hits: there were the Diddley Daddies, the Roadrunners and the Cops 'n' Robbers, but most notorious of all were Phil May, Brian Pendleton, Viv Prince, John Stax and Dick Taylor – known collectively as the Pretty Things.

The Pretties burst onto the scene in June 1964 with 'Rosalyn' [Fontana TF-469], an uncompromising 'Bo Diddley'-beat thrash taken at breakneck speed. The record was only a minor hit, but the Pretty Things became famous overnight as the group that had out-Stoned the Stones: they were uglier, scruffier and ruder, and their music deliberately cacophonous and aggressive – precisely the sort of thing to win them credibility with the rapidly-growing British 'punk' contingent.

Their second single, 'Don't Bring Me Down' [Fontana TF-503], went to No. 10 and their third, 'Honey I Need' [Fontana TF-537], made No. 13. Their first Fontana LP, *The Pretty Things*, sold well too, climbing to No. 6 on the 'Top Albums' chart in June 1965 – its success due in no small part to the inclusion of the thumping 'Honey I Need' and six other Bo Diddley-styled numbers: 'Judgement Day' (a slow tune based on 'I'm A Man'), '13 Chester St' (actually Slim Harpo's 'I Got Love If You Want It' set to the 'Bo Diddley' beat), 'Road Runner', 'She's Fine, She's Mine', 'Mama, Keep Your Big Mouth Shut' and 'Pretty Thing', on which they acknowledged their debt: *'We thank you, Bo/For the name/We thank you all/For the fame'*.

At the end of the day, however, it was the Rolling Stones who proved themselves the most inventive of all the 'long hair and maracas' groups. Not content with cutting convincing interpretations of Diddley compositions like 'I'm Alright' [Decca EP *Got LIVE If You Want It*] and 'I Need You Baby' [Decca LP *The Rolling Stones*], they also incorporated many of his musical idiosyncrasies into their own material (heavy reverb on 'Empty Heart' [Decca EP *5x5*] and 'I'm Free' [Decca LP *Out Of Our Heads*]; the 'Diddley Daddy' riff and descending bass runs on 'Nineteenth Nervous Breakdown' [Decca F-12331]; and a pounding 'Bo Diddley' beat laced with feedback on 'Please Go Home' [Decca LP *Between The Buttons*]), creating a unique sound of their own that was to remain popular for many years to come.

Hey, Good Lookin

By 1965, however, hard-edged Chicago R&B was already beginning to lose prominence in Britain, as public tastes shifted towards the subtler, more modern sounds of a younger generation of black entertainers – most notably those recording in Memphis for Stax, and in Detroit for Berry Gordy's Motown Corporation.

Although featured on several mid-sixties' black dance hits like Marvin Gaye's 'Baby, Don't You Do It' [Tamla 54101], Ben E. King's 'Let The Water Run Down' [Atco 6315], the Kolettes' 'Who's That Guy' [Checker 1094], the Miracles' 'Mickey's Monkey' [Tamla 54083], the Supremes' 'When The Lovelight Starts Shining Through His Eyes' [Motown 1051] and Rufus Thomas's 'Jump Back' [Atlantic 4009], the jerky, thumping 'Bo Diddley' beat was essentially unsuited to the smoother R&B styles now in vogue and quickly fell out of favour.

Once again facing the prospect of anonymity on both sides of the Atlantic, Bo had little choice this time but to soften his style and go with the crowd.

His first step in that direction was 1964's 'Hey, Good Lookin'' [Checker 1098] – a sequel to the 'Gunslinger' saga (mysteriously credited to Chuck Berry Music Inc) on which he experimented with a muzzy, ringing guitar sound, rumbling bass and an unusual piano-led rhythm section.

Though unsuccessful in the States, the single was selected to inaugurate Pye's new Chess label in the UK, where [as Chess CRS-8000] it peaked at No. 39 in April 1965 – no mean feat considering the competition. Reaction to the eponymous LP that followed it, however, was decidedly cooler.

Despite flashes of brilliance like 'Brother Bear' (a violent Br'er Rabbit-style reinterpretation of the *Goldilocks & The Three Bears* story), the bizarre cock-fighting yarn, 'Rooster Stew', and the bittersweet 'I Wonder Why (People Don't Like Me)', the album was ill-served by a preponderance of aimless (and generally faceless) dance tracks and a disastrously muddy mix that made it sound like it had been recorded inside a cardboard box.

Whatever Chess's intentions may have been, it signalled the beginning of a downward spiral for Bo Diddley – which he vainly tried to resist by making further concessions to the styles of the day. 'Durin' that time, everybody started havin' girl groups to back 'em up, so I said: "If I'm gonna *survive*, I've gotta get me some *girls*!" An' so, I hired Bee Bee an' Gloria, an' named 'em the Bo-ettes. They were both from DC*.

'At first, I didn't wanna do it, because I didn't want any bother on the road. You know, everybody says: "Man, you ain't gonna have nothin' but trouble." They told the *truth*!

'But, I *needed* girls to put that "flower" on stage, you know, prettiness, where guys is gonna go: "Hey man, did you see those *chicks* on stage with Bo Diddley?" Damn *me*, y'understand?

'It did that, but, aside from the "flower", it was troubles, hassles. The guys in the group would say: "Hey, I don't wanna be *bothered* with them broads",' (laughs) 'you know, so I was always left to baby-sit the girls, an' then everybody would say: "Bo Diddley's got a *harem*", you know, an' I didn't like that. *Always* give *all* the girls to the leader of the group! He's *gotta* be the one that's makin' it with the chicks, y'understand? *Can't* be nobody else in the group – they ain't got enough sense!' (Laughs.)

'An' so, I went through hell an' destruction, man – but, you know, it put me where I am today.'[1]

Bo's next album, *500% More Man*, was closer to soul than anything he had done before, with Motownish vocal backings, tambourine-accentuated

---

*Lily 'Bee Bee' Jamieson and Gloria Morgan were the two girls from Bo's neighbourhood who had sung backing vocals on the *Gunslinger* sessions. They were the first of several Bo-ettes line-ups between 1965 and 1969, which also included at various times Dorothy Holliday (Bo's niece), Della Horne, and sisters Cornelia and Delores Redmond.

140

dancebeats and bubbling, stuttering guitar rhythms (a development of his celebrated 'string-scratching' technique) that laid the musical foundations for future black music styles like disco, funk and hip hop. 'It's the thing that *I* started, an' *nobody* recognizes where it came from, nobody mentions this is an old Bo Diddley lick! If you listen to the song 'Bo Diddley', that's actually where it came from. There's a lot of it in there – the "muffled" sound – you know.'[1]

Recorded in July 1965, the record thankfully turned out to be much better than its predecessor, with a beautifully crisp sound, a variety of moods, and some truly memorable compositions including 'Let Me Pass', a magnificently dramatic companion to Chuck Berry's 'Nadine' [Chess 1883], with the singer tearing the town apart looking for his girl; 'He's So Mad', a variation on the classic 'husband-discovers-item-left-behind-by-wife's-lover' theme; 'Somebody Beat Me', the story of an hotel-room theft inspired by a true incident in Norfolk, Virginia, when Clifton James had his clothes stolen while he slept; and the bouncy 'Greasy Spoon', a visit to a true 'soul food' restaurant serving such mouth-watering delights as *Etta James Peach Melba*, *Chuck Berry Upside-Down Cake*, *Jimmy Reed Chicken à la King* and *Muddy Waters Corn Bread & Muffins*, as well as the rather more exotic *Barbecued Alligator Navels*, *Snake Feet* and *French Fried Toe Jam On Rye*.

In Britain, the album was stripped of its US title track and retitled *Let Me Pass*, but received an exciting (and otherwise unissued) instrumental cut, 'Stinkey', by way of compensation.

Released in September 1965 (three months ahead of its American counterpart) to coincide with Bo's second UK tour, it received an undeservedly frosty reception from disappointed hard-line Diddleyists, and no reaction at all from the soul/mod camp.

Despite an impressive itinerary of club, ballroom and college dates and an equally impressive itinerary of television appearances including *The Eamonn Andrews Show* (26 September), *Gadzooks* (27th), *Scene At 6.30* (30th), *Thank Your Lucky Stars* (2 October), *Discs A Go-Go* (6th) and *Ready, Steady, Go* (8th), Bo fared equally badly on the road, with many fans voicing their disapproval of his new, toned-down style and many more demanding to know why he hadn't brought his dynamic maraca-shaker with him.

'Jerome got married, an' his wife said she'd leave him if he didn't leave me – I don't think she liked him touring. So, the cat had to choose

141

between shakin' his maracas or stayin' with his wife. He went where his heart was.[35]

'Jerome never came back, but he used to call me every year on New Year's Eve, you know, an' one year he never called. I started tryin' to find out where he was livin' in New York, you know, because I'd moved. But he *had* my number, an' if he *didn't* have it, it wasn't no problem for him to get it, 'cause all he had to do was call the record company, y'understand?

'I started wonderin' about it, an' – don't really take my word for it, I'm repeatin' somethin' that I got from someone else in New York that knew him also – they told me he had passed away. Then, I got a few people in other cities that's asked me: "Is it true that Jerome's passed away?"[32]

'I don't really know what happened to him, only that he never called me again. It must be nine or ten years at least, so he probably is dead – which is very, very sad. Jerome was the *greatest*!'[1]

Plagued by equipment problems, car breakdowns and disappointing attendances, the ill-fated tour finally ground to an ignominious halt on 18 October when Bo abandoned it in the midst of a dispute over payment.

His popularity in the UK declined rapidly thereafter and, when he returned to Britain in the spring of 1967 for a couple of gigs, he was once again a cult figure playing for a minority audience.

His influence, however, continued to make itself felt in British rock music throughout the second half of the decade on records like Jess Conrad's 'It Can Happen To You' [Pye 7N.15849], the Cryan' Shames' 'Ben Franklin's Almanac' [CBS CS-9389], Billie Davis's 'I Want You To Be My Baby' [Decca F-12823], Donovan's 'Hey Gyp (Dig The Slowness)' [Pye 7N.15984], the Freaks Of Nature's 'People, Let's Freak Out' [Island WI-3017], the Misunderstood's 'Who Do You Love' [Fontana TF-777], the Rolling Stones' 'Honky-Tonk Women' [Decca F-12952], Johnny Shadow's 'Talented Man' [Parlophone R-5308], the Troggs' 'Gonna Make You' [Page One POF-001] and 'Mona' [Page One LP *Trogglodynamite*], the Truth's 'Hey Gyp' [Deram DM-105], the Wheels' 'Road Block' [Columbia DB.7827] and the Who's 'I'm A Man' [Brunswick LP *My Generation*] and 'Magic Bus' [Track 604.024].

Chapter 7

I Wonder Why People
Don't Like Me

The Day The Music Died

In a little under five years, beat and the R&B explosion transformed British popular music from an imitative, second-rate irrelevancy into a vibrant, innovative, compelling art form all of its own. The effects of this unexpected development were felt all over the world – particularly in the USA, whose domination of the pop industry and youth culture had for so long remained unchallenged.

First to strike a blow were the Beatles, who crossed the Atlantic in February 1964 and took the whole country by storm. Not only did the freshness and vitality of their music compare favourably with anything else on offer in the States at the time, but the novelty of their mop-top haircuts and English accents gave them instant mass appeal, opening up the way for a wholescale 'invasion' by other combos from across the Pond like the Animals, the Dave Clark Five, Gerry & The Pacemakers, Herman's Hermits, the Kinks, the Rolling Stones, the Searchers and the Zombies (all of whom enjoyed 'Hot 100' successes during the course of 1964).

'The Beatles definitely did *somethin'* to help the rock 'n' roll business,' affirms Bo, 'because, in the United States, it was most certainly goin' downhill.

'They came up with somethin' that kept the music for teenagers alive for a while, an' played a very important part in – I would say – *redesignin'* the style of music. They didn't make any different *notes*, but they came up with a thing which was entirely different from anythin' that had ever been done before – *weird* changes an' all – an' the teenagers here grabbed a hold of it, an' *ate it up!'* [15]

The unprecedented popularity of the British groups had a massive impact both in the United States and in Canada, inspiring many teenage musicians to copy their style: by 1965, there were literally hundreds of amateur British beat outfits practising in garages and playing high school hops all over the North America.

Those who modelled themselves on R&B groups like the Animals, the Kinks, the Yardbirds and (of course) the long-haired, loutish Stones, assumed the arrogant, rebellious stance of their heroes and quickly developed a unique sound of their own – 'punk rock' – characterised by snarled, rasping vocals, fuzztone guitars, tinny electric organs, and mounds of feedback.

The music itself was, however, still largely derivative of R&B and rock 'n' roll – in many cases deliberately so – and, as in Britain, the era also begat many memorable Bo Diddley-influenced recordings ranging from straightforward covers like the Accents' 'You Don't Love Me' [Bangar 629] and 'Road Runner' [Bangar 648], the Avanties' 'Say Boss Man' [Twin Town 705], the Baker Street Irregulars' 'I'm A Man' [Large 402], the Barbarians' 'Bo Diddley' [Laurie LP *The Barbarians*], the Barracudas' 'I'm A Man' [Justice LP *A Plane View*], the British Walkers' 'Diddley Daddy' [Try 502], the Bumps' 'You Don't Love Me' [Sin-A-Way 351], the Cavemen's 'Bo Diddley' [Capitol Star Artists 18285], the Chancellors' 'I'm A Man' [Soma 1435], Jerry Dee & The Intruders' 'Bo Diddley' [Sara 6352], Jim Dovall & The Gauchos' 'Hey Mama, Keep Your Big Mouth Shut' [Diplomacy 17], the Gants' 'Road Runner' [Statue 605], 'Crackin' Up' [Liberty 55844] and 'Oh Yeah' [Liberty LP *Gants Again*], Jack Horner & The Plums' 'Who Do You Love' [Panorama Various Artists LP *Battle Of The Bands*], the Iguanas' 'Mona' [Forte 201], the Invictas' 'I'm Alright' [Bengel 113], the Jades' 'I'm Allright' [Ector 101], the Juveniles' 'Bo Diddley' [Jerden 770], the Little Boy Blues' 'You Don't Love Me' [IRC 6939], the Mersey Men's 'I Can Tell' [Wildwoods 2001], the Moonrakers' 'I'm All Right' [Tower 180], the New Colony Six's 'Cadillac' [Sentar 1203], the Ones' 'Didi Wa Didi' [Ashwood House LP *The Ones*], Our Generation's 'I'm A Man' [Barry B-3461X],

Peter & The Wolves' 'Hey Mama' [PW 501], the Preachers' 'Who Do You Love' [Moonglow 223], the Remains' 'Diddy Wah Diddy' [Epic 10001], the Royal Guardsmen's 'Bo Diddley' and 'Road Runner' [both on Laurie LP *Snoopy vs The Red Baron*] and 'I'm A Man' [Laurie LP *Return Of The Red Baron*], the Shadows Of Knight's 'Oh Yeah' [Dunwich 122] and 'You Can't Judge A Book By The Cover' [Dunwich LP *Gloria*], the Starliners' 'Bo Diddley' and 'I'm A Man' [both on Lejac LP *Live At Papa Joe's*], the Stepping Stones' 'Pills' [Diplomacy 21], T.C. Atlantic's 'Mona' [B-Sharp 272], the Teddy Boys' 'Mona' [Cameo 448], the Ugly Ducklings' 'I Can Tell' [Yorktown Y-45001] and 'Mama, Keep Your Big Mouth Shut' [Yorktown LP *Somewhere Outside*], and the Woolies' 'Who Do You Love' [Spirit 113] to inspired adaptations like the Barons' 'Don't Burn It' [Brownfield 1035], the Beau Brummels' 'In Good Time' [Autumn 20], the Descendants' 'Lela' [MTA 112], the Fallen Angels' 'Bad Woman' [Eceip 1004], Finni Cum's 'Come On Over' [Ruff 1011], Dale Gregory & The Shouters' 'Did Ya Need To Know' [B-Sharp 271], the Just VI's 'Bo Said' [Wax 213], the Kingsmen's 'Bo Diddley Bach' [Wand 1184], the Outcasts' 'I'm In Pittsburgh (& It's Raining)' [Askel 102], Passing Fancy's 'I'm Losing Tonight' [Boo LP *Searching In The Wilderness*], ? & The Mysterians' 'Ten O'Clock' [Cameo LP *96 Tears*], the Remains' 'Don't Look Back' [Epic 10060], Mitch Ryder's 'Jenny Take A Ride' [New Voice 806] and 'Baby Jane (Mo-Mo Jane)' [New Voice LP *Take A Ride*], the Seeds' 'Lose Your Mind' [GNP Crescendo LP *The Seeds*], the Shadows Of Knight's 'Gospel Zone' [Dunwich 128] and 'I'll Make You Sorry' [Dunwich 141]', the Strangeloves' 'I Want Candy' [Bang 501], 'No Jive' and 'Just The Way You Are' [both on Bang LP *I Want Candy*] and 'Hand Jive' [Bang 524], the Ugly Ducklings' 'She Ain't No Use To Me' [Yorktown LP *Somewhere Outside*] and the Young Monkey Men's 'I'm Waiting For The Letter' [P&M 3649].

Despite its pervasiveness, however, punk rock always remained essentially a local phenomenon. Too crude, too intense ever to gain mass acceptance, it was none the less an important milestone in the history of rock, for these unsophisticated garage bands not only reintroduced the rawness and energy of R&B into North American popular music, but also revived its use as a vehicle for teenage rebellion.

Folk artist Bob Dylan was a different kind of rebel – a 'protest' singer, whose acerbic compositions had by the mid-sixties already earned him a reputation as spokesman for pacifists and civil rights campaigners across the nation.

Intrigued by the possibilities of fusing folk music with rock, he went 'electric' in 1965, earning the derision of purists and widespread acclaim from everyone else. Many others followed his lead, casting their musical nets ever wider and drawing in influences from other white traditional sources, blues, gospel, rock 'n' roll and (somewhat improbably) even Bo Diddley.

The Byrds, for instance, used his famous beat on 'Don't Doubt Yourself, Babe' [Columbia LP *Mr Tambourine Man*], John Paul Hammond cut fine versions of 'I'm A Man' [Vanguard LP *Big City Blues*], 'I Can Tell' [Atlantic LP *I Can Tell*], 'You Can't Judge A Book By The Cover' [Vanguard LP *So Many Roads*] and 'Who Do You Love' [Vanguard LP *Country Blues*] (the latter two also being covered by Tom Rush on his 1966 Elektra LP *Take A Little Walk With Me*), while New York's Mugwumps reworked 'Book' on their Warner Bros LP *Mugwumps* and expatriate Brit Ian Whitcomb experimented with harmonica, drums and maracas on 'Fizz' [Tower 120].

Remarkably, Dylan himself appears to have been inspired by Diddley time and again, imitating his guitar-chopping technique on 'Mixed Up Confusion' [Columbia 42656], quoting from 'She's Fine, She's Mine' on 'Obviously 5 Believers' [Columbia 43792] and slipping in the immortal line *'She walks like Bo Diddley and she don't need no crutch'* on 'From A Buick 6' [Columbia 43389].

All this renewed interest in Bo Diddley was a very encouraging sign for Bo, and an invitation he received to appear on *The Big TNT Show* in Hollywoood, California on 29 November, 1965* alongside top acts of the day like Joan Baez, the Byrds, Ray Charles, Donovan, the Lovin' Spoonful, the Modern Folk Quartet, the Ronettes and Ike & Tina Turner particularly so – for the entire event was also to be filmed as a sequel to the previous year's immensely successful *TAMI Show* movie.

Even in black and white, Bo's big screen debut was nothing less than glorious as he tore through 'Hey Bo Diddley' and 'Bo Diddley' to rapturous applause from a screaming, hand-jiving audience. Sadly, very few people actually got to see the finished product, because the picture ran into distribution problems shortly after its release in 1966 and received only limited exposure thereafter.

As it turned out, it would all have been too late anyway, for a number of dramatic and far-reaching changes had taken place in the meantime –

---

*This was one of the last occasions that Duchess appeared with the group. She was replaced by Bo's sixteen year old guitarist nephew, Ricky Jolivet, in 1966.

changes that would ensure that rock music would never be the same again. The popularity of marijuana and the hallucinogenic drug, LSD, had spread like wildfire throughout high schools and college campuses during 1965 and 1966, and the Californian city of San Francisco – long a refuge for artistic or political radicals and misfits (popularly known as hippies) – had given birth to a completely new form of music known as 'acid rock'.

An amalgam of folk, blues and punk rock styles impregnated with Eastern, classical and jazz influences, acid rock was conceived as a free flowing, spontaneous musical re-creation of the psychedelic drug experience. Characterised by long, meandering improvisations (frequently discordant, or laden with frantic guitar work), exotic instrumentation (sitars, chimes, bells and so on), electronic effects (notably phasing) and a hazy, relaxed mood, it was a complete antithesis to the driving dance music played by Diddley and his contemporaries, and an arena in which they could not hope to compete.

Once psychedelia had gained national attention via the *Monterey Pop Festival* of 16–18 June, 1967 and the record industry moguls decided that 'flower power' was to be the Next Big Thing, rock 'n' roll's fate was sealed. New idols appeared virtually overnight, while all the old ones – Bo Diddley included – went out of the window.

Understandably, this sudden unwarranted rejection proved to be a painful and bitter experience for Bo. 'Music is a cut-throat business here. I've found that, in this country, they tend to drop you like a hot potato whenever a new thing comes along.[28] Today, it's one thing; six weeks later, it's somebody else. You are *already* a has-been! Cat say: "I make a record. If this one hits, I gotta worry 'bout another one" – an' they ain't got *room* for another one, 'cause the motherfuckers drop you too quick.[10]

'People said I faded out. I didn't *fade out*: they pulled the switch on us![4] We were cut off, like you turn off a lightbulb![7] There was no fade-off of rock 'n' roll, it was a clear *cut*-off. You turn on the radio an' – *boom!* – there's this whole new thing. I said: "Oh-oh, I'm goin' down the drain" – because I heard it before it happened. I *saw* it comin'.[56] When the acid rock thing came in, I was in *big* trouble, man. I couldn't even get a gig playin' for a *cat show*![1]

'I've gotten very bitter about it, an' it's time I said somethin': you see guys get on stage drunk an' dirty, an' it looks like the rowdier you are, the more you're uplifted. I *refuse* to be rowdy. I'm a clean dude,[38] an' I don't fool with no dope. People were *very* upset because I don't do any of these weird things. If you don't smoke joints, an' all this kinda stuff, you're a *square*! I don't dig it. How am I gonna teach my kids the beautiful things of life if I do it? It's my belief that you don't have to do all this to be beautiful.[47]

'Some kids say: "Well, I got problems at home." So, they go out an' swallow a bunch of pills. That is *stupid*! The problem ain't goin' away by your swallowin' pills unless you wanna go to sleep an' *never wake up*! You got to train yourself to see farther than your nose! Maybe drugs won't affect some people, but how can you be *sure*? It might not show up in *you*, but it show up in your *kids*. Then they wonder why their offsprings is screwed-up, an' they're the ones that's *carryin'* it!

'Drugs can leave you screwed up for *life*, man. Reds, downers, all sorts of ol' crap as that. I have no use for people that are dealin' with this type of stuff, because I don't wanna be their victim. You're not a chemist or scientist to tell what some guy is givin' you. You don't know *what* you are takin' when you swallow somethin' that some guy gives you: "Hey man, take this, it'll really *get you off*!"

'Yeah, you might be gone *forever*! You take a cat like Jimi Hendrix. He had everythin' in the *world* goin' for him, an' look what happened: he went an' *blew* himself!

'I guess there was reds an' stuff around back in the fifties, but I was too dumb to know anythin' about 'em. Most of the cats I knew, they'd go an' get a 39¢ bottle of wine, man, an' they'd have more fun than a boatload of mice on a pound of cheese!' (Laughter.) 'A 39¢ pint of wine! An' *everybody'd* have a good time! Was that good, or was that bad? I don't know. All I know is that nobody *died*. What I'm sayin' is: you *can* have a good time! Look how happy I am, an' I ain't takin' *nothin'*!'[1]

Super Blues

The changes in musical fashions proved to be a major headache for Chess – and one which the company never really managed to overcome. Blues, the label's staple, had been decidedly 'out' since the fifties, rock 'n' roll had likewise died a death, and even the R&B/soul hits which had done so much to sustain business throughout the first half of the sixties were now proving increasingly harder to get. Chuck Berry, their biggest seller, had been tempted away from the fold by Mercury's big bucks, and their other stars were by now too old-fashioned to appeal to the mass teenage audience.

Clearly, a drastic rethink of marketing strategy was called for, and September 1965 saw Muddy Waters, Howlin' Wolf and Sonny Boy Williamson quaintly repackaged on LP as *Real Folk Blues* singers, while Bo (whose sharp rock 'n' roller image didn't lend itself to the same treatment) was saluted a year later as *The Originator*.

A sort of musical scrapbook spanning the years 1959–66, the album contained reissues of 'Puttentang' [from *Have Guitar – Will Travel*], 'Pills' [Checker 985], 'Lazy Woman' [from *Bo Diddley & Company*], 'Jo-Ann' [Checker 1083], and the engaging flip of 'Hey Good Lookin'' [Checker 1098], 'You Ain't Bad (As You Claim To Be)', alongside seven previously unreleased gems: 'What Do You Know About Love', one of the most beautiful ballads Bo has ever recorded; 'Limbo' and 'Love You Baby', two frantic rockers left over from the experimental 1959 session with sax ace Gene Barge; 'Yakky Doodle', a song about the Yogi Bear cartoon character recently written by Bo for his daughter; 'Africa Speaks', an unintelligible ethnic chant with percussion accompaniment; the hilarious 'Two Flies' (who cheekily threaten Bo with a cudgel and a knife when he tries to empty their garbage can, but get their come-uppance when he returns armed with some Real-Kill spray); and the brilliant 'Background To A Music', in which Bo impresses a prospective employer by demonstrating how well he can '*background*' various styles and, of course, gets the job!

This superb anthology was the beginning of a concerted effort by Chess to re-establish Bo Diddley with the contemporary rock audience, and the closing months of 1966 witnessed the reissue in stereo of his first LP (rechristened *Boss Man* to avoid confusion with the 1962 *Bo Diddley* album), *Go Bo Diddley* and *Bo Diddley's A Twister* (judiciously retitled *Road Runner*), and the release of a 25-minute black and white featurette funded by the company titled *The Legend Of Bo Diddley*.

'It wasn't a very good movie, 'cause I had started gettin' *smart*! Nobody said nothin' to me about *dollars*, ain't seen no *contract* or nothin', so I wouldn't do anythin' in it, you know.

'Marshall Chess came out to my house in Chicago, an' took some shots of me in my front yard. I had on a brown leather suit, brown hat, an' I was wearin' some guns.

'Later on, they took some shots of me in the studio, an' also at the Le Coq D'or – which was a nightclub in Toronto – but I never knew what happened to that damn thing. It didn't *do* nothin', an' I ain't never seen a *dime*!'[1]

149

An invaluable publicity exercise nonetheless, the film also doubled as a promotional vehicle for Bo's latest single, 'We're Gonna Get Married' [Checker 1142], a powerful slab of wild rock 'n' roll with shrieking girls and crashing guitar breaks. Great, but hopelessly outdated, it was a stiff before it hit the racks.

Clearly, something had to be done to modernise Bo Diddley's sound – but what? The solution lay with Marshall Chess who, at the age of twenty-four, was by now becoming increasingly responsible for determining the company's musical direction: 'I'd started smoking pot, taking LSD, so I was trying to make records for that audience, and at the same time make money for my family – and it *did*! I'll tell you the truth: Muddy Waters *never* made more money than he did on *Electric Mud**. That album sold 150,000 – that's more than it would *ever* have sold, you know. He was thrilled, it *totally* revitalised him, and I did the same thing with Howlin' Wolf.

'You know, it bothered me *horribly* that people put 'em down, but it don't bother me anymore. I find that, when you make records, you don't make 'em to please anyone but *yourself* – otherwise you're in big trouble. And, you make some bad ones, and you make some good ones, you know.

'I guess I shouldn't have maybe used Muddy or Wolf, I should have found some young black guy – because the bands were really, like, the most hip young black musicians around Chicago – but I didn't have no qualms about it: they were experiments. I mean, if you don't take chances making records, you'll never make anything different.

'My father was real pleased with those records: I had *tremendous* opposition, you know, and he liked the fact that I put 'em out and made 'em with *all* the opposition. They sold, and I laughed in the people's faces!' [19]

Chess's influence was indeed unmistakable on Bo's next single, a reworking of Fred Hughes's 1965 hit, 'Oo Wee Baby, I Love You' [Vee-Jay 684] titled simply 'Ooh Baby' [Checker 1158], whose unusual electric violin lead (played by Eddie Drennon**) carried it to No. 17 on the *Billboard* 'Rhythm & Blues' chart and No. 88 in the 'Hot 100' in the early months of 1967. This, however, was little consolation for the indignity of

---

*Muddy's notorious 'psychedelic blues' album (Cadet Concept LP-314) came out in 1968.
**Later a chart artist in his own right (with BBS Unlimited).

being relegated to the role of guitar-playing sideman on one's own record – and the wounds still haven't healed.

'It was a *disaster*! Why you kill my day by mentionin' Marshall Chess? That was one kid I wanted to *choke*, an' still ain't too far off it, y'understand?'[36]

Two days after 'Ooh Baby' entered the charts, Diddley and Drennon were back in the studio cutting a carbon copy follow-up, 'Wrecking My Love Life' [Checker 1168]. This time, sadly, their efforts were in vain, for the single made no impact whatsoever, and Chess discovered that the electric violin sound was not the magic formula he was seeking.

Under constant pressure to come up with something that would sell, Bo had meanwhile been doing some hard thinking himself, and suggested: 'Let's do somethin' *different*: call Muddy Waters an' Little Walter before I come to Chicago, an' set it up with them, an' let's see if we can't do somethin'. All the other record companies are combinin' their artists on albums, so why is it Chess an' Checker can't do it?'[58]

The blues 'super sessions' duly took place in the early weeks of January 1967 under the watchful eye of veteran producer Ralph Bass, and yielded an enjoyable (if somewhat chaotic) 'jam' album containing reworkings of eight of the trio's biggest hits.

Although sales of *Super Blues* were by no means phenomenal, they were encouraging enough for Chess to repeat the experiment in September – this time combining the awesome talents of Bo, Muddy Waters and Howlin' Wolf.

'Muddy, Bo and Wolf stay out of each other's way, step all over each other, laugh at and with each other. They intimidate each other, shrug off and ignore each other, groove on and with each other,' babbled the sleevenotes, though in reality *The Super Super Blues Band* was a comparatively turgid affair, with over-long versions of Waters's 'Long Distance Call', Willie Dixon's 'Little Red Rooster' and 'Spoonful', Robert Nighthawk's 'Sweet Black Angel', and 'St Louis Jimmy' Oden's 'Goin' Down Slow' – thankfully interrupted by the rather livelier 'Ooh Baby'/'Wrecking My Love Life' medley and 'Diddley Daddy'.

'The *Super Blues* albums did pretty nice, but I got tired of Chicago because there wasn't nothin' happenin' – *plus* I was havin' hassles outa Chess, so I moved to Los Angeles*.

---

*Actually to Granada Hills.

'I had to break California open by *movin'* to California! The agency in New York did not book me in California – didn't book me anywhere past Oklahoma City. You got a dividin' line: you work to Oklahoma, then from Oklahoma to California is another country. When I went to California, nobody knew who the hell I was! I had to make a new start for myself.'[1]

Bo's move to the music industry's new capital did not solve his dilemma. His only 1968 release, 'I'm High Again' b/w 'Another Sugar Daddy' [Checker 1200], was a heavy electric mess far below his usual standard and deservedly sank without trace, while his stab at the bubblegum market the following year, 'Bo Diddley 1969' b/w 'Soul Train' [Checker 1213] fared equally badly, despite a first-rate production job by the otherwise successful Kasenetz–Katz outfit.

Forgotten by his fans, unable to get a hit and barely managing to find live work, Bo must have felt as if the whole world were against him, but there was still worse to come. Much, much worse.

'A pencil is worse than a pistol'

'We had a bad accident in California. I wasn't in it, but all the rest of the band was. Some guy hit my bus, knocked it off the San Diego Freeway. My nephew, Ricky Jolivet – which was the guitar player in my group at the time – was drivin', because the driver that I had had been drinkin', an' Ricky took the bus away from him an' was tryin' to bring it back home. This cat ran into the back of him, hit him on the back wheel, an' knocked him down a sixty-foot embankment!

'They was all shook up pretty bad. My guitar got ran over in the middle of the San Diego Freeway: it was flat as a pancake! The man that hit my bus had tore up his car pretty bad, an' I said that, since I was just a little better off, I would offer him a few bucks so he could feed his family. I was tryin' to be nice, you know. When they found out I was Bo Diddley, that turned the whole thing around: "Get *money!*"

'I was sued for a *lotta* money, you know, *big* figures – but I feel I was sued unjustly. I didn't have any insurance, an' I was *wrong* for havin' my vehicle on the highway, but the person that hit me didn't have any insurance either! So, the way I look at it, *both* of us was wrong. I was at home *in bed*, this cat come out of the clear blue sky, tear up *my* bus, break some woman's arm, an' *I* get sued! They were threatenin' to clean me out totally, an' I didn't have no money, man.

'See, all of this happened just after I'd found I was bein' shafted by my manager – which was the *second* time I'd gotten into that type of predicament.

'When I started out in the business, my manager was Dr Jive, but things got so he couldn't handle it, so he turned me over to a dude named Phil Landwehr. They was hooked up in some kinda way.

'To cut a long story short, my lawyer told me one day he'd heard that Phil hadn't paid my taxes, or filed 'em or somethin'. Phil Landwehr got me into a *lotta* problems an' then flew the coop. I haven't seen him since that day, because I politely said: "If I *ever* lay eyes on him again, I'm gonna do somethin' *nasty* to him."

'I *trusted* him! He was bringin' me tax things an' had me sign 'em. So, if he's my manager, I don't have nothin' to worry about: my manager's takin' care of business, all I gotta do is play my rock 'n' roll for people.

'I *know* he got the money from Shaw Artists, 'cause they charged me with it, but he didn't pay my taxes like he was supposed to. He got a $1,200 or $1,300 advance, an' it was *supposed* to have been for taxes. This was told to me by their accountant *and* Mrs Shaw, an' when they heard he hadn't done it, *they* wanted him also. So, he ran out, left me in the trick bag that I was in. But I paid up, an' I'm straight. I got no problem with the government.

'All this shit started *way back*, when I first started in the business. Shaw Artists was the first booking agents I ever had, an' I was with 'em until they folded. From 1955 up until Billy Shaw an' then Lee Shaw, an' then their son, Milt, died. I was with 'em for *years*.

'That was *another* rip-off, 'cause cats was sellin' me for $175 a night, an' they were probably gettin' $1,200 an' puttin' the rest in their pocket, see? I didn't know you could do that, but it's a common practice, because the artist don't know what the contract is. All you do is get it in the mail, an' if you accept the price, you sign. So, yeah, I'm a lil' country boy outa Chicago, don't have no education, an' I ain't never seen more than $50 in one pile at the same time. $175? Man, that looked *good*!

'Back then, Shaw Artists was bookin' me for, like, $700–750 a week – I still got the contracts. I *believe* I was bein' booked for *more*, but Shaw Artists is out of existence now, you dig? But, back then $700 sounded like a lotta money: I'm makin' $700 a week, an' I'm payin' the musicians $35–40 a night. When we all first started, I was payin' 'em $15 a night – because I wasn't makin' but $275, an' had to drive a automobile, eat, an' then send money home for the wife an' babies.

'So, I thought I was *raisin' hell*, workin' four or five nights an' sendin' $200 home a week maybe, but there should have been about another $1,000 with it, 'cause that was probably the goin' price then.

'Phil Landwehr used to keep me workin' in New York *all* the time. I'd be in the Apollo Theater for, like, two weeks at a shot, an' I didn't know it was *his* show! He'd made enough money offa me as manager in a couple of years to start doin' his *own shows*! Then he'd put me on 'em, because I was a guaranteed draw!

'I was *packin'* places, man, people all 'round the block an' stuff. It was really the height of it, an' it was the time to make money. There's just *no way* they were sellin' me for $175, or, if they *were* bookin' me right, an' *not* doin' some crap under the table, I was started off in the wrong price bracket – an' it's *hard* to get out of that rut, because the Musicians' Union cannot set a fee over Scale, an' $175 was over Scale anyway: "Scale is $35, so you done already made $140. What you hollerin' about?"

'When I was younger, I was a person that didn't trust *nobody*. I had a *very* bad inferiority complex, because it looked to me like everythin' I touched turned to shit. I just didn't wanna be bothered with people, just wanted to be left alone. My oldest sister, Lucille, kept talkin' to me an' finally got me out of it. She told me, she says: "You gotta trust *somebody*!" an' I finally said: "Okay."

'I dropped my guard an' – *bam*! – I fell victim to a bad manager which was a thief, an' I wish I had a rubber leg so I could kick myself in the ass for ever bein' involved with a man like that, but how do you know? You never know *who* you are dealin' with, but you *hope* that the man that's handlin' your business is honest. There ain't no way you can keep up with it when you're playin' three hundred gigs a year.

'Okay, so then Frank Kocian, who was the book-keeper for Shaw Artists, got this big idea about managin' me, because I didn't have nobody. So I says: "Hmm, Frank's the *book-keeper*, so he should be able to keep track of my money." It sounded good, man, you know, like what other dude is better to watch stuff than the book-keeper?

'That was the *worst* fuckin' mistake in the *world*! But, see, I wasn't hip to the idea that a book-keeper is worse than a dude with a gun. A *pencil* is worse than a *pistol*, you dig? I went to Europe – it was supposed to have been a promotion tour for an album – an' I caught him stealin' from me!

'Frank would come an' give us all a couple of bucks, an' we'd all go get somethin' to eat, you know, like birds in a fuckin' cage. I didn't dig it, but we were doin' this tour for nothin', to push the record. So, we got to the theater to do a show, an' I seed the promoter come through with another dude. I stopped him, an' I told him I needed an advance because I didn't have enough money with me. The cat looked at me an' says: "Uh? I just gave your manager $2,000 last night."

'I said: "For what?"

'He said: "Well, you worked last night. All together I've given him – I think – $6,000. Where is the guy anyway?"

'I said: "I don't know. He's probably in the hotel."

'So he says: "Well, you sound like you didn't know about this."

'I said: "To tell you the truth, man, I *didn't*, an' I wanna see him. *Quick*!"

'So, they got him on the phone, an' he came an' tried to tell 'em he didn't have the money, that he'd banked it, sent it to America. They told him they was gonna have his ass locked up if he didn't get that money, 'cause they *knew* he didn't send it out on Saturday, y'understand, an' it was too late to do it on Friday, an' he was tryin' to bullshit the people.

'They had to keep me off him, because I wanted to *eat him alive*! This was really the *pits*: this cat was gonna make all this money off of us, an' send us back home with ten bucks in our pocket! So, at that point I just said: "Well, here's *two* in a row! Who is honest? *Who is honest*? How do you find a *honest* manager?"' [1]

The Big One

By this time, Bo Diddley was in dire financial straits and, as if management problems were not enough, the trouble that had been brewing between him and Chess since the early sixties erupted into an ugly and bitter wrangle over allegedly unpaid royalties.

'Nobody was doin' me any favors at that time. I was definitely *not* havin' much fun at Chess, an' it came to where we started lookin' at each other sideways. That started in 1965. I remember that distinctly, because I bought my wife a new Fleetwood gold brougham Cadillac, an' when I bought that Cadillac, the whole shit hit the fan!

'Phil went out in the parking lot 'cause he thought I was pullin' his leg, an' when he seed it, he says: "You beginnin' to act like a *white* boy!"

'I just looked at him an' laughed, an' went off about my business. I didn't think nothin' about it, but I didn't know that I had the Devil in my pocket, an' that one day he was gonna stick me.

'After that, they began tellin' me: "Your records aren't sellin', they have all been returned", an' they would have as many returns down there as they had record sales – but I never got a countin' from the record plant on how many they *pressed*, you dig what I'm sayin'? Later on, I found out why: Chess Records *owned the pressing plant*!

'If they wasn't sellin' no records, why did they keep doin' new contracts? They wasn't *in love* with me, you know: they were makin' *money*!'[1]

'When I first started out recordin' for Chess – an' for years after – I thought they was just sellin' my records in the United States. *Now* I found out they've been sellin' 'em *for years* all over the *world*! I'm sellin' records in Australia, I'm sellin' records in Germany, England, France, Italy, Japan. I don't see this on my statement. Every time I ask 'em: "Where's the foreign royalties?" they tell me it's about eight or nine months behind. I can't live off no "behind", it's gotta be *upfront*! But it's *not* behind: it takes 'em that long to get their lie together, to make it look nice to you.[8]

'I don't appreciate 'em sellin' my records to my fans because, to me, that's a form of rippin' 'em off: my fans buy my records because they like *me*, y'understand? It's a form of helpin' Bo Diddley. Man, it *hurts* me to take a *dime* from anybody, but they *survived* on doin' this to other people!

'There's a *lotta* things that went on, man, that *nobody* knew about. Like, if you produce a record, or you co-write it, you supposed to get paid. My wife produced the *Gunslinger* album, but she never got any recognition from Chess for it, an' somebody else picked up the producer's fees on it – which was *another* fraudulent thing that they did. These people just took money an' stuck it in their pocket 'cause we didn't know anythin' about the business.

'One girl that worked in the accounting department at Chess Records was ordered to stop talkin' to me because they was afraid that she was gonna tell me somethin'. She *wanted* to tell me, but she was afraid because Phil an' Leonard Chess had the whole goddamn building *bugged*!

'They say it's hearsay, but I *know* it! They would do all these funny little things like go to the corner, pick up a phone, push a button an' listen in. I never said anythin', so they figured I didn't know what it was. When they moved to East 21st Street*, that's when that started happenin'.

---

*The building at 320 East 21st Street was officially opened in March 1967.

'When they started buyin' radio stations an' stuff, I began to wonder where they was gettin' the money from. Now, after I'm older, I've figured it out: they used *my* money, an' Muddy Waters's, an' Willie Dixon's, an' everybody else they never paid.

'Jimmy Rogers got shafted around by Chess Records. They got rid of him *right quick* because he started to askin' about money. They did Willie Mabon the same way. Anybody that start to askin' about money, you just didn't hear of 'em anymore.

'I figured these cats was just causin' problems – but what really made me realize what was goin' on was, I started hearin' less Bo Diddley records bein' played on the station that *they owned**! They was tryin' to cut my throat *quick*, popularity wise. You know: let's shut this nigger down, because this nigger is *dangerous*!'

'I remember I had one record, 'Bo Meets The Monster', which was a *disaster*, a total *bomb*. The dude earned $1,800 in the publishing! *This* is what told me I had a lotta money layin' around: not no million, but maybe two or three – an' that's *after* taxes! I'm *serious*!'

'So, I had the Library Of Congress do a search on all of my tunes, an' they found some with "Eddie McDaniel" on 'em. Who the hell is *Eddie* McDaniel? Nobody's name should appear on a composition that didn't write it, an' there can't be *that* many mistakes. The woman there told me: "We don't make mistakes in this building. We double-check and double-check, and then somebody checks my work, and we keep the papers that we took it from."

'Now, maybe Eddie McDaniel *is* gettin' my check, but I don't think Eddie McDaniel is gettin' no check, y'understand?

'I never got *nothin'* from Arc Music for the song 'Bo Diddley' – which was *another* rip-off. They always said to me: "It's a PD** song, Bo. We can't pay you on that." All those other cats that made 'Bo Diddley', I believe Arc sold 'em the rights to do it – but, if you look there on the record label you won't find "Arc Music" anywhere, you dig what I'm sayin'? They'd do it through somebody else, so nobody could trace the money that was comin' in off the song.[1]

'They finally admitted that the song is mine by signin' a release for it to be used in that *Fritz The Cat* movie – because how can they give someone

---

*WVON.
**Public Domain.

permission to use somethin' which they say they don't own?[59] So I said: "That's cool, but where's the bread?"

'Arc told me: "If you think we're beatin' you, *sue* us!"

'They knew I couldn't sue 'em, 'cause I didn't have shit to sue 'em *with*! A lawyer will want $5,000 up front before he'll even take somethin' like that, an' I didn't have no doggone money. I knew they was rippin' me off, an' couldn't do anythin' about it!

'You know what happened? I ended up sellin' 'em my songs! It was the *last* thing I wanted to do, but I had gotten into a problem with a house that I had bought, an' the people was gonna sue me if I didn't come up with the bread.

'I'd bought a fourteen room *mansion* in Chicago.' (Laughs.) 'That sucker had eight bedrooms, eight *bathrooms* in it! It was my *dream*! See, I had always been raised up in Chicago, an' we all had to sleep in the same bed crammed in one room, an' stuff of that sort. I said if I *ever* got my hands on enough money, I was gonna buy me a *big* house, so that my family would not have to sleep all over each other. Everybody would have their *own* room. Leonard an' them guaranteed me $10,000 a year, an' I figured in five years I'd have the house paid for, so I bought this monster!

'One night, I sat up tryin' to figure out how we was payin' for this doggone thing. I worked it out the best I could usin' my little dots an' lines, but the figures got a little too big for me, so I went to ask Kay.

'We was payin' a house note which was $521 a month, but only $49 of it was goin' toward me *ownin'* it! The rest of it was *interest*! It looked good when the guy had wrote it on a piece of paper, but I *never* would have paid for that sonofabitch! I'da been *four hundred years old*!' (Laughter.)

'Leonard an' Phil had me right where they wanted me, because they were the *only* people I could get any money from. I would rather have *borrowed* money from a bank an' paid interest, but I couldn't borrow nothin' from nobody 'cause I was a musician.

'You go to a bank an' say: "I need $10,000." "What are you, some kinda nut? Where you work at? How long you been there?" "Uh – I'm a musician." "*What*? Well, er, wait a minute: I'll go speak to Mr So-an'-so-an'-so."

'Cat go in the back an' say: [whispers] "...musician... yeah..."

'Other cat say: "Musician? *No way*!"

'So he say: "But he's *Bo Diddley*!" "What? Bo Diddley? What's he need $10,000 for? He should *have* 10,000!"

'You dig what I'm sayin'? This is what came out of the bank executive's mouth. Then, I get sick in the stomach, because I know *exactly* what they're thinkin'. I *shouldn't* be there! I even feel shitty goin' down there to ask 'em for it!

'If I'da got paid what's due to me, I wouldn't have needed to sell my songs. They found out I was in a trick bag an' said: "We'll buy some of 'em from ya!" I *needed* the bread, an' I couldn't get it anyplace else, so I made a deal with Arc, sold 'em my rights in everythin' I'd written up until then.

'Chess Records helped a lotta people, an' then destroyed 'em: led you to a trough of poisoned water. In other words: lead you to success, an' you don't reap the rewards that success is supposed to bring.

'Take David Essex for instance, an' 'Rock On'. The dude made a lotta money offa that, I understand, an' now he's into a whole lotta other things from just that one record: he was dealin' with *honest* people. I've been out here forty fuckin' years, an' what am *I* doin'? I don't mind that I'm still *workin'*, but what am I *doin'*?

'I was *happy*, because I thought they were *honest*. I'm not happy anymore. I've got a name that's all over the fuckin' world, everybody knows who the hell I am – an' I *thank* Leonard an' them for givin' me the chance to make somethin' of myself, but I ain't got no love for 'em on the part where they ripped me off. We made *agreements* on a piece of paper. I just want what I *worked* for.'[1]

Needless to say, Marshall Chess strenuously denies Diddley's allegations: 'I don't think there was any ripping off at all. We paid *low* royalties, but everyone did, you know. I used to see my father go through all the royalty statements, and all I ever saw him do was *once* take money from one artist and give it to another because *he* needed the money to *live*. But I'll say this: they were 2–3 percent artists' royalties, all these cheap royalties.

'We paid Union Scale, you know, we paid Union sessions. We used to cut a tune an hour: three-hour sessions, three tunes. The leader would get double, and his band would get single. Or, if the band owned him money, he'd get all their checks. That's the side that no one ever tells, you know? An artist will say that we stole from him; how about when he took all the checks from his band?

'You know, I think at the end of it all there wasn't *any* artists that wasn't in the red to us. We *buried* Little Walter! You know something? They owed us a *lot*! They came in *all* the time: every time they needed something, they came in.

'You have to understand, we were dealing with people from the South, illiterate people, *wild* people. Drink! Partying! Little Walter had all these vicuna coats, buying Cadillacs and rings. $70,000 they could spend in *two days*, you know, shootin' dice. *Shootin' dice*! They'd be drunk and lose all their money, and two days later they'd be saying: "You cheated me", because they wanted more money.

'People don't realize this. Everyone looks at 'em like these old folk singer-type guys. *No way*! They were women-beaters, you know, wild, "cowboy" kinda people. These guys wasn't what you think. These were dice-shootin'... "motherfuck" was *every other word*, man! Since I'm five years old, all I've heard is "motherfucker". *All* I heard was "motherfucker". They used to send my father Mother's Day cards on Mother's Day, that's how much that word was used!

'Bo Diddley's disappointed me a lot. I've seen a lot of interviews when he's said a lot of bad shit, and I think that's really uncalled for, because I *know* what went down with him: he used to *suck* money out, you know. Bo Diddley thought *everyone* was cheating him!' [19]

Bo, however, remains unswayed by Chess's denials: 'Sure, I went through a spendthrift era, buyin' a lotta crap, like things that I didn't have when I was a kid. I bought a motorcycle, an' I used to buy these little model airplanes an' crash 'em in the ground but, you know, we're not even talkin' 'bout $10,000. When I bought Cadillacs an' stuff like that, I bought 'em from *workin'*, not from what I got from Chess. The payments I got from Chess were a *joke*!

'The reason why I've been tellin' everybody about this, is because I thought I'd wake somebody up, an' they'd get a little scared an' say: "Let's send him a check for $10,000 or somethin'. Maybe that'll keep him quiet."

'If they had been smart at that time, they probably would have got away with it, because I had no idea how much stuff there was that was runnin' loose.

'But I never got no check, an' so I've been gatherin' stuff for a *long* time. You know: in order to whup a giant, you gotta have a big rock – an' I got a motherfuckin' *MOUNTAIN*!!!

'These people go to church, hide behind the Good Book. They don't *believe* in the Bible: it's just to make you think they're real straight – an' they're the biggest crooks in the world! If these people die an' go to Heaven, I'm goin' *higher*! I ain't been no *angel* in life, but I ain't never done *this* – I don't do this to other people. I figure if you make a deal with someone, then give the man what you told him you was gonna do.

'I was on the point of *doin'* somethin', an' I thank God that I had my family, because if it hadn't've been for them, I feel I might have done somethin' *drastic* to these people.

'I *saw* what happened to Little Walter! The man to me was the greatest – an' he was also a great friend – but he started drinkin'. He got his last two cuts out of Chess because I begged 'em to give him a chance! I told 'em: "He *ain't* finished. The man is *down*, an' he needs helpin' *up*. You cats have made all of this money off of him, an' now you gonna shove him out the door because he drink a little liquor?"

'Walter was in bad trouble mentally. I don't mean he was *crazy* or nothin' like that, but he'd got run down an' lost all dignity of himself, lost all his self-control, because of the same stuff that is goin' down with me now – except that he had it earlier, an' with less records. He just didn't *care* anymore, an' it was a tragedy that should never have been.*

'You can say that you understand a person's feelings when they're hurtin', but really you don't. People say: "Water under the bridge." I was usin' that for a while, then I says: "That's *bullshit*! Uh-uh, there ain't *nobody* gettin' away *that* easy! I *worked* for this! This is what's supposed to come from *my talent*. I've been *fortunate*, but I can't go back an' be twenty-six again. I haven't anythin' to lay back on, to spring back from another direction an' do somethin' else, because everythin' changed on me. I can't go get a *job*.

'I would like to be able *not* to depend on the government to send me out a old-age pension every month: that's the only reason why I've been workin' so hard, an' it look like I've been workin' for nothin' so far. It makes me wanna crawl in a corner somewhere an' just *die*! Everybody say: "It's over an' done with. *Forget* about it!" I don't feel that way: it's my life. It's my fuckin' *life*!'[1]

---

*Walter suffered a rapid artistic decline during the sixties because of his alcoholism, and his resulting slide from popularity only made his habit worse. His unhappy life finally ended on 15 February, 1968 when he died from injuries sustained in a drunken brawl.

Stalemate

'I was in Los Angeles an' walked up to the elevator an' pushed the button. The doors opened, an' Etta James walked out of it. She had tears in her eyes, an' she says: "Do you know Leonard sold Chess Records? Can you *believe* that, Bo?"

'I said: "No, somebody bought *in* on him or somethin'... "

'She said: "No man, they *sold* the company! Can you believe that shit? What's gonna happen to everybody?"

'This is exactly what she said. She had tears in her eyes – because Etta was, at that time, tryin' to kick that drug habit that she had gotten herself involved in.[1]

'Then I found out they *had* sold the company, an' nobody told anybody. A man doesn't *have* to, but I think it's *courtesy* to tell the artists: "Hey, look, we're sellin' out. Do y'all wanna stay here with the new people?" They didn't tell nobody *nothin'*!

'Course, I wouldn't have left no way, you know. I had no *intention* of leavin'.[3] Chess was always good to me. We laughed, we talked, you know – an' that's what took me in. I never got the impression that they were bein' dirty, because we were all – uh – look like one big happy family.

'I think Muddy had the same problem I got, but in a different way. Take it like this: a bunch of winos hang on the corner by an old liquor store, an' they hustle bottles for ten or fifteen years, an' they're buyin' wine from this store. Finally, the guy closes the place, gives the place a facelift, new bricks around the front. When the winos find out the joint's still open, they come back, an' he's behind the counter with a *suit* on. He done made all this money offa these winos, but now he doesn't want 'em in the door, you dig? Is this *right*?

'Well, Chess did the same thing to us: we walked in there one mornin', an' they had a receptionist sittin' out there in the front. Over the weekend they'd built a little booth, an' the guy had installed a buzzer on the damned door. When I walked in, the girl asked me: "Who should I say...?"

'I said: "What *is* this shit?"

'That was to keep us from just walkin' into Leonard's office. I think it should have been just privileged artists: me – well, *first* of all, Muddy Waters, Little Walter, Howlin' Wolf.

'Wolf kicked the door off its hinges, an' I hear tell Billy Stewart blasted it with a gun, but I kinda accepted it in a way an' didn't raise no hell about it. They had a *right* to put that up there, but I still think there should have been exceptions, otherwise they shouldn't have started off with us in that way.

'When they moved from 2120, bought the new buildin' down on East 21st, that's when things got really weird an' they fell on their face.'[1]

By all accounts, the Chess family business had outgrown itself, losing the very intimacy upon which its success depended. Paul Gayten, long-time talent scout for the company, watched the rot set in...

'Leonard's timing was good to sell out: he was *too* big. Leonard had a lot of things going: two or three radio stations, four record companies*. He couldn't put his hands on everything. He and Phil couldn't take care of it: they couldn't trust everybody.

'GRT approached him – I was right there when they approached him. A *lot* of people wanted to buy. He wanted out of the business because we'd got too big: we had too many artists. He couldn't have that rapport with everybody. Leonard wanted to see *everybody*. I used to call him – I had a *private* line – and *I* couldn't get him half the time!'[60]

On the day of the take-over, Gayten went into retirement but Bo stayed on, only to witness the systematic dismembering of the company by its new owners.

'At first, when GRT moved in, I didn't understand what was happenin', but I knew it was a fuck-up, because they had a bunch of dudes sittin' around a table with slide-rules, tryin' to count how much money they was goin' to make. Leonard didn't run that business that way!

'When they came in, Chess was *boomin'*! They decided to change everythin' an' started to *demand* payment from customers! Leonard *never* demanded stuff from his customers!

'He'd say: "Hey man, just send me a check for what you got." This is the way Leonard used to do business, an' they wasn't *hurtin'*, they used to get their money.

'So, when GRT started this bullshit, cats said: "Hey man, fuck you! I ain't dealin' with *you*!" an' they wouldn't buy Chess products. That led to a decline in sales.

'Leonard was mad about it, too. He used to walk around, say: "It's *crazy* in there!" It was pathetic, but there wasn't nothin' he could do about it.

'I don't know the exact reason why they sold, but the big talk was that they signed up the Five Blind Boys, an' Don Robey sued 'em, an' won a

---

*Chess, Checker, Cadet and Janus.

lotta money from 'em*. GRT was lookin' for somebody to buy, an' Chess was a prime target.'[1]

Whatever the reasons, Marshall Chess for one was not at all happy about selling out. 'The record business was always just – you know, that was *it*. For me, that was *all* there was, you know? I was raised with the idea that there was a family business to be left, and I *wanted* it that way, but I was out-voted by my father and my uncle, and their wives, who desperately wanted them to get out of that business. They thought they'd see more of their husbands, you know – which never really happened.

'My uncle's still alive. I guess for him, it did change his life. My father had already left the record business at the time when we sold it. He was in the radio business, and died shortly after**.

'Before my father died, he'd already sold WVON, but it hadn't been signed yet. After he died, we finished the sale. Then my uncle bought this other radio station we had, WSDM – which was the FM side of it – from my mother and I. Then he sold *that*, and now he's in real estate and horses out in Arizona. My uncle's a *cowboy* now, believe it or not!

'The publishing is still owned by my mother and my uncle, and the other two partners, Gene and Harry Goodman – which is Benny Goodman's two brothers: my father and my uncle felt they needed a New York publisher. It was a very complex business thing where they initially really only worked on cover records. They really had nothing to do with the new work: they only shared in what other artists did of those songs, not what Chess artists did. It was a complex deal.'[19]

Leonard Chess's death marked the end of an era. After GRT moved in, Phil stayed on to handle A&R, while Marshall concentrated on production work - but the arrangement proved short-lived. 'They made me president, because they wanted my uncle out of there. Then they started really to manipulate me and piece-by-piece dismantle this organisation. They were going to dismantle Chess Records, not even knowing what it was to begin with! I became very frustrated and I quit on the spot.'[19]

Before the Chess family were finally ousted, however, Bo managed to cut one more record under their auspices – a fine 'greasy soul' album called *The Black Gladiator*'.

---

*The Five Blind Boys Of Mississippi were still under contract to Peacock Records of Houston at the time.
**16 October, 1969.

'I just decided to do somethin' *different*. Everybody was wearin' funny lookin' crap – Isaac Hayes had come out with chains an' stuff on, an' it was kinda flowin' in that area at that particular time – so I got me some belts an' stuff, an' said I was the *Black Gladiator*, you know.'[1]

Surrounded by funky guitars, tambourines and a churchy organ, Bo sounded fresher and more exciting than he had done in years – an impression reinforced by the topicality of titles like 'Hot Buttered Blues' (a tribute to Chicago's musicians), 'Black Soul' and 'Funky Fly', and the subject matter of 'Shut Up, Woman' (a parody of male chauvinism wittily set to the 'I'm A Man' riff) and the racial harmony 'message', 'If The Bible's Right'. But there were flashes of the old Bo too, like the two amusingly overblown self-promotions, 'Power House' and 'You, Bo Diddley', another recycled toast ('Elephant Man'), and the unusual 'I Don't Like You', a hilarious signifying exchange between Bo and his 'sassy woman', topped off with some of the craziest operatic singing this side of Screamin' Jay Hawkins.

His partner on the latter track was the beautiful Cornelia Redmond, last remaining survivor of numerous Bo-ettes line-ups, who was by now becoming an increasingly important part of his act: 'People are always askin' me about her, 'cause she looked good on stage, an' she added a lot to what I was doin'. I taught her how to be comical: she was a good lookin' chick an', puttin' up with all the crap I was gonna be talkin' 'bout her, she had to be *together*. You can't find too many girls who'll do a comical act on stage where the dude's gonna be talkin' about 'em: they can't hack it.[4]

'She is the only one who stayed from the original group. When things got very bad, with a gig every week or every two weeks, everybody started driftin' away. They said: "Man, I can't live on *this*!"[61] That's how I lost Clifton James: he was a *very* important member of the group – the *foundation* of the 'Bo Diddley' beat – but I didn't have any money, so I had to let him go.'[1]

'Connie was a *helluva* entertainer, an' I saw this an' persuaded Chess to let her make a record*. We came up with the name "Cookie Valdez" for her, but after we found out that people was havin' problems with it, we shortened it to "Cookie V."**. The songs were arranged by a piano player

---

*'You Got The Wrong Girl' b/w 'Queen Of Fools' [Checker 1222], recorded and released in mid-1969.
**The spelling was subsequently altered to 'Cookie Vee' in 1970.

from California that was a hippy or somethin', an' he played on 'em too. I wasn't on the record, but I produced it.

'They let me do that – I think – to pacify me, because I had so much confidence in the girl, but they didn't do anythin' with it. As far as I know, they didn't even try to get it played, 'cause they sold the company right after that.'[1]

Sadly, a similar fate also befell the excellent *Black Gladiator* album, which appeared only in the USA and was quickly strangled by chronic under-promotion, dragging Bo Diddley further down the path to obscurity.

Chapter 8

I've Had It Hard

On The Road Again

As psychedelia and the sixties faded out together, underground music fragmented into a variety of 'hard' and 'soft' rock styles, but remained essentially committed to its traditions of eclecticism and experimentation with many 'progressive' musicians began returning to their roots – blues, gospel, jazz, country, folk and rock 'n' roll – for inspiration, rekindling a widespread interest in their original exponents in the process.

Of the rock 'n' rollers, Chuck Berry had succeeded in maintaining the highest public profile – thanks largely to commendable efforts like his 1967 Mercury album with the Steve Miller Band, *Live At The Fillmore Auditorium*, and 1969's experimental *Concerto In B. Goode* [also on Mercury] – but Bo Diddley was not far behind, his music and reputation having been kept alive in the late sixties by adventurous reinterpretations of his compositions like Captain Beefheart's 'Diddy Wah Diddy' [A&M 794], the Blues Magoos' 'Who Do You Love' [Ganim 1000], Canned Heat's 'Pretty Thing' [Janus LP *Vintage*], David Clayton-Thomas's 'Say Bossman' [Decca 32556], the Great Impostors' 'Who Do You Love' [Dad's 102], the Haunted's 'Mona' [Jet 4002], Kaleidoscope's 'You Don't Love Me' [Epic LP *Beacon From Mars*], the Litter's 'I'm A Man' [Warwick LP *Distortions*],

Rabbit Mackay's 'Somebody Beat Me' [UNI 55112], the Quicksilver Messenger Service's 'Mona' and ambitious 'Who Do You Love Suite' [both on Capitol LP *Happy Trails*], the Mood's 'Who Do You Love' [Cove QC-467], the Sonics' 'I'm A Man' [Jerden LP *Introducing*], the 13th Floor Elevators' 'Before You Accuse Me' [International Artists 113] the Yellow Payges' 'I'm A Man'/'Here 'Tis' medley [UNI LP *Volume 1*] and the Youngbloods' 'I Can Tell' [RCA-Victor LP *Earth Music*], and equally inspired adaptations like Captain Beefheart's 'Mirror Man' [Buddah LP *Mirror Man*], Big Brother & The Holding Company's 'Women Is Losers' [Mainstream LP *Big Brother & The Holding Company*], the Chocolate Watch Band's 'Gone & Passes By' [Tower LP *No Way Out*], Driving Stupid's 'The Reality Of (Air) Fried Borsk' [ICR 0116], the Electric Prunes' 'Get Me To The World On Time' [Reprise 564], Tommy Jett's 'Groovy Little Trip' [Jox 060], the Life's 'Snake Bite' [Hi 2138], Love's 'Bummer In The Summer' [Elektra LP *Forever Changes*], Ken Stella's 'Hey Hey, Where You Goin'' [Decca 32486], Steppenwolf's 'Magic Carpet Ride' [Dunhill 4161] and 'Round & Down' [Dunhill LP *At Your Birthday Party*], the Stooges' 'Little Girl' [Electra LP *The Stooges*], and Tony Joe White's 'Soul Francisco' and 'Don't Steal My Love' [both on Monument LP *Black & White*], and 'Woodpecker' and 'I Want You' [on Monument LP *...Continued*].

The time for a comeback was drawing ever closer, and Bo's fortunes received a massive boost when (along with Chuck Berry, Little Richard and Jerry Lee Lewis) he was invited to appear at the *Toronto Rock 'n' Roll Revival* on 13 September, 1969. *NME's* Roy Carr reported...

> *'The festival proved to be one of the very best of this season's events. This was not just another Pop On A Summer's Day featuring the very latest "in" names; it was a historic get-together, with producers John Brower and Ken Walker assembling a cavalcade of the original innovators of pop music through to the Southern Cajun styles of Tony Joe White and Doug Kershaw, the jazz–rock fusions of the Chicago Transit Authority, the revived rock sounds of Cat Mother & The All-Night Newsboys, the antics of Screaming Lord Sutch, the outlandish theatrics of Alice Cooper, the sombreness of the Doors – and the Plastic Ono Band, which managed to embrace all these influences and throw in a few of their own.*
>
> *'With the temperatures way up in the eighties, MC Kim Fowley*

introduced Bo Diddley, who immediately set the pace for the remainder of the day. Sporting one of his famous guitars, he romped through a selection of his better-known songs such as 'Love Is Strange', 'Hey Bo Diddley', 'Mona', 'Have Mercy' and 'Live It Like You Feel It'... Actually, Bo & Co did an extra set when Junior Walker failed to show.'[62]

Fronting a trimmed-down band consisting of Chester Lindsey (bass), Clifton James (drums) and a mini-skirted Cookie Vee (vocals and tambourine), Bo was an instant hit with the 25,000-strong crowd at the Varsity Stadium. This welcome exposure was not confined solely to the youngsters who attended the festival, either, for the entire event was also filmed Monterey Pop-style by director Donn A. Pennebaker.

With its hand-held camera work and intimate on-stage shots, *Sweet Toronto* contained some of the most exciting footage ever assembled of rock 'n' roll's superstars in action, and was released in 1970* to great critical acclaim.

Although Bo's appearance in the movie was disappointingly brief (reportedly because the camera crew was unprepared and missed most of his act), his energetic renditions of 'Hey Bo Diddley' and 'Bo Diddley' were generally well received by the contemporary rock audience. He quickly realised, however, that he would have to cultivate a more with-it image if he was to retain his new-found credibility.

'I was always groomed-up to be the nice-lookin', clean-cut rock 'n' roller with the lil' tuxedo on, an' the ruffled shirts with a bow-tie, an' the patent-leather shoes – which is *great*! Now, I'm tryin' to figure out how I'm goin' to penetrate this new wave of music that's come in – this is the "tied 'n' died" jeans era, you dig?

'So, I went out an' bought me some jeans, tied 'em all up, bleached 'em an' everythin', put 'em on, jumped on the stage in San Francisco, an' the kids went *berserk*: "Aaaaargh!!!"'

'I says: "Hey, I'm in!"' (Laughs.)

'I did that because of an incident which happened to me when I was waitin' to do the *Mike Douglas Show* over in Philly. I was standin' in the hallway with my $200 suit on, waitin' to go on, an' the guy passed by me

---

*An edited version showcasing the talents of Bo, Chuck Berry, Little Richard and Jerry Lee Lewis, *Keep On Rockin*, followed in 1972.

an' says: "Uh, Bo, when you gonna change?"

'This was in the seventies, when cats was goin' on television with sweatshirts on, an' *dirty* jeans, all raggedy, you know, hair all over their heads an' stuff, an' I thought this was the *worst* thing in the world, you know. How can the public accept you lookin' like *that*? I came from the old school. You did *not* do that, y'understand? You wore a *tie*. If you'da jumped up on the Apollo stage in 1955 or '56 – even 1965 – lookin' like that, Bobby Schiffman woulda run you outa the theater out onto 125th Street! You did *not* do that!

'An' so, it was kinda hard for me, after bein' groomed an' taught this is what you do, to accept it. To tell you the truth, when cats start goin' on TV like they do today, I think it's *ridiculous*! I'm not gonna bite my tongue about it: I don't like it, an' it hurts my feelings, but if I've *gotta* do this to make money, then I have to fall in line – otherwise I'll be standin' on the outside lookin' in, you dig?

'So, the guy asked me: "Aren't you going to change?" I thought he was bein' funny, but then he says: "You gonna wear *that* shit?"

'Man, I got just about hot enough to *fight*! I looked down an' says: "What's *wrong* with me? I'm goin' on television, it's goin' to be shown all over Philadelphia, an' probably New York too."

'I could *not* be a total disgrace to the profession that I was in, but I guess that's the way it goes. I'm tryin' to accept it.

'After that incident, I started lookin' for somethin' I could wear on stage. I went to play a big jazz an' rock festival with Ike & Tina Turner, Santana, Sly & The Family Stone, an' a whole host of others, an' I saw Ike come out on stage with this hat on his head. I says: "Now, if *that* dude can get away with that, I know darn well *I* can!"' [1]

The change of image worked, and the broad-brimmed stetson has remained on Bo's head ever since. A string of bookings followed, including one in the summmer of 1971 supporting chart sensations Creedence Clearwater Revival – a tour he would in all honesty prefer to forget.

'My name wasn't mentioned on a single billboard in the country! I didn't necessarily like that.[25] Then, the suckers got *nasty*: there was only one of 'em that would talk to me – he was really nice – but the other two had *attitudes*, you know, an' I think they got on *his* shit.

'I said: "You're makin' all the money, an' I'm just the goddamn warm-up band, but, since you wanna be stuck up,[1] I might as well go out there an' warm up the stage!"

'So, I tried to *set it on fire* everywhere I went![25] They *really* hated me then – 'cause I had pulled some shit outa the bag that they didn't even know I had, an' made it *hard* for their ass to get off stage!'[1]

Cops & Robbers

'The year 1971 was also the year that I became a cop. We moved to a place called Los Lunas, New Mexico – near Albuquerque – an' I didn't see nothin' 'round there but Anglos, an' indians, an' Chicanos. No blacks. So I says: "Here I am, a mixed marriage, movin' in here. Hmm, great. I'll go an' try to do somethin' for the neighborhood, or the area." So, I went up to the Police Department to find out if I can join.

'I became a cop, an' I think it was very successful. I was Deputy Sheriff for two and a half years in the Valencia County Citizens' Patrol. I had the keys to the jailhouse, a revolver, an' the whole dress gear. There should be a lot more of these type of patrols, 'cause the police can't be everywhere all the time, an' there are a lot of respectable citizens who can look out.

'I gave the Citizens' Patrol in my county three Highway Patrol pursuit cars, because the equipment that we were usin' had seen its days, an' we couldn't get the County to come up with more bread for what we needed. I had access to obtainin' police cars from Los Angeles, 'cause a friend of mine had a club there which I played that was next to a used car lot. He asked me: "How much do you want?"

'I say: "I don't want no money, man. I want that car right there, an' that one over there."

'I had all the little nicks an' dents taken out, had 'em painted, an' then my cousin drove 'em from Los Angeles to New Mexico, an' I gave 'em to the Citizens' Patrol. They freaked out,' (laughs) 'because, here is a black dude just moved into the neighborhood – all of the whites that was there, nobody was interested in tryin' to help, an' I came in just like that, you know. I told 'em there wasn't any strings attached, it's just that I could do this, an' felt it *should* be done, so I *did* it. I ended up givin' 'em three in all.

'I'm a very law abidin' citizen. I'm in Florida now*, an' I'm thinkin' 'bout tryin' to start a Citizens' Patrol in Florida. We need one *bad*, because a *lot* of criminals are around in the streets when the cops ain't around, an' by the time the officers get there, the criminals is *gone*!

'I used to be the dude that didn't like cops, but they sure look good

---

*Bo moved to his ranch near Hawthorne, Florida in 1978.

when somebody's whuppin' on your head. The reason why I used to be that way is, there's a *lotta* policemens that are very *arrogant*. They don't realize that they were once teenagers, just the same as the kids they're harassin'. The harassin' – I guess – just came normal to black kids in Chicago: you didn't have to be *doin'* anythin'.

'I had gotten very funky about policemens because I figured they were out there to *help* us, you know, not to be jumpin' on me for somethin' I didn't do, an' didn't know nothin' about. A *lot* of that happened to me: "Oh yeah? It sound like somethin' you did!" *Sound* like somethin' I did? That's not a thing to put on a person! I just thought it was *horrible*! I've got a dent in the back of my head now from gettin' hit with a blackjack for standin' on the damned street-corner! I'm a *citizen*! That gives me the *right* to stand on that corner! I wasn't doin' *nothin'*! So, for a while, I hated every cop I seen, because I thought every one was the same way.

'A lotta cops durin' that time came from the South, which was super-redneck people, y'understand? You didn't have to be *black* for 'em to hate you: if you wasn't for what they was, they hated you. They were strictly head-busters: this is the way they were taught. A lot of 'em couldn't read or write, but: "If you can bend a horseshoe, you *my* man! Let's make him a *Sergeant* in the Police Department!" – this is what was goin' on.

'One of the cops around Chicago at that time was Two-Gun Pete. He was a *bad* man. He was black, an' he was known for beatin' up black kids – this was his shot. He was a *very* evil man, an' I'm pretty sure I heard people say he'd killed a *lotta* people. He was already, like, forty or fifty years old when I was a kid.

'He once got a hold to me: I was walkin' down the street, an' it was kinda late in the evenin'. I had on a brand new zoot suit, an' I was *sharp*, y'understand? I was *clean*!' (Laughs.) 'The cops pulled up in their car an' Pete says: "You a *jitterbug*, aintcha?" He tore my pants leg, told me he didn't wanna catch me out there no more with that suit on. I thought that was the *worst* thing in the *world* for him to do that. Who was *he*?

'There was another policeman in Chicago called Indian Joe, an' he was also classified as a *very* mean policeman in the black community. An' also the three Seabury brothers.' (Laughs.) 'We used to call 'em the "King Cole Trio". They patrolled the South Side, an' they'd beat on your head till the cows come home. They called that "keepin' law an' order", but I feel that they overstepped their power.

'Lemme tell you 'bout the time I got gassed in Washington, DC: this was in the sixties, an' the colleges was raisin' hell about somethin' or another. I was there to play a gig, an' the cops ran everybody down the street that we was playin' on. We're inside playin'. All of a sudden, the doors fly open, an' all the people run in with the cops after 'em.

'This dude walked up on the stage an' told us: "The dance is over!" Just snatched the mike: "Pack up an' get outa here. You got fif-teen minutes!" Threw the microphone on the floor. Big tall dude dressed in black leather, with a helmet over his face, an' a big stick, an' a riot gun over his shoulder. The cat acted just like a German stormtrooper – just imagine how them people treated people back in the Second World War. I mean they spoke, an' the next thing, they shot you with no explanation or nothin'.

'I says: "Sir, there's no way we can pack this up..."

'He says: "You can be packin' while you're talkin' to me. You got *fifteen minutes* to vacate this joint!"

'So, we start packin', an' I *know* my life is fixin' to end, because I've never been in any shit like this *in my life*! We look outside, an' there's a *riot* in the street! The cops was firin' tear-gas, or salt-an'-pepper gas, or somethin' – which burns the eyes, it burns your throat, an' you can't breathe it. The stuff was seepin' through people's windows, goin' into their houses. Man, people was tryin' to put paper, an' towels an' shit along their doors an' stuff, an' the stuff was *still* gettin' in!

'I jump in this cat's car, lock the door, an' I figure I'm saved, 'cause no air's gonna come in unless we open the vents. We had to go down a one-way street, an' here's cops standin' all over the road with these big tear-gas guns in front of 'em. They shot one, an' it hit right under the car. We were all sittin' in there, cryin': the driver couldn't see, so I was bein' his eyes.

'After we got across the bridge out of DC into Virginia, we ran into a restaurant that said "White this way, black this way", y'understand? All three of us burst in the door, ran down the stairs, an' into the "white" bathroom, puttin' water in our eyes, you know. I'm standin' there with two white dudes: we're all in the same shit together.

'So, this dude comes down there, gonna throw us all out because we done broke the code. I wasn't supposed to *be* with 'em in the first place: in Virginia that was a no-no. Not two white cats an' one black one in the "white" bathroom that didn't set too good.

'We told him: "Man, we've been *gassed* out there! They're *riotin'* in DC!"

'An' the cat turned around an' says: "Well, y'all wash in Washington, an'

173

get outa *here!*" You'd be surprised how cruel people can be in some circumstances.

'I had to go back outside an', you know, for *weeks* I had a burnin' in my throat an' my eyes – an' I think till today I still suffer from some of that. That stuff is *dangerous* to you, you know: if you breathe it, it burns your lungs an' shit. I think that a water-hose is better to break up a riot, you know, get some cold water to cool 'em off. But shootin' gas an' stuff on other humans, man, it just ain't civilized!

'Of course, in some instances the cops *have* to be firm, because you never know *who* you are walkin' up on today. But you don't treat a man like a *child* – or a *dog* – an' then hit him in the mouth with a stick just because he said somethin' back to you, beat him up, knock his teeth out, an' then tell lies that he fell down the stairs, an' all that ol' kinda stuff. To me, that is the *worst* kinda thing that one human being could do to another one in a free society. You don't have to be that *cold* to people just because you've got a stick an' a badge.

'A lotta things that went down when I was a kid, man, I didn't agree with – but I was a kid, couldn't do nothin' about it; now, I'm sixty years old, an' *still* can't do nothin' about it!' (Laughs.) 'But I'm glad we've got policemens, because you get so many treacherous people that's out there, that you gotta deal with every day, if there *wasn't* no police on the streets, *I* wouldn't go out there!'[1]

Rock 'n' Roll Is Here To Stay

Much of the credit for Bo's re-emergence at the beginning of the seventies must go to Richard Nader, a young promoter's assistant whose fond memories of the halcyon days of rock 'n' roll prompted him to stage his own *1950s Rock & Roll Revival* show:

> *'January 1965 PFC Jim Pewter and I used to sit near the oil stove at Radio Cavalier, Armed Forces Radio Network in Man-Son Ni, Korea, talking about the great rock 'n' roll shows that came to town in the mid- and late 1950s. I remembered driving all the way to Pittsburgh – 55 miles – from Masontown, Pennsylvania in my brother's car.*
>
> *'It was a light green '55 Merc with white-walls, fender skirts, duals, nylon rugs, glasspak mufflers and an eight-foot whip antenna. Going through the Liberty Tubes it sounded like the*

soundtrack from Bombs Over Tokyo. Up Fifth Avenue at the Syria Mosque I dove into my seat in the sixth row and slouched down. There was electricity in the air – the loud whisper before the show seemed to cover me like a blanket: I was about to see my first rock 'n' roll concert!

'The lights went dim and Porky Chedwick from WAMO stepped out through the opening in the curtain. The building rose three feet with the cheer. I was about to see the people who recorded all of the hit records that were on sale in my father's drug store.

'The magic moment of that concert night never left me, never really left any of us. While the Beatles had eight of the top tunes on the charts here in the States, Jim and I were sitting in Korea selecting artists for our make-believe rock 'n' roll shows, arguing for hours about billing and who would close the show. I decided then that the rock 'n' roll artists of the fifties were not to be forgotten and that someday I would get them back to center stage again.'[63]

Nader's first concert (featuring the talents of Chuck Berry, Jimmy Clanton, the Coasters, Bill Haley & His Comets, the Platters and the Shirelles) was held at New York's Felt Forum on 18 October, 1969. A resounding success, it became the first of almost one hundred similar events he was to promote over the next three years. His unswerving commitment to rock 'n' roll's original acts put many faded stars back into the limelight to receive the public acclaim they deserved – not least the ever-dynamic Bo Diddley, who was delivered from a miserable existence tinkering with wrecked cars in his back yard to become a regularly featured attraction and one of the show's top draws.

'If it hadn't been for Richard Nader, my name wouldn't be before a whole lotta people.[25] I think he did a great thing when he brought about the idea of bringin' all of us back, the people who *started* this stuff.[47] We are *strugglin'* to let people know that we are still alive an' kickin', an' that we *know* what a stage is built for!'[1]

'Some of the younger kids are now just beginnin' to pick up on all of the rock stuff that really started the whole thing, the people who started it. They're beginnin' to find out there are cats like myself, Chuck Berry, Little Richard, who were there, who laid the groundwork, an' are still *alive*.[57]

When they see me doin' all these funky rhythms, these kids *freak out* because they don't understand it: "Hey, why is he doin' this? He's old enough to be my *daddy*!"[1]

The *Rock & Roll Revival* era was immortalised in the 1973 Columbia movie, *Let The Good Times Roll*, a thoughtfully assembled montage of recent concert footage featuring Bo, Chuck Berry, Chubby Checker, the Coasters, Danny & The Juniors, Fats Domino, the Five Satins, Bill Haley & His Comets, Little Richard and the Shirelles, intercut with atmospheric period TV and newsreel clips.

Bo's sequence showed him chatting in his dressing room, enjoying a joke with the Coasters, shopping for chicken in a supermarket, and tearing New York's Madison Square Garden apart with rousing versions of 'I'm A Man' and 'Hey Bo Diddley' (both of which were included on the soundtrack album). He also made an unscheduled appearance at the end of the film, joining Chuck Berry for an energetic stage jam that provided it with a fittingly exciting climax.

His renaissance as a rock star was by this time all but complete. Ecstatically received in live performance, eulogised in songs like Elephant's Memory's 'Chuck & Bo' [Apple LP *Elephant's Memory*], George 'Harmonica' Smith's 'McComb, Mississippi' [Deram LP *Arkansas Trap*] and Thunder & Lightnin's 'Good Ol' Rock 'n' Roll Feelin'' [Tommy ZS-71752], and acknowledged as a major influence through recordings like the Allman Brothers Band's 'You Don't Love Me' [Capricorn 2-LP *At Fillmore East*], Captain Beefheart's 'I'm Gonna Booglerize You Baby' [Reprise LP *The Spotlight Kid*], Mike Bloomfield, John Hammond & Dr John's 'Pretty Thing' [Columbia LP *Triumvirate*], Brownsville Station's 'Road Runner' [Warner Bros LP *Brownsville Station*], Cactus's 'You Can't Judge A Book By The Cover' [Atco 6792], Creedence Clearwater Revival's 'Before You Accuse Me' [Fantasy LP *Cosmo's Factory*], Dr John's 'Iko Iko' [Atco LP *Gumbo*], the Doors' 'Who Do You Love' [Elektra 2-LP *Absolutely Live*], Guess Who's 'American Woman' [Nimbus 9], LA Getaway's 'Bring It To Jerome' [Atco LP *LA Getaway*], John Mayall's 'Play The Harp' [Polydor 14117], the New York Dolls' 'Pills' [Mercury LP *New York Dolls*] and Bob Seger's 'Who Do You Love'/'Bo Diddley' medley [Reprise 1117], Bo Diddley was no longer a has-been.

'All of a sudden, I became a celebrity! They have set a quota of years, I guess, to identify the "legend" trip, an' I have lived all over into that era, an' I'm still playin', so they started sayin' I'm a "living legend". It's almost like "hero", you know. It's *great!*' [1]

In the UK, meanwhile, the demise of flower power had also sparked off a 'back to the roots' movement, engendering both a folk music revival and another blues boom (though this time around the accent was on 'progressive' blues–rock fusions, rather than the slavish imitation of American originals).

Not surprisingly, Bo Diddley's lively rhythms and raunchy style once again proved extremely popular – as is testified by recordings like Bacon Fat's 'Manish Boy' [Blue Horizon LP *Grease One For Me*], Long John Baldry's 'You Can't Judge A Book By The Cover' [Warner Bros 7597] and 'Let Me Pass' [GM GMS-015], David Bowie's 'The Jean Genie' [RCA-Victor RCA-2302], Climax Chicago's 'Cubano Chant' [Parlophone LP *Plays On*], 'That's All' [Harvest LP *Tightly Knit*] and 'Shake Your Love' [Harvest LP *Rich Man*], Free's 'Trouble On Double Time' [Island LP *Free*], the Groundhogs' 'You Don't Love Me' [Liberty LP *Scratching The Surface*], Juicy Lucy's 'Who Do You Love' [Vertigo V-1], the Rolling Stones' 'Hipshake' [Rolling Stones 2-LP *Exile On Main Street*], Savoy Brown's 'Waiting In The Bamboo Grove' [Decca F-12310] and 'You Don't Love Me' [Decca LP *Boogie Brothers*], Stackwaddy's 'Road Runner' [Dandelion S-5119], 'Bring It To Jerome' [Dandelion LP *Stackwaddy*] and 'Mama, Keep Your Big Mouth Shut' [Dandelion Various Artists LP *There Is Some Fun Going Forward*], Screaming Lord Sutch's 'Flashing Lights' [Atlantic LP *Lord Sutch & Heavy Friends*], Ten Years After's 'I'm Going Home' [Chrysalis LP *Recorded Live*], Toe Fat's 'Working Nights' [Parlophone LP *Toe Fat*], UFO's 'Who Do You Love' [Beacon LP *UFO*] and Chris Youlden's 'Nowhere Road' [Deram LP *Nowhere Road*].

The rock 'n' roll revival itself, however, made less of an impact in Britain than it had in the States, though a mammoth show featuring Bo, Chuck Berry, Emile Ford, Billy Fury, Bill Haley & His Comets, Heinz, the Houseshakers, Jerry Lee Lewis and his sister Linda Gail, Little Richard, Screaming Lord Sutch and (somewhat incongruously) Gary Glitter, the MC5 and Wizzard, managed to attract a crowd of 87,000 to London's Wembley Stadium on 5 August, 1972.

Peter Clifton (who later directed Led Zeppelin's *The Song Remains The Same*) captured the historic event on celluloid with more than a modicum of style, but the effect was ruined by an inexcusably muddy soundtrack. Even so, Bo came across surprisingly well duetting with Cookie on 'Road Runner', 'Bring It To Jerome' and 'Mona', with the Houseshakers supporting.

177

Unfortunately, copyright problems prevented *The London Rock 'n' Roll Show* from being shown until 1978, by which time it had lost most of its topicality and much of its relevance. It never appeared in the USA, in fact, although subsequent TV screenings in various European countries helped to redress at least some of the damage caused by the delay.

Adios!

With Bo Diddley now firmly back in the running, GRT were not slow to capitalise on his popularity, reissuing many of his classic recordings in the United States and in Europe between 1972 and 1975, and even presenting him with a unique 'super-gold' record *'in recognition of his outstanding contribution to contemporary music, and for being the Originator who created many of the exciting rhythms of rock 'n' roll'*.

Diddley, of course, also continued writing and recording new material during this time, though the company's efforts to update his sound resulted in a series of patchy and embarrassingly lacklustre albums.

The 1971 *Another Dimension* was a case in point, with a plainly uncommitted Bo struggling to inject some feeling into songs by Al Kooper, Elton John, the Band and – in what must have been a particularly galling experience – Creedence Clearwater Revival. All in all, the album had the air of one of those anonymously recorded supermarket cheapos, and even the inclusion of two excellent McDaniel originals – 'Pollution' (a topical 'message' song with a solid funk groove akin to Sly & The Family Stone's recent 'Thank You (Falettinme Be Mice Elf Agin)' [Epic 10555]) and 'I Said Shutup Woman' (a remake of the *Black Gladiator* cut – this time with a great 'answer' part sung by Cookie) – failed to save the day.

His three cuts on the double live album, *Blues/Rock Avalanche* (a collection of performances by various Chess artists at the 1972 *Montreux Jazz Festival* in Switzerland) were even worse, with unbelievably leaden backings by the Aces and an uncomfortable, bass-laden mix*.

By contrast, *Where It All Began* was easily the most artistically satisfying of all of Bo's seventies' releases. Sympathetically produced by Pete Welding and Johnny Otis in a hard rock/soul format, he came across well on a variety of songs including 'Take It All Off' (Eva Darby's intriguing commentary on how so-called beauty aids can camouflage the real person

---

*Bo's act was also filmed and broadcast on Swiss television in two twenty-minute instalments.

underneath), a beautiful 'Love Is Strange' rewrite called 'Infatuation', buttshakers like 'I've Had It Hard' and 'Bo Diddley-itis', and his wickedly satirical jibe at geriatric teenyboppers, 'Look At Grandma':

Bo: *Look at grandma, wearin' her hot pants.*
            Look at grandma, tryin' to give the young boys a chance.
            Look at grandma, she's really outasite.
            Look at grandma, tryin' to make everythin' alright.

Chorus: *Grandma, grandma, what you tryin' to do?*
            Grandma, grandma, everybody's watchin' you!

© Heavy Music/BoKay Music (BMI)

However, the record's subsequent prevalence in the cut-out bins suggests that its success in commercial terms was rather less resounding. Despite this, producer Esmond Edwards opted for a similar approach on *The London Bo Diddley Sessions*, but failed miserably, swamping Bo's guitar and vocals with a top-heavy organ and layers of messy brass. Indeed, the only cut to do the Diddler any real justice was 'Make A Hit Record', a tongue-in-cheek portrayal of a young hopeful doing the rounds of the record companies, boasting: *'I-I-I even got one like Joe Tex when he sings 'I Gotcha!''*.

Shortly after the album's release in April 1973, Cookie left Bo's group: 'She got married, and that was the end of that. She was pretty loyal, you know – she stayed with me longer than anybody else – but I don't know where she's at now.'[1]

In the closing months of 1973, Bo recorded what was to be his final album for Chess, *Big Bad Bo*. A collection of laid-back, jazzy blues (including Bobby Charles's 'He's Got All The Whiskey', Odetta Gordon's 'Hit Or Miss', Van Morrison's 'I've Been Workin'' and his own 'Evelee'), it was both competent and enjoyable, but not a patch on his trailblazing fifties' and sixties' offerings.

'I was tryin' to go forward, to get away from that thing I'd been doin' all the time, because people were beginnin' to tell me I was in a rut. What I tried to do, was try to update things a little bit by usin' horns. It was a good album, but I found that horns don't work with me too well: people don't understand me with horns.'[1]

When his contract finally expired in 1974, Bo seized the opportunity to extricate himself from his legal strait-jacket: 'I was a tax deduction, an' they got *awfully* mad when their little sucker refused to sign another contract: they ain't got any more suckers now, y'understand, all their suckers is *gone*! So, when they claim they lost $80,000, they've gotta find somebody *else* to put it on!

'When I found out what was happenin', I told 'em I'll sign another contract – but I asked for a *ridiculous* price, 'cause I knew they weren't gonna do it. I told 'em I wanted $70,000 – $30,000 when I signed, an' the rest in two pieces, before the year's out – an' they said: "No, we're not gonna do it."

'So, I said: "Adios, amigo!"

'I *knew* they wasn't gonna do it, y'understand me, an' that was my way out: I made 'em think I was *crazy*. That was for *one year*! Now, who's gonna give up $70,000 unless the cat is *sizzlin' hot*?'[8]

Unbeknown to Bo, however, GRT were themselves in deep financial trouble at the time, and were forced to sell off all their interests in Chess less than a year later.

The lucky buyers were All Platinum, the successful New Jersey independent run by Joe and Sylvia Robinson – the 'Sylvia' of Mickey & Sylvia – who immediately launched an ambitious reissues programme. However, after only a handful of releases, they too ran into difficulties and the project was shelved.

Suddenly finding himself with no material on the market, Bo opted for a one-album deal with RCA that teamed him with an impressive array of rock luminaries – among them Carmine Appice and Tim Bogert (of Vanilla Fudge/Cactus fame), Elvin Bishop (ex-Paul Butterfield Blues Band), Joe Cocker, Billy Joel, Corky Laing and Leslie West (Mountain), Albert Lee (Love), Alvin Lee (Ten Years After), Roger McGuinn (Byrds) and Keith Moon (Who) – for a celebration of *The 20th Anniversary Of Rock 'n' Roll*.

Regrettably, he was also saddled with an insensitive producer who turned what could (and should) have been one of rock's finest moments into an over-indulgent, tedious cacophony that easily qualifies for the dubious distinction of Bo Diddley's worst-ever LP.

'The idea was okay, but I didn't like the album,'[36] admits Bo. 'They didn't stop an' ask me how to produce Bo Diddley, an' they *should* have done: I'm the *only* dude that knows what to do with Bo Diddley[35] but, you know, all entertainers are *dummies*, they don't know what they're talkin' about. All *you* do is play!'[1]

180

'Ron Terry was a very brilliant producer with ideas, but he screwed it up on the way. When he brought in a guy from New York to play like me, I wanted to *kill* him!'[35] But what can you do if you've signed a contract? You can't just get up an' walk out of the studio if you don't like what they're doin' with you, because they *got* you.

'But *I'm* the one that's gotta live this down! It hurt *me*, an' I'm sufferin' for it. I lost a *lotta* fans through that album, an' the world don't know that I didn't have anythin' to do with it – but, *my name* was on it.'[1]

Still smarting from the RCA fiasco, Bo signed another one-off deal, this time with M.F. Productions Inc, an obscure New York venture financed by one equally obscure Manny Fox. *I'm A Man*, an enjoyable double album featuring live versions of fifteen of his best-known songs duly appeared in 1977, but died an undeservedly early death due to poor distribution and a total absence of promotion.

By now thoroughly disenchanted with the record business, Bo declared himself reluctant to enter into any new commitments:

'Everyone looks at me an' says: "Man, you're *crazy* not wantin' to record!" Maybe I am, but I just don't dig bein' ripped off. People are buyin' my records thinkin' they're pushin' Bo Diddley to the top, an' I'm *sinkin'*![8] I don't sign anythin' with anybody anymore.[1] *Nobody* owns me now!'[36]

Gotta Be A Change

While Bo was busy trying to rescue his career, changes were being wrought that would ensure the seventies turned out to be no less eventful musically than the previous two decades.

In the USA, market research revealed that young adults, rather than teenagers, now constituted the largest sector of the record market, and the industry duly began gearing itself towards 'adult-oriented rock', a sort of modern 'easy listening' music whose suitability for radio airplay represented a virtual guarantee of success for anyone recording in the idiom. As a result, artists from all fields began watering down their styles to conform to the bland AOR stereotype, wiping out much of America's musical heritage they did so.

These changes did not bode well for Bo Diddley and, although a handful of roots rockers kept the flame burning in the latter half of the decade with recordings like Roky Erickson's 'Bo Diddley's A Headhunter' [released in 1992 on Swordfish CD *Mad Dog*], John Hammonds's 'Mama, Keep Your Big Mouth Shut' and 'Pretty Thing' [both on Vanguard LP *Hot*

Tracks], Roy Head's 'Who Do You Love' [Crazy Cajun LP *Boogie Down*] and 'Bring It To Jerome' [Crazy Cajun LP *Rock 'n' Roll My Soul*], Delbert McClinton's 'Before You Accuse Me' [ABC LP *Genuine Cowhide*], the New Riders Of The Purple Sage's 'Home Grown' [MCA LP *Who Are Those Guys*], Neil Sedaka's 'Bad Blood' [Rocket 40460], Bruce Springsteen's 'She's The One' [Columbia 10274], George Thorogood's 'Ride On Josephine' [Rounder LP *George Thorogood & The Destroyers*] and 'Who Do You Love' [Rounder 4519] and Townes Van Zandt's 'Who Do You Love' [Tomato 10003], he was completely ignored by the soporific AOR acts that now dominated rock's mainstream.

Black music, too, had become increasingly sophisticated during the seventies, with Isaac Hayes' orchestral funk and the slick 'Philadelphia sound' of Kenny Gamble, Leon Huff and Thom Bell initially supplanting earthier soul styles, and subsequently degenerating into 'disco' – lowest common denominator dance music with a simple, repetitive beat and inconsequential lyrics, which rapidly went on to achieve global popularity.

Sadly, although Bo had created the stuttering guitar sound that graced so many disco hits (indeed, records like La Belle Epoque's 'Miss Broadway' [Harvest HAR-5146], Hamilton Bohannon's 'Disco Stomp' [Oak 54599], Eddie Drennon & BBS Unlimited's 'Let's Do It Again' [Friends & Co LP *Collage*], Hello's 'New York Groove' [Bell 1438], Margie Joseph's 'How Do You Spell Love' [Atlantic LP *Margie Joseph*], Linda Lewis's 'It's In His Kiss' [Arista 17] and Shirley & Company's 'Shame, Shame, Shame' [Vibration 532] even used his famous beat), the new music left him cold.

'As far as I was concerned, disco *sucked*! You know, it didn't have no *meanin'*! They took a marchin' beat, hung a little cymbal on top of it, an' they called it "disco". It's "hup, two, three, four!" If you was ever in a school band marchin' in the parade, that's the same identical beat. Soldiers *train* by it!'[1] (Laughs.)

'It's a lazy man's music for cats who don't wanna work. The bass player hits the same two licks for about nine minutes, an' another guitar player hits a lick every now an' then. You could go to McDonald's an' buy a hamburger while you're waitin' for the next one! Back in the fifties we *worked*, but today you don't have to do nothin'. They got enough knobs in the studio to make you sound like a million dollars!

'I don't believe in disco, but I've written songs *related* to disco.[28] Things I played in 1955 an' earlier, before I even started recordin', people are just startin' to get hip to now. I can *prove* what I'm sayin': a few weeks ago, I just happened to pick up one of my old tapes an' bring it into the house to see what was on it, an' just about went through the floor! *1961* I had all these funny rhythms goin', an' I was still too far ahead of myself!

'The kids back then were just startin' to get into dances like the "chicken" an' the "bop", an' all that kinda stuff. It was more on the primitive side, an' they weren't geared to that yet.

'Now, I'm right in the middle of it. You could play it in a disco right now, an' they would go: "Oh!"[5] – but the kids today are too young to go that far back, to deal with that real authentic 'Bo Diddley'-type sound I had goin'. That authentic "raggedy" sound that I had back then – which was actually deliberate – is difficult to duplicate, because the electronic instruments today have a much cleaner sound an' everythin'. We're usin' new techniques an' updatin' everythin' – like young people that would play Beethoven today would probably put a little bit more feelin' into it than the cat that wrote it all them years ago, because they are usin' new instruments, an' gettin' more effects an', you know, makin' the song – uh – more lovelier. Kids today are more advanced *already* than I was at that time, an' I respect that.[1]

'Really, I'm glad to be a part of *whatever's* goin' on,[5] but if I had to go totally disco in order to survive, I don't know what I'd do.'[28]

Once again, it was Britain that was to come to Bo's rescue. In the UK, the sterility of studio-created pop, the pomposity and increasing inaccessability of the major rock acts, and a sobering economic recession had created a demand among teenagers for unpretentious, exciting live music at realistically-priced local venues. A thriving 'new wave' group scene quickly developed, encompassing a variety of styles from good-time 'pub rock' to a hardcore 'punk' thrash – which by 1976 was already beginning to attract world-wide attention.

'When the punk rock first came out, I thought it was *ridiculous*, groups pukin' on stage, an' all that crap – as everybody usually do when they first hear somethin' until they figure out that it's really not that dangerous.[1] Punk rock is nothin' but 1969 acid rock. Same *noise*, just a different generation of kids got hold of it, so they had to put a different name to it.[4]

'Today, I like some of it, but there's a specific problem with it, which is that the groups play too loud. They could make just as much of an impact by playin' *softer*, an' I've told 'em this. If it's too loud, kids that are doin' this at nineteen an' twenty years old are gonna be *deaf* when they get to thirty-five, an' they don't know it. Experience is that you *protect* your ears, because when they're gone, there's no ear transplants yet, y'understand? So, I'm just tryin' – as a older man – to tell 'em that it's *dangerous*.'[1]

Despite his initial reservations, Bo was generally well-served by the new wave on both sides of the Atlantic. Its basic precept – a return to the musical ideals of the pre-hippy era – and the relative inexperience of its young protagonists led many of them to re-examine and rework earlier rock styles including his own.

Almost inevitably, the latter half of the seventies saw a plethora of Diddley-inspired releases like the B-52s' '52 Girls' [Warner Bros LP *B-52s*], the Barracudas' 'I'm A Barbarian For Your Love' [Coyote LP *The Big Gap*], the Bishops' 'I Want Candy' [Chiswick CHIS-101], the Clash's 'Hateful' and 'Rudie Can't Fail' [both on Columbia LP *London Calling*], Dr Feelgood's 'I Don't Mind' [United Artists LP *Down By The Jetty*], 'I Can Tell' [United Artists LP *Malpractice*], 'I'm A Man' [United Artists LP *Stupidity*] and 'Hey Mama (Keep Your Big Mouth Shut)' [United Artists LP *Sneakin' Suspicion*], the Steve Gibbons Band's 'No Spitting On The Bus' [Polydor LP *Down In The Bunker*], Kilburn & The High Roads' 'Huffety Puff' [Warner Bros LP *Wotabunch*], Lene Lovich's 'Say When' [Stiff BUY-46], Nick Lowe's 'I Love The Sound Of Breaking Glass' [Radar ADA-1], the Lurkers' 'Pills' [Beggar's Banquet BEG-9], Matchbox's 'Buzz Buzz A-Diddle It' [Magnet 157], the 101ers' 'Don't Let Go' [Andalucia LP *Elgin Avenue Breakdown*], the Pork Dukes' 'Three Men In An Army Truck' [Wood LP *Pig Out Of Hell*] and Suicide's 'Girl' [Red Star LP *Suicide*], as well as the occasional nod in the same direction from rock's elder statesmen like Jess Conrad's 'Lock Up Your Daughters' [EMI 2682], Eno's 'Blank Frank' [Island LP *Here Come The Warm Jets*], Peter Gabriel's 'Solsbury Hill' [Charisma CD-301] and Rick Wakeman's 'Pedro Do Gavea' [A&M LP *Rhapsodies*].

Although these records were undeniably derivative, they were also important in that they introduced the exciting 'Bo Diddley' beat to a new generation, simultaneously investing it with sufficient street credibility to gain it both respect and acceptance with the contemporary popular music audience.

In Britain, Bo received a further (and equally unexpected) boost from a spin-off 'rockabilly' craze that saw him return to Europe in 1978 to tour with Matchbox and Carl Perkins, and again the following year with Ray Campi and George Thorogood.

The widespread recognition that followed finally enabled Bo to transcend his 'golden oldie' tag and re-establish himself as a composer and musician of contemporary relevance.

Much of the credit for this breakthrough must go to the Clash's Joe Strummer, a self-confessed Diddley fanatic who insisted on booking his idol as support act on the group's first major US tour in early 1979.

'They requested that I be on the show with 'em, an' I enjoyed workin' with 'em,' says Bo. 'Our music is entirely different, but it was a *gas!*[51] When they first met me, I think they were scared to death, you know, but they finally came around an' we began talkin' an' laughin' an' jokin' an' stuff. When they found out that I was a cool dude, then everythin' was really *beautiful*, you know. We rode up an' down the highway in the snow, you know, in the bus. It was *great!*[32]

'I had one guy say: "Oh, Bo Diddley won't work on this tour because this is a new type of music, an' he's just not gonna fit in." He didn't wanna have me on the show with the Clash, so they stood up an' said: "We *want* him on the show" – an' I *love* 'em for that, because I *destroyed* the place!' (Laughs.) 'Just totally destroyed it, an' the promoter was left with his mouth *gapped open!* See, you *cannot* say what people are gonna like, or not gonna like: you have to stick it out there an' *find out!* If they taste it, an' like the way it tastes, you can bet they'll *eat* some of it!'[1] (Laughs.)

'I had somethin' for the bubblegum trip, we did encores, an' everybody was happy. We shocked *everybody*, an' in a way it shocked me too. See, a lotta kids don't know me. They say: "Bo Diddley? What is *that?* Somethin' you get in Safeway's?"[9] There *are* people who have never heard of Bo Diddley, who don't know I even exist, but I'm not surprised at that, an' it doesn't bother me.[1]

'You know, some people may look down – uh – like I saw somethin' in the paper about *"Bo Diddley has to rely upon being an opening act for a young group just coming out of England"*, or somethin' like this – but I could be one of the guys that *can't get* a telephone call! When *nobody* calls you, *that's* bad news, but right now I don't have any problems: I have to turn work *down*, you know. So, the person that wrote that, I feel he doesn't know what he was talkin' about, because they paid my price, an' I was *happy* doin' it, an' that's all it is.'[51]

185

Into The Nineties

The 1980s brought with them an air of optimism and a promise of better things to come – a promise which, for once, was fulfilled.

With his popularity on the increase, Bo took advantage of the many opportunities that now presented themselves, bolstering lengthy tours of North America, Europe and Australia with guest appearances on TV spectaculars like *American Bandstand*'s 30th and 33¹/₃rd anniversary specials and *Live Aid* (on which he performed 'Who Do You Love' with George Thorogood & The Destroyers), and in the Chuck Berry film bio-documentary, *Hail! Hail! Rock 'n' Roll*; he tackled cameo acting roles in *Trading Places*, *Eddie & The Cruisers II*, *Rockula* and George Thorogood's *Bad To The Bone* video [EMI America]; he advertised Dean Markley amps and strings, Budweiser beer and Nike sportswear; he sat in on recording sessions with the BMTs, Freddy Cannon and the Belmonts, the Snakes, Canada's Paul James Band and Jannetta, and Norway's Vazelina Bilopphøggers; his songs were featured on the film soundtracks of *Sunnyside*, *Forever Young*, *La Bamba*, *The Big Town*, *The Colour Of Money*, *Tapeheads* and *Shag*; and many of his classic fifties' and sixties' recordings were made available once again by MCA, who acquired the Chess catalogue from Sugar Hill/All Platinum in 1984.

Needless to say, this unprecedented level of exposure (highlighted by Bo's election to the Rock 'n' Roll Hall Of Fame in 1987 and his immortalisation in concrete on Sunset Boulevard's Rock Walk in 1989) stimulated enormous interest in the man and his music, engendering a flurry of reverential articles in authoritative publications like *Guitarist*, *Guitar Player*, *One-Two-Testing* and *Rolling Stone*, and a plethora of covers and imitations including the Blasters' 'I Love You So' [Slash LP *The Blaster*], the Blue Caps' 'Silly Song' [Magnum Force LP *Unleashed*], Blues 'n' Trouble's 'Cadillac' [Ammunition Communications BNT-3], Bow Wow Wow's 'I Want Candy' [RCA-Victor 238], the Len Bright Combo's 'Mona' [Empire LEN-1], Eugene Chadbourne's 'Bo Diddley Is A Communist' [Fundamental LP *Vermin Of The Blues*], Eric Clapton's 'Before You Accuse Me' [Duck LP *Journeyman*], Elvis Costello's 'Lover's Walk' [WEA LP *Trust*], the Cramps' 'Call Of The Wighat' [Enigma LP *Smell Of Female*] and 'Cornfed Dames' [Big Beat LP *A Date With Elvis*], Link Davis Jr's 'Catalina, Catalina' [Goldband LP *Catch A Train To New Orleans*], the Del Fuegos' 'Out For A Ride' [Slash LP *The Longest Day*], Dr Feelgood's 'A Case Of The Shakes' [Liberty BD-386] and 'You Don't Love Me' [Line LP *Doctor's*

Orders], Thomas Dolby's 'Europa & The Pirate Twins' [Parlophone
R-6051], John Dummer & Helen April's 'Own Up (If You're Over 25)' [Red
Shadow REDS-009], Bob Dylan's 'Got My Mind Made Up' [Columbia LP
Knocked Out Loaded], Steve Earle's 'I Love You Too Much' [MCA LP
Exit 0], the Fabulous Thunderbirds' 'Diddy Wah Diddy' [Chrysalis LP
T-Bird Rhythm], Tav Falco's Panther Burns' 'Do The Robot' [New Rose LP
The World We Knew], the Gibson Bros' 'Bo Diddley Pulled A Boner'
[Homestead Records LP *Big Pine Boogie*], Ian Gomm's 'Images' [Decal LP
Images], the Gun Club's 'Bo Diddley's A Gunslinger' [Dojo LP *Two Sides
Of The Beast*], the Hawks' 'Looking For More Good Times' [Ronnie
Hawkins Epic LP *Hello Again... Mary Lou*], the Highliners' 'Henry The
Wasp' [ABC ABCS-017], Catfish Hodge's 'A A-political Blues' [Adelphi LP
Bout With The Blues], the Jesus & Mary Chain's 'Who Do You Love'
[blanco y negro NEG-24T] and 'Bo Diddley Is Jesus' [blanco y negro
SAM-360], the Jets' 'Yes, Tonight Josephine' [EMI 5247], Joan Jett's 'Be
Straight' [Boardwalk LP *I Love To Rock 'n' Roll*], Willy Jive's 'Mona'
[Cheapskate CHEAP-33], Johnny & The Roccos' 'Go! You Rebel' [Big Beat
LP *Tearin' Up The Border*], Wilko Johnson's 'Down By The Waterside'
[Rockburgh ROCS-220], Mickey Jupp's 'Hot Love' [A&M LP *Shampoo,
Haircut & Shave*] and 'Lover By Night' [Waterfront LP *X*], King Kurt's 'Bo
Diddley Goes East' [Stiff LP *Ooh Wallah Wallah*], Sleepy LaBeef's
'Gunslinger' [Rounder LP *Nothin' But The Truth*], Lindisfarne's 'Fog On
The Tyne' [LMP LP *Lindisfarntastic*], Lone Justice's 'East Of Eden' [Geffen
LP *Lone Justice*], Roy Loney's 'Fast & Loose' [Double Dare LP *Fast &
Loose*], Mahogany Rush's 'Mona' [Columbia LP *What's Next*], Paul
McCartney's 'Crackin' Up' [Melodiya LP *CHOBA B CCCP*], George Michael's
'Faith' [Epic EMU-3], the Milkshakes' 'Bo Diddlius', 'Little Girl' and
'Gringles & Groyles' [Big Beat LP *They Came, They Saw*], the Nighthawks'
'I Can Tell' [Varrick LP *Live In Europe*], Omar & The Howlers' 'Wall Of
Pride' [Columbia LP *Wall Of Pride*], the Only Ones' 'Me & My Shadow'
[Columbia LP *Baby's Got A Gun*], the Pretenders' 'Cuban Slide' [Real
ARE-12] and 'Dance' [WEA LP *Get Close*], Eddie Rabbitt's 'Gotta Have You'
[Elektra LP *Rabbitt Trax*], Carlos Santana's 'Who Do You Love' [Columbia
LP *Havana Moon*], the Smiths' 'How Soon Is Now' [Rough Trade RTT-
176] and 'Rusholme Ruffians' [Rough Trade LP *Meat Is Murder*], Bruce
Springsteen's 'Ain't Got You' [Columbia LP *Tunnel Of Love*], Talking
Heads' 'Ruby Dear' [Sire/Fly LP *Naked*], Tenpole Tudor's 'There Are Boys'
[Stiff Various Artists EP *Son Of Stiff Tour 1980*], the Texana Dames' 'The

Mall Parade' [Sonet LP *Texana Dames*], Moe Tucker's 'Ellas' and 'Bo Diddley' [both on Trash LP *Playing Possum*] and 'Bo Diddley' and 'Hey Mersh!' [on 50,000,000,000,000,000,000,000 Watts LP *Life In Exile After Abdication*], U2's 'Desire' [Island IS-400], Westworld's 'Bubble Bo Diddley' [RCA BOOMT-1], 'Silvermac' [RCA BOOM-4] and 'Mix Me Up' [RCA LP *Where The Action Is*], Link Wray's 'Walk Away From Love' [Viva LP *Live At The Paradiso*] and Warren Zevon's 'Bo Diddley's A Gunslinger'/ 'Bo Diddley' medley [Asylum LP *Stand In The Fire*].

Happily, this trend has continued into the 1990s, with more high profile appearances (most notably the Expo '92 *Guitar Legends* concert in Seville and a series of gigs in 1994 supporting the Rolling Stones), movie soundtrack work with Ben E. King and New York rapper Doug Lazy (a remake of the old Monotones hit, 'Book Of Love'), videotape releases of film and television performances from various stages of his career (including some ultra-rare footage from a 1962 appearance on WPIX-TV's *Clay Cole Show*, and the magnificent *I Don't Sound Like Nobody*, forty-five minutes of pure Diddley dynamite filmed in a Swedish club in 1987), a healthy number of reissues and compilations of his Chess classics and rarities, and, of course, yet more Diddley soundalikes/retreads including Belinda Carlisle's 'Love Is A Big Scary Animal' [Virgin VSCDT-1472], Big Daddy's 'Lovely Rita' [Rhino CD *Sgt Pepper's*], Junior Brown's 'Sugarfoot Rag' [Curb CD *Guit With It*], the Chicasaw Mudd Puppies' 'Movin' So Fast' [Polydor LP *Movin' So Fast*], Julian Cope's 'Beautiful Love' [Island 483], Dick Dale's 'Tribal Thunder' [Hightone CD *Tribal Thunder*], Everything But The Girl's 'Love Is Strange' [blanco y negro EP *Covers*], the Gibson Bros' 'Road Runner' [Homestead LP *The Man Who Loved Couch Dancing*], Guitar Crusher's 'Don't Stop' [Blue Sting CD *Googa Mooga*], INXS's 'Suicide Blonde' [Mercury/Phonogram INXS-14], Mickey Jupp's 'No Place Like Home' [On The Beach CD *As The Years Go By*], Bill Kirchen's 'Rockabilly Funeral' [Demon CD *Tombstone Every Mile*], Little Richard's 'Twinkle, Twinkle, Little Star' [Walt Disney CD *Shake It All About*], Charles Mann's 'Borderline' [Gumbo LP *Walk Of Life*], Craig McLachlan's 'Mona' [Epic 655784], Dawn Penn's 'You Don't Love Me (No No No)' [Big Beat/Atlantic A.8295], Pirates Of The Mississippi's 'Redneck Blues' [Capitol CD *Walk The Plank*], the Pleasure Barons' 'Who Do You Love' [Hightone CD *Live In Las Vegas*], Soho's 'Hippychick' [S&M SAV-106], the Thin White Rope's 'Roadrunner' [Frontier LP *Squatters' Rights*], Thunder's 'Backstreet Symphony' [EMI EM-137], Moe Tucker's 'Lazy' [New Rose LP *I Spent A*

Week There The Other Night], World Party's 'Is It Too Late' [Ensign LP *Goodbye Jumbo*] and the entire *Cub Digs Bo* CD [Garageland] by former Brownsville Station member, Cub Koda.

But, probably most exciting of all was Bo's decision to reactivate his recording career: he resurfaced in 1983 after a break of five years with *Ain't It Good To Be Free*, a limited edition cassette of new songs released via his own company, BoKay Productions.

Side One featured six funky numbers he had cut that summer with the help of Offspring (a four-piece featuring his daughters Terri Lynne (keyboards and vocals) and Tammi Deanne (drums and vocals)), while *Side Two* contained four bluesier items recorded back in 1978 with Lady Bo & The Family Jewel.

The poignancy of his commentaries on human rights ('Ain't It Good To Be Free'), unemployment ('I Don't Want Your Welfare') and the state of the nation ('Gotta Be A Change'), the outlandishness of his sci-fi fantasy, 'Stabilize Yourself', the infectious humour of the boozy escapade, 'I Don't Know Where I've Been', and the sheer verve of his punchy self-promotion, 'Bo Diddley Put The Rock In Rock 'n' Roll', all provided conclusive proof that Bo Diddley had not run out of steam – though many of his older fans found it difficult to wholeheartedly embrace his modern, synthesizer-laden sound.

Commercially released on vinyl in 1984 by the French new-wave indie, New Rose, the album nevertheless sold well enough to justify a follow-up, *Bo Diddley & Co Live* on their Fan Club subsidiary a year later.

Sadly, what might have been another *Beach Party* turned out to be a disappointing collection of five overlong and uncharacteristically subdued live cuts dating from the same Woodstock, NY club dates that had yielded the 1977 MF Productions *I'm A Man* double. Indeed, apart from the witty 'He's A Hell Of A Man' and some nice cover shots, the record's only redeeming feature was its length – an unusually generous 55 minutes.

Thankfully, amends were made in 1986 with the UK release of *Hey... Bo Diddley In Concert* on the Conifer label, an atmospheric set of tough live performances culled from his September 1984 European tour with the British blues–rock outfit, Mainsqueeze.

In 1987, Bo Diddley's cause was espoused by Rolling Stone and former Face, Ronnie Wood, and the ensuing two years saw them playing short concert tours together in the USA, Europe and Japan. A recording of a November 1987 gig in New York City, *Live At The Ritz*, surfaced in Japan in mid-1988, but the performances included thereon – with the notable exception of 'Hey Bo Diddley' – were generally overblown and frustratingly drab.

In the summer of 1989, however, the Diddler returned with a new sound for the Nineties on the aptly-titled *Breakin' Through The BS** [Triple X Records] (released in Europe with several different tracks as *Living Legend* [New Rose]).

The result of various sessions at his Bad Dad Studios in Archer, Florida that summer, Bo's new opus contained some interesting (if not always successful) fusions of R&B with contemporary black music styles like funk, hip hop, rap and even reggae, and clearly signalled his intention to aim for the younger end of the market. It wasn't a great album, but it did have its moments – like the heartfelt 'Wake Up America', the gospelly rocker, 'Are You Serious', the bizarre 'Bo Pop Shake' (where, thanks to the miracle of electronic voice reprocessing, Bo ends up sounding like De La Soul) and, of course, the touching story of the boy who wants to play guitar 'Jus' Like Bo Diddley'.

Sadly, family and health problems slowed things down for Bo in the early Nineties, and almost four years elapsed before his next new release.

A superbly produced seamless blend of blues, gospel, soul, funk, highlife, hip-hop, rap, and any number of other influences, 1993's *This Should Not Be* [Triple X] was certainly well worth the wait, containing a number of strong cuts including the socially conscious 'This Should Not Be' and 'My Jesus Ain't Prejudice', a great instrumental reworking of 'Bo Diddley' titled 'Bozilla's Groove', and the lush ballad 'Let Me Join Your World', which gradually and quite unexpectedly develops into a thumping piledriver of a rap.

Even more unexpected was the title cut of 1994's *Promises* [Triple X]: a stomping country rocker-cum-rap which might just have dented the charts had it been pushed as a single. Disappointingly, the rest of the album was far more downbeat, with Bo continuing his crusade against drugs on 'Kids Don't Do It' and 'Hear What I'm Sayin'', and causing consternation in some quarters with the outspoken 'She Wasn't Raped'.

Although they may not be to everyone's taste, Bo Diddley's recent recordings not only testify to his uncanny ability to move with the times, but also augur well for his continued survival in the music business.

---

*Bull-Shit.

Bo certainly remains optimistic and, if everything goes according to plan, more releases are likely to be forthcoming in future:

'I've got my own record company now, I'm recordin' lots of new tunes, an' I've got tons of material that I'm fixin' to release as collectors' tapes on my own label – you know, old stuff I probably won't perform on stage. I've got a *lotta* tapes from back in the sixties: things that I recorded an' kept. Even though Chess have got all these titles, they *still* don't have what I call "the best of the bunch". I *never* put all my eggs in one basket. You might get *one* basket, but you ain't gonna get 'em all!

'I still write tunes *all* the time. I write some of my best tunes sittin' in the bathroom – 'cause that's where your mind relaxes, you know.' (Laughs.) 'The white kids now are growin' into blues real heavy, an' I'm fixin' to back up, an' do as much blues as I can. I've got a *lot* of ideas an', since technology has got so fantastic, it falls right into what I've had in my mind for a lotta years, an' never had a chance to do it. I use synthesizers an' all that stuff. Some of 'em *already* sound old-fashioned, but I don't throw nothin' away: I'll keep 'em, an' then maybe I'll come out with somethin' – but it will have a *different sound* to what everybody else is doin'.

'I just did a religious thing called 'In The Beginning' that I'm thinkin' about puttin' out. It's not a song, but it's some really weird music in the background, an' I say: *"In the beginning, God created the Heaven an' the Earth – dum-dum-dum-dum – An' the Earth was without form, an' the Spirit of God moved upon the face of the waters"*. It would *shake* people, me doin' that. It would shake *everybody*. That would even shake my *brother*!' (Laughs.)

'My mother predicts me to be a minister one day. I probably will, but I'm not ready yet: I gotta finish my rock 'n' roll first. I'm relaunchin' Bo Diddley again *by myself*. Everybody is askin' how I'm doin' this. Whaddya mean, *how* am I doin' this? Just get off your ass an' do it, that's all. I've been in the business for forty years now, so I *should* know what it's all about. It's really weird that I had to do this myself but, if people are eager to do somethin' with 'em, it must prove a point: it proves I'm *not* finished!'[1]

Speaking shortly before his untimely death in 1992, Marty Otelsberg (Bo's friend and manager since 1969) was equally buoyant: 'I think Bo Diddley is getting stronger, more popular now than ever, ever before. I don't think he's been this hot since 1955. We're going into April now, and I've got him booked for the rest of the year already, you know. How many managers can say that about their artists?

'Bo works a *lot* in the States. *Very* much. In fact, he's been begging me for some time off. Like, we've just got a tour coming up: we start in Tucson, Arizona, and then we go to Memphis, then Texas, then to New Orleans – where he does the *New Orleans Jazz & Heritage Festival*, and then in May we go to Maui, Hawaii. We play rock 'n' roll revival shows. Bo doesn't *need* to play them, but they're good to do.

'We've been going to Australia and New Zealand now for twelve years. Fifteen tours, and it's *never* been less than two months. They *love* Bo Diddley in Australia. The press has been very good to him, the people have been very good, and so has the promoter we use.

'We're now creating a market for Bo Diddley all over Europe: Germany, Austria, France, Italy, Spain, Holland, Belgium; all the Scandinavian countries; East Germany, Hungary, Poland. I can't believe that a place like Poland or Yugoslavia could give Bo Diddley standing ovations and have the kind of turnout that he gets, consisting of *thousands* of people. We did 19,000 people in *four days* in Yugoslavia! That's saying something, you know. In Poland, there was one woman that took off her *cross* to *give* to Bo Diddley! You know, it was just a beautiful sight.

'As far as new markets go, I don't think Bo Diddley would fit in too well in South America, but I know once we get to Israel, we're gonna go back there. I know that for a *fact*! I think Bo Diddley would do really well in Japan, but I think it would be better if we had a release there of his latest album and do it together with them, because I *know* the "Bo Diddley" beat will drive the Japanese people crazy! I would love to do Russia, but so far there's been no nibbles on that, you know. Russia I would like to do just for the sake of doing it. It's not really a question of the money: sometimes you just wanna create new territories and see the different reactions of different people.

'Bo and I have a very beautiful relationship. We understand each other *totally*. I know his likes and dislikes, I know how he thinks, and I'm pretty sure he's got the same vibes with me. Bo Diddley is not just "Bo Diddley the artist" to me: it's his whole family, it's a *lifetime* situation. I'm there for making sure that Bo's family and Bo are well taken-care-of in all aspects of life.

'Bo has been very good to me. When I'm sick on tour, he brings me breakfast in bed, orange juice, jello, you know, he makes sure that I eat. Every chance he gets, he buys me a present. Sure, sometimes I also get a lot of pressure, but then that's to be expected: he's *Bo Diddley*!'[64]

Postscript

The 1990s find Bo Diddley enjoying a higher public profile than ever before. Now a sprightly sexagenarian, he still tours constantly and, although his good fortune was soured in 1985 by the breakdown of his marriage to Kay, his future prospects seem reassuringly bright.

'I work all the time because I haven't priced myself out of the market. I got *smart*! Instead of workin' for all the big bucks that you see everybody tryin' to get from club owners, an' stuff like this, I brought my price *down*. It's almost like a guy that pass you speedin'. You goin' 55 miles an hour an' he's runnin' 80 miles an hour, an' there's a red light up there. When you get there, he's just pullin' off from the light – so why was he doin' all the speedin'? Get my point?[1] I know dudes that made more records than me, made a *lotta* money, an' they can't even get a telephone call now![5]

'To be truthful about it, my life has been beautiful, an' I *love* my fans, but I *am* tired of the road. I'm what you call a "black gypsy": always *goin'*. If I could have everybody come in my back yard, then I'd sit there an' play for 'em all day! All *night*! Wake up next mornin', an' do it again.

'In actual fact, I think electronics is gonna dominate the whole music scene, an' live entertainment is fixin' to go out of the window for a short period, so I'm settin' myself up now to try an' help people. That's what I wanna do: that's my alternate thing.

'I'm not losin' interest – because if I *was*, I wouldn't be sittin' here talkin' to you – but I got other levels that I wanna explore in my lifetime an' pass on my talents, you know. Maybe I wasn't very smart about previous things that happened, but I feel that I've got *somethin'* to give to the world.[1] There's a lotta kids out there got more talent than Bo Diddley, but that don't mean they're gonna make it like I did.[9] I can *help* other people, plus train 'em a little bit, so that they don't step in the same holes that I stepped in.[1]

'There are some pretty rotten dudes in the business. I hate to say this, but it's true. I don't think a girl should have to go to bed with some dude to make somethin' of herself. I tell 'em: "Come under my supervision." They can look like Marilyn Monroe or whatever, I say: "Hey, strictly business! I'm not tryin' to go to bed with you. I'm after that Almighty Dollar!" They look at me like I'm some type of weirdo: they ain't used to this happenin'.[47]

'I swore that, when I got asked for help, I was goin' to try to help people. I don't turn away *nobody*, you know, an' it's really great when you pick up a paper an' you see somebody said: "Bo Diddley gave me my first chance." That makes you feel *good*: it's a feelin' you've *helped* somebody.

'There was a time when work wasn't that plentiful, an' all the money that I got my hands on had to go toward our survival, so I wasn't in a position to be able to help other people. Then, not long after we moved to Florida in 1978, my eldest daughter, Terri Lynne, was in a bad car accident – an almost fatal head-on collision. She's okay now, you know – but that dealt a *helluva* blow to the family because, after somethin' of that sort, you don't know whether the person is goin' to come out of it stable, or what.

'So, I wasted a *lotta* time, but it's comin' together now, an' I'm goin' to do what I set out to do. It's a *must*! This is a goal that I have just gotta get out of my blood. In a way of speakin', everything's always gotten in the way of what I wanted to do. You know, everybody's always got somethin' for you to do, but what *you* wanna do.

'What people don't know about me, is that there are other things I do besides play a guitar. My talent don't stop with "chinka-chinka-chink-chink". My capabilities are not known to the world because I haven't been given the chance to let people know what Ellas McDaniel is all about. I am put into a little box, an' nobody looks outside of that box to see if Bo Diddley does anythin' else. I'm not at a standstill by a *long* shot. *No way*! I done *forgotten* more than some cats will ever know!' (Laughs.) 'I hate to put it that way, but I'm serious! That's the reason I came up with the idea of doin' a videotape on me: to give people just a little outlook on some of the things I know how to do.

'I was told it couldn't be done. In other words, *I* couldn't do it – because no one knows me as a person that fools around with cameras. There's a *lotta* things that people don't know about my potential, about what I can do, because I don't talk about it. I can't explain things in technical terms, so I prefer to shut up an' just do it. I can't read superbly, an' don't know all of the big words, an' all this ol' kinda stuff – but, had I stayed in school, I might not be talkin' to you now. I would have been somebody else, because I'da been programed by a *book*! This way, I learn it myself, an' *still* know the same thing that the cat got out of a book – but I know it *my* way, which makes it *different*, an' I'm happy about that.

'A lotta things that I wanted to do, I was talked out of by people sayin': "How can *you* do that?", "You haven't been to school for that", an' all this ol' kinda stuff. People have got the biggest "No" bag in the world: "*No*, you can't do that", "*No*, it'll never work", "*No*, I don't see how it can work", "*No*, not in a million years", "*No*, how you gonna do that", "*NO*!" – y'understand what I mean? The word "No" can be very damaging in some cases.

'Well, I done built a studio in my barn, got me some cameras an' stuff, an' – because I think I'm just as smart as the next dude – I'm gonna shoot my *own* video movie!

'I do a whole lotta things that people don't know about: I cut up old cars, I make pottery, I cook... I've been cookin' ever since I was old enough to get up on a milk-crate an' reach the stove. Momma Gussie taught me: she used to be a cook at school. Man, you oughta check out some of the stuff I cook! I barbecue a lot, an' I also smoke fish, but it's weird: I cook *in the ground* – which is not really weird, it's just a cheap way of doin' it – an' it *works*! You've never tasted anythin' like it *in your life*! It's somethin' else!

'What made me do this is, when we had the energy crisis in the United States, I started runnin' scared. I says: "Hey man, I ain't used to eatin' no *raw meat* – an' all we got is a *gas* stove in the house, *electric* plates, an' all this kinda stuff. I gotta figure out a way to *cook*, because I can't handle no raw meat!" I remembered seein' Hawaiians cook with leaves an' stuff, so I went an' dug me a hole in the back yard an' burned up $300-worth of meat before I figured it out, you know.' (Laughs.) 'I was tryin' to cook 'em *too fast*, but now I got it down to the minute. *To the minute*!

'I was playin' Sparks, Nevada once,' (laughs) 'an' the Coasters wanted to try some Bo Diddley chicken. We found a place in the desert where we could dig a hole, an' got down in-between the rocks an' built us a fire there. The Fire Department came, wanted to lock up everybody for buildin' a fire in the desert – 'cause if you set *that* shit on fire it'll just burn up everythin'! So, I just fed everybody. They *killed* themselves! The meat was just *fallin'* off the bones, you know, an' they say: "Hey man, all you need is a shovel, a vacant lot an' some tinfoil, an' you're in *business!*"[1] (Laughs.)

'I'm home quite often now. I got a garden out in the back, an' I'm growin' me some sweet potatoes, beans an' corn. I'm tryin' to learn how to become self-sufficient. I don't wanna have to depend on the Safeway, because I got this firm belief that the corner store isn't gonna be there too much longer: with the price of oil, the truck drivers can't afford to carry the stuff, an' the trains are goin' broke. Who's gonna carry the food to the stores? How are we goin' to survive? I'm sayin' to everybody to get off your buns an' grow somethin' of your own *other* than marijuana. There are a lotta people who are connoisseurs of all different kinds of marijuana, an' they can't even grow a head of lettuce![65]

'Everybody look at me real strange because I like doin' this kinda stuff, but I can't play that ol' phoney role of bein' dressed up all day lookin' like a million dollars. That's not *me*, man. I *gotta* be me *sometime*, an' I *won't* play that plastic role!

'People ask me: "How do you keep goin'?" I get my rest. I realize that I'm gettin' on in years now, y'understand, an' I don't intend to keel over on *anybody's* motherfuckin' stage! I've gotta take care of *me*, an' that's the way it is – but I ain't over the hill yet.

'I've had people come up to me, say: "Bo, you don't play like you used to."

'I just look 'em dead in the eye an' say: "An' you don't *run* like you used to, baby!"'[1] (Laughs.)

'My mother told me when I was a kid that, if I was goin' to be a thief, be a good thief; an' if I was gonna be a preacher, be a good preacher; an' if I was gonna be a musician, be a good musician. I don't try to be the *best*; I just try to be a good 'un.[27] Anytime that I hit the stage, look out there an' see all them pretty faces, you're gonna get the *best* that I know how to give ya![4] Before I leave this business, I'm gonna leave a dent in it! I was ten years too soon, they tell me. Maybe I'm in time now.[27] When I leave this Earth, man, they'll *know* I've been here!'[16]

They already do, Bo.

Quotations

1   George R. White, *Various interviews with Bo Diddley, 1982–85* (unpublished).
2   Michael Lydon, *Boogie Lightning* (Dial, New York), 1974.
3   Lenny Kaye, *Sound Scene* (*Cavalier* 22.4), February 1972.
4   Brian Case, *Bo Diddley's A Gunslinger* (*New Musical Express*), 6 May, 1978.
5   John Dalton, *I Can Go Down The Highway To A Little Town And Totally Destroy The Place* (*Guitar* 7.1), August 1978.
6   Bill Dwyer, *Bo Diddley: Part 1* (*Blues Unlimited* 71), April 1970.
7   Charles White, *Interview with Bo Diddley, 13 April, 1978* (unpublished).
8   Keith Macphail, *Bo Diddley Interview* (*Crazy Music* 5), May 1975.
9   Val Wilmer, *The Grand-Diddley Daddy Of Rock 'n' Roll* (*Observer Magazine*), 6 May, 1979.
10 Cliff White, *Interview with Bo Diddley, November 1975* (part-published in *Shout* 110), September–November 1976.
11 Jeff Hannusch, *Bo Diddley Is A Guitarslinger* (*Guitar Player* 174), June 1984.
12 Robert Neff & Anthony Connor, *Blues* (Latimer, London), 1976.
13 Max Jones, *The Men Who Make The Blues: Bo Diddley* (*Melody Maker*), 20 September, 1969.
14 Mike Rowe & Bill Greensmith, *Billy Boy Arnold: I Was Really Dedicated (Part 3)* (*Blues Unlimited* 128), January/February 1978.
14A Mary Katherine Aldin, *Billy Boy Arnold: I Had No Intention Of Stopping* (*Living Blues*), January/February 1994.
15 Marilyn Doerfler, *Bo Diddley, Idol Of Stars* (*Record Beat*), 1 March, 1966.

[16] Karl Dallas, *Bo: Rocking Up To 1990* (*Melody Maker*), 10 June, 1978.

[17] Mike Rowe, *Dirty Mother Fucker* (*Blues Unlimited* 130), May/August 1978.

[18] Stuart Colman, *Radio interview with Marshall Chess* (*Echoes*, Radio London), 16 August, 1980.

[19] Ray Topping, *Interview with Marshall Chess* (part published in *Blues Unlimited* 142), Summer 1982.

[20] Dorah Elworthy, *Readers' Letters* (*TV Times*), 1963.

[21] Stanley Sadie (*Ed*), *The New Grove Dictionary Of Musical Instruments* (Macmillan Press Ltd, London), 1984.

[22] Daddy Cool, *Various interviews with Bo Diddley, 1970s* (unpublished).

[23] Robert Pruter, *Windy City Soul: The Hambone Kids* (*Goldmine* 52), September 1980.

[24] Alan Lomax, *The Penguin Book Of American Folk Songs* (Penguin, Harmondsworth, Middx), 1964.

[25] Mike Jahn, *A Bo Diddley Revival* (*New York Sun*), 28 November, 1971.

[26] George R. White, *Interview with Rev Kenneth Haynes, 19 March, 1982* (unpublished).

[27] Beverley Creamer, *He Wants Everyone To Get Case Of Bo Diddley-itis* (*Honolulu Star-Bulletin*), 26 January, 1972.

[28] William D. Kerns, *Bo Diddley Now A R&R Legend* (*Lubbock Avalanche-Journal*), 5 September, 1980.

[29] Bill Millar, *Echoes: Diddley Daddy's Offspring* (*Melody Maker*), 14 April, 1979.

[30] Unknown, *Bo Diddley: Diddley Daddy* (*Rock 'n' Roll Stars* 2), 1957.

[31] Dick Tatham, *Bo Diddley: Dick Tatham Phones Him In The States* (*Disc*), 15 June, 1963.

[32] Stuart Colman, *Radio interview with Bo Diddley* (*Echoes*, Radio London), 11 March, 1979.

[33] Allan Jones, *Banging On The White House Door* (*Melody Maker*), 24 February, 1979.

[34] Rick Coleman, *Bo Diddley* (*Wavelength*), June 1982.

[35] Spencer Leigh, *Stars In My Eyes* (Raven, Liverpool), 1980.

[36] Clive Richardson, *Ain't Nobody Gonna Steal My Good Thing* (*Black Echoes*), 6 May, 1978.

[37] Stuart Colman, *Radio interview with Bo Diddley* (*Echoes*, Radio London), 28 March, 1982.

38 Alfred G. Aronowitz, *Pop Scene: Bo Diddley's Complaint* (*New York Post*), 22 October, 1971.
39 Bob Greene, *Only Nostalgia Paying Bo Diddley Now* (*Richmond Times-Dispatch*), 13 September, 1978.
40 Leonard Ferris, *Peggy Malone: Just Call Her Lady Bo* (*Guitar Player*), September 1974.
41 George R. White, *Various interviews with Peggy Malone (Lady Bo), 1987–91* (unpublished).
42 Tom Honig, *Lady Bo Steps Out Of The Shadows* (*Santa Cruz Sentinel*), 5 December, 1980.
43 Norman Jopling, *Bo 'n' Chess: The Tender Story Of A Love–Hate Relationship* (*Record Mirror*), 6 May, 1967.
44 Maureen Paton, *Up Baker's Street* (*Melody Maker*), 11 February, 1978.
45 Mike Leadbitter, *It Was All Alley Music* (*Blues Unlimited* 93), July 1972.
46 George R. White, *Interview with Kay McDaniel, 14 February, 1982* (unpublished).
47 Loraine Alterman, *I Opened The Door For A Lot Of People And They Just Ran Through And Left Me Holding The Knob* (*Melody Maker*), 18 December, 1971.
48 John Goldrosen, *Buddy Holly – His Life & Music* (Charisma, London), 1975.
49 Ted Scott, *Rock, R&B? It's All The Same, Says Bo* (*Disc*), 28 September, 1963.
50 Unknown, *Bo Diddley: I'm A Man* (*Boston After Dark – Spring Music Supplement*), 1972.
51 Christoph Ebner, *Interview with Bo Diddley, 14 March, 1979* (unpublished).
52 Bill Millar, *Interview with Billy Lee Riley, 11 April, 1983* (unpublished).
53 Norman Jopling, *My Music's Not R&B – Bo* (*New Record Mirror*), 28 September, 1963.
54 Chris Hutchins, *Swinging Act By The Everlys* (*New Musical Express*), 4 October, 1963.
55 Vernon Gibbs, *The Return Of Bo Diddley* (*Crawdaddy*), 5 March, 1972.
56 Peter Leslie, *Fab: The Anatomy Of A Phenomenon* (McGibbon & Kee, London), 1964.

[57] Max Jones, *Breakfast With Bo* (*Melody Maker*), 12 August, 1972.

[58] Bill Dwyer, *Bo Diddley: Part 2* (*Blues Unlimited* 72), May 1970.

[59] James Hamilton, *Bo: On The Hectic Art Of Playing 30 Clubs A Night* (*Record Mirror*), 19 August, 1972.

[60] John Broven, *Paul Gayten: I Knew Leonard At The Macomba* (*Blues Unlimited* 130), May–August 1978.

[61] Pat Griffith, *Bo Diddley: Where It All Began* (*Blues & Soul* 98), 1 December, 1972.

[62] Roy Carr, *Canada's Toronto Turns On Rock* (*New Musical Express*), 11 October, 1969.

[63] Richard Nader *Let The Good Times Roll* album sleevenote (Bell Records), 1973.

[64] George R. White, *Interview with Marty Otelsberg, 27 March, 1984* (unpublished).

[65] Tom Honig, *Rock Music's Big Daddy* (*Santa Cruz Sentinel*), 1 May, 1981.

Suggested Further Reading

African Influences
Francis Bebey, *African Music – A People's Art* (Harrap, London), 1975.
Paul Oliver, *Savannah Syncopators – African Retentions In The Blues* (Studio Vista, London), 1970.
John Storm Roberts, *Black Music Of Two Worlds* (Allen Lane, London), 1973.

Caribbean Influences
John Storm Roberts, *Black Music Of Two Worlds* (Allen Lane, London), 1973.
John Sealey & Krister Malm, *Music In The Caribbean* (Hodder & Stoughton, Sevenoaks, Kent), 1982.

Latin Influences
John Storm Roberts, *The Latin Tinge – The Impact Of Latin-American Music On The United States* (Oxford University Press, New York), 1979.

Afro–American Folk Traditions (Music)
Harold Courlander, *Negro Folk Music, USA* (Columbia University Press, New York), 1963.
Paul Oliver, *Blues Fell This Morning* (Cassell & Co, London), 1960.
Paul Oliver, *Screening The Blues – Aspects Of The Blues Tradition* (Cassell & Co, London), 1968.
Newman Ivey White, *American Negro Folk Songs* (Harvard University Press, Cambridge, MA), 1928.

Afro–American Folk Traditions (Toasts)
Roger D. Abrahams, *Deep Down In The Jungle-Narrative Folklore From The Streets Of Philadelphia* (Aldine, Hawthorne, NY), 1970.
Daryl Cumber Dance, *Shuckin' & Jivin' – Folklore From Contemporary Black Americans* (Indiana University Press, London), 1978.
Bruce Jackson, *Get Your Ass In The Water & Swim Like Me* (Harvard University Press, Cambridge, MA), 1974.
Paul Oliver, *Screening The Blues – Aspects Of The Blues Tradition* (Cassell & Co, London), 1968. [Includes a lengthy dissertation on the 'dozens']

Blues/Rhythm & Blues/Rock 'n' Roll
Willie Dixon with Don Snowden, *I Am The Blues – The Willie Dixon Story* (Quartet Books, New York), 1989.
Gillian G. Gaar, *She's A Rebel – The Rise Of Women In Rock & Roll, 1950s–1990s* (Seal Press, Seattle, WA), 1992. [Includes a profile of Peggy Jones, *aka* Lady Bo]
Charlie Gillett, *The Sound Of The City* (Sphere, London), 1971.
Peter Guralnick, *Feel Like Going Home* (Outerbridge & Dienstfrey, New York), 1971. [Includes chapters on Chess Records and Muddy Waters]
Michael Lydon, *Boogie Lightning* (Dial, New York), 1974. [Includes a lengthy chapter on Bo Diddley]
Mike Rowe, *Chicago Breakdown* (Eddison Press Ltd, London), 1973.

Miscellaneous
Hal Rammel, *Nowhere In America – The Big Rock Candy Mountain & Other Comic Utopias* (University Of Illinois Press, Champaign, IL), 1990. [Includes a detailed examination of *Diddy Wah Diddy*]

Appendix I

Bo's Records 1955–94

US releases

SINGLES
1955
Checker 814   'Bo Diddley'/'I'm A Man'
1956
Checker 819   'Diddley Daddy'/'She's Fine, She's Mine'
Checker 827   'Pretty Thing'/'Bring It To Jerome'
Checker 832   'Diddy Wah Diddy'/'I'm Looking For A Woman'
Checker 842   'Who Do You Love'/'I'm Bad'*
Checker 850   'Cops & Robbers'/'Down Home Special'**
1957
Checker 860   'Hey Bo Diddley'/'Mona'
Checker 878   'Say Boss Man'/'Before You Accuse Me'
1958
Checker 896   'Hush Your Mouth'/'Dearest Darling'

---

*On some early pressings, the title was misspelt 'In Bad'.
**On some later copies, the title appeared as 'Down Home Train'.

Checker 907	'Willie & Lillie'/'Bo Meets The Monster'
Checker 914	'I'm Sorry'/'Oh Yea'

1959

Checker 924	'Crackin' Up'/'The Great Grandfather'
Checker 931	'Say Man'/'The Clock Strikes Twelve'
Checker 936	'Say Man, Back Again'/'She's Alright'

1960

Checker 942	'Road Runner'/'My Story'
Checker 951	'Walkin' & Talkin''/'Craw-Dad'
BoKay	'Bo Diddley's A Gunslinger'*
Checker 965	'Gunslinger'/'Signifying Blues'

1961

Checker 976	'Aztec'/'Not Guilty'
Checker 985	'Pills'/'Call Me'
Checker 997	[Reissue of Checker 814]

1962

Checker 1019	'You Can't Judge A Book By The Cover'/'I Can Tell'

1963

Checker 1045	'Surfer's Love Call'/'The Greatest Lover In The World'
Checker 1058	'Memphis' [live]/'Monkey Diddle'

1964

Checker 1083	'Mama, Keep Your Big Mouth Shut'/'Jo-Ann'
Checker 1089	'Chuck's Beat'/'Bo's Beat' [both sides with Chuck Berry]
Checker 1098	'Hey, Good Lookin''/'You Ain't Bad (As You Claim To Be)'

1965

Checker 1123	'500% More Man'/'Let The Kids Dance'

1966

Checker 1142	'We're Gonna Get Married'/'Do The Frog'
Checker 1158	'Ooh Baby'/'Back To School'

1967

Checker 1168	'Wrecking My Love Life'/'Boo-Ga-Loo Before You Go'

1968

Checker 1200	'I'm High Again'/'Another Sugar Daddy'

---

*Bo recalls that he had 'four or five hundred' copies privately pressed up, which he gave away by way of promotion. It is not known whether there was a flipside or if any copies have survived.

1969
Checker 1213   'Bo Diddley 1969'/'Soul Train'
1971
Checker 1238 [GRT]   'The Shape I'm In'/'Pollution'
Chess CH-2117 [GRT]   'I Said Shutup Woman'/
                     'I Love You More Than You'll Ever Know'
1972
Chess CH-2129 [GRT]   'Infatuation'/'Bo Diddley-itis'
1973
Chess CH-2134 [GRT]   'Husband-In-Law'/'Going Down'
Chess CH-2142 [GRT]   'Make A Hit Record'/'Don't Want No Lyin' Woman'
1974
Goldies 45 D-2838 [ABC/Dunhill] [Reissue of Checker 931]
Chess Blue Chip 9031 [GRT]   [Reissue of Checker 814]
1975
Chess Blue Chip 9052 [GRT]   'Say Man'/'Gun Slinger'
Chess Blue Chip 9053 [GRT]   'Diddley Daddy'/'I'm Sorry'
Chess Blue Chip 9054 [GRT]   'Diddy Wah Diddy'/
                     'You Can't Judge A Book'
Chess Blue Chip CH-9031   [Reissue of [GRT] Chess Blue Chip 9031]
[All Platinum]
Chess Blue Chip CH-9052   [Reissue of [GRT] Chess Blue Chip 9052]
[All Platinum]
Chess Blue Chip CH-9053   [Reissue of [GRT] Chess Blue Chip 9053]
[All Platinum]
Chess Blue Chip CH-9054   [Reissue of [GRT] Chess Blue Chip 9054]
[All Platinum]
1976
RCA PB-10618   'Not Fade Away'/'Drag On'
1982
Eric 239   'Bo Diddley'/[Other side by Dale Hawkins]
1983
Chess CH-104 [Sugar Hill]   [Reissue of Checker 814]
Chess CH-124 [Sugar Hill]   'You Can't Judge A Book'/
                     [Other side by Dave 'Baby' Cortez]
1984
Chess CH-91003 [MCA]   [Reissue of [Sugar Hill] Chess CH-104]
Chess CH-91023 [MCA]   [Reissue of [Sugar Hill] Chess CH-124]

1987

Collectables COL-3424	'I'm A Man'/'Say Man'
Collectables COL-3425	'You Can't Judge A Book By Its Cover'/ 'Who Do You Love'
Collectables COL-3453	'Cops & Robbers'/[Other side by Jimmy McCracklin]
Collectables COL-3455	'Bo Diddley'/'I'm Sorry'

1988

Collectables COL-3485	'Road Runner'/'Hush Your Mouth'
Collectables COL-3486	'Bring It To Jerome'/ [Other side by Billy Stewart]

4" 'HIP-POCKET' SINGLE
1967

Philco–Ford Corporation HP-33   'Song Of Bo Diddley'/'I'm A Man'

7" EP
1958

Chess EP-5125   Untitled
'I'm A Man'/'Bo Diddley'/'Willie & Lillie'/'Bo Meets The Monster'

12" LPs
1958

Chess LP-1431   Untitled
'Bo Diddley'/'I'm A Man'/'Bring It To Jerome'/'Before You Accuse
Me'/'Hey Bo Diddley'/'Dearest Darling'/'Hush Your Mouth'/'Say
Bossman'/'Diddley Daddy'/'Diddey Wah Diddey'/'Who Do You
Love'/'Pretty Thing'

1959

Checker LP-1436   *Go Bo Diddley*
'Crackin' Up'/'I'm Sorry'/'Bo's Guitar'/'Willie & Lillie'/'You Don't
Love Me (You Don't Care)'/'Say Man'/'The Great Grandfather'/'Oh
Yea'/'Don't Let It Go'/'Little Girl'/'Dearest Darling'/'The Clock Strikes
Twelve'

1960

Checker LP-2974   *Have Guitar – Will Travel*

'She's Alright'/'Cops & Robbers'/'Run Diddley Daddy'/'Mumblin' Guitar'/
'I Need You Baby'/'Say Man, Back Again'/'Nursery Rhyme'/'I Love You
So'/'Spanish Guitar'/'Dancing Girl'/'Come On Baby'

Checker LP-2976   *Bo Diddley In The Spotlight*
'Road Runner'/'Story Of Bo Diddley'/'Scuttle Bug'/'Signifying Blues'/'Let
Me In'/'Limber'/'Love Me'/'Craw-Dad'/'Walkin' & Talkin''/'Travelin'
West'/'Deed & Deed I Do'/'Live My Life'

Checker LP-2977   *Bo Diddley Is A Gunslinger*
'Gunslinger'/'Ride On Josephine'/'Doing The Craw-Daddy'/'Cadillac'/
'Somewhere'/'Cheyenne'/'Sixteen Tons'/'Whoa Mule (Shine)'/'No More
Lovin''/'Diddling'

1961
Checker LP-2980   *Bo Diddley Is A Lover*
'Not Guilty'/'Hong Kong, Mississippi'/'You're Looking Good'/'Bo's
Vacation'/'Congo'/'Bo's Blues'/'Bo Diddley Is A Lover'/'Aztec'/'Back
Home'/'Bo Diddley Is Loose'/'Love Is A Secret'/'Quick Draw'

1962
Checker LP-2982   *Bo Diddley's A Twister*
[Reissued in 1967 as *Road Runner*]
'Detour'*/'She's Alright'/'Doin' The Jaguar'*/'Who Do You
Love'/'Shank'*/'Road Runner'/'My Babe'*/'The Twister'*/'Hey Bo
Diddley'/'Hush Your Mouth'/'Bo Diddley'/'I'm Looking For A
Woman'/'Here 'Tis'*/'I Know'* [*Previously unissued]

Checker LP-2984   *Bo Diddley*
'I Can Tell'/'Mr Khruschev'/'Diddling'/'Give Me A Break (Man)'/'Who May
Your Lover Be'/'Bo's Bounce'/'You Can't Judge A Book By The
Cover'/'Babes In The Woods'/'Sad Sack'/'Mama Don't Allow No
Twistin''/'You All Green'/'Bo's Twist'

Checker LP-2985   *Bo Diddley & Company*
'(Extra, Read All About) Ben'/'Help Out'/'Diana'/'Bo's A Lumber
Jack'/'Lazy Women'/'Mama Mia'/'Gimme Gimme'/'Put The Shoes On
Willie'/'Pretty Girl'/'Same Old Thing'/'Met You On Saturday'/'Little Girl'

1963

Checker   LP-2987   *Surfin' With Bo Diddley*
'What Did I Say'/'White Silver Sands'/'Surfboard Cha-Cha'/'Surf, Sink Or
Swim'*/'Piggy Back Surfers'/'Surfer's Love Calls'*/'Twisting Waves'/'Wishy
Washy'/'Hucklebuck'/'Old Man River'*/'Oops, He Slipped'/'Low Tide'*
[Bo Diddley only plays on cuts marked *. Others are by Billy Lee Riley
and his group, the Megatons.]

Checker   LP-2988   *Bo Diddley's Beach Party* [live]
'Memphis'/'Gunslinger'/'Hey Bo Diddley'/'Old Smokey'/'Bo Diddley's Dog'/
'I'm Alright'/'Mr Custer'/'Bo's Waltz'/'What's Buggin' You'/'Road Runner'

1964

Checker   LP-2989   *Bo Diddley's 16 All-Time Greatest Hits*
[Some copies were numbered LP-2959 in error.]
'Bo Diddley'/'Bring It To Jerome'/'Hey Bo Diddley'/'Dearest Darling'/'I'm A
Man'/'Diddley Daddy'/'Pretty Thing'/'She's Alright'/'You Can't Judge A Book
By The Cover'/'Road Runner'/'Say Man'/'I'm Sorry'/'Bo Diddley's A Gun-
slinger'/'I'm Looking For A Woman'/'Who Do You Love'/'Hush Your Mouth'

Checker   LP-2991 (mono)   *Two Great Guitars*
          LPS-2991 (stereo)   (Bo Diddley[1] & Chuck Berry[2])
'Chuck's Beat'[1+2]/'When The Saints Go Marching In'[1]/'Bo's Beat'[1+2]/[Plus
one cut by Chuck Berry]

1965

Checker   LP-2992 (mono)   *Hey! Good Lookin'*
'Hey Good Lookin''/'Mush Mouth Millie'/'Bo Diddley's
Hootnanny'/'London Stomp'/'Let's Walk Awhile'/'Rooster Stew'/'La, La,
La'/'Yeah, Yeah, Yeah'/'Rain Man'/'I Wonder Why (People Don't Like
Me)'/'Brother Bear'/'Mummy Walk'

Checker   LP-2996 (mono)   *500% More Man*
          LPS-2996 (stereo)
'500% More Man'/'Let Me Pass'/'Stop My Monkey'/'Greasy
Spoon'/'Tonight Is Ours'/'Root Hoot'/'Hey Red Riding Hood'/'Let The
Kids Dance'/'He's So Mad'/'Soul Food'/'Corn Bread'/'Somebody
Beat Me'

1966

Checker LP-3001 (mono)   *The Originator*
          LPS-3001 (stereo)
'Pills'/'Jo-Ann'/'Two Flies'*/'Yakky Doodle'*/'What Do You Know About
Love'*/'Lazy Woman'/'You Ain't Bad'/'Love You Baby'*/'Limbo'*/
'Background To A Music'*/'Puttentang'/'Africa Speaks'*
[*Previously unissued]

*Between 1966 and 1969 the following LPs were reissued in
'electronically-reprocessed' stereo:*

Checker LPS-3006	*Go Bo Diddley*	[Reissue of Checker LP-1436]
Checker LPS-3007	*Boss Man*	[Reissue of Chess LP-1431]
Checker LPS-2980	*Bo Diddley Is A Lover*	
Checker LPS-2982	*Road Runner*	[Reissue of Checker LP-2982, *Bo Diddley's A Twister*]
Checker LPS-2984	*Bo Diddley*	
Checker LPS-2985	*Bo Diddley & Company*	
Checker LPS-2987	*Surfin' With Bo Diddley*	
Checker LPS-2988	*Bo Diddley's Beach Party*	
Checker LPS-2989	*Bo Diddley's 16 All-Time Greatest Hits*	
Checker LPS-2992	*Hey! Good Lookin'*	

New releases continued to appear in both mono and stereo formats:

1967

Checker LP-3008 (mono)   *Super Blues*
          LPS-3008 (stereo)   (Bo Diddley, Muddy Waters, Little Walter)
'Long Distance Call'/'Who Do You Love'/'I'm A Man'/'Bo Diddley'/'You
Can't Judge A Book By The Cover'/'I Just Want To Make Love To You'/'My
Babe'/'You Don't Love Me'

Checker LP-3010 (mono)   *The Super Super Blues Band*
          LPS-3010 (stereo)   (Howlin' Wolf, Muddy Waters, Bo Diddley)
'Long Distance Call'/'Ooh Baby & Wrecking My Love Life'/'Sweet Little
Angel'/'Spoonful'/'Diddley Daddy'/'The Red Rooster'/'Goin' Down Slow'

From this point, new releases were available only in stereo:

1970
Checker LPS-3013 [GRT]   *The Black Gladiator*
'Elephant Man'/'You, Bo Diddley'/'Black Soul'/'Power House'/'If The Bible's Right'/'I've Got A Feeling'/'Shut Up, Woman'/'Hot Buttered Blues'/'Funky Fly'/'I Don't Like You'

1971
Chess CH-50001 [GRT]   *Another Dimension*
'The Shape I'm In'/'I Love You More Than You'll Ever Know'/'Pollution'/'Bad Moon Rising'/'Down On The Corner'/'I Said Shutup Woman'/'Bad Side Of The Moon'/'Lodi'/'Go For Broke'

1972
Chess CH-50016 [GRT]   *Where It All Began*
'I've Had It Hard'/'Woman'/'Look At Grandma'/'A Good Thing'/'Bad Trip'/'Hey, Jerome'/'Infatuation'/'Take It All Off'/'Bo Diddley-itis'

Chess 2CH-60005 [GRT]   *Got My Own Bag Of Tricks* [2-LP]
'Bo Diddley'/'I'm A Man'/'Bring It To Jerome'/'Diddley Daddy'/'Before You Accuse Me'/'Pretty Thing'/'Road Runner'/'Mona'/'Cops & Robbers'/'Story Of Bo Diddley'/'Say Boss Man'/'Hush Your Mouth'/'Who Do You Love'/'Dearest Darling'/'You Can't Judge A Book By The Cover'/'Hey Bo Diddley'/'Say Man'/'I'm Looking For A Woman'/'500% More Man'/'Bo's Blues'/'Nursery Rhyme'/'Whoa, Mule (Shine)'/'Live My Life'/'Bo Diddley Is Loose'

1973
Chess 2CH-60015 [GRT]   *Blues/Rock Avalanche*
                         (various artists) [live 2-LP]
'I Hear You Knockin''/'You Can't Judge A Book By The Cover'/'Diddley Daddy'/[Other tracks not by Bo Diddley]

Chess CH-50029 [GRT]   *The London Bo Diddley Sessions*
'Don't Want No Lyin' Woman'/'Bo Diddley'/'Going Down'/'Make A Hit Record'/'Bo-Jam'/'Husband-In-Law'/'Do The Robot'/'Sneakers On A Rooster'/'Get Out Of My Life'

Bell 9002   *Let The Good Times Roll*
(various artists) [live 2-LP]
'Introduction'/'Documentary'/'I'm A Man'/'Hey Bo Diddley'/[Other tracks not by Bo Diddley]

1974

Chess CH-50047 [GRT]   *Big Bad Bo*
'Bite You'/'He's Got All The Whiskey'/'Hit Or Miss'/'You've Got A Lot Of Nerve'/'Stop The Pusher'/'Evelee'/'I've Been Workin''

1976

RCA-Victor APL1-1229   *The 20th Anniversary Of Rock 'n' Roll*
'Ride The Water (Part 1)'/'Not Fade Away'/'Kill My Body'/'Drag On'/'Ride The Water (Part 2)'/'Bo Diddley Jam (I'm A Man)'/'Hey Bo Diddley'/'Who Do You Love'/'Bo Diddley's A Gunslinger'/'I'm A Man (Reprise)'

1977

M.F. Productions Inc   *I'm A Man* [live 2-LP]
MF202/2 (77-1002)
'Bo Diddley'/'I'm A Man'/'You All Green'/'Mr Kruschev'/'Somebody Beat Me'/'Tonight Is Ours'/'I'm Sorry'/'Little Girl'/'Hey Bo Diddley'/'Say Boss Man'/'Bring It To Jerome'/'Mona'/'Before You Accuse Me'/'You Can't Judge A Book By Lookin' At The Cover'/'Road Runner'

1982

Accord SN-7182   *Toronto Rock 'n' Roll Revival 1969 (Volume 5)*
[Chess studio cuts overdubbed with audience noise. Original titles are shown in parentheses.]
'Cracklin'' ('Mumblin' Guitar')/'Rockin'' ('Bo's Bounce')/'Dancin' Girl'/'Let The Kids Dance'/'Mess Around' ('Give Me A Break (Man)')/'Somebody's Crying' ('Who May Your Lover Be')/'Hong Kong' ('Hong Kong, Mississippi')/'Can I Go Home With You' ('Little Girl')/'I'm Going Home' ('Down Home Special')/'Rhyme Song ('Nursery Rhyme')

1983

Chess CH-8204 [Sugar Hil] *His Greatest Sides (Volume 1)*
'Bo Diddley'/'Pretty Thing'/'Bring It To Jerome'/'I'm A

Man'/'Mona'/'Diddley Daddy'/'Dearest Darling'/'Who Do You Love'/'Road
Runner'/'Say Man'/'Bo's Bounce'/'You Can't Judge A Book By The
Cover'/'Crackin' Up'/'Hey Bo Diddley'

1984
Chess CH-9106 [MCA]   *His Greatest Sides (Volume 1)*
[Reissue of [Sugar Hill] Chess CH-8204]

Chess CH-9168 [MCA]   *Super Blues*
                         (Bo Diddley, Muddy Waters, Little Walter)
[Reissue of Checker LP(S)-3008]

Chess CH-9169 [MCA]   *The Super Super Blues Band*
                         (Howlin' Wolf, Muddy Waters, Bo Diddley)
[Reissue of Checker LP(S)-3010]

Chess CH-9170 [MCA]   *Two Great Guitars*
                         (Bo Diddley & Chuck Berry)
[Reissue of Checker LP(S)-2991]

Chess CH-9225 [MCA]   *Blues/Rock Avalanche*
                         (various artists) [live 2-LP]
[Reissue of [GRT] Chess 2CH-60015]

1985
Chess CH-9187 [MCA]   *Have Guitar – Will Travel*
[Reissue of Checker LP-2974]

1986
Chess CH-9194 [MCA]   Untitled
[Reissue of Chess LP-1431]

Chess CH-9196 [MCA]   *Go Bo Diddley*
[Reissue of Checker LP-1436]

MCA/Silver Eagle   *Goodtime Rock 'n' Roll*
MCA-6171   (various artists) [live]
'Bo Diddley'/[Other tracks not by Bo Diddley]

1987
Chess CH-9264 [MCA]   *Bo Diddley In The Spotlight*
[Reissue of Checker LP-2976]

Slash 25605-1   *La Bamba* (various artists)
'Who Do You Love' [re-recording]/[Other tracks not by Bo Diddley]

Checkmate LP-1960*   *Give Me A Break*
'Give Me A Break'/'Who May Your Lover Be'/'Bo's Bounce'/'Don't Let It
Go'/'The Twister'/'Pretty Girl'/'Congo'/'Little Girl'/'Deed & Deed I
Do'/'Aztec'/'Hong Kong, Mississippi'/'Detour'/'Gimme Gimme'/'Scuttle
Bug'/'Say Man, Back Again'/'Sad Sack'/'Bo Diddley Is Loose'/'Same Old
Thing   .

1988
Island 91030-1   *Tapeheads* (various artists)
'Surfer's Love Chant'/[Other tracks not by Bo Diddley]

Chess CH-9285 [MCA]   *Bo Diddley Is A Gunslinger*
[Reissue of Checker LP-2977]

1989
Chess CH-9293 [MCA]   *Wrinkles* (various artists)
'Mess Around'/[Other tracks not by Bo Diddley]

Chess CH-9296 [MCA]   *The London Bo Diddley Sessions*
[Reissue of Chess CH-50029]

Triple X51017-1   *Breakin' Through The BS*
'Turbo Diddley 2000'/'Bo-Pop Shake'/'Deeper'/'Down With The
Pusher'/'Slipped-n-Fell-n-Love'/'You Tricked Me'/'Wake Up
America'/'Jeanette, Jeanette'/'I Broke The Chain'/'RU Serious'/'Home To
McComb'/'Jus' Like Bo Diddley'

---

*The label states 'Made In USA', and is therefore listed as such, although there is strong
evidence to suggest that it is actually of European (most likely Dutch) origin, and probably a
bootleg.

1990

Chess CH3-19502 [MCA]   *The Chess Box* [3-LP box set]
'Bo Diddley'/'I'm A Man'/'You Don't Love Me'/'Diddley Daddy'/'Pretty Thing'/'Bring It To Jerome' (unedited master)*/'Bring It To Jerome'/'Diddy Wah Diddy'/'I'm Looking For A Woman'/'Who Do You Love'/'Down Home Special'/'Hey Bo Diddley'/'Mona'/'Say Boss Man'/'Before You Accuse Me'/'Say Man'/'Hush Your Mouth' (alt take)*/'The Clock Strikes Twelve'/'Dearest Darling' (alt take)*/'Crackin' Up'/'Don't Let It Go (Hold On To What You Got)'/'I'm Sorry'/'Mumblin' Guitar'/'The Story Of Bo Diddley'/'She's Alright' (LP version with overdubbed chorus)/'Say Man, Back Again' (alt take)*/'Road Runner'/'Spend My Life With You'*/'Cadillac'/'Signifying Blues' (extended version)*/'Deed & Deed I Do'/'You Know I Love You'*/'Look At My Baby'*/'Ride On Josephine'/'Aztec'/'Back Home'/'Pills'/'Untitled Instrumental'*/'I Can Tell'/'You Can't Judge A Book By Its Cover'/'Who May Your Lover Be'/'The Greatest Lover In The World'/'500% More Man'/'Ooh Baby'/'Bo Diddley 1969' [*Previously unissued]

LIMITED EDITION CASSETTE TAPE
1983

BoKay BK-069   *Ain't It Good To Be Free*
'Gotta Be A Change'/'Bo Diddley Put The Rock In Rock 'n' Roll'/'Ain't It Good To Be Free'/'I Don't Want Your Welfare'/'Mona, Where's Your Sister'/'Stabilize Yourself'/'I Don't Know Where I've Been'/'I Ain't Gonna Force It On You'/'Evil Woman'/'Let The Fox Talk'

UK releases

SINGLES

1959

London 45-HLM-8913   'Crackin' Up'/'The Great Grandfather'
[=US Checker 924]

London 45-HLM-8975   'Say Man'/'The Clock Strikes Twelve'
[=US Checker 931]

1960

London 45-HLM-9035   'Say Man, Back Again'/'She's Alright'
[=US Checker 936]

London 45-HLM-9112   'Road Runner'/'My Story'
                              [=US Checker 942]

1962

Pye Intl R&B 7N.25165   'You Can't Judge A Book By The Cover'/
                              'I Can Tell' [=US Checker 1019]

1963

Pye Intl R&B 7N.25193   'Who Do You Love'/'The Twister'

Pye Intl R&B 7N.25210   'Bo Diddley'/'Detour'

Pye Intl R&B 7N.25216   [Reissue of Pye Intl R&B 7N.25165]

Pye Intl R&B 7N.25217   'Road Runner'/'Pretty Thing'

Pye Intl R&B 7N.25227   'Bo Diddley Is A Lover'/'Doin' The Jaguar'

1964

Pye Intl R&B 7N.25235   'Memphis'/'Monkey Diddle'
                              [=US Checker 1058]

Pye Intl R&B 7N.25243   'Mona'/'Gimme Gimme'

Pye Intl R&B 7N.25258   'Mama, Keep Your Big Mouth Shut'/'Jo-Anne'
                              [=US Checker 1083]

1965

Chess CRS-8000 [Pye]   'Hey, Good Lookin''/
                              'You Ain't Bad (As You Claim To Be)'
                              [=US Checker 1098]

Chess CRS-8014 [Pye]   'Mush Mouth Millie'/'Somebody Beat Me'

Chess CRS-8021 [Pye]   'Let Me Pass'/'Let The Kids Dance'

1966

Chess CRS-8026 [Pye]   '500 Percent More Man'/'Stop My Monkey'

Chess CRS-8036 [Pye]   'We're Gonna Get Married'/'Easy'

1967

Chess CRS-8053 [Pye]   'Ooh Baby'/'Back To School'
                              [=US Checker 1158]

Chess CRS-8057 [Pye]   'Wrecking My Love Life'/
                              'Boo-Ga-Loo Before You Go' [=US Checker 1168]

1968

Chess CRS-8078 [Pye]   'I'm High Again'/'Another Sugar Daddy'
                              [=US Checker 1200]

1969

Chess CRS-8088 [Pye]   'Bo Diddley 1969'/'Soul Train'
                              [=US Checker 1213]

1971

Chess 6145 002	'I Love You More Than You'll Ever Know'/
[Phonogram]	'I Said Shutup Woman' [=US [GRT] Chess 2117]

1984

New Rose NEW-42   'Ain't It Good To Be Free'/'Bo Diddley Put
The Rock In Rock 'n' Roll'

7" EPs

1956

London RE-U-1054   *Rhythm & Blues With Bo Diddley*
'Bo Diddley'/'I'm A Man'/'Bring It To Jerome'/'Pretty Thing'

1963

Pye Intl R&B NEP-44009   *Chuck & Bo* (Chuck Berry/Bo Diddley)
'Pills'/'The Greatest Lover In The World'/[Other tracks by Chuck Berry]

Pye Intl R&B NEP-44012   *Chuck & Bo (Volume 2)*
                              (Chuck Berry/Bo Diddley)
'She's Fine, She's Mine'/'Bo Meets The Monster'/[Other tracks by Chuck
Berry]

Pye Intl R&B NEP-44014   *Hey! Bo Diddley*
'Hey Bo Diddley'/'Hush Your Mouth'/'I'm Looking For A Woman'/'Before
You Accuse Me'

1964

Pye Intl R&B NEP-44017   *Chuck & Bo (Volume 3)*
                              (Chuck Berry/Bo Diddley)
'Deed & Deed I Do'/'Diana'/[Other tracks by Chuck Berry]

Pye Intl R&B NEP-44019   *The Story Of Bo Diddley*
'Story Of Bo Diddley'/'Little Girl'/'Put The Shoes On Willie'/'Run Diddley
Daddy'

Pye Intl R&B NEP-44031   *Bo's A Lumberjack*
'Bo's A Lumberjack'/'Let Me In'/'Hong Kong, Mississippi'/'You're Looking
Good'

Pye Intl. R&B NEP-44036 *Diddling*
'Diddling'/'You All Green'/'I Can Tell'/'Babes In The Woods'

1965
Chess CRE-6008 [Pye] *I'm A Man*
'I'm A Man'/'Dearest Darling'/'Pretty Thing'/'I'm Sorry'

1966
Chess CRE-6023 [Pye] *Rooster Stew*
'Hey Good Lookin''/'Brother Bear'/'Rooster Stew'/'Mush Mouth Millie'

1972
Chess 6145 012 *Big Daddies*
[Phonogram] (Chuck Berry/Bo Diddley)
'We're Gonna Get Married'/'You Can't Judge A Book By The
Cover'/[Other tracks by Chuck Berry]

1985
Chess CHES-4001 [PRT] *Chess Mini Masters: Bo Diddley*
'Bo Diddley'/'Road Runner'/'Pretty Thing'/'Say Man'

12" EPs
1983
Red Lightnin' RLEP-12 0045 *It's Great To Be Rich* (various artists)
'Don't Know Where I've Been' [with the BMTs]/[Other tracks not by Bo Diddley]

1987
London LONX-152 Untitled (various artists)
'Who Do You Love' [from *La Bamba* soundtrack album]
[Other tracks not by Bo Diddley]

1990
Old Gold OG-7704 Untitled
'Bo Diddley'/'Pretty Thing'/'Road Runner'/'You Can't Judge A Book By Its
Cover'

12" LPs
1960
London HA-M-2230   *Go Bo Diddley*
[=US Checker LP-1436]

1961
Pye Jazz NJL-33   *Bo Diddley Is A Gunslinger*
[=US Checker LP-2977]

1963
Pye Intl R&B NPL-28025   *Hey! Bo Diddley*
'Hey Bo Diddley'/'I'm A Man'/'Detour'/'Before You Accuse Me'/'Bo Diddley'/'Hush Your Mouth'/'My Babe'/'Road Runner'/'Shank'/'I Know'/'Here 'Tis'/'I'm Looking For A Woman'

Pye Intl R&B NPL-28026   *Bo Diddley*
[=US Checker LP-2984]

Pye Intl R&B NPL-28029   *Bo Diddley Rides Again*
'Bring It To Jerome'/'Cops & Robbers'/'Mumblin' Guitar'/'Oh Yea'/'You Don't Love Me (You Don't Care)'/'Down Home Train'/'Bo Diddley Is Loose'/'Help Out'/'Call Me (Bo's Blues)'/'Don't Let It Go'/'Nursery Rhyme'/'Dearest Darling'

1964
Pye Intl R&B NPL-28032   *Bo Diddley's Beach Party*
[=US Checker LP-2988]

Pye Intl R&B NPL-28034   *Bo Diddley In The Spotlight*
[Different tracks from US Checker LP-2976]
'Gimme Gimme'/'Not Guilty'/'Scuttle Bug'/'Say Man'/'Let Me In'/'Hong Kong, Mississippi'/'Craw-Dad'/'Bo's A Lumberjack'/'Walkin' & Talkin''/'I Need You Baby'/'You're Looking Good'/'She's Alright'

---

*Not the track on US Checker LP-2974, but an unknown cut from 1959.

Pye Intl R&B NPL-28047   *Two Great Guitars*
(Bo Diddley & Chuck Berry)
[=US Checker LP-2991]

Pye Intl R&B NPL-28049   *Bo Diddley's 16 All-Time Greatest Hits*
[=US Checker LP-2989]

1965
Chess CRL-4002 [Pye]   *Hey Good Lookin'*
[=US Checker LP-2992]

Chess CRL-4507 [Pye]   *Let Me Pass*
[=US Checker LP(S)-2996 *500% More Man* except 'Stinkey' included
instead of '500% More Man']

1966
Golden Guinea [Pye]   *Hey! Bo Diddley*
GGL-0358
[=Pye Intl R&B NPL-28025 except 'Hush Your Mouth' and 'I'm Looking
For A Woman' omitted]

1967
Chess CRL-4525 (mono)   *The Originator*
     CRLS-4525 (stereo) [Pye] [=US Checker LP(S)-3001]

Chess CRL-4529 (mono)   *Super Blues*
     CRLS-4529 (stereo) [Pye] (Bo Diddley, Muddy Waters, Little Walter)
[=US Checker LP(S)-3008]

1968
Marble Arch (mono)   *Surfin' With Bo Diddley*
MAL-751 [Pye]
[=US Checker LP-2987 except 'Piggy Back Surfers' and 'Twisting Waves'
omitted]

Marble Arch (mono)
MAL-814 [Pye]   *Hey! Bo Diddley*
[=Pye Intl R&B NPL-28025 except 'Detour' and 'Shank' omitted]

Chess CRL-4537 (mono)   *The Super Super Blues Band*
       CRLS-4537 (stereo) [Pye] (Howlin' Wolf, Muddy Waters,
                             Bo Diddley) [=US Checker LP(S)-3010]

The following new releases were available only in stereo:

1971
Chess 6310 107 [Phonogram]   *Another Dimension*
[=US [GRT] Chess CH-50001]

1972
Chess 6310 123 [Phonogram]   *Bo Diddley's Golden Decade*
[=US Checker LP-2989 *Bo Diddley's 16 All-Time Greatest Hits*]

1973
Checker 6467 304   *Got Another Bag Of Tricks*
[Phonogram]
'Cops & Robbers'/'Mumblin' Guitar'/'Say Man, Back Again'/'Live My
Life'/'Background To A Music'/'Run Diddley Daddy'*/'Diddling'/'Mona (I
Need You Baby)'/'Cadillac'/'When The Saints Go Marching In'/'I Love You
So'/'Nursery Rhyme'/'Aztec'/'Bo's A Lumberjack' (unedited version)

Chess 6499 476 [Phonogram]   *The London Bo Diddley Sessions*
[=US [GRT] Chess CH-50029]

Bell DUBL-9002/3   *Let The Good Times Roll* (various artists)
                            [live 2-LP] [=US Bell 9002]

1976
RCA-Victor RS-1042   *The 20th Anniversary Of Rock 'n' Roll*
                            [=US RCA-Victor APL1-1229]

---

*Not the track on US Checker LP-2974, but an unknown cut from 1959.

1981

Chess CXMD-4003 [PRT]   *Chess Masters: Bo Diddley* [2-LP]
'Bo Diddley'/'Bring It To Jerome'/'Road Runner'/'Who Do You
Love'/'Hush Your Mouth'/'Pretty Thing'/'Pills'/'Mona'/'You Can't Judge A
Book By Its Cover'/'Hey Bo Diddley'/'Hucklebuck'/'Mumblin'
Guitar'/'She's Alright'/'Diddley Daddy'/'I'm A Man'/'I'm Looking For A
Woman'/'Say Man'/'I Can Tell'/'My Babe'/'Cops & Robbers'/'I'm
Sorry'/'Before You Accuse Me'/'Dearest Darling'

1982

Chess CXMD-4009 [PRT]   *Chess Masters: Bo Diddley*
                             (Volume 2) [2-LP]
'Crackin' Up'/'Blues Instrumental' (Spanish Guitar)/'The Great
Grandfather'/'You Don't Love Me' (alt take of 'She's Fine, She's
Mine')*/'What Do You Know About Love'/'Lazy Woman'/'Come On
Baby'/'Dancing Girl'/'Diddy Wah Diddy'/'Little Girl' (alt take)*/'Nursery
Rhyme'/'The Clock Strikes Twelve'/'She's Fine, She's Mine'/'Down Home
Special'/'Say Boss Man'/'Bo Meets The Monster'/'Willie & Lillie'/'Oh
Yea'/'Mama, Keep Your Big Mouth Shut'/'You're Looking Good'/'The
Greatest Lover In The World'/'Little Girl'/'Let Me In'/'Bo's Guitar'
[*Previously unissued]

1984

New Rose ROSE-34   *Ain't It Good To Be Free*
[=US BoKay cassette BK-069 except positions of 'Gotta Be A Change' and
'Ain't It Good To Be Free' reversed]

1985

Chess CXMD-4056 [PRT]   *Blues/Rock Avalanche* (various artists)
                             [live 2-LP] [=US [GRT] Chess 2CH-60015]

Fan Club FC-009 [New Rose]   *Bo Diddley & Co-Live* [live]
'He's A Hell Of A Man'/'Don't Handle The Merchandise'/'Get Up, Get
Down'/'Bad Dad'/'Can I Put My Finger In It'

1986

Conifer CFRC-507   *Hey... Bo Diddley In Concert* [live]
(Bo Diddley with Mainsqueeze)
'Intro & Bo Diddley Vamp'/'Dr Jeckyll'/'Everleen'/'I Don't Know Where
I've Been'/'You Can't Judge A Book'/'Road Runner'/'I'm A Man'/'Mona'

Magnum Force MFM-021   *Hey, Bo Diddley*
[=US Accord SN-7182 except 'Dancin' Girl' and 'Let The Kids Dance'
omitted]
Chess GCH-8002 [Charly]   *Have Guitar – Will Travel*
[=US Checker LP-2974]

Chess GCH-8005 [Charly]   *His Greatest Sides (Volume 1)*
[=US [Sugar Hill] Chess CH-8204]

1987

Chess GCH-8021 [Charly]   *Go Bo Diddley*
[=US Checker LP-1436]

Chess GCH-8026 [Charly]   *Bo Diddley*
[=US Chess LP-1431]

London LONLP-36   *La Bamba* (various artists)
[=US Slash 25605-1]

Chess GCH-8038 [Charly]   *Bo Diddley In The Spotlight*
[=US Checker LP-2976]

1988

Stylus SMR-849   *Chess Masters*
'Mona'/'Hey Bo Diddley'/'Road Runner'/'Bring It To Jerome'/'Pretty
Thing'/'Pills'/'I'm A Man'/'Hush Your Mouth'/'Say Man'/'Cops &
Robbers'/'Mumblin' Guitar'/'Diddley Daddy'/'Memphis' [live]/'She's
Alright'/'Who Do You Love'/'You Can't Judge A Book By The Cover'

Chess GCH2-6033 [Charly]   *Blues/Rock Avalanche* (various artists) [live 2-LP] [=US [GRT] Chess 2CH-60015]

Chess GCH-8111 [Charly]   *Bo Diddley's Beach Party* [live]
[= US Checker LP-2988]

1989

Instant INS-5004 [Charly]   *Road Runner*
'Bo Diddley'/'I'm A Man'/'Pretty Thing'/'Who Do You Love'/'Mona (I Need
You Baby)'/'Say Man'/'Hush Your Mouth'/'Road Runner'/'You Can't Judge
A Book By Looking At The Cover'/'Cops & Robbers'/'Hey Bo
Diddley'/'Crackin' Up'/'Diddley Daddy'/'Bring It To Jerome'

New Rose ROSE-188   *Living Legend*
'Turbo Diddley 2000'*/'RU Serious'*/'Jeanette, Jeanette'*/'I Broke The
Chain'*/'Bo-Pop Quake'/'The Best'/'I'll Lick Yo' Face'/'U Killed It'/'Goin'
Home To McComb'*
[cuts marked * also appeared on US Triple X 51017-1, *Breakin' Through The BS*]

1990

Instant INSD-5038 [Charly]   *Bo Diddley – Hey! Bo Diddley* [2-LP]
'Bo Diddley'/'I'm A Man'/'Little Girl'/'You Don't Love Me (You Don't
Care)'/'Diddley Daddy'/'She's Fine, She's Mine'/'Pretty Thing'/'Bring It To
Jerome'/'Spanish Guitar'/'Dancing Girl'/'Diddy Wah Diddy'/'I Am Looking
For A Woman'/'Who Do You Love'/'Cops & Robbers'/'Down Home
Special'/'Hey Bo Diddley'/'Mona (I Need You Baby)'/'Before You Accuse
Me'/'Say Man'/'Hush Your Mouth'/'Bo's Guitar'/'The Clock Strikes
Twelve'/'Willie & Lillie'/'Crackin' Up'/'I'm Sorry'/'Mama Mia'/'Bucket'*/
'What Do You Know About Love'/'Nursery Rhyme'/'Story Of Bo
Diddley'/'Road Runner'/'You Can't Judge A Book By The Cover'
[*Previously unissued]

1991

Edsel ED-318   *Bo Diddley – The 20th Anniversary Of
Rock 'n' Roll* [=US RCA-Victor APL1-1229

See For Miles SEE-321   *Bo Diddley –The EP Collection*
'Little Girl'/'Put The Shoes On Willie'/'Run Diddley Daddy' (actually

'Diddley Daddy')/'Bo Diddley'/'I'm A Man'/'Bring It To Jerome'/'Pretty Thing'/'The Greatest Lover In The World'/'She's Fine, She's Mine'/'Hey Good Lookin'/'Deed & Deed I Do'/'I'm Sorry'/'Dearest Darling' (actually 'Crackin' Up')/'Bo Meets The Monster'/'Rooster Stew'/'Bo's A Lumberjack'/'Let Me In'/'Hong Kong, Mississippi'/'Hey Bo Diddley'/'Before You Accuse Me'/'The Story Of Bo Diddley'/'You're Looking Good'

Appendix II

Bo On CD

US releases

3" CD EPs
1989
Chess CHD-37281 [MCA]
'Bo Diddley'/'Say Man'/'I'm A Man'/'Diddley Daddy'

Chess CHD-37326 [MCA]
'Who Do You Love'/'Road Runner'/'I'm A Man'/'You Can't Judge A Book
By Its Cover'

5" CD ALBUMS
1987
Chess CHD-5904 [MCA]   *Two On One*
                         [Reissue of Chess LP-1431 + Checker LP-1436]

Slash 25605-2   *La Bamba* (various artists)
                         [Equivalent of Slash 25605-1]
'Who Do You Love' [re-recording]

1988

Chess CHD-9264 [MCA]   *Bo Diddley In The Spotlight*
                        [Equivalent of [MCA] Chess CH-9264]

Island 91030-2   *Tapeheads* (various artists)
                        [Equivalent of Island 91030-1]

Chess CHD-9285 [MCA]   *Bo Diddley Is A Gunslinger*
[Equivalent of [MCA] Chess CH-9285 plus two bonus cuts, 'Working Man'
and 'Do What I Say', both previously unissued]

1989

Chess CHD-9293 [MCA]   *Wrinkles* (various artists)
                        [Equivalent of [MCA] Chess CH-9293]

Chess CHD-9296 [MCA]   *The London Bo Diddley Sessions*
                        [Equivalent of [MCA] Chess CH-9296]

Triple X 51017-2   *Breakin' Through The BS*
                        [Equivalent of Triple X 51017-1]

1990

Chess CHD2-19502 [MCA] *The Chess Box* [2-CD box set]
                        [Equivalent of [MCA] Chess CH3-19502]

1991

Chess CHD-9331 [MCA]   *Rare & Well Done*
'She's Alright' (unedited version)*/'Heart-O-Matic Love'*/'I'm A Man' (alt
take)*/'Little Girl' (alt take)*/'She's Fine, She's Mine'/'Bo Meets The
Monster'/'I'm Bad'/'Blues Blues'*/'Rock 'n' Roll'*/'No More Lovin'' (alt
take)*/'Cookie-Headed Diddley'*/'Moon Baby'*/'I Want My Baby'*/'Please
Mr Engineer'*/'We're Gonna Get Married'/'I'm High Again' (alt
mix/overdubs)*[*Previously unissued]

1992

Victory 383480008-2   *Live At The Ritz*
                        (Ronnie Wood & Bo Diddley) [live]
'Crackin' Up'/'Hey Bo Diddley'/'I'm A Man'/'Money To Ronnie'/'Road
Runner'/'Who Do You Love'/[Other tracks by Ronnie Wood only]

Chess CHD-9168   *Super Blues*
(Bo Diddley, Muddy Waters, Little Walter)
[Reissue of Checker LP(S)-3008 plus two bonus cuts, 'Sad Hours' and 'Juke']

Chess CHD-9169   *The Super Super Blues Band*
(Howlin' Wolf, Muddy Waters, Bo Diddley)
[Reissue of Checker LP(S)-3010]

Chess CHD-9170   *Two Great Guitars*
(Bo Diddley & Chuck Berry)
[Reissue of Checker LP(S)-2991 plus three bonus cuts by Bo ('Fireball',
'Stay Sharp' and 'Stinkey') and one by Chuck]

1993

Triple X 51130-2   *This Should Not Be*
'This Should Not Be'/'I'm Not The One'/'Rock Patrol'/'U Don't Look So
Good'/'Mind Yo Business'/'Put Your Suitcase Down'/'My Jesus Ain't
Prejudice'/'Turn Me Loose'/'The Best' (remix) /'I'll Lick Yo Face'
(remix)/'Yum I Yay'/'Let Me Join Your World'/'I Love My Baby'/
'U Ugly'/'Bozilla's Groove'/'Rock Titan'

TVT TVT-9447-2   *The Sullivan Years: Rhythm & Blues Revue*
(various artists)
'Bo Diddley' [live on Ed Sullivan show, 1955]/[Other tracks not by Bo
Diddley]

1994

Triple X 51162-2   *Live*
[Reissue of 1985 UK Fan Club LP FC-009]

Triple X 51192-2   *Promises*
'Promises'/'Kids Don't Do It'/'Hear What I'm Sayin''/'I'm Gonna Get Your
Girlfriend'/'She Wasn't Raped'

1995

MCA MSP-20872   *Bo Knows Bo*
'Gunslinger'/'Hey Bo Diddley'/'Doing The Craw-Daddy'/'Road
Runner'/'Diddlin''/'Diddley Daddy'/'Diddy Wah Diddy'/'Crackin' Up'/'Who
Do You Love'/'You Can't Judge A Book By Its Cover'

Triple X 51161-2   *The Mighty Bo Diddley*
                          [Equivalent of UK New Rose ROSE-34CD]

UK releases

5" CD EPs
1989
Charly CDS-11   *The Charly Originals*
'Bo Diddley'/'Road Runner'/'You Can't Judge A Book By The
Cover'/'Mona (I Need You Baby)'

5" CD ALBUMS
1987
London 828058-2   *La Bamba* (various artists)
                         [Equivalent of London LONLP-36]

1988
New Rose ROSE-34CD   *Ain't It Good To Be Free*
                       [Equivalent of New Rose ROSE-34]

Stylus SMD-849   *Chess Masters*
                       [Equivalent of Stylus SMR-849]

Spectrum U.4049   *Good Time Rock 'n' Roll* (various artists) [live]
                       [Equivalent of US MCA/Silver Eagle MCA-6171]

Chess CDRED-2 [Charly]   *Diddley Daddy*
'Bo Diddley'/'I'm A Man'/'You Don't Love Me (You Don't Care)'/'Diddley
Daddy'/'She's Fine, She's Mine'/'Pretty Thing'/'Bring It To Jerome'/'Diddy
Wah Diddy'/'I'm Looking For A Woman'/'Who Do You Love'/'Cops &
Robbers'/'Hey Bo Diddley'/'Mona'/'Before You Accuse Me'/'Say
Man'/'Hush Your Mouth'/'Bo's Guitar'/'Willie & Lillie'/'Crackin' Up'/'I'm
Sorry'/'Nursery Rhyme'/'Story Of Bo Diddley'/'Road Runner'/'You Can't
Judge A Book By The Cover'

1989
Instant CDINS-5004   *Road Runner*
[Charly]   [Equivalent of Instant INS-5004]

New Rose ROSE-188CD   *Living Legend*
[Equivalent of New Rose ROSE-188 plus one bonus cut, 'Just Like Bo Diddley']

1990
Chess CDRED-21   *London Sessions*
[Charly]   [Reissue of US [GRT] Chess CH-50029]

Instant CDINS-5038   *Hey! Bo Diddley*
[Charly]
[Equivalent of Instant INSD-5038, excluding 'I'm Sorry', 'Mama Mia, What Do You Know About Love' and 'Bucket']

Double Play GRF-061   *Hey Bo Diddley*
[Tring International]
'Bo Diddley'/'Hey Bo Diddley'/'I'm A Man'/'Bring It To Jerome'/'Diddley Daddy'/'Before You Accuse Me'/'Pretty Thing'/'Who Do You Love'/'Dearest Darling'/'You Can't Judge A Book By The Cover'/'Say Man'/'I'm Looking For A Woman'/'Road Runner'/'Mona'/'Cops & Robbers'/'Story Of Bo Diddley'/'Say Bossman'/'Hush Your Mouth'/'Nursery Rhyme'/'I'm Sorry'/'Live My Life'

1991
Object OR-0118   *Bo Diddley*
'Bo Diddley'/'Hey Bo Diddley'/'Pretty Thing'/'Bring It To Jerome'/'I'm A Man'/'Mona'/'Diddley Daddy'/'Dearest Darling'/'Who Do You Love'/'Roadrunner'/'Story Of Bo Diddley'/'Before You Accuse Me'/'I'm Looking For A Woman'/'Say Bossman'

Edsel EDCD-318   *The 20th Anniversary Of Rock 'n' Roll*
                               [Equivalent of Edsel ED-318]

Chess CDRED-31 [Charly] *Oh Yeah!*
'Bo Meets The Monster'/'I'm Bad'/'Dearest Darling'/'Say Boss Man'/'Mumblin' Guitar'/'Oh Yea'/'Run Diddley Daddy'**/'I Love You

---

**See footnote to UK LP Checker 6467 304 on page 220

So'/'Don't Let It Go'/'Live My Life'/'Signifying Blues'/'Let Me In'/
'Craw-Dad'/'Walkin' & Talkin''/'Gunslinger'/'Travelin' West'/'Ride On
Josephine'/'Cadillac'/'Bucket' (alt take)*/'Sick & Tired'*/'Huckleberry
Bush'*/'Bo's A Lumberjack' (unedited version)/'Diddling'/'All
Together'*[*Previously unissued]

See For Miles SEECD-321   *The EP Collection*
[Equivalent of See For Miles SEE-321 plus two bonus cuts, 'Hush Your
Mouth' and 'I'm Looking For A Woman']

Magnum Force   *The Chess Masters*
CDMF-077
'Bo Diddley'/'I'm A Man'/'Diddley Daddy'/'Pretty Thing'/'Bring It To
Jerome'/'Diddy Wah Diddy'/'Who Do You Love'/'Hey Bo Diddley'/
'Mona'/'Say Boss Man'/'Before You Accuse Me'/'Say Man'/'Hush Your
Mouth'/'Dearest Darling'/'Crackin' Up'/'I'm Sorry'/'Mumblin'
Guitar'/'Road Runner'/'Sixteen Tons'/'Ride On Josephine'/'You Can't
Judge A Book'

1992
Charly Blues   *The Super Super Blues Band*
Masterworks CDBM-26   (Howlin' Wolf[1], Little Walter[2], Muddy
                          Waters, Bo Diddley)
Selected tracks from US Checker LP(S)-3008 and LP(S)-3010: 'Long
Distance Call'[1]/'Goin' Down Slow'[1]/'You Don't Love Me'[2]/'I'm A
Man'[2]/'Who Do You Love'[2]/'The Red Rooster'[1]/'Diddley Daddy'[1]/'I Just
Want To Make Love To You'[2]

Victory 8283662   *Live At The Ritz* (Ronnie Wood & Bo Diddley)
                          [Equivalent of US Victory 383480008-2]

Charly Classics   *I'm A Man*
CDCD-1019
'Bo Diddley'/'I'm A Man'/'Pretty Thing'/'Who Do You Love'/'Mona (I Need
You Baby)'/'Say Man'/'Hush Your Mouth'/'Road Runner'/'You Can't Judge
A Book By Looking At The Cover'/'Cops & Robbers'/'Hey Bo
Diddley'/'Crackin' Up'/'Little Fool' (actually 'Little Girl')/'Dancing
Girl'/'Diddy Wah Diddy'/'Bring It To Jerome'

1993
Charly Blues   *Signifying Blues*
Masterworks CDBM-43
'I'm A Man' (alt take)/'Little Girl' (alt take)/'You Don't Love Me (You Don't Care)'/'I'm Looking For A Woman'/'I'm Bad'/'Who Do You Love'/'Down Home Special'/'Before You Accuse Me'/'The Clock Strikes Twelve'/'Oh Yea'/'Blues, Blues'/'Let Me In'/'Signifying Blues' (extended version)/'Live My Life'/'Call Me'/'I Want My Baby'/'Mama, Keep Your Big Mouth Shut'

Ace CDCH-396   *Bo's Blues*
'Down Home Special'/'You Don't Love Me (You Don't Care)'/'Blues, Blues'/'500% More Man'/'Live My Life'/'She's Fine, She's Mine'/'Heart-O-Matic Love'/'Bring It To Jerome'/'Pretty Thing'/'You Can't Judge A Book By The Cover'/'The Clock Strikes Twelve'/'Cops & Robbers'/'Run Diddley Daddy'/'Before You Accuse Me'/'Diddy Wah Diddy'/'Bo's Blues'/'Little Girl'/'I'm A Man'/'I'm Bad'/'Who Do You Love'/'I'm Looking For A Woman'/'Two Flies'

Charly Rhythm & Blues   *The Chess Years*
CD RED BOX 8   [12-CD box set]
Every Bo Diddley Chess recording issued to date including alt takes, cuts with Billy Boy Arnold, Chuck Berry, the Impalas, Little Walter and Billy Stewart, and both 'Super Blues' albums – as well as six previously unissued demos ('Pretty Baby', 'Can You Shimmy', 'I'm Hungry', 'Oh Yea', 'Watusi Bounce' and 'The Soup Maker') plus 'Hey Go Go' from the *Legend Of Bo Diddley* film soundtrack. Contains 282 tracks in all.

1994
See For Miles SEECD-391 *Bo Diddley Is A Lover... Plus*
[Reissue of US LP Checker LP-2980 plus six bonus cuts: 'Two Flies', 'Help Out', 'Diana', 'Mama Mia', 'What Do You Know About Love' and 'My Babe']

See For Miles SEECD-392 *Let Me Pass... Plus*
[Reissue of LP Chess CRL-4507 plus four bonus cuts: '500% More Man', 'Mama, Keep Your Big Mouth Shut', 'We're Gonna Get Married' and 'Easy']

Charly R&B CDRB-1   *Hey! Bo Diddley*
'I'm A Man'/'Bo Diddley'/'Diddley Daddy'/'Pretty Thing'/'Bring It To
Jerome'/'Cops & Robbers'/'Hey Bo Diddley'/'Mona (I Need You Baby)'/'Say
Man'/'Crackin' Up'/'I'm Sorry'/'Mumblin' Guitar'/'She's Alright'/'Say Man
Back Again'/'Road Runner'/'Ride On Josephine'/'Sixteen Tons'/'Pills (Love's
Labours Lost)'/'I Can Tell'/'You Can't Judge A Book By The Cover'

Charly 2 On 1 CDTT-2   *Two On One* (Chuck Berry/Bo Diddley)
'Bo Diddley'/'Hush Your Mouth'/'Pretty Thing'/'Who Do You
Love'/'Mona'/'Little Girl'/'Crackin' Up'/'Dancing Girl'/'Diddy Wah
Diddy'/'Road Runner'/[Other tracks by Chuck Berry]

Charly Classics   *Before You Accuse Me*
CDCD-1208
'Before You Accuse Me'/'I'm Bad'/'Down Home Special'/'Working Man'/ 'The
Story Of Bo Diddley'/'I'm Sorry'/'Cadillac'/'Bo Diddley's A Gunslinger'/
'Dearest Darlin''/'I'm Looking For A Woman'/'Say Boss Man'/'Bo's Twist'/'My
Babe'/'Bo Meets The Monster'/'Bo Diddley's Dog'/'Mr Custer'

1995
Triple X TX-511302CD   *This Should Not Be*
                         [Equivalent of US Triple X 51130-2]

Triple X TX-511612CD   *The Mighty Bo Diddley*
                         [Equivalent of US Triple X 51161-2]

Triple X TX-511622CD   *Live*
                         [Equivalent of US Triple X 51162-2]

Triple X TX-511922CD   *Promises*
                         [Equivalent of US Triple X 51192-2]

Beat Goes On   *Hey! Bo Diddley/Bo Diddley*
BGOCD-287
[Reissue of Pye Intl R&B LPs NPL-28025 and NPL 28026]

*As this book goes to press it has been announced that Bo is shortly to
begin recording a 'superstar' album for Mike Vernon's Code Blue label.*

Appendix III

Other Recordings Of Interest

Billy Boy Arnold   'I'm Sweet On You Baby'   1955
                           'You Got To Love Me Baby'
Two cuts from Bo's first recording session on 2 March, 1955 featuring
Billy Boy on vocals. A third cut, 'Rhumba', is listed in company
files as 'rejected'.
LP: Red Lightnin' RL-0012 *Blow The Back Off It* (UK) 1975
CD: Charly Blues Masterworks CDBM-34 *I Wish You Would* (UK) 1993

Little Walter   'I Got To Go'   1955
                     'Roller Coaster'
The results of Bo's second recording session, playing guitar behind
Chicago blues harmonica king, Little Walter Jacobs.
Single: Checker 817 (USA) 1955

Billy Stewart   'Billy's Blues' (Part 1)   1956
                     'Billy's Blues' (Part 2)
First solo recordings by singer/pianist Stewart, backed by Bo and
his group. Unfortunately, the famous Diddley guitar is virtually

inaudible throughout, though Jody Williams contributes some neat
licks. A third cut, 'Cryin'', remains unissued.
Single: Chess 1625 (USA) March 1956
　　　　 Argo 5256 (USA) October 1956

Continentals　　　'Picture Of Love'　　　　　　　　　1956
　　　　　　　　　'Soft & Sweet'
Peggy Jones's first recordings (playing guitar).
Single: Whirlin' Disc 105 (USA) 1957

Schoolboys　　　'Pearl'　　　　　　　　　　　　　1957
Recently discovered contract sheets have revealed that Bo was
drafted in to play guitar on this distinctly average doo-wop cut.
Disappointingly, his contribution is restricted to some perfunctory
and almost inaudible rhythm playing, with an unknown lead guitarist
stealing the show.
Single: OKeh 4-7090 (USA) 1957

Billy Stewart　　　'Baby, You're My Only Love'　　　1957
　　　　　　　　　'Billy's Heartache'
Good second effort by the Diddley protegé, this time with Bo's beefy
guitar well to the fore. Vocal backing by the Marquees [see next item].
Single: OKeh 4-7095 (USA) 1957

An alternate take of 'Billy's Heartache' appeared on the following:
3-CD: Epic/OKeh/Legacy E3K-48912 *The OKeh Rhythm & Blues Story*
(USA) 1993
3-CD: Sony Europa E3K-48912 *The OKeh Rhythm & Blues Story*
(UK) 1994

Marquees　　　'Hey Little School Girl'　　　　　　1957
　　　　　　　　'Wyatt Earp'
Vocal quartet from Washington, DC discovered by Bo. Line-up
consisted of Marvin Gaye, James Nolan, Reese Palmer and Chester
Simmons. Bo produced and arranged both sides, but did not play
on either.
Single: OKeh 4-7096 (USA) 1957

An alternate take of 'Wyatt Earp' featuring Bo on guitar appeared on the following:
3-CD: Epic/OKeh/Legacy E3K-48912 *The OKeh Rhythm & Blues Story* (USA) 1993
3-CD: Sony Europa E3K-48912 *The OKeh Rhythm & Blues Story* (UK) 1994

Bopchords   'Baby'   1957
                   'So Why'
Peggy Jones's second venture onto wax, singing backing vocals.
Single: Holiday 2608 (USA) 1957

Greg & Peg   'Honey Bunny Baby'   1957
                   'Why Do I Love You Like I Do'
Duet by Gregory Carroll of the Orioles (who also composed both songs) and Peggy Jones. Four other titles recorded at the same session remain unissued.
Single: Ro-Nan 1001 (USA) 1957

Bob & Peggy   'Everybody's Talking'   1959
                   'I'm Gonna Love My Way'
Duet by bass player Bobby Baskerville and Peggy Jones. Peggy wrote and arranged both sides.
Single: Peacock 1927 (USA) 1959

Terry &   'DJ Stomp'   1959
The Pirates   'How Can You Do This To Me'
                   'I've Lost You'
                   'Pack My Bags'
                   'Peacock Rock'
Everly Bros-style material cut for Chess by Washington outfit fronted by vocalists Terry West and Stephen Foster with Bo supporting on guitar.
Unissued

L.C. Cooke   'I Need Your Love'   1960
                   'The Letter'
Two sides cut at the January 1960 *In The Spotlight* sessions with Bo and crew backing Sam Cooke's brother. The chaotic 'I Need Your

Love' was finally released in 1995, but 'The Letter' remains in the can.
Various Artists
CD: CHD4-9352 *Chess Rhythm & Roll* (USA) 1995

| Impalas | 'For The Love Of Mike' | 1961 |
| | 'It Won't Be Me' | |

Vocal quartet from Washington, DC: Sandra Bears, Margie Clark,
Carrie Mingo and Billy Stewart's first cousin, Grace Ruffin. Bo
produced and played on both sides. 'For The Love Of Mike' was issued
with 'I Need You So Much' (a later recording) on the flipside. The
Impalas later became the Four Jewels/Jewels.
Single: Checker 999 (USA) 1961

| Jewels | 'I'm Forever Blowing Bubbles' | 1961 |
| | 'We've Got Togetherness' | |

Outfit fronted by Peggy Jones, not to be confused with the renamed
Impalas [see above]. 'Bubbles', a rocked-up version of the well-known
standard, was a minor hit in New York in 1961.
Single: M-G-M K.13577 (USA) 1961

Les Cooper &	'Wiggle Wobble'	1962
The Soul Rockers	'Dig Yourself'	
	'Owee Baby'	
	'Bossa Nova'	
	'Hippity Hop'	
	'Wobble Party'	
	'Garbage Can'	
	'Jungle Pony'	
	'Rockin' With The Shimming'	
	'At The Party'	
	'Boston Monkey'	
	'Peter Piper'	

Recordings by singer/pianist Cooper featuring Peggy Jones on guitar.
'Wiggle Wobble' b/w 'Dig Yourself' were also released as a single
[Everlast 5019], which made No. 12 on the *Billboard* 'R&B' chart
and No. 22 in the 'Hot 100' in the summer of 1962.
LP: Everlast ELP-202 *Wiggle Wobble* (USA) 1962

Cookie Valdez   'I'm In Love'   1965
Early solo recording by Connie Redmond (later Cookie Vee). Produced
by Bo Diddley for possible release on his own BoKay label.
Unissued

Little Walter   'Juke'   1967
                    'Sad Hours'
Two sub-standard out-takes from the January 1967 *Super Blues*
sessions featuring Walter, Bo and Muddy Waters.
EP: Red Lightnin' RLEP-0027 *Superharps* (UK) 1979
Remixed versions of both cuts appeared on:
CD: Chess CHD-9168 *Super Blues* (USA) 1992

Cookie V   'Queen Of Fools'   1969
                    'You Got The Wrong Girl'
Worthy solo effort by long-time Diddley backing vocalist, Connie
Redmond (later Cookie Vee). Bo produced both sides, but did not
play on either.
Single: Checker 1222 (USA) 1969

Bo Diddley   'Introduction'   1972
A short spoken introduction by Bo. Unissued elsewhere.
Various artists LP: Chess/Sun NQCS-1 *Rock Smuk* (Netherlands) 1972
Various artists LP: Bellaphon BI-15119 *4 Rock Giants – Talks & Hits*
(West Germany) 1972

Linda Ellas   'Blues Is Here To Stay'   1978
                    'I Can Feel It Coming On'
                    'I'm Confessing'
                    'Looking Back'
                    'Thank You Love'
C&W recordings produced by Bo. Backing was provided by Lady Bo &
The Family Jewel, who also laid down several instrumental tracks
for vocal overdubbing at a later date.
Unissued

Belmonts   'Shake It Sally' 1981
'Bo Diddley'-beat song recorded in New York with Bo on guitar and
Freddy Cannon on lead vocals.
LP: Downtown D-20001 *Rock 'n' Roll Traveling Show* (USA) 1982

Vazelina   'Hallingsprætten'   1983
Bilopphøggers
Norway's top rock 'n' roll band tackle a 'Bo Diddley'-beat number with
assistance from Bo on guitar.
LP: Slager SLP-99002 *På Tur* (Norway) 1983

Paul James Band 'The Ugliest Girl In Town'   1984
Jokey outing by Canadian blues-rocker Paul James Vigna. Bo helps out on
vocals and percussion.
LP: Lick 'n' Stick CSPS-2340 *Almost Crazy* (Canada) 1984

Bo Diddley   'Make Up Your Mind'   1985
with Jannetta
Attractive duet recorded in Toronto with singer Patti Jannetta and the
Paul James Band in support.
Various artists promo CD: Trilogy TRCD-289 *A Trilogy Of Stars
(Volume 1)* (Canada) 1989

Ronnie Wood & 'Road Runner'   1987
Bo Diddley   'I'm A Man'
       'Crackin' Up'
       'Hey Bo Diddley'
       'Money To Ronnie'
       'Who Do You Love' [bonus track on CD]
Below average live cuts from a New York concert on 25 November, 1987.
Originally released only in Japan, they were eventually issued in the
USA and UK in 1992. [Other tracks feature only Ronnie Wood]

LP: JVC/Victor VILZ-28122 *Live At The Ritz* (Japan) 1988
CD: JVC/Victor VDPZ-1329 *Live At The Ritz* (Japan) 1988

Ronnie Wood &	'Bo Diddley'	1988
Bo Diddley	'Do You Love The Rock 'n' Roll [sic]	
	'Crackin' Up'	
	'I'm A Man'	
	'Money To Ronnie'	
	'Hey Bo Diddley'	
	'It's All Over Now'	

Poorly recorded live cuts from a concert in Nuremburg, West Germany on 9 July, 1988. [Other tracks feature only Ronnie Wood]
Bootleg LP: *Headhunter Boogie* (West Germany) 1988

Snakes	'Pay Bo Diddley'	1989

A classic recording by the Memphis-based blues-rock outfit featuring Bo on guitar and vocals. Wonder if he got paid?
LP: Curb CRB-10616 *The Snakes* (USA) 1989

Ben E. King &	'Book Of Love'	1989
Bo Diddley		
featuring Doug Lazy		

Execrable revamp of the Monotones' 1958 smash arranged by bassist Stanley Clarke (who also plays on the cut), with rap vocals by Doug Lazy. Bo is way down in the mix somewhere, playing guitar and making the odd vocal interjection.
Various artists CD: Atlantic 82155-2 *Book Of Love* (USA) 1991

Hamilton	'I Know Bo Diddley'	1994

A tribute to Bo by his young Texan prodigy, Hamilton Loomis. Bo contributes guitar, maracas and vocals.
CD: Ham-Bone Records HB-101CD *Hamilton* (USA) 1994
CD: Ham-Bone Records CD-301 *Hamilton* (UK) 1995

Lady Bo &   Unknown titles   1995
The Family Jewel
At the time of writing, Peggy Malone is busy working on a new album
with her group.

Appendix IV

Bo's Hits

US charts

BILLBOARD 'RHYTHM & BLUES' SINGLES CHART

Size of chart	Date of chart entry	Highest position attained	No. of weeks in chart	Title	Label & Cat No.
15	4 May 1955	2	15	'Bo Diddley'/'I'm A Man'	Checker 814
15	6 July 1955	11	4	'Diddley Daddy'	Checker 819
30	15 Mar 1959	17	5	'I'm Sorry'	Checker 914
30	9 Aug 1959	14	5	'Crackin' Up'	Checker 924
30	13 Sept 1959	3	15	'Say Man'	Checker 931
30	27 Dec 1959	23	1	'Say Man, Back Again'	Checker 936
30	17 Apr 1960	20	2	'Road Runner'	Checker 942
30	25 Aug 1962	21	9	'You Can't Judge A Book By The Cover'	Checker 1019
50	21 Jan 1967	17	9	'Ooh Baby'	Checker 1158

BILLBOARD 'HOT 100' SINGLES CHART

Peak of popularity	Date of chart entry	Highest position attained	No. of weeks in chart	Title	Label & Cat No.
Jul 1959	12 Jul 1959	62	5	'Crackin' Up'	Checker 924
Nov 1959	27 Sep 1959	20	12	'Say Man'	Checker 931
Mar 1960	6 Mar 1960	75	6	'Road Runner'	Checker 942
Sep 1962	18 Aug 1962	48	10	'You Can't Judge A Book By The Cover'	Checker 1019
Feb 1967	21 Jan 1967	88	7	'Ooh Baby'	Checker 1158

BILLBOARD 'TOP LPs' CHART

Date of chart entry	Highest position attained	No. of weeks in chart	Title	Label & Cat No.
24 Nov 1962	117	4	*Bo Diddley*	Checker LP-2984

© Record Research Inc and *Billboard Publications* Inc

UK charts

RECORD RETAILER 'TOP 50' SINGLES CHART

Date of chart entry	Highest position attained	No. of weeks in chart	Title	Label & Cat No.
10 Oct 1963	34	6	'Pretty Thing'	Pye R&B 7N.25217
18 Mar 1965	39	5	'Hey Good Lookin''	Chess CRS-8000

RECORD RETAILER 'TOP ALBUMS' CHART

Date of chart entry	Highest position attained	No. of weeks in chart	Title	Label & Cat No.
3 Oct 1963	11	8	*Bo Diddley*	Pye R&B NPL-28026
7 Nov 1963	20	1	*Bo Diddley Is A Gunslinger*	Pye Jazz NJL-33
28 Nov 1963	19	1	*Bo Diddley Rides Again*	Pye R&B NPL-28029
13 Feb 1964	13	6	*Bo Diddley's Beach Party*	Pye R&B NPL-28032

© The British Market Research Bureau and *Music Week*

Appendix V

Bo In The Movies

The Big TNT Show
American International Pictures (Larry Peerce) 1966
Black and white film of the all-star concert held at the Moulin Rouge,
Hollywood, CA on 29 November, 1965. Bo plays 'Hey Bo Diddley' and
'Bo Diddley' backed by Clifton James, Chester Lindsey, Duchess, and
Bo-ettes Gloria Morgan and Lily 'Bee Bee' Jamieson.

The Big Beat
This Could Be The Night
Edited versions of *The Big TNT Show* with additional footage from 1965's
The TAMI Show.

The Legend Of Bo Diddley
**Chess Records/Mar-Ken Enterprises (Gary Sherman & Peter Weiner)
1966**
A 25-minute black and white promotional film sponsored by Chess. Bo is
seen touring Chicago, recording 'We're Gonna Get Married', and performing
at the Le Coq D'or club in Toronto, Canada. Although the soundtrack relies
almost entirely on Bo's hit records, the movie also features a magnificently
ragged live performance of a song unavailable elsewhere, 'Hey, Go Go'.

Sweet Toronto
Leacock-Pennebaker Inc (D.A. Pennebaker) 1970
Colour film of the *Toronto Rock 'n' Roll Revival* held at the Varsity Stadium

on 13 September, 1969. Bo plays 'Hey Bo Diddley' and 'Bo Diddley', supported by Cookie Vee, Chester Lindsey and Clifton James.

Keep On Rockin'
Edited version of *Sweet Toronto*.

Let The Good Times Roll
Metromedia Producers Corp (Sid Levin & Bob Abel) 1973
Colour film of a *Rock 'n' Roll Revival* concert staged at New York's Madison Square Garden in May 1972. Bo plays 'I'm A Man' and 'Hey Bo Diddley' supported by the Bobby Comstock band, and reappears at the end to join Chuck Berry for an exciting stage jam. Bo's sequence is intercut with footage of him talking in his dressing room, shopping for chicken and telling jokes.

The London Rock 'n' Roll Show
Notting Hill Studios (Peter Clifton) 1978
Colour film of the London Wembley Stadium spectacular held on 5 August, 1972. Bo plays 'Road Runner', 'Bring It To Jerome' and 'Mona' supported by the Houseshakers and Cookie Vee.

Trading Places
Paramount Pictures (John Landis) 1983
Highly acclaimed moralistic comedy. Bo appears in one scene playing a ghetto pawnbroker.

Hail! Hail! Rock 'n' Roll
Universal (Taylor Hackford) 1987
Nostalgic semi-documentary about Chuck Berry built around the preparations for his 60th birthday celebration concert. Bo appears in several sequences reminiscing about old times with Chuck and an over-exuberant Little Richard, but sadly makes no musical contribution.

Eddie & The Cruisers II: Eddie Lives!
Les Productions Alliance Ltée/Scotti Bros (Jean-Claude Lord) 1989
A rock 'n' roll star thought to have died in a car accident in 1964 re-emerges twenty-five years later when his record company starts hyping his old recordings. Bo appears in one scene being interviewed on television about Eddie's last legendary sessions.

Rockula
Cannon Films (Luca Bercovici) 1990
Feeble plot about a 400 year old teenage vampire who decides to form a rock band called 'Rockula'. Bo plays a low-key role as a bar bluesman (the quaintly nicknamed 'Axman') who is drafted into the band.

Appendix VI

Notable TV Appearances

1955
Toast Of The Town [The Ed Sullivan show] (CBS-TV) USA

1962
The Clay Cole Show (WPIX-TV) USA

1963
Scene At 6.30 (Granada TV) UK
Thank Your Lucky Stars (ABC-TV) UK

1965
Discs A Go-Go (TWW) UK
The Eamonn Andrews Show (ABC-TV) UK
Gadzooks! (BBC 2) UK

Ready, Steady, Go (Rediffusion) UK
Shindig (ABC-TV) USA
Thank Your Lucky Stars (ABC-TV) UK

1970
Music Scene (ABC-TV) USA

1971
The Mike Douglas Show (CBS-TV) USA

1972
Jazz Montreux (TV-SSR) Switzerland
Rollin' On The River [Kenny Rogers show] (CTV) Canada

1973
Dick Clark Presents The Rock & Roll Years (ABC-TV) USA

1974
Chuck Berry & Friends In Concert (ABC-TV) USA

1975
BST [Blood, Sweat & Tears special] (CBC) Canada
Midnight Special (ABC-TV) USA

1976
Donny & Marie (ABC-TV) USA

1977
Dick Clark's Good Old Days (NBC-TV) USA

1978
Dick Clark's Live Wednesday (NBC-TV) USA

Sha Na Na (NBC-TV) USA

1983

American Bandstand's 30th Anniversary Special (ABC-TV) USA
Unforgettable (Channel 4) UK

1984

The Tube (Channel 4) UK

1985

Fabian's Goodtime Rock 'n' Roll (Choice Channel) USA
Live Aid (Various) World-wide
Whistle Test (BBC 2) UK

1986

American Bandstand's 33¹/₃rd Anniversary Special (ABC-TV) USA
The 30th Anniversary Of Rock 'n' Roll (Western-World TV/MTV) USA
Late Night With David Letterman (NBC-TV) USA

1987

I Don't Sound Like Nobody (Channel 1) Sweden
The Late Show Starring Joan Rivers (Fox Network) USA

1989

The Legends Of Rock 'n' Roll – Cinemax Sessions (Cinemax/RAI) Italy
The Legends Of Rock 'n' Roll – Once More With Feeling
(Channel 7) Australia

1992

Guitar Legends – Expo '92, Seville (BBC 2) UK

1994

Hoodoo U Voodoo [Rolling Stones live in Miami] (Pay-Per-View TV) USA
1995
Music City Tonight (TNN) USA